T0244704

By ALEX WINTERS

Treading Water

Published by DREAMSPINNER PRESS
www.dreamspinnerpress.com

Treading Water

ALEX WINTERS

DREAMSPINNER PRESS

Published by
DREAMSPINNER PRESS

5032 Capital Circle SW, Suite 2, PMB# 279, Tallahassee, FL 32305-7886 USA
www.dreamspinnerpress.com

Treading Water
© 2023 Alex Winters

Cover Art
© 2023 Reece Notley
reece@vitaenoir.com
Cover content is for illustrative purposes only and any person depicted on the cover is a model.

Trade Paperback ISBN: 978-1-64108-582-3
Digital ISBN: 978-1-64108-581-6
Trade Paperback published October 2023
v. 1.0

Printed in the United States of America
∞
This paper meets the requirements of
ANSI/NISO Z39.48-1992 (Permanence of Paper).

ONE

Tucker

"Dɪᴅ ʏᴏᴜ ever go to *real* summer camp?"

Tucker Crawford was about to answer when the rental car hit another pothole in the middle of the one-lane dirt road and rattled his teeth. Summer Stevenson gripped the steering wheel tighter and made an apologetic pearly grin beneath her oversized, bug-eyed black *Breakfast at Tiffany's* sunglasses.

"Sorry," she mouthed dramatically as she steered dutifully down the rutted dirt road toward their final destination. Hollywood royalty of a sort, Summer wasn't necessarily used to driving herself places, let alone into the ass crack of Middle of Nowhere, Georgia.

"I was a little too busy working two jobs for those kinds of shenanigans," Tucker muttered, clutching the strap of his seat belt a smidge tighter and girding his loins as if they were back on location setting up another "driving a rigged car through a crowd of zombie extras" stunt scene.

Summer clucked her tongue, and even though he couldn't see them, he was pretty sure she rolled her predictably blue eyes just for good measure. "At thirteen, Tucker? Exaggerate much?"

She favored him with another frosty glance from behind her stylish sunglasses even as she gave him one of her trademark smiles—the kind that had been appearing on America's TV screens since well before Summer herself was a teenager. "I mean, that's when most kids go to summer camp."

He braced himself as another pothole loomed, but his stunt-driving chauffer managed to avoid it. "Look, Summer, if we're going to be fake dating for better ratings this season, you should probably know enough about me to remember that I didn't come from the same, uh, silver-spoon background as you. You know, when reporters start asking?"

The GPS screen on the rental car's glowing dashboard guided her closer and closer to Camp Run-A-Mok with every blinking purple arrow and whispered suggestion to "turn right in three-quarters of a mile" in just the most pleasant tone ever. "Please, Tucker, you make it sound like you were some kind of street urchin or something."

The camp sign finally came into view. It was a giant arch, constructed of wrought iron on either side and the words Camp Run-A-Mok spelled out in giant pieces of distressed wood, like something you'd see entering the Triple R Ranch in an old-timey western. His stomach did another flip-flop, and not from Summer's famously bad driving this time. He was nervous as hell about the next two weeks and what they might mean for his acting career, and holding it all in while acting like he wasn't holding it all in wasn't helping much.

It seemed oddly fitting that his fake girlfriend should be the one to drop him off at fake summer camp. Though they weren't necessarily friends per se, they were at least friendly after four seasons together on the set of *Suburban Dead*. And their opposites-attract sarcasm had definitely kept the conversation on the way from the airport light, vaguely hostile, and occasionally humorous, all of which had served to take his mind off the unpleasant matter at hand.

At least until this very moment.

"No, you're right. I wasn't exactly homeless growing up, but I didn't grow up in Beverly Hills being babysat by famous actors and actresses on the set of my mother's movies either."

Summer's response was calm and measured, as if she'd had to defend herself enough times over the years to have a pat answer ready for clueless Neanderthals like Tucker, who probably should have known better. "Look, Tucker, it's not my fault I was born to folks who were already in the acting game long before I came along, and I've spent every job since I started on TV proving myself worthy of what little career I have. So yeah, maybe you should know a little bit more about me before reporters start asking about us, *Boo*."

The manicured brows arching over her sunglasses indicated she was aware she'd just made a verbal mic drop and that he should be as well. But they'd never spent much time alone together on set, and this forced proximity in the front seats of the rental were the longest they'd spent together, just the two of them, ever.

He glanced over at her with a curious, almost tentative smile. "Sorry, Summer, I guess we both have a lot to learn about each other, huh?"

Her façade was a practiced cool; she was not used to such personal revelations from her far less famous costars. "I'm an open book, Tucker. Everything you ever need to know about me you can find on my IMDb.com page. You're the Mystery Man with the 'salt of the earth' background, remember? That's what our little relationship ruse is designed to counteract this summer, remember?"

"I know, I know," Tucker grumbled, as if to quiet the butterflies doing the jitterbug in his taut belly.

She sighed and joined him in glancing up at the towering rustic sign just before they drove under it, and the ominous gloom he'd been feeling all morning grew as the deserted camp stretched out in front of them like something straight from the set of, well, a horror movie.

Summer gripped the steering wheel tighter and sat up a smidge higher and nodded at him sympathetically. "Listen, I know you're skeptical about all this fake romance business, but trust me, it's going to be good for me, for the series, for getting us renewed next season, and especially for you."

"So everyone keeps telling me."

"Listen, between you and me? I think this whole 'costar charade' thing is an outdated piece of old Hollywood bait and switch, clearly. But it works, trust me. The fans love it, even if most of them know it's total BS. And from a pure business sense? You're the one getting the most out of this arrangement, Tucker, trust me."

Summer was right, obviously. And even if she wasn't, she talked so quickly, so confidently, Tucker had no choice but to nod and believe her. It had always been this way. Summer had been blessed with famous parents, boundless opportunities, and flawless good looks, but she'd made the business of Hollywood her business since she made her first million at twelve, probably. She knew her looks would one day fade and that her future lay behind the camera at some point, but until then Summer seemed bound and determined to put on her best dog and pony show in front of the camera. This year Tucker was along for the ride, whether he wanted to be or not. He just wasn't sure which role he was playing yet—the dog or the pony.

Tucker supposed he should be grateful that she'd chosen him to parade in front of the photographers and reporters in the buildup to the next season of their long-running zombie series, which was streaming exclusively on the Nightmares Network.

And he was. But the whole situation of "pretend dating" vaguely icked him out, particularly since, in a way, he'd been "pretend dating" with every girl he'd ever hooked up with. But how was poor Summer supposed to know that? How were any of them supposed to know that, after so many years of practice? The show's producers and publicists were all for it, but Tucker wasn't so sure it was such a good look for him—or his career, such as it was.

Still, what could it hurt? A few staged kisses at random coffee shops, cafes, nightclubs, premieres, and downtown hot spots back in LA between filming, and a few "leaked" photos from on location down in Georgia would keep the PR campaign going until the series premier in the fall and ensure a big uptick in new viewers.

How hard could it be?

"Are you... sure about this place, Tucker?" Summer was pulling up to a small rustic cabin with a matching sign out front that said Camp Welcome Center. Her uberconfident voice and practiced steely exterior finally faltered just a smidge. Tucker only wished she'd let it happen more often, for both of their sakes. It had to be a terrible burden, fighting to prove her own worth at every turn when all anyone ever wanted to do was compare her to her famous parents or assume she got where she was because of them.

Tucker checked the address on the back of the business card that Costas Imperial, head of Scream Studios and the show's executive producer, had given him on the way to the airport in LA that morning. "No, but... it's the right place."

"Yeah," Summer warned ominously, clutching the steering wheel with two sets of white knuckles. "The right place for some cheesy '80s slasher flick." They shared a conspiratorial chuckle, no doubt for very different reasons.

She put the car in Park in front of the welcome center and leaned in closer, smelling of cinnamon and spice and old Hollywood money. "Are you sure you're not filming some low-budget indie flick while we're on hiatus this summer, Tuck? You know that's against union rules, right?" she teased, skin sultry and shimmering from the cloying Georgia heat. If only he'd found her half as attractive as the rest of the world seemed to, being Summer's fake boyfriend might lead to more than just higher ratings come fall. Then again, she was no more into him than he was into her. As she'd reminded him at least a dozen times on their way from the airport, this was strictly business.

"I wish to hell I was." With the same trepidation he'd felt all morning, Tucker watched the cabin's screen door open with an ominous creaking sound. "Then at least I'd have an excuse for feeling scared to death at the moment."

Beside him, Summer's leather seat shifted, and moments later, she squeezed his hand on the armrest between them. It was such a surprising gesture, he almost flinched. In the end, he was glad he didn't. The very last thing Tucker wanted to do in response to the first genuine moment they'd shared off set was rebuff his notoriously private costar.

The tenderness in her grip almost matched the raw empathy in her voice as she said, "You're gonna be fine, Tucker. You've got this, okay?"

He nodded as he reached for his door, wishing he was half as confident in himself as she was in him. Or, for that matter, half as good an actor as she was.

TWO

Reed

"MR. CRAWFORD? Miss Stevenson?"

Reed Chancelor stood just behind the pudgy businessman in the ill-fitting suit and glanced curiously as the pretty young couple exited the sleek luxury sedan that looked as out of place in the deserted summer camp as, well, a pretty young couple standing on either side of a sleek luxury sedan.

The leggy blond in the skintight summer dress gave a Hollywood-worthy smile and slid her round black sunglasses atop her slicked-back hairdo. She stepped slightly forward and nodded coyly at the diminutive property manager, as if quickly deciphering which of them was in charge.

"Mr. Tatum, I presume?" Her voice was as immediately commanding as her sultry blue eyes.

Oscar Tatum, local real estate developer, property manager, and the de facto owner of humble Camp Run-A-Mok, beamed, the summer sun reflecting off his ebony skin like a mirror. "One and the same, Miss Stevenson. It's an honor to meet you and, if I may, I'm a big fan."

Reed choked on an ironic smile. The guy certainly wasn't kidding. He'd been talking about her nonstop as they waited in his office back in the welcome center.

"Please," the leggy blond oozed, offering a hand that featured fingernails polished to a glossy supermodel sheen, "call me Summer." She endured the older man's brisk handshake and preening gaze and then turned to Reed and glanced slightly upward to meet his eyes with her own.

He smiled down at her.

"Nice to meet you." He offered his right hand, and she took it with papery skin still chilly from the big car's air-conditioning.

"The pleasure's all mine," she purred, as if reading from a script. "So you're the guy who's going to teach Tucker how to swim this summer, huh?"

"I know how to swim, Summer." The pretty boy who accompanied the radiant starlet was still lingering by the trunk of the car. He hoisted a single gym bag over one shoulder and stared daggers at his girlfriend as he growled not-so-playfully, "I'm just going to learn how to swim better, right?" The kid glanced up at his new swim coach as if for confirmation.

Reed chuckled, wondering what the handsome new stranger might look like in a skimpy blue bathing suit, dripping wet and out of breath. He scrubbed the thought from his mind—or at least tried to—and replied in a neutral tone, "That's the assignment I was given, *sir.*"

The kid made a face and glanced around dramatically. Reed kept forgetting they were both actor types, though he'd never quite found the time to watch whatever show it was they actually starred in. "Sir? What, is my dad standing behind me?"

"My apologies, *Tucker.*" Reed pinned the kid's soft green eyes with his own. They shared a moment that made him shiver despite the radiating summer heat, and he instinctively felt that the kid wasn't just playacting.

"Well, now that you've met…."

Mr. Tatum waved a ring of keys and broke the spell. The leggy blond, retreating from the middle step and back to stand near the sleek black sports car, keys of her own in hand, matched the older man's "hurry, faster, let's go and leave these two to their own devices" energy. After enduring nearly an hour of the Realtor's breathy enthusiasm for their guests of honor, Reed wasn't exactly complaining.

Tatum risked a glance away from the radiant young starlet and pinned her tall drink of a costar with a no-nonsense scowl. "I assume your producer has given you the rundown of the camp's parameters for the duration of your stay?"

The kid known as "Tucker" dropped his bag on the top step and took the keys with an almost proprietary air. He was clearly used to getting what he wanted. Or perhaps simply being surrounded by people who did things for him, like teach him how to swim or hand over the keys to entire deserted summer camps for his private pleasure.

"For the most part, sure." His fuzzy response made it clear the kid was still a little vague on the details.

"Join the club," Reed wanted to grunt, but didn't. Between the well-to-do real estate mogul he'd spent the last hour with and the dazzling stars at his feet, Reed was clearly outclassed. The only thing he and Tucker seemed to have in common was a vague sense of confusion about what lay ahead.

From the moment he'd been approached by Scream Studios to coach their "big star" for a surprise twist in the upcoming season of their hit zombie show, whatever *that* was, Reed's quiet, steady workaday world had been turned upside down and inside out. Then again, getting paid an exorbitant sum to stand around and look at a sexy young movie star in a bathing suit for two weeks wasn't the worst assignment in the world.

Mr. Tatum hooked a thumb back at the vaguely rustic welcome center door behind him. "I left a dossier on the desk in there," he huffed, clearly eager to get on to bigger and better things that didn't include babysitting Hollywood royalty or down-on-their-luck swim coaches. "Basically, you two have got the run of the place for the next fourteen days, minus a few exceptions that are made clear in the papers on my desk. In short, the kitchen fridge in the mess hall is stocked to the gills, you each have a cabin as accommodations with central bathroom and showers nearby, as well as the rec center to include, of course, the Olympic-size pool and accompanying locker room. My business card and all pertinent numbers are attached to the dossier, and I'll try to pop in next week to see how things are going unless you need me before then, so...."

He approached the young actress with the stunning legs and gym-perfect body to match and extended a business card, which she took with the uncertain air of a Hollywood veteran indulging an obvious stalker. "Oh no, I'm... I'm not sticking around. I just came to show support for my, uh, boyfriend here before jetting back to LA?" The question mark at the end of her declaration made it clear she thought the obsessive Realtor already knew the score.

Mr. Tatum nodded, produced a pen, and handed it over with an almost butler-like bow. "No, of course not, dear. But do you mind signing it?"

Summer brightened and signed the card with an accomplished flourish. Mr. Tatum regarded the finished product with all the scrutiny of a legal document and then placed it into his top pocket and patted it for effect, like a character in an old Dickens novel securing their pocket watch after assuring themselves it was, in fact, tea time.

"Life goal accomplished," he boasted to the group with an abashed grin. Then he gave the gents on the porch a wave that felt more like an afterthought, piled into his own sleek sedan, and peeled away in a cloud of red Georgia clay and stringy peat moss.

Reed looked back at Tucker, who looked back at Summer. He suddenly felt like an intruder. She made a face that most resembled the nervously smiling "teethy face" emoji and then shrugged her shoulders. "You sure you don't need anything else before I bail on you, Tuck?"

The two shot each other a knowing glance that made it clear they had a shared history, one that was far more interesting to Reed than any mere Hollywood zombie series. "I guess not," the young actor sighed in a very young-actor way. "I'll just waste away here in the boondocks while you're out and about enjoying the high life without me."

Reed struggled not to snicker. Summer ignored him with a practiced ease and cocked out one practically nonexistent hip, as playful as she was polished. "I mean, it's not as bad as that, now is it, *darling?*" Her arched eyebrow and emphasis on that last word gave the comical interaction an old-married-couple air that didn't quite mesh with their fashion-magazine good looks.

"Oh no, not bad at all. Between you and me, getting eaten alive by mosquitos between repeated dunkings in a giant swimming pool sounds like the vacation of my dreams, *sweet cheeks.*"

Summer rolled her eyes comically, then gave the Tucker kid a "let's not argue in front of strangers" look that was as comical as it was vaguely threatening. "Either way, *dear*, I'll check in on you in a few days to see how things are going, okay?"

Tucker nodded resolutely and sounded every bit the fifth grader getting dropped off at real summer camp by his mommy. "Sounds great, *darling*. Hopefully this guy won't drown me by then."

They both glanced at Reed, who shrugged playfully. "I mean, if it keeps you two from arguing like cats and dogs, it may be worth it, *Tuck.*"

THREE

Tucker

"EVERYTHING OKAY, kid?"

Tucker leaned against the porch railing of the rustic welcome center and admired the man who was to be his swim coach for the next two weeks. He was long and lean and angular and aloof, clever brown eyes peering back at him above a curious, crooked smile, his chiseled face framed by a layer of sleek brown stubble.

He shrugged. "It's fine. I'm just a little out of my comfort zone is all."

The handsome stranger glanced at the last of the fragrant Georgia clay kicked up from Summer's rental sedan. "I meant, with you two."

"Us?" Tucker was still getting used to being part of an "us," however fake it might be. "Oh, we're fine. I guess I shouldn't have been so short with her. I'm just feeling a lot like a kid stuck in detention at the moment. Not Summer's fault, I suppose."

The big guy gave him a curious glance. Tucker found it hard to peer back into Reed's eyes for too long, lest he reveal too much of his interior monologue. "Are you together?"

Tucker shrugged, surprised at how homesick he felt watching Summer's taillights disappear down the long, snaking drive under the big rustic camp sign. "Only for the ratings, I suppose." Then he seemed to realize something and extended his hand almost... shyly. "I'm Tucker, by the way."

"I gathered." He took Tucker's hand and gave it a surprisingly firm shake back. "Reed. It's nice to meet you."

The handshake lingered a moment longer than it should have—not a full minute, not anything weird or creepy or suggestive like that, but just a moment longer than normal. Long enough for Tucker to slip his hand out first and give Reed a curious glance back.

"Well," Tucker said, a smidge louder than he intended, righting himself from where he'd been leisurely leaning against the porch railing. "I've got the keys now. Do you want to get settled in?"

Reed gave him a curious wink and took a stutter step closer. "I thought you'd never ask," he said, his voice as winking as his expression.

Tucker grabbed his gym bag, slung it over his arm, and glanced slightly upward. The late afternoon sun cast a flattering glow across Reed's masculine, vaguely sporty face as they hesitated, still in front of the welcome center. "Are you being serious right now? I can't tell."

Reed gave another sly wink and started walking. Tucker followed. "Good," he said in a vaguely syrupy Southern accent. "I like to keep my swimmers on their toes."

"So that's what you do? Coach swimmers?"

Reed glanced over and, Tucker noticed, slightly up at him. He'd always been tall and gangly, something he'd felt slightly self-conscious about ever since high school. But what Reed lacked in height he more than made up for in wrought-iron cocky machismo.

Reed gave him a soft, slow eye roll. "I know you're some kind of big Hollywood dude, apparently, but yeah, I have a life too, and that's what this sweatshirt means."

Tucker gave it a good study, wishing it weren't so big and baggy. "So you work at Eastern Georgia State on the… swim team?"

Reed chuckled as they strolled toward a long, low building just to the right of the welcome center that closely resembled a barn. "I'm assistant coach, kid."

"But over the summer?"

They were at the door to the barn-looking building now. Tucker didn't know what else to call it until he looked closer and saw a sign in the same wood-log font as the welcome center that read Mess Hall.

Reed glanced over and said, "I take it you dropped out of college to strike it big in Hollywood, kid?"

Tucker glanced back. "I take it you never read my IMDb page."

"Which means?"

"I never went to college in the first place."

"So maybe you don't realize that we pretty much practice all year long to get ready for the official season to kick off in September or that they had to scramble to find someone to replace me for your little private lessons over the next two weeks."

"So maybe *you* don't realize I'm not the producer of the show and had no control over who they picked to coach me or why or when, just so we're clear about the pecking order here?"

They stood, face to face and toe to toe, until Reed winked and put his hand on the door. He cocked his head. "Are we fighting already, kid?"

Tucker chuckled despite himself and softened his fight-or-flight posture. He'd immediately regretted snapping at Summer before she left, and now, apparently, had done the same with his new swim coach. "Sorry, no. Just a long day, I guess. Long flight, you know?"

"Not really." Reed pointed at something behind them, and Tucker noticed a shiny white Jeep with a variety of Eastern Georgia State bumper stickers on the back. "The school's not far from here, so I drove."

"When? How long have you been here?"

Reed pushed through the mess hall door as Tucker followed, struggling to ignore the way the track pants clung to Reed's firm, athletic backside. "Last night?"

"What? So why are you acting like we're both discovering this place for the first time together?"

"Relax, dude. You're already on the defensive. I didn't want to intimidate you any more by acting like I already knew the run of the place."

Tucker smirked. "Even though you already know the run of the place?"

Reed winked and squeezed Tucker's shoulder with a taut, viselike grip. "Speaking of, Tuck, why don't we skip the nickel tour and I'll take you straight to the heart of this little operation?"

FOUR

Reed

"THIS? IS the heart?"

They stood in the kitchen. Well, Tucker leaned back against the counter like a cool, long, tall drink of water while Reed lingered near the gleaming row of towering walk-in coolers that lined the opposite wall. "Could you wait until I unveil the reason why it's the heart of this operation before you start casting stones, please?"

Tucker gave another one of his casually resistant smiles. Dude was going to be a hard one to spend time with, Reed had already realized.

Then again, he'd always liked a good challenge.

"Sorry, yes." Then the pretty boy brightened, his smile curious and warm. He seemed vaguely conflicted and self-conscious, even shy, for an actor type. Not that Reed had spent much time around actors, but he'd known swimmers on his team more ballsy, confident, cocky, and camera-ready than Tucker. "By all means, please reveal what's so special about this nerve center of yours."

Reed nodded. "That's more like it. Now, please witness the splendor, the majesty, of a well-stocked fridge." With that, he whipped open the double doors of the nearest cooler to reveal shelves jam-packed with every sort of tallboy can and bottle known to man, from imported bottled water to savory iced coffee to hard seltzers to imported beers and absolutely everything in between.

He turned back to Tucker with a "ta-da" face but found the youngling far from impressed. "Are you not entertained?" Reed teased in a gladiator-like tone.

Tucker smirked. "No, I am, it's just…." The kid waved his hand to encompass the big gleaming kitchen, stainless steel as far as the eye could see. "I guess I'm a little more used to these things by now, that's all."

Reed supposed he should have been offended, but he wasn't quite sure why. He kind of enjoyed the way Tucker gave it back to him every time he was excited or confused by something. "Well, we can't all be big

Hollywood movie stars with caviar wishes and champagne dreams, okay? This is, like, genuinely impressive to the other ninety-nine point nine percent of the population, just so we're clear. So, what's your poison?" Reed turned back to the gleaming fridge with all the gurgling excitement of an actual kid in an actual candy store with an actual twenty- dollar bill in his pocket. "I've got imported beers, craft beers, fruity beers, ciders, extra hard ciders—"

"TV," Tucker muttered, interrupting him as he inched closer to the open fridge door.

Reed turned to find the kid standing surprisingly close. "Pardon?"

Tucker grinned, reached past him for a couple of cold brown bottles, and took a step back. "I'm on a TV show, *Coach*. I've never been in a movie, so, just clearing things up now before these kick in, you know?" He winked and held up the bottles in one hand, the frosty glass clinking between his long, agile fingers.

Reed closed the fridge door and did a little mock-bow thing that suddenly made him feel awkward for the first time since the famous actress had left them alone together. He knew instinctively that it wouldn't be his last. He could feel the twinges of a crush forming, quickly, inevitably, undeniably. He knew the signs well enough. Knew also how hard it would be to deny them over the next two weeks in the face of Tucker's undeniable straightness. And wondered if it was that obvious straightness that somehow supercharged the crush factor. Tucker's aloofness, his uncertainty, the challenge of denying himself, and the "Don't you dare" vibe to the whole exchange were maybe contributing to the crush in the first place. Nothing made Reed want something more than being told he couldn't have it.

He gave Tucker a smoky gaze and murmured reply, just to make it clear he was definitely, in no way, entirely not into him at all, whatsoever. "Sorry, kid. Here I thought I was working for a big-time movie star or something."

Tucker gave him a kind of "tut-tut" scoff. "You sound disappointed."

They drifted back through the swinging kitchen doors and into the cafeteria proper. It was as big and cavernous on the inside as it had appeared on the outside, with gleaming hardwood floors and endless rows of wooden picnic tables to match the vaguely down-home aesthetic that the designers of Camp Run-A-Mok were clearly so intent on conveying.

Reed winced as he imagined what it might look, sound, and even smell like with a hundred or more noisy, rowdy, hormonal, sweaty, sunburned, snobby preteens clamoring to find their favorite table come chow time every evening.

"On the contrary," Reed said as they drifted past the rows of tables and out through a clattering screen door to a massive wraparound porch that looked out on the vast wooded acreage that was the central focus of their own private summer camp. "I'm honored."

Tucker chose one of the wooden rocking chairs from the seemingly endless row beside them. "I guess it's hard to tell with that smartass tone of yours."

"Is it?" Reed sank into the chair beside him, feeling a strange mix of weariness tinged with anticipation. It was something he hadn't felt in quite some time, if ever. The night he'd spent in his cabin alone, getting adjusted to the sound of nature outside his open window, the curtains fluttering, the bed empty, the crickets outside chirping, the moon his only nightlight, had been lonelier than he'd imagined. But with Tucker around—with his youthful enthusiasm and Hollywood cred and those cheeky dimples—he was looking forward to a very different night indeed.

Tuck was long and lean in the creaky rocking chair, green eyes peering out from beneath the jaunty brim of his weathered ball cap as he handed Reed one of the beers. "I suppose that's my default conversational style, Tuck, so if we're going to survive the next two weeks together, maybe, I dunno, get used to it?"

Tucker chuckled, easily twisting off the cap of his frosty brown bottle in a way that seemed surprisingly masculine for such a pretty-boy Hollywood type. Maybe there was more to this lanky young kid than met the eye. Not that Reed was complaining.

"Or what, exactly?"

Reed hoisted his own beer in a mock toast. "Or I scrounge around in the tool shed for a lock and use it on the door to all these fancy beers someone in your camp stocked up for us this week. That's what."

Tucker rolled his eyes but tapped Reed's bottle top just the same. It clicked with a resounding, satisfying vibration that sent a pleasant shiver through his hand. "Over my dead body, Coach."

Reed chuckled. "Hmmmm, big words for somebody who probably has, like, half a dozen stunt doubles doing his fighting for him all the time."

Tucker's bottle was halfway to his mouth. He paused it to smirk. "Who says I didn't bring them along, huh?" He took a quick swig after his halfhearted boast, then waved the bottle at the scenic camp vista laid out before them, the leaves of the towering trees wafting in the late afternoon breeze, the shimmering green lawns, and the smattering of cabins scattered across the landscape. "Maybe they're hiding in one of those cabins out there."

Reed took a long hard pull of his beer. The rich imported lager felt cold on his parched throat and good in his empty belly. He glanced back over at Tucker, in his effortlessly flattering black V-neck and khaki shorts. Before he could chicken out, he blurted something he would probably regret but could no longer deny.

"If they all look like you, Tuck, that might not be such a bad thing."

FIVE

Tucker

"WAS THAT a compliment?"

Tucker struggled to hide his blush. He righted the de rigueur *Suburban Dead* ball cap atop his unruly brown curls and avoided the big guy's roving brown eyes as Reed glanced over.

His voice was low and cryptic in reply. "Take it any way you want it, kid."

Tucker grinned nervously and seized on the very first opportunity to change the subject. "I'm not an actual kid, you know." He waved his beer bottle menacingly. "I mean, I'm old enough to drink these legally, okay? By a few good years, even."

Reed smirked knowingly. "Oh, I know you're not exactly jailbait. I just like the way it makes you flinch every time I say it."

Tucker rolled his eyes. Sipped his beer. It was cold and rich and good and soothing, just the right tonic after the long, anxious day. "Are you this way with your swimmers back home?"

"Let's just say I'm not like most college coaches, Tucker." Reed gave him an almost guarded glance, more evasive than the ones they'd shared so far. "Then again, I suppose that's what Costas wanted for his favorite TV star?"

Tucker rolled his eyes, imagining his producer and de facto boss, Costas Imperial, sitting in his plush penthouse office back in LA, no doubt plotting his character's eventual demise as they spoke. "How did you two get hooked up together in the first place?"

Reed was glancing out at the campgrounds, at the lush woods and rustic outbuildings and the massive fire pit in the middle that pulled it all together. Tucker followed his admiring gaze and wondered what it might look like at night. Then he realized he only had a few hours before he found out.

The thought—a night alone with a handsome stranger, cold beers and a warm fire, under a blanket of stars and not another soul around to interfere, judge, or admonish—gave Tucker delicious goose bumps full of risky, unwanted anticipation.

For years he'd struggled to tame his hidden desires in Hollywood's sexually fluid environment, despite the many opportunities to indulge them any way he saw fit. Tuck wondered if all of that hard work and temperance would come undone his first night in a deserted campground with some randy swim coach.

"I was his last choice," Reed finally grunted in reply. "Trust me."

"Really? Why?"

"Everyone else turned him down," Reed confessed. "I guess they didn't want to leave their teams mid training, you know?"

Tucker was vaguely surprised. Everything about Reed screamed uptight, adult, professional so loudly that his sudden admission seemed vaguely out of character. "And you did?"

Reed shrugged, avoiding Tucker's curious gaze. "It's not that I did, per se. I just wasn't entirely opposed to *not* doing it, I guess. That and the fact that my current, uh, position made it easier for me to take a break than it normally might have. Make sense?" He turned to Tucker with an almost vulnerable expression, something as new as it was suddenly endearing. He didn't mind the abrasive, cocky, older jock aesthetic, exactly, but it warmed him even further to think there was a vulnerable man with actual emotions lurking just underneath. Wondered too what it might take to get him to come out completely.

No pun intended.

Tucker shook his head. "Not really, no."

Reed sighed and confessed. "I guess it's not like the transition team really needs me in the first place, but they're stuck with me for now, so...."

"Transition team?"

Reed shrugged, voice monotone, as if reading from his resume. "Think of it as a bridge between high school seniors and college freshmen, the best coed swimmers in the district prepping for the big time with an actual college coach as their guide. I'm part recruiter, part coach, part cheerleader, part dance mom all rolled into one, scouting out the best and the brightest and prepping them for the big league."

"Sounds cryptic enough for Hollywood," Tucker teased, sensing something vaguely rehearsed in Reed's soliloquy, the longest the dude had spoken since they met.

"I kind of got thrust into it, for lack of a better term, midway through last season. Kira, my head coach, is far more qualified than me, as are the rest of the coaching staff. But since I have seniority, well, she's kind of stuck with me now. Either way, let's just say she'll be fine without me for a few weeks, that's all."

Tucker gave him a curious grin and a sly, chaste wink. "So what I'm hearing so far, Coach, is that they sent me the new guy this summer."

Reed replied with a knowing smile. Then he dropped a bombshell he'd probably been sitting on ever since they met: "Hey, pal, I've seen the video they leaked of your test swim on set, and let me put it this way, beggars can't be choosers."

SIX

Reed

"YOU SAW that?"

Reed took a long, leisurely sip from his beer, enjoying the pleasant vibe of a rocking chair beneath his ass, the late afternoon sun on his face, and the warm, soft glow of a day-drinking buzz deep in his surprisingly fluttery belly. He couldn't remember the last time a guy had made him feel that way.

"Tucker, everyone's seen it. You know that by now, don't you?" Reed remembered the first time he'd seen the viral video in question, when he broke up a gaggle of freshman swimmers outside the locker room as they hovered around one of their cell phones, squealing with delight and hitting Repeat over and over and over again. Grainy and wobbly, it nonetheless clearly showed a hapless young stud, bare except for a pair of cutoff denim shorts, slapping helplessly at the surface of a lap pool. At first glance it looked like someone drowning, but upon closer inspection, it was just a really pretty boy with really, really bad form. Nothing that couldn't be improved with a little discipline and know-how under Reed's expert tutelage, but that's certainly not how it must have looked to the untrained eyes of the millions of people who'd seen it and commented on it online.

Suddenly Reed felt bad for the guy all over again. In fact, now that Reed was sitting face-to-face with Tucker, he felt even worse.

"No, I'm aware it's gone viral. I just choose to kind of block it out of my mind, you know? Like maybe it's happening to someone else and not me."

Reed gave him a cool, steady glance, if only to admire the adorably thin stubble of Tucker's wispy five-o'clock shadow. "That's the only logical choice, yes."

Tucker suddenly looked miserable. Reed felt bad for the poor kid. All the looks, fame, and money in the world, and one clandestine video of him slapping around in that big Hollywood pool like a cat with three legs had made him the latest TikTok laughingstock. "You know how these things are, Tuck. People watch for one day and then forget about it."

Tucker gave him a world-weary frown over the lip of his beer bottle. "Easy for you to say, non-viral video guy."

"Fair enough. Who do you think leaked it, anyway?"

Tucker seemed to squirm in his chair, as if it wasn't an easy topic to discuss. "Supposedly it was some random crew member, one of only a handful that were there that day. It was a closed set, so it limits the potential suspects to less than two dozen, but so far it's still a mystery, and no one's rushing to confess, especially now that it's gone viral."

"Just seems like a shitty thing to do, is all."

"Shitty? Sure. Good for ratings? You bet."

Reed struggled to remain impartial. Even with all that had happened to him back at school, this seemed particularly cruel. "What, you think someone did it on purpose?"

"Not at first," Tucker explained. "I think it was just something that looked funny to someone who didn't know any better. And maybe they shared it with a few friends and those friends shared it with a few friends, and it might have died that way if the folks in charge of the network didn't notice and maybe play a hand in making it go viral."

"They'd do that?"

"If it meant more viewers, more often, who'd never tuned into the show before? Sure, I think so. I'm certain of it, actually."

"Even if it means making you look like a fool?"

"I'm not sure they look at most of us as 'people' anyway, so I'm not really taking it personally. I just want it behind me so I can move on and not be 'that guy who can't swim' anymore."

"That's gross, Tucker."

"Which part?"

"Every part, I guess. College athletics can be catty, trust me, but that is some next-level BS."

Reed sipped his beer, quietly fuming and not sure why. He barely knew this kid, but if it had happened to one of his swimmers? He would have been pissed. Reed wondered what kind of support system Tucker had, if he even had one at all.

"What?"

Tucker's question jolted Reed out of his protective reverie.

"What, 'what'?"

Tucker waved his empty beer bottle toward Reed's eyes. "Just trying to get a read on those judgey brown eyes of yours, man."

Reed squirmed deeper into his rocking chair, the warm Southern air on his face and the soft, worn wicker beneath his ass. He wondered, mildly, what it meant that Tucker already knew what color his eyes were.

If it meant anything at all.

"Anyway, whoever it was kind of did you a favor."

Tucker looked surprised by the comment. "Oh yeah? Like what? Making me a laughingstock who will probably never work again?"

"Listen, they got that producer of yours to get in touch with all the swim coaches in Georgia, which led you to me when none of them would touch this with a ten-foot pole, and led me to here. And after the next two weeks, we'll have you looking like Michael Phelps, and just think what that's gonna do when somebody leaks a video of that shit on purpose."

"That's gonna be a tall order," Tucker mumbled.

Reed saw his chance to tease his new charge out of his blue Hollywood funk. "Speaking of orders," he reminded, waving his empty beer bottle suggestively.

Tucker's eyes grew wide above an inevitable smile. "What, why am I the one getting the beers?"

Reed next waved the empty bottle at the screen door. "You're the one who sat closest to the fridge, bro. Rookie move, that's all I'm sayin'."

Tucker narrowed his eyes and, with a huff and a puff, announced, "Aren't I technically your boss for the next two weeks?"

Reed winked. "Hardly, kid. If anything, I'm your boss until we whip that nonswimming ass of yours into Olympic shape, okay? And the sooner you realize that, the better it will be for both of us. So...." He made a hurry-up gesture with the bottle that really got Tucker's nostrils to flaring. It was quite the sight. Reed was suddenly enjoying himself immensely. "Chop-chop, kid."

"Fine," Tucker huffed as he scooted from his chair. "But you're getting the next round."

Reed listened to the screen door slam shut behind him and squirmed delightedly in his chair. Suddenly a third round with Tucker was the best thing he'd heard in a good long while. To say nothing of a fourth.

SEVEN

Tucker

"WAIT, WHEN did you get here again?"

Tucker stood outside Reed's cabin, aglow with warm light and an already made bed. Beside it, an unzipped duffel had spilled from the center zipper outward, track pants and hoodies and rolled-up tube socks bulging out in the middle like a loaded baked potato.

"Yesterday," Reed admitted a tad sheepishly as they stood uncomfortably close on his front porch. "I didn't want to get lost."

"So you came a day early?" Tucker was no world-famous explorer himself, but even *he* thought that was a tad excessive.

Reed avoided his eyes. "I mean, it's an important gig. I didn't want to show up late."

Tucker narrowed his eyes and nodded knowingly at his new coach. Maybe there was a heart under that big, bad exterior. "I thought you took it as an afterthought, tough guy."

Reed leaned against the frame of the open door. From above, an intermittently flickering porch light cast flattering shadows across his masculine face. Tucker struggled not to stare and even harder not to drool. Hollywood was full of handsome men, but they were often so generically beautiful as to be bland and vaguely boring. Antiseptic, even.

Reed had a natural, rugged quality that not only invited the eyes but practically demanded them. Tucker wasn't sure how it would translate in front of the camera, if his charm would have the same magnetic effect on film as it did in person, but up close?

He was all but irresistible. He was also exceedingly flirtatious, even coy in his own cocky, testing-the-waters way, and the last thing Tucker needed after going viral with his flailing-in-the-pool video was to add an illicit affair with his swim coach to the mix. A viral video with his shorts on was one thing. Being caught with his pants down—with another man no less—was quite another.

"I wasn't gonna take the gig at all," Reed insisted, "but when the kids on the transition team heard who I'd be teaching, they wouldn't let me *not* take it."

"I thought it was supposed to be confidential," Tucker teased. He'd forced himself to stop after three beers, though he'd been sorely tempted to crack open a fourth. Even so, the short walk to Reed's cabin in the sultry Georgia heat had left him breathless, buzzed, and ballsy, in all the best ways.

They still stood in front of the cabin's screen door. Reed had made no move to ask him in, and despite the crumbling inhibitions of an unexpected buzz, Tucker had made no move to be asked. They'd had no problem sitting side by side on the mess hall porch, rocking—and drinking—steadily. But suddenly, standing face-to-face in front of an empty cabin full of tempting beds, they seemed to have drawn the line on moving forward. He regarded his coach curiously and tried to keep the topic light and nonflirtatious. "So you've really never seen an episode of my show? Not even one?"

Reed looked immediately uncomfortable, apologetic even. "It's not you, Tuck, it's me. I just don't watch a lot of TV, that's all."

"I get it," Tucker teased. In a way, he was almost relieved Reed had never seen any of *Suburban Dead*. It would make things easier going forward. None of that hype and fawning and stiffness that came along with being around someone so-called famous. "Big player like yourself, you're probably out on a date every night while the rest of, you know, the civilized world is binging our next episode."

Reed scoffed. "Hardly."

"Hardly you're out boffing babes every night?" Tucker teased, as if on a fact-finding mission, stealthy as it might have been. "Or hardly only half the civilized world is watching our show?"

Reed gave Tucker a playful hip check and winked. "Probably a little bit of both. I'd ask you in, but…." He inched a little closer—close enough for Tucker to see the hints of gold in his brown eyes. "Mr. Tatum made it clear we had our own bunkhouses for the duration, sorry."

Reed nodded to the next cabin over. Where his coach's was painted a cheery tortilla yellow, Tucker's was a rustic pine green. "That's yours over there."

Reed's hand was on the screen door handle, but he hadn't opened it yet. They seemed to be sharing a moment. Which kind, Tucker wasn't quite sure, but the air between them was definitely charged.

"Probably for the best anyway," Tucker muttered playfully, as if unwilling to let the evening end without at least a smidge of halfhearted take-it-either-way flirtatiousness. "You look like a snorer to me."

Reed snorted, as if that were the last thing he expected Tucker to say. "Not sure about the snoring part, but I've been known to sleep in the altogether, and that can get a little, uh, *intimidating* for guys like you."

Tucker snorted and backed away as flashes of Reed—all of Reed— flooded the back of his fluttering eyelids. "Guys like me?" he asked, finding himself on the bottom step as Reed lingered in the doorway, bathed in the glow of the cabin lights behind him.

Reed gave Tucker another one of his long, lingering up-and-down takes. When their eyes met again, his smile was soft and teasing. "Yeah, you know, you Hollywood types with your big egos and your little, well...."

Tucker was still chuckling when he finally got to his cabin. He turned back only once, to find Reed safely behind his door, a shadowy figure bathed in orange light, half turning as if expecting something else to happen.

Eight

Reed

"You did bring a bathing suit, right?"

Tucker stood, midway through the double doors that led to the mess kitchen. He looked pleasantly rumpled, casually dressed in khaki shorts and a faded *Suburban Dead* T-shirt. His eyes were still at half-mast when Reed handed him a coffee mug steaming from the bittersweet black brew inside.

He looked disappointed, and not just from the lackluster coffee. "Yeah, but I mean, are we starting *today*?"

Reed gave him a playfully stern growl. "No time like the present, kid. What, you maybe had other plans for filling your time at a deserted summer camp all day?"

Tucker frowned beneath his adorably slept-on curls. "It's just, we didn't really set anything in stone last night, so I figured today was an off day."

Reed watched Tucker blow on his coffee, the tendrils of steam swirling and separating under his plump, kissable lips. "I guess I just assumed you'd wanted to get started right away, that's all."

Tucker looked uncomfortable, and it wasn't just from the black coffee. He swallowed audibly, like something out of a movie. Or in his case, a hit TV show about suburban zombies or whatnot. When he glanced back over at Reed, his eyes were beseeching and wide. "I mean, I can change if… if…."

Reed took pity on the poor guy. He hadn't been planning much for that day in the first place—a little kickboard action, some paddling exercises, a few strength and conditioning drills—but suddenly he toned down even those basics-for-beginners antics in response to Tucker's miserable face and pathetic body language. "Look, we'll start slow, okay? You're the boss here. We'll just get our feet wet this morning, okay? Like, literally, just our feet." As if for emphasis, Reed dangled one foot ridiculously an inch off the floor.

Tucker's relief was palpable. "Promise?"

Reed gave in with a sigh. "I promise to only get as wet as you want us to, Tucker. How about that?"

Tucker was coming back to life somewhat. His face took on a dubious grin above the half-empty coffee mug. "That sounds like a trick, Coach."

"Hardly, kid. I'm trusting you to know your limits, and if you want to get more than your feet wet, we'll do that. But it'll be up to you either way, okay?"

"Scout's honor?"

"I was never a Scout."

Tucker frowned. "Me either. Coach's honor, then?"

Reed chuckled, relieved to see the kid so relieved. "That I can cop to, Tuck."

"Can we eat first?" Tucker was not only bashful this morning, Reed noticed, but particularly boyish as well. Not that Reed was complaining. He much preferred boyish to bossy, especially in the bedroom. Not that that was ever going to happen, of course, but everything in his imagination was fair game, so why not a fantasy or two? Particularly the kind that had boyish, gawky Tucker in Reed's soft white sheets, naked and writhing under Reed's tutelage for good measure.

He tossed the kid a granola bar from a wicker basket full of vaguely healthy snack treats on the counter between them.

"Sure thing."

Tucker gave the snack bar a woeful frown, then glanced helplessly at Reed, like perhaps he needed to learn how to unwrap breakfast treats as well as swim an entire lap without flailing like a wounded seal. "Wow, thanks."

Now that they were both awake and the plans had been settled on for that day, Reed was enjoying their playful exchange in the massive kitchen. "What? You were expecting five-star Hollywood service?"

Tuck smirked as if he'd been caught doing something dirty. "Hardly, but cinnamon, bro? There's no banana nut bread in there or anything? Even plain is better than this mess."

"Wow, you really are a spoiled A-lister, huh, Tuck? I thought Summer was the diva, but I guess I was wrong."

Tucker rolled his eyes. They barely knew each other at all yet, but of the few distinct moods Reed had witnessed so far, he liked Tuck at his sarcastic, flirty best.

"Hardly, I just know there's better snacks in there if you'd looked a little harder."

Reed clucked his tongue, grabbed the basket off the counter, and wiggled it in front of Tuck's face. "Feel free, snack food detective. I hope you can do better than I did if, you know, you just fend for yourself?"

"Fine, yes, okay. This is great, super, thanks." Tucker waved the basket away and opened his bar. Reed snickered and set it back on the counter. It was vibrant and stocked with gaily colored treats galore, enough to last them the rest of their duration at Camp Run-A-Mok.

"Thought so." He finished his own coffee and prepared to get wet.

Tucker nibbled at the granola bar with small, tentative bites that indicated he hadn't actually been hungry. Just stalling for more time before hitting the pool, probably. Reed could give him that much. He wasn't in much of a hurry, either way.

This whole deal—the deserted camp, the time away from a school where he'd been made to feel like a pariah, the lack of prying eyes from the nosy, cloistered coaching staff or the constant chatter of the vindictive administrative staff—had him feeling vaguely vacation-y.

Reed tried to remember the last time he'd been on an actual vacation and couldn't, for the life of him. Since high school he'd either been in competition mode on a swim team or, after college, coaching one team or another. There had been little time in between for anything other than working or swimming or both. Up until now it had kept him busy and, if not jumping for joy, at least satisfied with his life choices, such as they were. Suddenly, here in this ghost town of a deserted summer camp with some Hollywood star who felt more like the boy next door, Reed was in a temporary state of absolutely *not* giving one single fuck.

He found he liked it.

A lot.

Tucker was done with his granola bar. He crinkled up the wrapper and tossed it into the trash can at his feet.

"Feel better, kid?"

Long, lean, and youthful in the kitchen's brightly lit landscape, Tucker leaned back against the counter. "Sorry, yeah, I guess I was a little hangry."

"A little?"

"I guess. I dunno. I was expecting a little more out of Scream Studios in the way of accommodations, you know?"

"Kid, we've got the run of an entire summer camp for the next, like, thirteen days." Reed tapped the massive stainless-steel cooler beside him for emphasis. "Three or four stocked fridges of random delicacies, an Olympic-size pool just for two, ten different cabins to choose from, walking trails, bikes and ATVs, what more do you want, exactly?"

Reed wondered what else the Hollywood hot guy could find to bitch about. As usual, Tucker didn't disappoint. "Fine, yes, but would indoor plumbing have killed anybody?"

Reed chuckled, big toe still sore from stubbing it on the way to the communal bathroom in the middle of the night. "I wondered when you might notice we weren't exactly staying at the Ritz."

"I noticed as soon as I got to my room, Reed. You could have warned me, at least."

"It's a summer camp, Tuck. What'd you expect?"

"I dunno. Maybe I am a little spoiled, but even on location we have private porta potties, geez."

Reed gave the kid a playful growl, tempted to chuck him under his chiseled chin for good measure. "It's a minor inconvenience, bro. Relax."

"I'm fine, but you could have warned me."

"What, and spoil all the fun?"

Reed wasn't about to admit that every time he used the bathroom-slash-shower area between their cabins the night before, he'd been half expecting, mostly hoping, positively wishing Tucker might stumble in, a wake-up boner half in, half out of his baggy boxer shorts or clingy cotton briefs.

Alas, he had had to stand there alone, relieving himself in the dead of night with only the sound of chirping crickets and buzzing mosquitos and his cheap, lurid dime-novel fantasies to keep him company.

Reed nibbled on a banana. "Why don't you call your big Hollywood producer bro, and maybe he can get one of those fancy movie star trailers in here so you can sleep in the manner of luxury you're accustomed to, hotshot?"

Tucker rolled his eyes but didn't quite back down. "Look, I'm fully aware I'm sounding like a giant-ass diva right now, but I feel like I'm being punished for not knowing how to swim."

"For the eight hundredth time, Tuck, you're not being punished. So you had to walk eight steps to the bathroom. It's okay. So you had to choke down a cinnamon granola bar instead of the organic, gluten-free non-GMO banana-bread kind you're used to back in Beverly Hills. You'll get over it. Promise."

Reed reached out with a tentative hand, squeezed Tuck's shoulder emphatically, and gave him an overdramatically comforting nod. "Today is a time for healing, my child. Would you like to share a moment of silence with me?"

Tucker shrugged his way out of Reed's grasp and shook his head with a playful snort, the hint of a smile indicating the kid might have a sense of humor. "I'm not a diva, okay?"

"If you say so, diva."

"Fine, let's just start over."

Reed winked over his half-dressed banana, the peels hanging down in all directions like a cheerleader's skirt. "Good idea."

"I'm just…."

Reed waited for the punchline, and when it never came, delivered it himself. "You're nervous, Tucker. I get that."

Tucker nodded, staring at his feet. "I just don't want to look like a fool again."

Reed felt the same swell of almost-parental concern he had when hearing why Tucker was in such a predicament in the first place. "To whom, Tuck? To me? I'm not filming our lessons, God knows, and I'm not working undercover for *Screen Scandal* magazine either. It's just you and me out here, Tuck. Even if you do look foolish from time to time, no one's gonna know except me, and by the end of our time together, you're gonna be swimming like a shark and any slight misstep along the way will be long forgotten."

Tucker looked painfully sincere as he finally glanced over. There was a slight pause before his voice cracked. "Promise?"

Reed tossed his empty banana peel into the trash at his feet. Then he reached inside the fridge beside him, grabbed two bottles of water, stood to his full height, and glanced back at Tucker, almost eye to eye across the industrial sized kitchen.

"Look, Tucker, real talk? You don't know me. I don't know you. But we've got two weeks to change all that, starting today, and when I make a promise, I don't break it, okay? I know you live in a different world than I do, where relationships are just for page views and ratings and contract negotiations, but you and me? We can't fake this. I'll make you a promise, but at the same time, you have to promise me something in return, capisce?"

"Like what?"

"I promise to teach you how to swim like a badass Aquaman mother trucker, and all you have to do, Tucker? Is promise to trust me and just release all this nervousness and self-doubt along the way. Deal?"

Tucker gave a sly, relenting grin and extended his hand to meet Reed's. They shook, and Tucker's grip was surprisingly firm for a guy who'd just gone on a ten-minute rant about having to walk to the bathroom in the middle of the night, heaven forbid. "It's hard for me to trust people, Reed. Okay?"

Tucker gave his fingers a good tight squeeze and then drifted from Reed's grip. "I may not be the star of yesterday's funniest viral video, Tucker, but it's not exactly easy for me to trust others either, so we've got that in common, at least."

Tucker cocked his pretty head to one side and examined him with gently curious eyes. "Why not?"

"Pardon?"

"Why don't you trust other people, Reed? You seem pretty easygoing, far as I can tell."

Reed winked, surprised the kid would even listen to what he had to say, let alone dig deeper. "Let's just say, you're not the only good actor in the room, Tuck."

Tucker grinned and slapped Reed playfully on the shoulder. "Aw, so you *do* think I'm a good actor."

NINE

Tucker

"FEELS GOOD, actually."

Tucker wriggled his toes in the clear pool water. He sat on the pool deck, Reed across from him. Unlike Tucker, he had worn a pair of faded red baggies that clung to him like a second skin, tight in all the right places and loose where it counted the most. It had been a challenge to make eye contact all afternoon, let alone to keep from popping wood in front of his new coach.

Reed brightened, face fresh and clean and damp under the hot Georgia sun. His stubbly black hair only added to the lean, masculine cut of his already intoxicating jib. "Right? You sure you don't want to actually, you know, get inside the pool? Cool off a little before you shrivel up like a piece of bacon sitting there in the sun?"

Tucker shrugged bare broad shoulders that actually felt like they might be on fire. "I'd love to, but I didn't bring my trunks this morning, remember?"

Reed snorted. He was leaning back slightly, palms out on either side of him as his tendons flexed in the flattering fall sunlight. His feet danced beneath the surface of the clear, blue water. Inviting indeed. "Yeah, well, I'm not walking my happy ass back to your cabin to get you some, that's for sure."

"Well, me either, so this is fine." Even as he said it, another rivulet of sweat ran down his face, bearing witness to the lie.

Reed rolled his eyes and jutted his chin out in Tucker's direction. Namely, the direction of his sweltering crotch. "Boxers or briefs?"

Tucker started, as if he hadn't heard right. "Beg pardon?"

"You heard me, kid. Do you wear boxers or briefs under those khaki cargo pants you seem to favor?"

Tucker struggled to contain the burst of excitement the question had elicited deep down in his very bone marrow. "I wear boxers, but they're, like, really thin and white."

Reed rolled his eyes again, making Tucker feel silly and, well, something else as well. He just wasn't sure what yet. Or maybe he was absolutely sure but just didn't want to admit it to himself. Yet. "Do you see any cameras here, bro? It's you, it's me, I mean…." He tugged at the waistband of the clingy red baggies that temptingly hugged his lean, narrow waist and generous package. "They can't be any thinner than these, right?"

Tucker was adamant. He was no prude, but Reed was basically asking him to go skinny-dipping in the middle of the day in front of a veritable stranger. "Uh, yeah they can."

Reed gave him a lurid little wink. "I mean, if you're worried about your little dinky-winky, just say that, bro. Use your words. Let it all out. I already told you, you're among friends here."

Tucker chuckled with a combination of relief, nervousness, curiosity, and more than anything, the rampant desire of being hot and sweaty with a handsome stranger and nothing more than a thin layer of damp boxer shorts between them.

He'd had wet dreams less sexy than that.

"It's not that, obviously."

Reed sat up, taut chest rippling with the effort. He clapped his hands together in front of him, guru style, pointing his fingers beneath his stubbly chin as if giving the matter much deep thought. "Remember our little discussion about trust, Tucker? I trust you, and more importantly, *you* trust *me*. This? Here? This is one of those moments."

Tucker jutted his chin back in reply. "As in?"

"As in, trust me when I say it's hot as shit out here and it's only gonna get hotter as the day goes on, so get in the damn pool if you want to survive."

"It's not the getting in I'm worried about. It's the getting out."

"So I'll look away, bro. Sheesh. When I accepted this gig, they didn't tell me you were a frickin' Mormon or something."

"I'm not. It's just that Hollywood has made me paranoid, I guess." As if to prove it, Tucker reflexively scanned the perimeter of the pool area for hidden cameras or quietly buzzing surveillance drones, all the better to add a clandestine picture of his wet willy to go along with his infamous swimming-fail video.

Reed spread his arms again, as if to signify his near nakedness. "Do you see any paparazzi here, Tuck? I'm not wearing a wire, and where the hell would I hide a camera in this getup? It's you, it's me, it's a pair of wet boxers. What's the worst that could happen?"

Tucker sighed. The minute Reed suggested it, he knew he was going to strip down to his skivvies and slip quietly into the clear, tempting pool.

Obviously. It just took him a while to work up to things like that. Not that things like that happened to him often, of course. Hardly ever, in fact.

Well, to be honest, almost never.

"Fine," he grumbled dramatically and pushed himself into a standing position, wet feet practically steaming on the sizzling concrete as he danced from sole to sole. He glanced around as if someone might see and took in the deck chairs stacked like cordwood along the chain link fence surrounding the Olympic-size pool.

His fingers drifted down to the button of his rumpled khaki shorts, eyes drifting across to where Reed sat peering back at him placidly as if this was just the most natural thing in the world. He supposed, in a way, it was. Two guys, hanging out at the pool, the unbearable heat making stripping down to one's skivvies and jumping into the pool the only logical choice.

So why were his hands suddenly trembling as he slowly unfastened his button and dragged down his zipper? Why was his heart pounding? Why was he so glad for the simmering shadows to hide the perspiration that had sprung out all over his body? Why was he so hungry for Reed's eyes as he drank in Tuck's plump lips, slightly parted, his body poised in anticipation.

Of what? Tucker shrugged his pants down his hips, then past his knees until he finally stepped out of them altogether, one foot at a time, feeling naked and exposed to the world.

Reed's voice was low, as if perhaps someone might overhear them. "Was that so hard, Tuck?"

Tucker shook his head. He absently folded his shorts and placed them on top of the *Suburban Dead* T-shirt he'd discarded as soon as they wandered onto the pool deck an hour or so earlier. Now he stood, naked save for the achingly thin boxer shorts that clung to his bony hips. He struggled to ignore Reed's ravenous eyes and awkward silence as he stepped first one foot, then the other, onto the pool steps, water swallowing his feet, then his ankles, then his shins, until he stood in waist-deep water, running his hands nervously along the surface on either side of his hips.

Already he could feel the boxers wrapping around his jewels like a glove, caressing his downturned staff like a mysterious lover. He was glad, at least, that most of him was beneath the water's surface.

"See there." Reed slipped into the water to lean against the pool deck at his back. "You're practically swimming already."

"Practically."

Tucker's voice was low and hoarse. The heat from above and the cool water from below were merging to bathe him in the most pleasant of sensations, making him worry he might react in some embarrassingly prominent way.

Reed's limber descent into the pool had left them surprisingly— suddenly—achingly close. He couldn't back away without seeming even more awkward than he already did when he balked at taking off his shorts, but being this close to Reed was testing Tucker's acting skills to the limit.

And he'd never been accused of being an Oscar contender in the first place.

Reed seemed to sense his partner's discomfort, perhaps even enjoyed it. "Something… bothering you, Tuck?"

"No, why?"

"You just seem nervous, that's all." Was it Tuck's imagination, or had Reed just taken another step closer? Either way, he was already too close by far.

Tucker met his eyes, struggling to bluff his way out of his sudden state of nervousness. "We're in a pool, right? That's not exactly my forte, remember?"

Reed clucked his tongue. "Correction, you seem nervous about more than just swimming, Tuck."

Tucker sighed and drifted away until his own back rested against the warm pool tiles and they stood, mirroring each other's posture from across the shimmering shallow end of the big blue pool.

"I have a lot to be nervous about, actually." This time he wasn't just bluffing.

"Yeah, like what?" Reed's eyes were at once hooded and curious, but he seemed genuinely interested in Tucker's reply.

Tucker didn't hesitate to open up. He found it quite easy to talk to Reed, in fact. Easier, he found, than he'd been able to talk to anyone in a very long time. "Like what's happening on set while I'm away. I haven't missed a season since we started this crazy ride four years ago, so...."

"I thought you guys were on hiatus."

"Yeah, I mean, we're not on camera every day, but there are still script pages to approve and costume fittings to show up for and Zoom calls to make and storyboards to weigh in on. I feel a little removed from it all at the moment, that's all."

"I'm no expert, but isn't that the point of a hiatus?"

"Yes and no, I suppose. I've always been Johnny on the spot before. Just tell me where to go and I'll be there, early, before anybody else. And now? Well, let's just say a lot can happen in two weeks, you know?"

Reed cocked his head curiously. "Like what?"

Tucker swallowed hard and fessed up. "Like getting replaced, for one. After something like that, there really is no number two."

Reed gave him another wide-eyed grimace. "Aren't you, like, the star?"

Tucker made a "how dumb can you be?" face before instantly regretting it. It wasn't necessarily his fault. Reed was so movie-star handsome, so Hollywood cool, so knowing and cocky and irresistible that Tucker had a hard time forgetting he wasn't actually a big star himself. "Yeah, the so-called star of a show where the shock appeal has always been that one of the stars dies every season, so...."

"I thought you didn't really care about all this Hollywood stuff in the first place, though."

"I don't. At least I didn't at first. But now that I'm in it, and in it so intensely, I'm not sure what I'd do without it at this point."

Reed squirmed where he stood, tan lines aglow atop the slipping-down waistband of his baggies. His skin was smooth and radiant, almost hairless. No, Tucker realized, he was hairless—smooth and slick as a baby's butt. Tucker let his eyes covet Reed's body from afar, admiring the place where his happy trail should be and finding none. The realization made him wonder if Reed was smooth everywhere else as well. All the way down, for instance. Hollywood, Tucker knew, was full of dudes who manscaped to various degrees. He hadn't taken Reed for a pretty-boy spa-day salon type, but maybe he preferred the feel of nothing, nowhere, anywhere. Tucker couldn't help but wonder what that might look like—

smooth and clean and hairless. He scrubbed the thought away as quickly as it had come. The last thing he needed to be doing at that moment was picturing Reed's smooth, slick junk.

Or at least, he tried to stop.

"I'm getting mixed messages here, Tuck."

Tucker chuckled, glad for the return to normal, civilized above-the-waist conversation that didn't necessarily involve manscaping and literal navel gazing.

He glanced up from Reed's bare waistline and grinned. "Yeah, I guess I'm all messed up. Hate the Hollywood game but am kind of addicted now. Maybe this hiatus will actually be good for me, you know?"

Reed nodded as he sank down slowly beneath the surface of the crystal-blue water until only his head poked out. His big brown eyes, soulful and searching, made it clear he wanted Tucker to join him.

He licked his lips, torso still broiling in the late August sun, bare shoulders already reddening from an early burn. He sighed and sank down to join Reed. The water claimed his sweaty bare skin and forced a sudden involuntary smile from his lips.

His feet were still firmly on the shallow-end concrete, knees slightly bent, chest buoyant as he clung to the pool deck with one hand, just in case. He realized, in that moment, he had gone deeper than he'd intended to go and far quicker.

Reed gave him a satisfied grin and nodded at his bobbing form. "Look at you, half-submerged and everything. And on your very first day, no less." His tone, as always, was part nurturing, part smartass. The sound was quickly becoming music to Tucker's ears.

"Don't get any ideas, Reed."

"Who? Me?"

Still, it felt good to cling to the pool deck, the water gently lapping him back and forth as Reed regarded him curiously. "What about you?" Tucker asked, bobbing safely. At least, as long as his wet fingers clung to the pool deck.

"What about me?"

"Are you gonna be able to enjoy this little break, or is coaching me gonna jam you up?"

Reed smiled. "I already am."

"Seriously, though. I hope we're paying you enough to make the break worth your while."

Reed's satisfied expression made it clear that, as usual, Scream Studios had spared no expense when throwing money at a problem. "And then some."

Tucker arched an eyebrow curiously. "Oh yeah? How much?"

"A gentleman never tells," Reed teased. "But let's just say it blows my coaching salary for the entire year out of the water." He lifted his hands from the pool's surface, long, pale fingers dripping temptingly with little beads of water. "No pun intended."

"Careful, that Hollywood money will hook you fast."

Reed made a face, and Tucker chuckled. "I mean, if you are looking for a change of pace, pretty sure you're Hollywood ready, bud."

"Sure, I mean, if we don't get you in swimming shape in time, I can always be your swim double."

Tucker nodded. That wasn't an entirely bad idea. Why didn't anyone on the set of *Suburban Dead* think of that? For that matter, why hadn't *he*? A simple title change from Coach to Stunt Swimmer could have saved him a few weeks of trouble here in the armpit of Bumsuck, Georgia.

Then again, he would have never gotten a gander at Reed in his wet, clingy baggies, and he wouldn't have wanted to miss that.

He gave Reed another appraising nod and struggled not to imagine him in the altogether. Then again, Reed hadn't been kidding—those wet, clingy baggies really did leave little to the imagination.

"Pretty sure I could do better for you than that, Reed."

Reed scoffed, and Tucker wondered if the poor guy knew what a stunner he really was. "Not quite sure I'm ready to give up my career as a washed-up swim coach just to be an extra on some zombie TV show, Tuck."

Tucker clucked. "Extra? We're talking leading man material here, bud."

Reed's eyes opened a little wider, and Tucker struggled to hide the blush that rose to his face. He hadn't meant to be so complimentary so soon, and not quite so loudly.

Then again, he hadn't meant to be so smitten with his swim coach either.

Reed was predictably surprised. "Was that an actual *compliment*?"

"Sorry," Tucker teased. "The heat must be getting to me."

Their eyes met across the pool. Tucker felt foolish for his poor choice of words. Or perhaps, his hasty ones. He knew sexuality was pretty fluid in Hollywood, but never his own. He wasn't one to go around flattering other men, no matter how tall, lean, limber, sexy, smooth, seductive, or wet one currently was, lounging lazily in the pool across from him with his drawers threatening to drift down those smooth, sultry hips at any moment.

It wasn't that Tucker was surprised by his powerful attraction to Reed. He'd had various crushes in the past—hotties in their steamy nakedness in the high school locker room, handsome actors waiting for an audition, random strangers in smoky nightclubs or private parties, eager reporters at red-carpet premieres, or tempting extras on location, but he'd either been too scared in the past or, like now, too invested in his future to indulge in his long-simmering but deeply buried desires.

He had crossed the line with one high school crush in his past, but never anything more and nothing since. Now, suddenly, alone in the sweltering Georgia heat with someone like Reed, who despite being macho and cocky as sin seemed to be pretty "fluid" himself, Tucker felt vaguely… unhinged.

In the past, he'd always been able to control his impulses before they got the best of him. He'd stopped drinking before his inhibitions lowered enough to invite a potential scandal, ended an interview before it got too obviously flirty, or shut down a sexy-ass intern before he had the chance to sneak into his dressing room. But now, removed from the trappings of his Hollywood lifestyle and far away from the prying eyes, alert ears, and gossip-ready tongues of reporters and paparazzi, he felt his resolve give way like the sagging waistband of Reed's swim trunks.

What's worse, he sensed Reed knew it as well.

TEN

Reed

"COMFY?"

Tucker leaned back in his deck chair, long since dried and smooth tan skin aglow in the day's waning light. Somehow, in between the kid's second and third beer, he'd given up on putting his shorts back on and now lay, in all his splendor, clingy white boxer shorts drying in the sun.

"Kinda. I mean...."

Reed chuckled, enjoying Tuck's discomfort. In or out of the pool, he invariably found himself "coaching" his younger charge in more ways than just swimming laps, to include the proper way to dry out after a long, tempting practice.

They had dragged two of the deck chairs down from the towering pile along the fence, and Tucker was still not happy with the way they were situated. His rumpled, confused, awkward expression gave Reed no end of subtle delight.

He couldn't help but chuckle at Tucker's obvious discontent. "What? Still?"

Tucker made a face, brown curls drying in the sun and hollow cheeks subtly flushed. Whether it was from an afternoon in the sun or spending all day half-naked and wet in Reed's company remained to be seen.

"I just, is this how you always lie out?"

Reed replied with a pleased tone. "I don't lie out on the regular, actually. It just seemed the most natural way to sit."

"Facing each other?"

Reed double-checked. They were, in fact, facing each other, his feet facing Tucker's head and vice versa. Still. Just the way he had arranged the chairs when he'd unstacked them, with a cooler full of cold green beer bottles within arm's reach between them. "Sure, I mean... you prefer we sit side by side like real housewives or some shit?"

"That's how they do it at hotels, sure."

"But we're not at a hotel."

"Don't remind me." Tucker must still have been sore about the communal restrooms.

"I mean, when you go out on a date, do you sit on the same side of the table as your lady friend?"

Tucker distractedly waved his half-empty beer bottle, light winking off its cool green surface the same way it did off the kid's matching green eyes. "God no, that's for rednecks and old people."

Reed chuckled. He couldn't argue with that logic. "Well, then."

"So, what? This is a date now?"

Reed sighed. They'd been dancing around each other all day, in and out of the pool and everywhere in between. Trading glances and inching closer, then away from each other, back and forth, closer then farther, wet and sticky and hot and smooth until it was finally Miller time and they'd decided to linger in the sun a little while longer, sipping beers and risking glances.

Bad idea.

Reed was no expert, but his gaydar was giving him the warm fuzzies and hot tingles and sharp stabs and everything in between. Then again, it could have been his second beer on an empty stomach. Or was it his third? He was no lightweight, but something about the heat and the sun and the pool and the beer and the prospect of what lay just beneath Tucker's damp, clingy boxers had him positively giddy.

And epically, perhaps even unstoppably, curious.

"I mean, it's a date if you want it to be," Reed teased, lobbing off a quick salvo in his fact-finding mission.

Tucker just rolled his eyes cryptically and sipped his beer. He stared back, unblinking for once. "Speaking of, is anyone missing you back home?"

Reed nearly spit out his latest sip of cold, crisp imported Hollywood-worthy beer. "Is that… I mean… are you asking me if I'm dating anyone at the moment?"

Tucker kept his eyes level with Reed's and nodded over the lip of his fast-emptying beer bottle. "I mean, I figure 'no' unless you're just really playing hard to get."

"Oh yeah, why's that?"

"Because I haven't seen you on your phone since we got here, and most people in relationships at least check in a few times a day."

Reed nodded, impressed. "So, like, do you play a detective on *Neighborhood Zombies*?"

Tucker chuckled good-naturedly, a most unexpected and agreeable sound indeed. Reed liked watching his flat belly flutter when he did that, smooth and firm above the waistband of his boxers. "*Suburban Dead*, and no. We're undercover zombie hunters living in suburbia, and you'd know all this already if you'd, you know, actually watched the show."

"I will soon, promise."

"I mean, it's kind of getting personal at this point. Like, now it just feels like an attack on my character or something."

"It's not an attack on your character, for God's sake."

"Then what is it, Reed? Exactly why can't you take one hour out of your precious day and watch one episode of my TV series? Like, seriously?"

"Well, for one, in case you haven't noticed, there are no TVs in our rooms, or computers, and I didn't bring my laptop, so that would be a bit of a challenge at the moment."

Tucker's nostrils flared. "Yeah, they have these things called apps? You know, on your cell phone? Which let you watch TV? Maybe check into it one of these days?"

Reed rolled his hand impatiently. "Yes, I will. We're getting to that, but since you asked, no, Tucker. No, there's no one waiting on me at home."

Tucker nodded knowingly, as if answering his own question. "Thought so. You look more like a 'catch and release' type, anyway."

Reed gave a startled, even flattered, little chuckle. "Oh, do I now?"

Their eyes met—Tucker's challenging and playful—right before he gave Reed a long, lingering gaze up and down his body. It was slow and purposeful, and so help him, Reed felt himself thicken despite himself, deep inside his drying baggies. He wondered if Tucker noticed.

And, if so, if he somehow approved.

"Yeah, you know." Tucker's voice was low and confidential, making Reed shiver despite the ungodly heatwave they were enduring under the unforgiving Georgia sun. "Walk into any bar on any given night, catch a young lady's eye, buy her a drink, an hour later you're back at your place doing your thing. Sound about right?"

"Uh, no." Reed chuckled. "I mean, I'm flattered, but those days are long over, kid."

"I'm not a kid," Tucker insisted with a low, teasing growl. It was more than a snippy comeback, Reed realized. It was a challenge, as if

Tucker wanted to be seen as more manly, more masculine, less childlike and playful. But Reed didn't want an equal, a carbon copy of himself. He wanted Tucker the way he was—lean and hungry and youthful, the very picture of a shimmering, magical moment in time, not quite innocent but neither grown tired of this world and his place in it.

Maybe he was as attracted to Tucker's innocent youth as he was to his tapered body.

Realizing he'd taken too long to answer, Reed rolled his eyes to keep things light and airy. "So you keep telling me, *kid*."

Tucker chuffed and grumbled and rolled his eyes. Then he gradually simmered down and sat back until, yet again, his lean body was splayed out atop the deck chair, radiant and aglow beneath the fading sunlight. Time had somehow slipped away from them.

Only moments ago they had been happily bickering over coffee and granola bars in the mess hall kitchen, then lounging lazily in the pool and wrestling the deck chairs from their stacks until, now, evening was approaching and with it the hunger and regret that another day with Tucker would soon be ending.

And a long night of wanting him, naked and writhing in his bed, would begin.

Reed scrubbed the thought and peered back, awaiting Tucker's next question. He didn't have to wait long. "So, what? You're a lone-wolf kind of dude?"

Reed chuckled dryly. If the kid only knew how solitary, sedate, and downright lonely his life had become ever since the scandal that had forced him to take the college crossover position in the first place. "You could say that."

Tucker nodded confidently, chin jutted out like he knew the score. "Same."

Suddenly it was Reed's turn to scoff. "Yeah, right."

The ancient rubber straps beneath Tuck's young body squeaked in protest as he writhed in reply. "What? Of course I am."

"Tuck, I saw that Hollywood hottie who dropped you off, bro. You're telling me you're not hitting that every possible opportunity you can get? I mean, every other guy in Hollywood would be."

"Every other guy in Hollywood but me."

Reed glanced over, one eyebrow arched curiously. "So it really *is* just for show, then?"

Tucker nodded. "That's the studio's strategy, anyway."

Reed shrugged and gave Tucker a withering glance. "What about *your* strategy, player?"

Tuck made a tongue-clucking sound and then sipped the last of his beer. "My strategy at this point is just get through the day without another scandal, you know?"

Reed gave him a stern, fatherly glance. "You've got to let that go, Tuck. You can't let it control your life."

"Easy for you to say, Reed."

"I know it, but that's what we're here for, right?"

Tucker sat up, and little ripples fluttered across his concave belly. Reed inched up as well and reached to open the cooler top so one of them could slip their hand inside. Tuck obviously had the same idea, and their fingers glanced across one another's as they reached for the lid.

"Sorry!" they blurted at the same time, descending into mirthful little beer-buzzed giggles until Reed noticed they were still lingering in each other's grip.

"I'll grab the beer." Reed reluctantly pulled his hand away.

"Okay, but it's gotta be my last."

Reed glanced at the two or three bottles left inside the shimmering ice. "Oh yeah?"

"Big day tomorrow, right?"

Reed sighed. For some reason, the last thing he wanted to do with Tucker at the moment was work. Coach. Admonish. Correct. Teach. "I mean, it's not like we have to set our alarms, though, right?"

Tucker gave him a wry grin. "This how you are with your swimmers back home?"

"Hell no," he barked, very much the same way he might at them. Then he softened. "But this is different."

They were still sitting up. The sun caressed Tucker's smooth, unlined face like an unseen hand, and they were mere inches away from each other now—so close Reed could smell the chlorine in Tucker's hair and feel the heat coming off his half-naked body in tempting, shimmering waves that Reed felt deep inside his clenched gut. "Oh yeah? How so?"

Their eyes met in the afternoon sun. Reed's answer was revealing in more ways than one. "I'm miles away from home, kid."

ELEVEN

Tucker

"IT DOES feel like we're the last two people on the planet at this point." Tucker drank in the quiet that surrounded them—the hushed, dulcet tones of the swaying trees and miles of vivid green grass and the unseen bugs chirping away out there, hidden all over the deserted summer camp.

Meanwhile Reed was grinning above his fresh beer. His face was glossy and surprisingly pale after their long day in the sun, torso still lean and bare as the pool lights began to illuminate them more than the softly setting sun. "No one around for miles and miles…," he emphasized, adding to the apocalyptic feel of the vacant campgrounds.

Tucker was feeling no pain either. "Just the two of us, drinking beers and sleeping in cabins and tripping over tree trunks on the way to the bathroom in the middle of the night."

Reed inched slightly forward and smirked as the vinyl straps of the retro deck chair squeaked beneath him. "Speaking of, and not to intrude on your cozy little 'end of the world' scenario, but… I've had to piss for the last two hours."

Tucker was playfully conspiratorial, grinning with fresh beer lips as if they were two bros at a frat party checking out the new girl. "You too?"

Reed nodded. Their skin was warm and fragrant with sun, chlorine, sweat, and beer as they stood with a flurry of scraping chairs, winded grunts, and bottles clanking at their bare feet.

They stood, vaguely awkward, in baggy board shots, boxers, bare feet, and warm smooth skin. "We should probably grab something to eat and head back, right?" Tucker said, not wanting to break the spell but feeling it had already lost something the minute they both stood.

Reed seemed just as mixed on the subject. "I suppose. But showers first?" He nodded behind him at a sign over a door that read Men's Locker.

Tucker followed, bare feet padding on the still warm but no longer volcanic pool deck. "Piss first," he corrected Reed. "And then shower."

He paused as they walked into the vast room, and Reed made his way to the first urinal he saw. Tucker had still been expecting something out of a five-star resort, for some reason—glittering marble, muted lighting, automatic sinks, and at the very least, urinal dividers.

Instead he was instantly transported back to junior high school, featuring one drab cement wall with nonstop urinals and the opposite wall with drains and shower spigots in another long, undivided row that was sure to leave nothing to the imagination once they stepped inside and turned on the individual spigots.

"Cat got your tongue?" Reed teased, already whipping out his junk and practically spread-eagled at the nearest urinal as he began to relieve himself with unabashed relish.

Tucker avoided a clandestine look at his coach's exposed package and instead focused on the wall just above Reed's head. "No, I just was expecting something different."

Reed chuckled, interrupting the sound of his steady stream of… relief. "Sorry it's not the lobby of the Beverly Hilton, pretty boy, but what did you expect from a summer camp?"

Tucker rolled his eyes and drifted a few urinals down, admiring the way Reed was still pissing all the while. He understood why moments later when, wrinkled, damp boxers pulled down, he began to relieve himself and didn't stop for what felt like an hour.

Reed was drifting gradually toward the showers as Tucker flushed, taking his time and stalling as he turned to find his lean, limber coach leaning nonchalantly against the half-wall partition that separated the shower drains from the rest of the bathroom. He had already grabbed fresh towels from a stack on a nearby bench and was laying them out along the waist-high wall.

"You okay?" Reed gave him a gentle tuck on the chin just to be sure.

Tucker smirked, a hand on the opposite partition. "I guess I'm just used to more privacy back home, yeah?"

Reed nodded with a merry grin. As usual, he seemed to be enjoying Tucker's discomfort. And despite the chill vibes and almost flirty ambiance of the swim session and beyond, Tucker was suddenly very uncomfortable.

"I bet you are, but come on. It'll be just like high school all over again."

He was already untying the string that held his baggies up, thin fingers on the damp nylon as if knowing the anticipation was only thrilling Tucker all the more.

"I never graduated," Tucker confessed.

"No shit?" Reed paused, string undone, a hand on either side of the Velcro that was all that was keeping them from knowing each other a whole lot better. "What? Because you wouldn't shower with the other guys?"

Tucker snorted. Reed was right, of course. This shouldn't have been a big deal. He'd done it all through junior high, most of high school, and a million times in gym showers up one side of Hollywood and down the other.

So why was he balking now?

"Long story, I suppose."

Reed nodded, and their eyes met as he seemed to kind of nod as if making a decision. "Right, well, maybe I'll tug it out of you sometime over the next two weeks, huh, Tuck?"

They both heard the Velcro rip, the swim trunks slither down, and just like that, Reed was tossing them over the half-wall partition like he owned the damn place and padding away, tan lines, bare asscheeks, and precious little dimples on full display. Tucker stood, one hand on the wall, the other on his waistband, literally transfixed by the sight.

He shouldn't have been. Hell, Reed had basically been on full display all day. But something about that pale round butt and what lay, glistening and wet, on the other side gave him pause in a most unexpected, even unsettling, way.

Reed turned the water on, and the frenetic spray dappled off the rich black stubble that coated his head. The water began to glide and snake down his broad shoulders, bare torso, and smooth, shapely legs.

"You don't have to be shy," he called over his shoulder. Then he turned to give Tucker a smooth, self-assured once-over as water pelted his smug, leering face. "I mean, if you think those thin wet boxers hid anything back there in the pool, you're wrong, pal. Dead wrong." He winked and slowly turned back to let the spray fully embrace him.

Tucker glanced down, afraid he might already be thick—too thick to let himself swing free—but certain there was no escaping the current situation. Instead he sighed, swallowed, and steeled his nerves as he stepped out of his boxers, one leg at a time. Then he folded them where he stood, slapped bare feet on the wet tile floor, and headed straight to the nozzle right next to Reed.

His coach, glistening and smooth, was oblivious beside him, eyes closed beneath the spray as he let it coat his entire body before he pulled slightly back to blink his eyes open and peer beside him.

"Wow, not even six nozzles away, huh? Ballsy." Reed chuckled and gave Tucker a good once-over. "No pun intended."

Tucker reached for the tube of shampoo affixed to the wall, pumped a few radioactive green spurts into his hand, and then rubbed them to a lather and dragged his fingers through his hair. Eyes closed, he could only feel the warm water pelting his naked body, tingly and brown from the day in the sun. It was refreshing and, as he feared, titillating.

Too titillating. He felt himself thicken and dance below his waist, balls full from over a month of self-imposed abstinence and cock just as aching with thick, curved need.

He made quick work of shampooing and rinsing off, then opened his eyes to catch Reed giving him not-so-furtive glances as he stood beneath his own spurting spigot. Tucker wasn't sure whether to feel flattered or amused and instead blinked, his eyes wide as he peered next door to return the favor while Reed began to lather himself with soap.

He was shorter than Tucker by a couple of inches, slight of build but strong and lean from his coaching job and, apparently, his passion for swimming in general. He definitely had a swimmer's body—smooth and lean and slight and tempting as the tendrils of soap slithered across his broad shoulders and down across the small of his back to drizzle down his pale, clenched cheeks. Reed slathered himself with his hands as Tucker did the same, risking an admiring glance every time Reed turned his head in the other direction.

While he'd seen nearly every spare inch of Reed's body by now, the question he'd been asking himself all day in the pool was now officially confirmed—Reed was altogether smooth. Shaved bare. As in… everywhere. As he casually lathered his pelvis, caressing and rubbing his gleaming package as if he were alone in his own bathroom, Tucker's eyes widened to see his balls smooth as a baby's butt, just like the rest of him.

"For swimming," Reed explained as he stepped back under the spray and the soap glided away to reveal his glistening manhood, shimmering wet and achingly curved beneath the shower spray. He glanced up until their eyes met. It was clear that Reed was hiding nothing. If anything, he was letting it all hang out, literally and figuratively, as if to challenge Tucker to look—to admire and savor and examine, perhaps even memorize every glossy, glistening inch.

"I got into the habit of shaving all over when I was still competing. It really did help me 'shave' seconds off my lap times, and, well, I guess old habits die hard."

Tucker could feel the heated blush rise to his face despite the cool shower water that splattered his entire body. "Sounds time-consuming," he sputtered helplessly, absently lathering soap around his hungry belly, if only for something to do with his hands.

As always, Reed noticed. Or perhaps he just wanted a chance to glance in that general direction.

TWELVE

Reed

"TOO TIME-CONSUMING for you, clearly."

Reed nodded at the unruly bush of dark brown pubes nestled between Tucker's wispy brown happy trail and his long, slim member. It was damp and dotted with shower water and dredges of the slick, foamy green soap provided by the summer camp shower stalls.

As if he knew Reed was watching—he certainly wasn't hiding it, he supposed—Tucker ran his lathered hand through his bush and down, soaping up his package thoroughly and impressing Reed with its floppy, soapy heft. He struggled not to lick his lips and returned eye contact instead.

Apparently Tucker's earlier hesitance had flown the coop, and now, smirking back at him, he grinned unabashedly. Even proudly. "I haven't had any complaints yet."

Reed chuckled as Tucker stepped tentatively into the spray, admiring the way it drizzled the soap off his body, inch by glorious inch. He'd had dozens of lovers over the years, no shortage of them dazzlingly handsome in one way or another. But something about Tucker—his innocence, his shyness, his uncertainty, and certainly that body—had his heart pounding and his own dick throbbing as shower water pelted it almost sensuously.

"Did I say I was complaining?"

Tucker smirked and rinsed off the lather until he was squeaky clean, dripping wet as the water lingered on his curved, downturned cock. His balls, wispy with hair and dripping wet, hung thick and heavy between his long, shapely legs. Reed found himself staring and, clean already, reached with an unsteady hand to turn off the gurgling spigot above his head.

He lingered, rubbing his stubbly scalp and shaking the excess water off his arms and legs before he drifted away to reach for his towel, still carefully folded atop the tile partition wall where he'd left it.

Tucker dawdled under the spray, rinsing himself off effortlessly, almost tenderly, as if he knew he was on display and was loving every minute of it. With the kid's back turned, Reed indulged himself in a long, lingering look at his firm bare ass, pale and dimpled and slick with shower water. He was still looking when the squeak of the spigot startled him, and when Tucker turned, gleaming and bronze from the sun, Reed's eyes took a leisurely trip up his body until their eyes met.

Tucker opened his lips as if about to say something and then seemed to think better of it. Instead he smirked, inched closer to the wall that separated the showerheads from the rest of the bathroom, and slowly reached for his towel.

"See?" Reed tossed the towel over the partition wall and reached for his baggies. "That wasn't so hard, now was it?"

Tucker chuckled and nodded down at his lap, still thick and softly downturned but unmistakably... lengthy. "Speak for yourself."

Reed rolled his eyes. Then he watched Tucker towel himself dry while casually covering the unmistakable bulge beneath his thin white towel. "So you're a shower *and* a grower, big deal."

"I'm just awkward, that's all. Socially awkward, I mean."

"Aren't you an actor?"

"An actor by accident." Tucker was drying himself still, gently rubbing his package as if it was the most natural thing in the world. Reed struggled to keep eye contact, forgetting for a moment that showering together had been his idea—and a bad one at that. "I started as a carpenter, though."

Reed's eyes bulged, and not, for once, at the beauty of Tucker's glistening bulge or enticing lean body. "Come again?"

Tucker tossed the towel aside to once again reveal his splendid undercarriage. "Do you always talk in double entendres?" he asked while bending to reach for his boxer shorts.

"Only when I'm nervous," Reed admitted, cracking his tough-guy exterior in the presence of Tucker's undeniable radiance. So far he'd sailed through life unencumbered, single and proud of it, more than ready to walk away from a one-night stand, weekend fling, or casual relationship at a moment's notice if necessary. Suddenly Reed feared he'd found his kryptonite in the form of this shy, goofy, aloof, vulnerable—and unlikely—Hollywood star.

Tucker paused, the boxers held aloft in front of his lap and only half hiding his low-hanging balls. "What are you nervous about?"

Reed gave him another admiring nod, afraid he was being too obvious by far but unable to help himself any longer. "Seeing some big-time actor naked, I guess."

Tucker leaned slightly forward to slip into his boxers and sank onto the bench opposite Reed after he was done. "Weren't you the one who insisted on showering together, Coach?"

"I might have been a little buzzed when I suggested that."

He stood at last. Tucker followed. "And now?"

"Now I'm just hungry."

Tucker paused near the door. "Another pun?" His voice sounded almost hopeful. Then again, it was probably just Reed's imagination.

He patted Tucker on the shoulder—the bare, clean, smooth shoulder. "No, actually hungry. Let's grab some dinner before we both pass out from sunstroke and imported beer."

Tucker nodded, found his pile of clothes near their deck chairs, and slipped into them. Once dressed, he looked sun-kissed and innocent, no longer the long, lean sex machine Reed had fantasized about in the showers.

Reed put on his T-shirt and flip-flops and watched as Tucker reached to return the deck chair to its rightful place. "We'll just use it again this week, right?" Reed reminded him. "Why not let it be?"

Tucker gave up and joined him for the walk through the gate that led away from the pool and across a grassy field to the barn-shaped mess hall. "I keep forgetting we're the only two here."

"Feels weird, right?"

"Like a deserted movie set," Tucker mused, bare feet crunching on the soft green grass. The sky was dark now, the moon aglow above as the porch light in front of the mess hall beckoned.

"Speaking of, you were saying back in the showers that, what, you built sets or something?"

Tucker sighed heavily, as if he'd told the tale a million times. Or maybe never before. The kid seemed wildly private and shy for an actual TV star. "Literally," he said as he opened the creaky screen door for them and Reed passed through. He followed, bare feet on the vinyl flooring. "They were filming just north of here, not far from my hometown of Worsham, Georgia. It was my senior year, and somebody in the drama department saw on some website where they were hiring a ton of people to work on some 'unnamed zombie series.' That's what they called it in the beginning."

They had made it to the kitchen, both of them peering shoulder to shoulder inside the stainless-steel fridge and snatching previously prepared dishes left and right.

Once dinner was acquired, they leaned back against their respective counters and nibbled contentedly while Tucker told the tale. "I was basically bailing on school already, just going through some stuff at home, totally not motivated, and I thought, sure, why not?"

He paused to chew on a toast point that had accompanied his personal charcuterie platter of assorted pickles, olives, meats, and cheeses. Hollywood indeed. "So a few friends and I went, and they were so desperate for warm bodies, they hired us on the spot."

"No shit?"

Tucker pretended to be offended. "You sound surprised."

Reed chuckled midway through a caprese sandwich that was downright delectable—toasted ciabatta bread, mozzarella, and tomato slices slathered with a delicate balsamic drizzle that had his tastebuds doing backflips. He put it down almost grudgingly and nodded at Tucker. "Let me see your hands."

Tucker set down his plastic platter and accompanying tallboy fizzy soda and offered them up. With Tuck's big palms and long, thin fingers extended, Reed took them and turned them over, leisurely running his own along Tucker's. He returned them reluctantly, the skin warm and smooth beneath his own. "What?"

"Nothing, you just don't seem like a carpenter to me."

Tucker blushed vaguely in that warm, gushing way he had. "I wasn't. I mean, I'd helped build a few sets for drama, but only because it was supposed to be an easy A, and besides, all the hot girls took it. And basically I just hung around, handing the real carpenter a hammer or nails or whatnot."

Reed was blushing himself, suddenly, inexplicably, and irrationally jealous of whoever those "hot girls" were back then. *The nerve of those Drama Babes!* He busied himself by nibbling on his sandwich and washing it down with a bottle of fancy club soda in a cool blue bottle. He realized he'd been a fool to think that he and Tucker could be anything other than a quasi-work relationship in the first place.

Then again, he had a history of such indiscretions.

"So what'd you do when you got the job?" Reed mumbled, mouth full of the crispy, savory Asian slaw that had been paired with his snooty, if savory, sandwich. "Fake it till you made it the whole time?"

"Basically," Tucker answered around a swiss cheese cube. "I just kind of tried to look busy and took a lot of breaks, but I didn't have to bluff for long, because on one of my breaks, the casting director asked my boss if he could 'borrow me' for a scene because one of his extras hadn't shown up. It was for a speaking role, and I guess I kind of, sort of looked like the missing extra, and it all happened so fast I didn't have time to be nervous about it, and boom, they were behind schedule, so it was one, maybe two takes and I was done. Somebody upstairs at the studio fast-passed a SAG card for me so everything would be aboveboard by the time it aired on TV.

"Then, by the next day, they had rewritten some stuff for continuity and that character had to come back for a few more scenes, and one thing led to another, and before the first season aired, I had a credited role. By season two I was officially a recurring character. By season three there were only four of the original actors left and I was one of them, and by season four, I was an actual leading man with a fan base and everything. So here I am." Tucker did a cute little bow, then made a face afterward like maybe he regretted it.

Reed ignored the instinct to golf clap and asked instead, "What was the line?"

The kid seemed surprised. "Beg pardon?"

"The line. The one you had to say as an extra on that first day of filming. Do you remember it?"

Tucker chuckled, set down his by now empty platter, and tugged off his shirt in one quick, effortless, and apparently shameless motion.

Reed pretended to be shocked. "Whoa there, now...."

"Relax." Tucker held his wrinkled T-shirt in his free hand and lifted his other arm. There, just under his left armpit, were three words, tattooed in blunt black cursive. Reed squinted but still couldn't quite make them out. He was surprised he hadn't noticed them in all the time he'd been staring at Tucker that day.

"Go on," Tucker practically purred. "You can come closer. I won't bite."

Reed smirked and came so close he could admire Tucker's sparse, softly brown armpit hair and smell the junior-high soap from back in the locker room. He still struggled to make it out.

"Lighten up, pop?"

Tucker snorted. Then he glanced down awkwardly to read it himself and lifted his long arm higher, as if that might help. "No, look closer."

Reed risked running a single fingertip along the phrase instead. He felt Tucker flinch at the first blush of contact, fingertip against skin, then shiver, then relax slightly, and Reed wondered if he might react the same way if Reed touched the rest of his body. He could hardly believe he'd done it, but like Tucker had said about his acting debut, it all happened so fast. He started at the top of the phrase and, swirl by loop by turn, carefully outlined it until he had reached the end.

"Oh, I see. 'Listen here, pal.'" Reluctantly Reed dragged his finger away, and Tucker slowly lowered his arm and quietly put his shirt back on. As if transfixed, Reed remained in place—which was to say dangerously close.

He had been fighting his attraction from the moment Tucker drove up to the welcome center that first day, all cheekbones and feathery brown curls and long, enticing limbs as he stood from the sleek rental sedan. Reed had ignored the impulses since then, played it all down, glanced left when he wanted to look right, down when he wanted to look up, kept eye contact, kept things professional.

But today, with the long, languid swim, the hot sun and clingy boxer shorts, the intensely seductive shower, and that thin, banana-curved package dangling beneath that full frat-boy bush of pubes, it had all come undone.

Unraveled, in every sense of the word.

All his resolve, all his willpower, was subtly eroding under the weight of one unavoidable fact—he wanted Tucker, wanted him in the worst of ways. And Tucker, the little shit, was doing nothing to prevent that. He'd yet to talk about his sexuality one way or the other, but the mention of "hot Drama girls" back in school and his obvious "fake girlfriend" from the TV show made it clear he possibly, probably, identified as straight. And yet, two days into their time together, he was giving off very confusing, very sexy, very curious signals. Reed wondered how long it might be until one of them caved and did, or said, or even touched the wrong thing.

And naturally who would be first.

"That's the line." Tucker tugged down his T-shirt, opened a tray of fancy cookies, and held it out to Reed. He took one—something thick and chocolate and rich—and savored it in his mouth as he nodded.

"So you had it tattooed under your arm. Nice."

Tucker grabbed some kind of coconutty thing and chewed quietly. "I just wanted to commemorate it, you know, in case it all comes crumbling down any minute."

Reed snatched another cookie and then shoved the tray back—forcefully—in Tucker's direction. "Why would it crumble down, Tucker? What makes you think that way?"

"Just the fickle nature of Hollywood, I guess."

"But dude, you're the star of some hit TV show, four seasons in, raking in the dough and in millions of homes every night. Even if this thing crapped out tomorrow, you've got a ticket to ride anywhere else in Hollywood for life, you know?" Reed made jazz hands and then held them up to portray, as best he could, a theater marquee. "Starring Tucker Crawford, star of *Household Zombies*!"

Tucker chuckled around another coconut cookie as he began to clean up. "*Suburban Dead*, clown!"

"I know, I know." Reed joined him as they added another layer to the rapidly filling trash can. "Just giving you the business. I never knew any of your backstory."

"Why would you? You don't even watch the show."

"I mean, I never knew that about *you*. As a person. That's quite an accomplishment."

"It is and it isn't." Tucker grabbed them both a bottle of water, their nightly ritual before shutting off the lights and leaving the mess hall as clean as they'd found it.

"How so?" Reed followed him through the swinging doors, out through the screen door, and onto the porch.

"Everyone else on the show has these big, long pedigrees. Summer, my costar, she was in some big award-winning independent film two years ago and comes from a long line of movie stars. Brandon, the director, has done, like, two major superhero-comic-book movies. My other costar, Ross, was this big child actor. Everyone on the set is someone very important and special, and I'm just some guy who wandered in with a hammer in my hand, literally, and got the job by accident. I am definitely the odd man out, and value-wise, the first guy to have his neck on the chopping block come contract renewal time every season."

Reed slugged Tucker playfully on the shoulder as they ambled across the lawn back to their respective cabins. Neither of them, he was happy to note, was eager for the day to end. "You might have gotten the job by accident, Tucker, but you wouldn't have lasted one episode if you had sucked, right?"

"I guess. It's just that they kind of never let me forget it, you know?"

Reed nodded as he walked quietly alongside his new friend. "Sounds kind of like a toxic environment, actually." He knew from whence he spoke.

"Duh." Tucker hip-checked him as they approached the rambling cabin on the left. Reed's cabin—the counselor's cabin, the only one with a big queen-size bed smack dab under the picture window in the back. "It's Hollywood, right?"

"I wouldn't know," Reed said, slowing his progress as they approached his porch. It had two chairs, wicker and worn. The left one was where he sat most nights, watching the sky change colors and the stars appear until it was time to hit the hay for another day with Tucker. He wanted to ask the kid to take the right seat but felt he'd been forward enough all day.

As if in reply, Tucker stood on the thick green grass below while Reed ascended the two steps it took to reach the rickety wooden porch. He turned and glanced back. "Keep it that way," Tucker said. He lingered at the railing instead of joining Reed on the porch.

Reed winked. "I don't really have a choice in the matter, so...."

Tucker smiled, but it didn't quite reach his eyes the way it normally did. Reed also struggled for something else to say. The stars were already out in a blue-black, cloudless sky. Crickets chirped in the near-awkward silence until Tucker's voice, low and rich, muttered almost abashedly, "Thanks. For today I mean."

"Thanks for what?"

Tucker shrugged, hands in his pockets. "I dunno, just hanging out, I guess. I don't have a lot of guy friends in Hollywood. I don't have a lot of friends, period, so today was nice. So just... thank you, okay?"

Reed held up his hands as if surrendering. "Okay, yes, same here."

Tucker cocked his head. "Same here what?"

"I'm pretty busy back home. The kids on the team are quite a bit younger, the other coaches are all kind of cliquey, and the teaching staff is quite a bit older, so I don't have a lot of friends, period."

Tucker seemed to take that in for a moment, his young face a curious mix of encouragement and sadness. He seemed about to say something else when, behind him, Reed's cell phone chittered on the scarred wicker bureau just inside the screen door.

"Shit," he said, suddenly remembering. "I've been expecting this call all day." He gave Tucker an almost panicked glance, practically begging him, "Hang out for a second till I'm done?"

Tucker seemed to consider it for a moment, then frowned resolutely. "Naw, you grab that and talk as long as you want. I'm pretty beat and should probably check in with the studio myself anyway." He was already half turning when he chirped, "Tomorrow, then?"

Reed struggled to hide his disappointment as he reached for the screen door and the phone continued to bleat. "Sure, yeah, tomorrow, then."

THIRTEEN

Tucker

"COSTAS?"

Tucker stood in front of the phone, glancing at his producer as he lounged in a desk chair amidst the splendor of his office in downtown LA. "Kid, where you been? I've been trying your phone all day!"

Tucker was still on the porch, the night so dark and still he could vaguely hear Reed on his own call in the cabin just around the way. He drifted inside, none too eager for Reed to overhear any scandalous Hollywood slander his producer, Costas Imperial, might throw his way on the surprise video call.

"I don't know if you remember this, Costas," Tucker teased as he sank onto a beanbag chair in the corner of the spacious, if rustic, cabin, "but I've been in the pool all day. Learning how to swim, remember?"

"Save it, smartass," Costas huffed back in his thick Mediterranean accent. Tucker set the phone against the desk beside him so they could be, virtually anyway, face-to-face. "Why'd we invest in that expensive waterproof case if you don't even bring your phone to the pool area with you?"

"I forgot, okay. Sue me."

Costas fiddled with something on his desk, clicked a keyboard next to it, and swiped on a large tablet next to that. He was impatient, distracted, blunt, and demeaning—in other words, business as usual. Tucker smiled. He'd been vaguely homesick ever since Summer drove away in a cloud of dry Georgia clay, and hearing Costas's loud voice and brash accent almost made him feel right at home.

"Yeah, well, listen," Costas barked, waving a slimy sub sandwich at the phone for emphasis. "You're still under contract during hiatus, so pretend you're on set, okay?" The minute he quit speaking, he took a massive bite, like a shark tearing into the flesh of its unwitting victim. Then he set the sandwich down and wiped his big, hairy hands on the side of a sweaty diet soda can.

Yup. Just like home.

"I don't hear any answer yet, kid."

Tucker rolled his eyes and smirked despite the tension in his gut. The day had gone so well, so unbelievably well, that the reminder that he was still a paid actor for some zombie series and working for this loudmouth shmuck made it clear how torn he already was between his two very different worlds.

"When's the last time you called me on set, Costas?"

"Tucker," Costas growled, only half joking. He was in his midforties, balding but with bad hair plugs no one was allowed to talk about. He was bursting out of his one-size-too-small suit, his voice as loud as his garish personality.

He'd never been a fan of Tucker and had fought actively against having an "amateur" star in their series. Unfortunately for Costas, the fans of *Suburban Dead* had rallied to keep Tucker around at the end of season one and then all but demanded he survive through seasons two, three, and four, and now, coming up on season five, he was the standout favorite among the surviving veterans. At least for now. Still, Costas never missed an opportunity to be an egregious dick when he had the chance.

Tucker responded in kind. "Fine, Costas, what was so important that you tried to call me at the pool while I would have been swimming and probably unable to hear the phone anyway, huh?"

Costas stopped doing the three other things he'd been doing the whole time they'd been speaking and glared into the phone. "You were swimming?"

Tucker dialed it back. He hadn't been eager to come to Camp Run-A-Mok in the first place, but now that he was falling under Reed's casual spell, he was in no hurry to get back to LA. "I mean, splashing was more like it," he stammered awkwardly, hoping Costas had been too busy multitasking to notice the slipup. "We're still in the shallow end of the pool, if that gives you any idea of my progress thus far."

Costas leaned back in his chair, garish, shiny pink necktie pulled halfway down and two buttons of his tailored shirt open to expose a veritable carpet of thick, shiny chest hair. "You had me excited there for a minute."

"Look, it's a process, okay?"

Costas rolled his eyes and reached for the can of his favorite diet soda. "That what your coach said, huh?"

"It's what my body said. I'm getting there, trust me. You'll be the first to know, Costas."

"I better be, kid. We could use you back here, pronto."

Tucker lurched forward in his cozy beanbag chair and inched closer to the phone as if to hear better. "What? Why?"

"No particular reason, I suppose. I was just hoping for a little better blowup from you and Summer's photo ops in the Atlanta airport, and well, so far the optics have been less than dramatic."

"Listen, I was against that fake-dating idea from the get-go, Costas. You know that."

"So was she, trust me, but ratings were off last season. So if you guys want to return for season six, we've got to make more of the on-set drama for season five."

"What, that stupid video of me practically drowning and getting seventeen million page views wasn't good enough 'optics' for you?"

Costas waved the soda can with one hand and the bursting-at-the-seams sandwich with the other. "Yesterday's news, kid. Already forgotten. We need shit like that every week if we're gonna stay on the air as long as all those other zombie shows on competing networks."

"Look, I'm doing my part, okay. Find some other dude to date Summer this summer. I'm trying to focus on what I'm doing here."

Costas sighed, crumpled up his soda can, and tossed it somewhere near the foot of his desk. He looked annoyed, but not necessarily with Tucker. "I know it, kid. Don't I know it? We'll do another video when you can swim like a dolphin, and that will buy us a week or more of social media wins. So I know what you're doing is important. I'm just under pressure back home, all right?"

Tucker felt for the guy. Kind of. Despite Tucker's character being on the chopping block at the end of every season and Costas the one in charge of doing the chopping, the two had somehow developed a grudging respect, even if they could hardly stand one another. "When aren't you, Costas?"

"Right, but this is preventable pressure."

Tucker fidgeted deeper into his beanbag chair and wondered what Reed was doing at that moment. If he was off his call already, changing into boxers for the night, creeping under the covers, turning off the light, his smooth, hairless body aglow under the moonlight slipping in through the open window beside his bed, curtains rustling and brushing across his pale, hard chest as his nipples hardened to the size of taut little erasers—

"Tuck? Tucker!"

Tucker tumbled, as if from a daydream. Make that a *wet* dream. "Shit, sorry. Yes?"

Costas seemed to chuckle despite himself. "I was considering a set visit later in the week, maybe bring Summer along for a little free publicity of you two doing the smoochy-smooch in front of some freelance photographers. So, do you think you'll be ready by then?"

Tucker struggled to keep a straight face, although he couldn't quite muster a smile. "No, but I suppose I can't stop you."

Costas visibly flinched. He wasn't in the habit of hearing "No," especially not from a Hollywood imposter like Tucker Crawford. "That doesn't sound like progress to me, kid."

"I mean, I'm not quite a dolphin yet, Costas. More like a turtle."

"Still, I don't think it's too much to ask for a progress report after a week of swimming lessons, right, kid?"

"You can ask, Costas. All I can do is my best."

Costas glared into the phone, and Tucker could feel the menace all the way in his cabin a thousand miles—and three hours by Learjet—away. "And I'm saying, see you in a week, kid. And your best better be damn good. This whole season's riding on it."

"Or what, Costas?"

Costas barely blinked. "Or what? Or the screenwriters can get busy writing you a fancy exit before the contracts for season six are even printed yet, that's what."

Tucker nodded. He wasn't exactly unfazed, but it wasn't the first time he'd been threatened by Costas. Every season, it seemed, his character's role was up for extinction. And every season, the fans clamored for him to stay alive.

"Hmmmm, as I've said in the past, Costas, if you want to talk contracts and negotiations and seasons and threats, my agent's all ears. Until then, like I said, I can't stop you from visiting me while I learn how to do something that, I'll remind you, was never in my contract to begin with. Anything else, *boss*?"

Costas sat back in his chair, chuckling humorlessly. "Wow, you're really getting good at this, Tuck. Used to be I'd have you quaking in your boots after one of these calls."

"I guess I just don't understand why you'd want to threaten one of your stars for no good reason. I said I'd be ready in two weeks. I'll be ready in two weeks. If you didn't go changing the finish line every season, we wouldn't have a beef like this. Every. Season."

Costas nodded and reached for his phone. "Fair enough, kid. See you soon, huh?"

Before Tucker could answer, his producer's side of the call went dark, a small square floating against his screensaver. Then it too disappeared.

Just like the great mood Tucker had been in all day.

FOURTEEN

Reed

"I'VE BEEN calling you all day, Reed."

"Sorry, Kira, I've been with my client all day. I guess I left my phone in the cabin."

Kira's face, stern and businesslike, peered out at him from a square that took up most of his cell phone screen. "Well, what if someone needed to get ahold of you for some reason?"

Reed chuckled as he sank into his favorite wicker rocking chair and propped the phone on the porch railing across from his nightly perch so the two could share an unobstructed view of each other. "You all barely need to get a hold of me when I'm there all day, let alone when I'm off for two measly weeks out of the year."

In the middle of his video screen, Kira's ebony skin glowed a radiant, shimmering blue. She must have had her TV on pause somewhere nearby. She sat at some kind of dinner table situation, cluttered and unruly, like the rest of her messy, successful, happy little life. "Yeah, well, what if, huh?"

Reed chuckled. They'd never been close, and considering how things went down after his recent scandal, it was a miracle they were friendly at all. "Well, I'm here now, boss, so what's up?"

As always, Kira's young, unlined face frowned at the forbidden word that should not ever be mentioned. "You know I hate when you call me that, Reed."

But he was feeling frisky all of a sudden. He had only been gone from the university campus for three days, but the sudden submersion into "camp life" and its isolated sexiness made him feel like he'd been gone forever. "But it's true, no?"

"Yeah, but it carries a lot of weight."

"Listen, I know I got foisted on you through no fault of your own, and I know I'm an unnecessary burden while I'm on academic probation, so I just want to give respect where it's due, that's all."

She rolled her young eyes. After being one of their strongest swimmers during her tenure there for four years as an undergrad, at twenty-three, Kira Emerson was head of the Aquatics Department at Eastern Georgia State, overseeing not just the men's and women's swim teams but the transition team as well. Once upon a time, Reed had been the men's coach, the yang to her yin, rooting her on from the sidelines, as she had done him. At least until his own career was derailed by a slight but apparently unforgivable transgression. Now that he'd been "strategically reassigned" to the transition team while "awaiting further determination," as the college board had deemed it, Reed was, officially anyway, in her direct employ.

Not that Kira had ever seen it that way, God bless her. "Anyway, I was just calling to check on you, not dredge up all this political BS. Sheesh."

Reed was visibly touched. "That's nice of you. I'm good."

Kira inched closer to the screen, the glow of her paused TV illuminating the stubble of her closely cropped black hair. Like Reed, they both swam as often as they coached, and the shorter the hair, the quicker the time. Not that it mattered anymore, officially, but competition—even with oneself—was as strong as muscle memory in competitive swimmers. "How's your client? Is he as dreamy in real life as he is on the show?"

"I can't tell about the show. I haven't watched it yet."

"What?" Kira squealed. Then she reined herself in and lowered her voice a notch. She lived with her wife, Saffron, and their adopted daughter, Chloe. Noting the late hour, Reed realized it must have been way past bedtime for most of the house. "How can you not have seen it? Dude's a legit star, and you're swimming with him every day and you haven't even made it a point to watch a single episode? Scandalous, dude. Purely savage."

Reed sighed. He wished Tucker had grabbed him a beer instead of a bottled water. Probably for the best for how he'd feel in the morning, but for tonight? One more cold one would have been just about right. "I keep hearing that, but he just seems like a sweet, goofy kid to me."

"Really? Cause he's quite the badass on the show."

Reed barked laughter and shook his head with both shock and glee. He all but slapped his knee at the sheer improbability of that statement. "Impossible."

Kira shot him a judgey glance through the phone. "He is, Reed," she insisted plaintively, as if she had a personal stake in the matter. "He's, like, the head of the zombie detectives, and he kills, like, a dozen of them every episode, in the most badass ways imaginable."

"I simply find that very hard to believe, Kira. He must have the best stunt double in the biz, because to me he seems like he wouldn't hurt a fly."

"It's called acting, Reed. You should try it sometime."

Reed rolled his eyes and rocked gently in his chair. From his perch, he could see the lights aglow inside Tucker's cabin, and he wondered what the kid was up to—and what he was wearing while he was up to it. "I do, every time I'm in the presence of Dean Whortley."

Kira rolled her eyes. "Speaking of, he was in my office just this morning."

Reed nodded, suddenly remembering why he'd been so eager to take this particular side gig in the first place. "So *that's* why you called. Wanted to check up on me, my ass!"

Kira rushed to defend herself and perhaps warn Reed. "Listen, I just... I hate to be the bearer of bad news while you're on kinda-sorta vacay, but that man has a hard-on for you like I've never seen before, pun intended."

"Oh, I'm well aware." Reed felt his gut tighten at the very mention of the man, his archnemesis back at the university. "So what was he bugging you about?"

"The usual—how you were doing in your 'new capacity' leading the College Crossover Program, were there any potential signs you wouldn't be able to perform your duties in an appropriate manner moving forward considering you were still dealing with young men, how were you handling being supervised so closely, yada yada. I shut him down, said all the right things, but he's obviously gunning for you, my man."

Reed sighed. He sank deeper into his chair and felt... nothing. "I wish I cared more, Kira, I really do. But after the way things went down, it's hard for me to muster anything but fight-or-flight when it comes to that place, you know?"

"I do know, Reed. I just, I'm here for you. I'm doing my best."

"Look, Kira, I appreciate everything you're doing on my behalf while I'm gone. Really, I do. It's nothing I didn't expect to happen the minute I left campus. It's just disappointing, is all. I kissed all the right asses, made all the right concessions, paid my dues, took the reassignment without fanfare, and they're still looking for ways to permanently delete my ass, you know?"

"I do know. I also know you've got choices, my man. You know that too, right?"

Reed nodded. "I like it there, Kira. Or at least I used to. I like you. I like the kids on the team. I think they like me. I don't want to bail on them."

"I know that, Reed. They know that too." She brightened, doing a little bit of acting herself. "They all want to know what Tucker's like."

"I bet they do." Reed chuckled. "He's sweet, actually. Shy as hell, nothing like what I thought some Hollywood hotshot would act like. I guess that's why I'm so surprised about his character on the show."

Kira wagged a literal finger, the fuzzy sleeve of her mustard-yellow bathrobe drifting down across her wrist in the process. "I can't believe you refuse to watch it, dude. That's mad disrespect for your boy."

"I'm going to, I promise. But after all that's happened this year, being away, out here in the real-ass woods, no computer or big-screen TV or amenities, I just zonk out after every day."

"I see your ass on that rocking chair, Reed. Careful you don't turn into a boomer while you're gone."

"Too late," he chuckled as, somewhere in the background of Kira's video call, a little girl in footie pajamas and a thumb jammed squarely in her mouth came stumbling around the corner, practically tripping over the blankie in her hands. "Listen, thanks for the heads-up. I miss you, 'kay? Tell the kids I miss them too."

"I will, Reed, and one thing? Watch that boy's show. His feelings are probably hurt." Before she hung up, though she'd already turned from the screen, Reed could hear Kira murmuring, "Come here, baby. What's that you've got up your nose now?"

He was still chuckling when her screen went blank. He sighed and glanced yet again at the cabin just a few yards away and down the sloping hill to the left. His belly ached with sexual tension, and he was sorely tempted to stand and stroll straight down the hill and see what Tucker was up to.

To just rap on the door, teeter from toe to toe outside the screen door, wait for Tucker to appear, probably in the same baggy white boxers and little else, fresh-faced and wondering what he was up to. He smiled at the thought, even considered it for a moment. Actually, realistically considered it.

Then thought better of it, obviously.

Instead he settled in and fiddled with his phone until he'd opened his rarely used TiVo app. A quick search and, moments later, he was balls deep into the first episode of the first season of *Suburban Dead*. It took a while for his character to show up, but minutes later, Tucker appeared on the screen, unpolished, rawboned, and looking all of sixteen. Reed couldn't help but flinch at the sight, belly and balls lurching with delight as his sexy neighbor muttered the single line he'd had tattooed on his arm—*Listen here, pal*. It all happened fairly quickly, and before long, the first episode was over and Reed wanted more. So much more. He watched the second episode, then another, almost leaping from his seat triumphantly the first time he watched as Tucker kicked and punched and eventually swung a crowbar to silence a horde of six hungry zombies toward the end of episode four. Or was it episode five?

Either way, Kira wasn't kidding—dude was a legit badass. At least his character was. Reed settled in for a long night of binge-watching and wondered why he'd never heard of the show before he was offered this job. And knowing now, no matter what happened—or preferably didn't happen—between him and Tucker, that he'd never be able to forget *Suburban Dead* ever again.

Let alone it's ass-kicking star.

FIFTEEN

Tucker

"THAT WAS some good work this morning, kid."

Tucker rolled his eyes as he used a long, gnarled tree branch to stoke the fire they'd built inside the rustic circular brick pit outside the mess hall. "If you call 'paddling like a six-year-old' for three hours work, then okay."

Reed's face looked both soft and hard in the glow of the flickering flames, lips full and moist from another sip of beer as they sat slightly across from but also near each other around the crackling fire pit.

His sigh was heavy and vaguely impatient. "Could you just trust your old coach for once and take a compliment? You showed good form. Your legs are strong. Consistent. You've got a lot of upper-body strength and good coordination to boot. We just need to get the arms and legs to match up in sync and you'll be swimming in no time."

"That's what I'm afraid of," Tucker muttered.

"Why afraid?"

Tucker rattled off a few nuggets from last night's call with his producer and watched Reed frown and turn pensive with each new detail. "And you say this happens every season?"

"It's just a negotiating tactic they use to make you fear for your job and be happy for whatever they offer you to come back for the next season. I learned that the hard way the first season, but now it's just part of the grind and hustle and the unwritten moves everybody dances to. It all just gets really old after a while, you know?"

"I'm starting to," Reed said cryptically. Then he explained, "That call I got last night? It was from the head of my athletic division. The dean was in her office sniffing around while I'm out of town, looking for ways to get rid of me."

Tucker sat up a little straighter. "What? Why?"

Reed glanced slightly away, eyes alive but dour in the glow of the flickering flames. Tucker marveled at how close they'd gotten in such a relatively short amount of time and yet how little they actually knew about each other.

Reed's voice was uncharacteristically low and somber. "You don't want to know."

Tucker jutted out his chin defensively. "I asked, didn't I?"

Reed turned back, and their eyes met under the vast starlit sky. His lips parted, full and ripe, and then he shook his head as if he thought better of it. "That's for another time, kid. Tonight? I've got to know—is that *really* you in all those fight scenes?"

Tucker frowned. "What fight scenes?"

"You know." Reed reached out to tap Tucker's bare knee, the touch resounding through his entire leg and up toward his eager, throbbing crotch. "In *Suburban Dead*, obviously."

Tucker glanced back in surprise. He had a hard time keeping the pleasant surprise out of his tone. "You got the name right."

"Of course I did. I watched all the way through most of season two last night."

"No shit?"

"No shit." Reed nodded, as if proud of himself. "I only tapped out because I nodded off halfway through episode nine."

Tucker marveled. "What? How? Which part?"

Reed wore a troubled expression, as if struggling to remember. "The zombies had just kidnapped that girl, Rena, and you were trying to find their lair so you could rescue her before the head zombie bit her and she turned."

"And you fell asleep through that cliffhanger?"

"Hey, I thought you'd be glad I watched the show at all."

Tucker nudged his knee and left it there for a smidge longer than was perhaps socially acceptable. Or, for that matter, particularly wise. The night was warm after another long, humid, tantalizing day in and out of the pool. Reed's skin, or perhaps it was just Tucker's, was soft and slick with the evening humidity. "I am. I'm actually impressed."

Reed nudged his knee back and then pulled it away. It was a subtle but noticeable gesture. Tucker felt vaguely confused. All day long, and certainly the day before—hell, ever since they met—Reed had been vaguely, subtly, but palpably flirtatious. Nothing flamboyant or frilly, but definitely unmistakable. Suddenly he was backtracking? "Listen, you're working hard for me, kicking and pulling in that pool every day, stretching your comfort zone, and last night I figured the least I could do was see why all of this is so important to you."

Tucker sighed and leaned back into his chair. "I wish it was as important as you think it is, Reed."

"What do you mean?"

"I really agreed to all this, kind of actually pushed for all this, because I just needed a break from it all, you know?"

Reed nodded like maybe he really did. Tucker, propelled by his third beer, the moonlight, the crackling fire, the solitude, and the handsome, willing stranger, continued to bare his soul. "I just, it's not that I'm complaining, because no one knows how lucky I am more than I do, but ever since that happy accident that started my acting career five years ago, it's literally been nonstop. And not just, like, nine-to-five nonstop, but day shoots, night shoots, middle-of-the-night shoots, rewrites, reshoots, publicity, negotiations, ratings, bonuses, budget cuts, no bonuses, comebacks, the works."

Tucker sighed, took a swig off his latest beer, and peered at the crackling fire. "I mean, I dropped out of high school to be in that show. I was eighteen. It was my graduation, my college, my frat house, my first apartment, my first million, my first success, my first failure, my first kiss, my first heartbreak, my first everything." Tucker sighed and paused to rejigger his thoughts before they spilled out of control. Reed sat and watched him patiently. Curiously.

"It's been like a boxing match, eighteen full rounds, only you never get to go to your corner and spit out your mouthpiece and guzzle water and talk to your trainer and catch your breath. You just run around the ring, bobbing and weaving, and sometimes you hit and sometimes you take a hit, but no rest, no peace. It's just me, and all these hits just keep on coming, and I was tired, you know? I just wanted a break, and this...."

Tucker spread his arms, sore from that day's workout in the pool, to encompass the deserted camp, vast and wild and dark and empty. It was gloriously quiet, save for the crackling of the fire and the sound of his own voice. He glanced at Reed with an almost grateful smile. "This seemed like the only ticket out for me. At least for a few weeks, anyway."

Reed nodded, voice soft and low. "Why alone?"

"Huh?"

"You heard me, Tucker. Why are you going through all this alone? Where are your people? I guess I should say, *who* are your people?"

Tucker glanced back at Reed's serene and expectant face. "My mom passed when I was little, and my dad's never been the same. He was a janitor at my elementary school growing up. Was still working there when I first started on *Suburban Dead*. I bought him a house with my first sign-on bonus check for season two, set up a trust fund with my bonus from season three. He gets a monthly allowance and drinks most of it away, but I pay a local lady to check on him, clean the house, do his laundry, buy fresh groceries, meal prep, stuff like that. I try to get home for the holidays every year, but we're usually on location shooting, and I don't try as hard as I should, even though Worsham isn't all that far from the set. But he's taken care of. I make sure of that much, at least."

Reed nodded. "Sounds familiar. Just flip it and reverse it."

"You and your mom?" Tucker asked.

"Dad's alive, just out of the picture. Left us high and dry when I was five and never looked back. Mom's remarried and lives in Florida with a guy twice her age, and we've never gotten along, so holidays I usually do solo. And that brings us up to tonight."

Tucker smiled. Reed noticed. "What?"

"Nothing, it's just that I haven't talked about myself for that long since I started this whole journey."

Reed frowned. "You would think with interviews and reporters asking you questions over the years, magazine articles and whatnot, you'd get tired of talking about yourself."

Tucker waved a hand. "They just want to know about the show, the dirt, the scandal, who's dying off at the end of this season, the ratings. You could be anybody and they'd ask you the same questions, over and over."

Tucker sagged, relaxed and all but deflated, if only in a good way. He waved his beer and gave Reed an appreciative grin. "All I'm saying is, this is nice. Talking, and not just about myself. Listening too. To you. Here, now. That's all. So thank you."

Reed rolled his eyes and scrambled in the cooler between them for another beer. "Thank *you*." He lifted two familiar-looking green bottles from inside, crushed ice gliding down his fingers, and he handed one to Tucker. "For having the connections to keep an endless supply of these bad boys stocked up for us."

Tucker cracked his open, the bottle cold and refreshing in his hand. "We're gonna have to call for reinforcements soon if we keep this pace up."

Reed winked, lips full above the mouth of his freshly opened bottle. "Like you said, it's kind of a vacation. I felt that, you know?"

Tucker nodded, tapped Reed's bottle with his own, and winked in the dark, crackling night. "To trying new things," he offered, the temptation of another long, sultry night getting the best of him. When Reed cocked a single eyebrow, Tucker added, "We're on vacation, right?"

Reed seemed to consider the notion, as if for the first time—or perhaps just in a different way. "I'll drink to that, Tuck," he agreed. Then he took a long, luxurious sip. "Here's to trying new things, then. Between *friends*, right?"

Tucker's mouth was busy savoring a slug from his new bottle. All he could do was nod and wonder, as usual, what Reed meant by that.

If he meant anything by it at all, of course.

SIXTEEN

Reed

"YOU COULD always stay here."

Tucker made a face that most closely resembled that nervously grinning, mouth-wide-open, no-lips "teethy face" emoji. On either side of him, his arms were raised in the human version of a question mark.

Reed gave him a curious glance as they stood on the porch, eyes glassy, skin flushed from the humid Georgia night, heat rolling off them both in seductive, risky ways. He'd simply been walking Tucker back to his cabin, both of them on unsteady legs.

For once he hadn't been hinting around. And even if he had been, tonight, like this, was not the way he wanted his teasing, vaguely flirtatious "hints" to go down. He didn't want what might happen between them to be the result of some drunken, lowered-inhibitions "mistake" Tucker made in the heat of the moment only to regret the next morning—and then for the rest of his life.

If something was going to happen, something special, he wanted Tucker clean and aware and sober and wide-awake for every aching, explosive moment of it. Wanted them both to feel every fingertip, every kiss, every eyelid flutter and moan and whisper and all that came after.

Tonight was not that night—no matter how badly he wanted it to be.

"Yeah, Tuck, but all my stuff's in the other cabin."

Reed struggled to come up with an excuse not to go inside, where temptation was just a bed, a chair, a mattress, or hell, at this point, a floor or a wall away. He'd never wanted anyone as much as he did Tucker, and never more so than at that very moment. He was proud of himself, actually, for offering up any excuse at all. Not when all he wanted to do was drop to his knees on the scruffy welcome mat and service the sexy TV star right then and there as the poor kid held on to either side of the doorway in hard, stiff surprise.

Jesus, Reed. Get a grip!

Tucker scoffed and crossed his arms playfully over his chest. "Like what?"

Reed was practically whining at this point. "I dunno, man, just... my stuff."

"What are you, some princess you need your makeup kit to go to bed? It's you, it's me, I've got mouthwash, twelve spare bunks to choose from, what more do you need?"

Tucker was standing with the screen door open, soft light from inside illuminating the veins in his forearms. It was clear he wasn't going to take no for an answer, and Reed was too tired, too buzzed, too flattered to fight anymore. "Jesus. Fine, but only until you fall asleep."

Tucker smiled, but only half so, as Reed drifted by, careful to keep his distance from his long, lean host. "What kind of sleepover is that?"

"It's not a sleepover, kid," Reed insisted as he inched deeper into the room and leaned against a nearby bunk bed. Tucker frowned, shut the door behind him, and stood by the next stack of bunk beds over.

"We're at camp, Reed. There's no TV, I forgot to charge my phone, so it's dead, and I didn't bring any books or magazines. What am I gonna do? Sit here and twiddle my thumbs all night?"

Reed rolled his eyes. "First of all, quit whining. Secondly, from the looks of your unsteady ass, it's not going to be long before you pass the hell out, so what are you worried about?"

"I'm not worried and I'm not drunk. Buzzed, maybe." Tucker wagged a long single finger to emphasize the point. "But not drunk."

"So what are you, then, smart guy?" Reed teased. Honestly, he didn't want to go home and stare at the four walls of his own cabin either. He just didn't want to lie in the same room with Tucker and fight temptation for the next eight hours, tossing, turning, imagining, savoring....

Tucker's voice was somber and dry. "Just lonely, I guess."

Reed nodded. He felt that, felt it deep down in his gut. Not just for himself, but in Tucker's plaintive, almost pitiful plea. He softened, sagging slightly, and Tucker's grin said he knew he'd been had. "Fine, kid, but where's this mouthwash you keep squawking about?"

Tucker clapped his hands together playfully and let out a comical little *squee* sound before offering up a bottle of travel-size mouthwash from a small collection of sundries and assorted toiletries on the nearest window ledge. "Minty fresh," the label promised.

Reed chuckled as they shared a snort, gargling and swishing until they both raced through the screen door and onto the porch and leaned side by side on the railing to spit their collective mouthfuls onto the grass below, breathless and giddy from the effort.

They turned to each other then, too close by far, Tucker grinning from ear to ear, lips glossy and slick and tempting. As. Hell. They stood too long in the dark.

In the quiet.

In the solitude of two strangers peering back at each other, the only two strangers in the world.

In the glow of the softly orange porch lamp, casting dramatic shadows on Tuck's sweet, young, even expectant face.

In the heat of the soft, sweltering night.

In the shimmer of glossy, slick sweat.

And in the safe, sheltering dark of anonymity. Total, complete, utter privacy—not a soul around to listen or see or judge or tamper with that perfect, private moment.

Reed should have inched away, reached for the screen door, rocked back on his heels, cracked a joke, something. Anything. Anything to distance himself from the temptation that stood right before his hungry, approving eyes.

He knew what was coming, had felt it dozens of times in the past— that seismic vacuum of desire, the sweet, patient sting of temptation, the gut-telling pause of anticipation and the inevitable, clumsy first attempt at intimacy. The secret, sacred type only two men could share.

But by the time the kid made his first move, it was already too late. Tucker was slick in his approach. Reed gave him that much. His fingers slithered, snakelike, along the rustic porch railing, until they laced smoothly, almost perfectly, with Reed's.

Reed indulged it, for the moment. It felt too good, too sincere, too shy and bashful and awkward and pitifully sweet to yank his hand back immediately. And Reed liked it. He wanted it. It was the most perfectly naturally innocent thing in the world—their hands, gently touching on the porch rail after a long, hot, sultry day together and before an even longer, even more sultry night.

But not this time. Not now. Not with him.

Reed made a sound partway between a cluck and a gurgle and then squeezed Tucker's hand and inched his slowly away. Their eyes met, shy and curious in the dim porch light. Tucker made an abbreviated grunt and then, "What?"

"Tucker, I...." Reed struggled to explain but then fell short.

Tucker shook his head as if arguing with himself. "I'm not mistaking this, right, Reed? I'm not misinterpreting what's going on here? This whole time? You? Me? The lingering stares? The puns and jokes and come-ons and the hot, steamy showers? And now you're gonna pretend none of that ever happened?"

Reed risked another touch, soft and velvet on Tucker's shoulder, and squeezed his firm bicep reassuringly and, he hoped, innocently. "It did happen, Tucker. Every bit of it. You're not mistaken at all. And I'm sorry for that. I shouldn't have confused you."

Tucker literally stamped one foot, temper tantrum style, on the hollow floorboards of the sagging front porch. "What *isn't* confusing about all this, Reed? I shouldn't... I shouldn't want you like this. I shouldn't want any of this.... I'm not...."

Before Tucker could blurt another word, give voice to yet another lie, Reed leaned in and kissed him, hard and fast and thick and rich, warm and sticky and hot. Tucker responded and melted beneath him, gripping his arms almost helplessly, opening his lips desperately, gasping out loud. But Reed pushed him away and then gingerly dragged him through the open screen door.

"What?" Tucker gasped as Reed sat him down on the corner of the unmade bed that was obviously his. "What was that for?"

Reed grabbed a desk chair, the same wooden kind from his own room, and dragged it in front of Tucker. He sank into it, and their knees were gently touching, faces inches apart. "That was it," Reed insisted. "That was me wanting you and, hopefully, you wanting me back, and that's gonna have to be the extent of it."

"What?" Tucker was halfway between amused and confused, right where Reed preferred to keep him. This could still go either way, he reasoned in the back of his muddled, desperate mind. Reed could still pass off the kiss as a drunken blur, a rash decision, a joke gone too far, an innocent overstep made in the heat of the moment. Hell, maybe Tucker wouldn't even remember it in the morning. That much he could salvage. He'd done it before. But anything more? Beyond a kiss?

It would already be too late.

"Listen, you probably won't even remember this in the morning, but I'm gonna tell you why whatever this is, between us, stops here. Why it has to stop here, okay?"

Tucker was indignant, but charmingly so. He sat back until he clumsily conked his noggin against the bunk above him, winced adorably, and then crossed his arms and scowled at Reed, as though just remembering he was supposed to be pissed about getting cock blocked at 1:00 a.m.

"Fine, tough guy. Spill it."

"The reason I'm on academic probation back home is because I basically got fired from coaching until the college board reviews my petition to be reinstated as head coach."

"Why?"

"I'm trying to tell you, Tucker." Reed's voice was a low, no-nonsense growl. If he didn't spill this now—right now—he might not ever. That... that didn't seem fair to either of them.

"Fine, okay, sure." Tucker crossed his arms and held out his hands in dramatic supplication. "Shoot."

Reed gritted his teeth and went on. "There was this kid on my team. It was my third year of coaching, I knew better, but he had this older brother that used to come to all his meets. He was my age, late twenties, quirky, funny, cute as hell—"

Tucker beamed. "Like me!"

Reed growled back playfully. The kid was making this too easy on him. "He was nothing like you, trust me. But he was fine and funny and we were obviously into each other, and he started showing up to practices, and while the guys were swimming or stretching or changing afterward, we'd get to talking. Just he and I. He was into scary movies and synthwave music and donut shops and good watches, so we had a lot in common. And one thing led to another, and one day after practice, he asked me out for coffee."

Reed paused, throat tightening with the memory. Although it had happened nearly two years earlier, that moment—that decision, the big pool all to themselves, the nervous hitch in his voice, the bolt of lightning that struck when Reed said, "Yes"—felt like it had just happened that morning.

A quick glance found Tucker nodding, eyes curious and soft. Reed resumed the grim tale.

"I agreed. I mean, he wasn't on my team, he wasn't a minor, we were two consenting adults who just happened to have this kid on my team in common. And I was lonely, you know? It was late in the season, and we'd been winning and grinding, and I was in between relationships. I was just needing somebody, and he was there. It got hot. Real hot, real fast, and then… his little brother found out. Saw one of my racy texts or maybe a dick pic or something, and short version, the guy ghosted me.

"Like, immediately. Then the kid on my team stopped talking to me. Turned the others against me, one by one. I waited for the other shoe to drop, for someone in the administration to find out. Took a while, but when it finally did, I got called to the dean's office. The head of the athletic department was there, the kid *and* his older brother were there, blaming everything on me, even though he was the one who had asked *me* out. No one in that room had my back. It was nauseating. Just telling you makes me sick right now. Anyway, I sat there and took it, and when the dust settled, when it was all over, they transferred me to the transition team, where I'd be, as they called it, 'less of a threat.' Under constant supervision, never actually alone with students, but basically barred from coaching altogether. I guess they were too afraid of the blowback if they fired me completely, since I'd done nothing legally wrong. Only morally."

"Morally?"

"It's Eastern Georgia State, Tuck. It's about as conservative as it gets, so I was lucky to keep my job, I guess."

Tucker reached out a hand—innocently, this time. He placed it on Reed's bare knee. "I'm sorry that happened to you, Reed."

"Me too, Tucker. Because…." He reached down and covered the kid's hand with his own. "I really would like there to be something more between us. You and me. Right here, right now, all alone in this place with no one to see. I could use that right now, and from the looks of it, from the feel of it, I bet you could too. But I can't risk another scandal, you know?"

Tucker turned his hand over until they were palm to palm, and they held each other's hand in the warm, quiet cabin. Still knee to sticky knee, sweaty in the stifling Georgia heat, they were close enough to kiss.

Only this time they didn't.

Obviously they couldn't.

"I understand, Reed. I respect your wishes, even if I really, really hate being punished because of some clown who can't handle a grown-ass relationship without putting the blame on someone else."

Reed would have taken a stagger-step back if he weren't sitting. "That's very astute of you, Tucker. Very mature, even."

"Yeah, well, don't sound so surprised." The kid yawned, and without another word, tugged off his T-shirt to reveal his glistening bare torso, making Reed breathless in the midnight heat. "I'm an actor, not an idiot."

"Right, sure," Reed mumbled as Tucker continued disrobing, unbuttoning, unzipping, and tugging down his khaki shorts to reveal soft, clingy gray boxer briefs beneath. They left absolutely nothing to the imagination. "Of course not, and listen, just for the record, I thought you were a boxers man."

Tucker glanced up at last, bare to the world save for his clingy underwear. "I am. Why?"

"Those aren't boxers."

Tucker winked as he bent and slipped into bed and lay atop the covers like a waking wet dream. "What do you care, Reed? You've made it clear you're not interested in me, so quit staring at my boxers bulge, you big perv!"

"Why, you little shit."

Tucker chuckled, squirmed to get comfortable, his tousled brown curls caressing a soft white pillow. Then he tucked his arms under his head and stretched out, long and limber and sleek.

Reed turned his head, tugged off his clothes near the desk by the door, and carefully folded them until he too stood clad only in his actual boxer shorts, alone in the middle of the room as Tucker, God love him, began to breathe heavily and then snore lightly.

Reed ogled him openly in the soft dark of the moonlit room. His brown curls against the white pillow. Nostrils flaring above his thick, smooth lips. Shoulders bare, nipples maroon, and belly flat where it dipped achingly, following his wispy brown happy trail where it drifted beneath the waistband of his light gray boxers. His bulge, as ever, prominent and curved beneath the front panel. Thighs pale from his swim trunks tan and legs long and lean as they stretched out toward the very edge of the bunk, one half falling off the end because he was so damn tall.

Reed swallowed, armpits sweaty and bulge thick in his own boxers. He knew he should leave, just put his clothes back on and duck out of the cabin, but something in that felt vaguely like a betrayal. He knew instinctively that if Tucker woke up the next morning or, more than likely, in the middle of the night, alone in the empty cabin, he would think less of Reed. And suddenly that was the last thing he wanted.

Instead he grabbed a comforter and a pillow and, quietly, so as not to rouse him, spread them out beside Tucker's bed. If he couldn't have the man himself, the least he could do was be as close to him as possible before the sun rose, the day dawned, and the spell they'd shared tonight was broken forever.

SEVENTEEN

Tucker

"ARE YOU awake?"

Tucker's voice was hoarse in the dark, barely above a whisper to match the surreal nature of the moment. All the same, Reed responded in kind, his voice as husky and hoarse as the deep, dark night that surrounded the rustic cabin, filling it with quiet mystery and the by-now-familiar thrum of humid temptation. "Of course."

Tucker snorted, just shy of a chuckle and mixed with a quiet gurgle of relief. He wasn't sure what he would have done if Reed had answered with a snort or a snore and then rolled over and gone back to sleep. He'd been waiting for over an hour to make his move, so he shifted over on his mattress and lifted himself up on one elbow to peer over the bottom bunk to the floor directly by his bed.

He smirked and rolled his eyes, trying his best to be alluring. "What are you doing down there, anyway?"

"You were so drunk last night." Reed glanced up from the fuzzy striped comforter splayed out beneath him, "I didn't want you to roll out of bed and bust your head open."

Tucker struggled to retain his composure at Reed's half-naked form, sprawled out on the floor literally at his feet. Moonlight caressed his quietly grinning face in a most flattering way. "What were you gonna do, catch me in your sleep?"

"If I had to, yeah."

He slid his hands beneath his chin and gazed down at Reed the way teenage girls stared at the posters of rock stars and screen idols from old black-and-white movies on their walls. "Besides, I wasn't that drunk."

Reed made a face. "Okay, bud."

Tucker was hungry. And thirsty. And hard as a rail beneath his boxer briefs, pressed thick and tight against the mattress beneath him. "Well, I'm not now."

Reed lay flat on his back, looking up, as if he'd been waiting for Tucker to open his eyes and look down at him. He lifted his hands and gave a little golf clap, the soft sound vaguely startling in the middle of the night. Outside the screen door, only a stray cricket chirped in the deep stillness of the forest. "Congrats. I guess I can get into an actual bed now?"

Reed made no move to leave, and Tucker was glad. He was enjoying the view—every smooth, savory, moonlit inch of it. Before Reed could stand, to make good on his promise, Tucker slid one hand away from beneath his chin and pressed it flat against Reed's chest. It was warm and hard and lean and softly humid in the cabin's almost stifling heat. It was also beating like a jackrabbit. The feel—the pulse—of Reed's pounding, frantic heart was vaguely encouraging.

"Let's not be too hasty, now."

Reed's playful smile froze into something less than amused, if not quite startled. He didn't say anything, not right away, but it was clear he wanted Tucker to move his hand. So he did. Moved it just a smidge lower down Reed's chest and drifted it lazily toward his suddenly stiff nipples.

"Tucker, stop." Reed's voice was a groan, his words a lie. Every fiber of his being, every slick sheen of sweat and rat-a-tat of his pounding heart, every thrum of vibration throughout his taut, pale skin said, "Go," not "Stop."

"Why?" Tucker croaked, voice thick with desire and brain riddled with indifference.

"I already told you. I knew you wouldn't remember." Still, Reed stayed in place and squirmed beneath Tucker's touch, nipples still stiff and enticing. The cabin was so quiet and still, Tucker could feel the vibration of each syllable through Reed's lean torso.

"I remember every word, Reed. And I've been lying here, hard as a rock, thinking about it all night."

Reed chuckled, and the soft vibration trilled under Tucker's open palm. Tucker used the lighthearted moment to almost imperceptibly glide his hand below Reed's chest. His heart was still pounding, harder, even, than before. "And?"

"And it's not fair. What happened to you, obviously, but the way you're holding it over me too. And this isn't even the same. You're not my actual coach, Reed. And there's no morals clause in your contract, no backwater college dean with a stick up his butt to find out, nothing to prevent you and me from doing whatever we want when no one's around to see it anyway."

"Tucker, I've already lost so much. I don't want to lose any more. Especially you."

Their eyes met, and in that moment, Tucker saw the lie in Reed's curious, hungry, leering glare. Heard it in his husky, turbulent tone. Felt it in the moistness of the skin under his hungry palm and in the pantherlike, coiled quiver of Reed's gut as it trembled just shy of Tucker's velvet touch.

Tucker smirked, bluffing almost triumphantly. "Okay, fine. If this is really something you don't want, here, in the middle of the night, deep in these woods, just you and me and…."

He began to lift his hand until Reed grabbed it by the wrist and held it just firmly and far more tenderly in place. "That's not what I'm saying, Tucker. I just… it's different, for me."

"And not for me? You don't think I have anything to lose? You think I'm scandal-proof?"

"So we both do, Tucker. We've both got lives, careers, at risk here. So why are you so willing to risk all that on some washed-up old swim coach?"

Tucker growled playfully. "You're not washed up." As Reed smiled, blushing from the touch and the heat and the moment, Tucker pressed his hand back against his pale, pounding chest. "So give me what I want, Reed, and I'll make it worth your while."

Reed shook his head, even as he raised his hands and tucked them casually behind his head, splaying out as if on full display. Tucker met his eyes, and they shared a quiet moment in the dark. "Tucker, you're grown. We both are. I obviously want this. It seems like you do too. I can't stop you, so…."

"You can," Tucker blurted, sensing a way to relieve his tense, coiled lover and give him the freedom to resist. If that was what he truly wanted. "If I'm doing anything you don't want me to do, just stop me."

Reed smiled. "You're sweet, kid. For real. I appreciate that, but…." He took a glance down the long expanse of his half-naked body. "If you'll notice, I probably couldn't stop now if I tried."

Tucker followed Reed's gaze, noting with a flattered blush that the mere glance of his palm against Reed's stomach had created a noticeably thrumming bulge beneath the thin cotton of his soft white boxer shorts.

Tucker thought about some snappy comeback, but at the prospect of Reed's smooth, thick cock in his hand, he suddenly lost the ability to speak.

Instead he let his fingers do the talking, inching them slowly toward Reed's waistband. He risked a glance away from his lover's fluttering belly to meet his eyes and saw the eagerness and hunger flickering there. Reed was right about one thing—it would have taken a nuclear blast to stop the freight train of desire rolling right over them at that moment.

Tucker smiled and squirmed atop his bunk bed, glad for once that Reed slept the same way he sat in a deck chair—his feet facing Tucker's head and his head at the foot of Tucker's bed. It was as if, subconsciously, or maybe consciously, he knew what might happen deep in the dark of night and wanted perfect placement for Tucker's hungry, eager hand to slather attention on his greedy prick.

Tucker wasted little time teasing and tugging at his lover's boxer shorts. He slid the waistband back and forth along Reed's flat belly and watched his girth slip and slide along with the easy motions. Reed began to purr and squirm and, eager as Tucker was to satisfy him, the control he suddenly had made him want even more than a quick tug job in the dark.

They spoke not a word in the stifling heat of the cabin, the only light source the moon through the open windows and the glow of a faint, fuzzy nightlight by the foot of the desk across the room. But Reed's body spoke volumes, shivering and tense in turn the closer Tucker's hand got to his emerging staff.

At last his hunger got the best of him, and with a decisive motion, he slipped his fingers beneath the waistband of Reed's boxers. Reed gasped, the sound so pure and erotic Tucker nearly came in reply. But it was too soon for that.

Too soon by far.

Instead Tucker crept, fingertip by fingertip, even lower, until at last the throbbing tip of Reed's cock glanced across his hand. It was hot and sticky and dappled with dew, the way Tucker's got when he stayed too excited for too long before he finally did something about it.

Reed gasped anew at the physical touch, helplessly, hungrily, and Tucker grinned as his lover squirmed and tugged until his boxers were halfway down his smooth, sticky thighs. Tucker marveled at the glossiness of his lover's shaft, slick with his own juices. Unlike the snatches and glimpses he'd stolen in the steamy locker room, now Tucker could gaze at Reed's member openly, admiring every veiny inch and pebbly wrinkle and the smooth, saggy skin of his perfectly shaved sac.

He ignored the girth of Reed's staff and cupped the heft of his meaty package, his balls warm and thick and rich and damp in the late summer heat. They shrugged and throbbed in his gentle clutches, Reed hungrily spreading his equally smooth legs and pushing the boxers down farther until at last they rested just below his knees.

Tucker's throat was dry, his heart pounding, his own cock throbbing and leaking eagerly against his thin mattress, forcing him to savor every inch and moment of this all-too-brief late-night encounter, as if it might be their last.

It was certainly his first, but not the first time he'd imagined such a scenario—a willing lover beneath his hands, smooth and sultry and helpless against the grip of his eager, trembling clutches. The night dark around them, boxer shorts below his knees, thighs spread, balls thick, a deep, husky male voice panting and grunting in delight. He'd just never had the balls to make good on the fantasy before.

If only Reed knew how much he'd wanted this moment or for how very, very long. It was up to Tucker to make him realize it, and at last he did. He released Reed's throbbing, sweltering sac to grip the base of his stiff, straining prick.

Reed gasped, skin aglow with a fresh glimmer of perspiration as he swallowed and turned his head from side to side, lips parted, eyelids fluttering with desire, biting down on his lower lip as if to squelch the real sounds, the desperate cries he surely wanted to make. And still he spoke not a word, merely watched Tucker's every move as he tentatively stroked and savored Reed's velvet cock with a quietly desperate grip.

It was thick and meaty, the skin pliant and supple as Tucker groped his way to the tip. It was pulsing and slick with excitement. Tucker gathered it instinctively and swirled hungry fingertips around the slit in the middle of his mushroom head until it was sufficiently slathered and he coated Reed's shaft with his own juices as, legs spread, ass grinding into the comforter beneath him, Reed pumped as eagerly as Tucker stroked him.

The teasing was over, the temptation at hand, Reed hungry and greedy as he thrust in and out of Tucker's sticky fist. He grunted, arched his ass one last time, and with a shivering surge, his cock erupted—a splash, then a stream, followed by a jet, then a spurt—and Reed's chest and belly were slick and splattered with his own goo, glistening and clotted in the pale moonlight, enhancing the appeal of Reed's shivering, panting torso.

Tucker's loose grip felt every surge and throb of the blast, and he smiled contentedly to himself that, at long last, he'd fulfilled at least one of his life's greatest curiosities and most tantalizing fantasies. He wondered if Reed would be up for satisfying the rest.

EIGHTEEN

Reed

"JESUS, KID!"

Reed shivered, Tucker's grip surprisingly tender as it clung to the base of his sticky, slathered shaft, squeezing it almost as an afterthought. "I thought you said you'd never been with a guy before."

Tucker smiled from atop his bed, face flushed and soft brown curls sticking to his perspiring skin as their eyes met and Reed struggled not to blush at his veritable explosion of appreciation. "I haven't, but I've had a little practice with my own."

Reed chuckled, deep and throaty, as if to match the panting in his chest, the pounding of his heart, and the quivering in his tumultuous gut. He hadn't wanted to give in like that, to succumb to Tucker's pretty-boy face, big, long fingers, and surprisingly forceful presence, but lost in the dark, hungry and eager and surprised by the power of Tucker's youthful lust, he simply hadn't been able to help himself. Any more than he'd be able to resist returning the favor. Just as soon as he could muster the strength to sit up after expelling half his body fluids in the last ten seconds.

"I'd say," Reed muttered, hardly recognizing the huskiness of his words or the light-headed bliss of such a powerful, earth-shattering climax.

Where moments ago he'd been servicing Reed's cock like a certified rent boy, suddenly young Tucker was exceedingly coy. "Why, was that good?"

"Good? If it had been any better, I might have blown a hole through the wall with that massive splooge explosion."

Tucker nodded and sighed contentedly as he continued to play his fingertips up and down the sticky splatter across Reed's belly and chest. It was an absent gesture and one Reed didn't think anyone had ever used on him before. Usually, after the money shot, the guy was either rolled over in the fetal position, fast asleep, or gathering up his clothes on his way out the door.

Tucker nodded at the sticky glaze coating Reed's chest. "It was a lot."

"Yeah, well, it's been a while, kid." Reed glanced at Tucker's body, lying flat on the bed, squirming with obvious anticipation. "What, like you're not ready to blow a gasket over there?"

Tucker glanced away and then quietly nodded. Reed smirked and at last found the power to bat Tuck's hand away and sit up. He kicked his boxers off all the way as he crossed his legs and scooted closer to his lover's bunk bed.

"Sit up," Reed commanded playfully, albeit quietly, still under the spell of the deep, dark night, throat too tight to speak above a hoarse whisper. "And we'll see if I can excite you half as much as you did me."

Tucker shifted slowly, as if unsure how to proceed. "Trust me, Reed, I've literally never been more excited. You could look at me funny and I'd explode."

Reed sat directly in front of Tucker's bed, covered in his own goo, cock wilting and sticking against his left thigh as they spoke, his sticky sack still throbbing with his most powerful orgasm ever. "Oh, I think I can get you a little more excited than you are right now."

"I mean it, Reed. Feel my chest." Tucker sat up, legs dangling over the bed and on either side of Reed, leaning slightly forward to avoid conking his noggin on the top bunk right above him. Reed ventured a tentative hand up to place flat against Tucker's broad chest. Sure enough, the kid's heart was practically pounding through his rib cage.

That wasn't the only thing pounding. By far. Straining against his dew-splattered boxer briefs as if trying to pull them off itself, that long, thin shaft of his throbbed and danced with every pounding heartbeat. Sated, but already eager for more, Reed let his hand glide down from Tuck's chest and across the throbbing bulge. He gripped it through the damp fabric and squeezed it tightly, but not too tightly. Tucker gasped, shivered, and murmured his approval in a raw, unfamiliar grunt.

"Not yet, stud," Reed moaned, wishing they were close enough for him to smother Tuck with an appreciative, hungry kiss that left the cocksure TV star breathless and gasping for air in its wake. Instead he'd have to settle for teasing him until he practically came hands-free. "Remember how long you teased me for, you sadistic little horndog?"

Tucker chuckled and blushed as, on either side of his lean, narrow waist, Reed ran hungry fingertips up his rib cage and back down again, glancing but not touching his throbbing prick.

Reed was lost in the moment, no longer abashed or inhibited or worrying about what might happen tomorrow, next week, or when he got back to Eastern Georgia State. He was here right now, in this room, with the hottest lover he'd ever had, and damned if he was going to turn back now. If anything, he was going to plunge straight forward until there was no turning back—for either of them.

"Lift up your arms," Reed grunted forcefully, and he smiled to himself as Tucker smirked but did his bidding, gripping the wrought iron bars that held the top bunk above him.

"Why?" Tucker asked, just before the breath caught in his throat as Reed playfully pinched a taut, stiff nipple.

"I just like looking at them, that's all," Reed mused even as his heart began to race anew to watch his lean, limber lover hang there, as if suspended in midair, arms wiry and taut, wispy underarm hair damp from the Georgia heat, body splayed out and stretched as if just for him.

Incredibly, Reed realized, it *was* just for him. All of this—every throbbing, glistening, damp, dewy inch. The smile, the smirk, the strain, the throb—it was all just for him. Right now, right here, Tucker was his and his alone, and Reed decided to enjoy every moment of it. He ran his hands up and down Tucker's body until the poor guy was visibly trembling, licking his lips as his eyelids fluttered open and shut with obvious quaking, shaking desire.

Amazingly, Reed was thickening again, legs crossed and Tucker's body so close he could have kissed it if he didn't think it would make the kid literally explode, detonating right off the bed and into the very stratosphere above the rustic cabin.

Instead he ran his hands one last time down Tucker's rib cage and settled on either side of his waistband, which was straining with the heft of Tucker's engorged staff. Although he'd tormented the poor kid within an inch of his life, suddenly Reed wasted little time in tugging the briefs down below his waist, quickly past his knees, then off. Tucker squirmed and grunted until they hung off one ankle like a forgotten grocery store bag in the wind.

At last Tucker was freed, fists gripping the bunk bed above, thighs gently spread on either side of Reed as he hefted the meat of Tuck's thick, sagging balls with one hand and the base of his thin banana cock with the other. Tucker was hot and slick, vibrating with desire and panting with every shift and heft of Reed's fingertips as they danced up and down the veiny shaft.

Reed forced himself to pause and soak in the moment—to admire every little detail, like the scruffy bush of his lover's pubes, damp and glistening in the somber moonlight, climbing upward into a thin, wispy happy trail that led to his belly button.

Tucker cooed approval as Reed stroked his cock, wet with desire and stiff with anticipation as the glistening actor writhed atop the bottom bunk, clenching his cheeks and gently thrusting into Reed's expertly gripping fist as his own hands clung desperately to the bars on either side of him.

Reed licked his lips, too hungry to resist, and held the prick aloft as, slowly, he leaned forward to slather the impressive staff with an appropriate amount of licking and kisses. Tucker opened his fluttering eyelids just in time and shrank, almost imperceptibly, away.

"N-n-nnnnooo, Reed," he panted.

Reed glanced up with a questioning look. "What's wrong, Tuck? I thought... I thought you wanted this."

"I do. God, I do, just not yet. Next time, okay? We'll both do that next time? Tonight I just want your hands, okay? I want your hands, all over me, just like they are. Just. That."

Reed smirked, squeezed Tuck's hefty sac, and watched him wince with desire. "Like a first-date kind of thing?"

"It's kind of a fantasy of mine," Tucker admitted. He smiled, almost bashfully, as if either of them could hide the abject, raw power of their sticky, naked bodies in the dark. "It's just that I've wanted this so long, Reed, I want it to last. I want it to stretch out, night after night, until I've indulged every fantasy I've ever had about being with... with...."

"Another guy?" Reed finished for him, sensing Tucker might not be able to say the words out loud just yet.

Tucker nodded feverishly. "Let's make it last as long as possible, before...."

Reed glanced at Tucker's throbbing, glistening prick. "Not sure how long you're going to 'last,' bro, but I'll just use my hands for now, okay?"

Tucker nodded and sighed with relief until Reed gripped the base of his staff tightly and he bit down on his lower lip as if to keep from making some ungodly noise that would give the lie to whatever control the kid might have thought he had.

It might have been Tucker's first time with another man, but it was hardly Reed's first rodeo. Grinning almost triumphantly, Reed stroked him in earnest, sensing the looming climax in every inch of his lover's slick cock and slippery, noisy thrust.

Every part of Tucker was trembling in concert as he struggled to hold on—his pale, flexing thighs, his flat belly, his hands, gripping the bars on either side of him, and his balls that throbbed and danced as Reed stroked him from base to tip and back again, savoring the slick, veiny heft in his grip and relishing the anticipation until, at last, Tucker shuddered with an almost violent release.

It coursed through his staff, throbbing and desperate, and into an explosion of epic proportion that spurted and sprayed Tucker's panting, heaving chest with a sweet, sticky glaze of pent-up lust. Reed gently milked him as he watched Tuck shudder and quake but never shy away from another softly squeezing stroke until at last his mighty fountain had slowed to a creamy trickle that ran across Reed's fingers like icing on a cupcake.

Only then did Reed release him and, teasingly, temptingly, lean forward to kiss a quivering thigh, dappled with Tuck's sweet, fragrant jizz and making for a savory, musky dessert to a most satisfying meal. He felt the kid buck at first, then relax on the edge of his bunk bed.

All the same, even after spending everything he had, Reed wanted more. He nodded at his lap. "Come here," he purred as he leaned back on the flat of his palms and stretched his body out for maximum exposure. Tucker nodded and disentangled himself from the rumpled bed to slither atop Reed's sticky, sated lap.

They wrangled until they were groin to groin, legs entangled, sweaty and slick and still humming from the aftershocks of their sated lust. Once Tuck was firmly wedged in place, his back to the bed frame, Reed inched closer to wrap his arms around his lover's waist and pull him in for the wet, wilting kiss he'd wanted to revisit ever since the night before.

Tucker's lips were full and fragrant, his mouth quickly open to meet Reed's intense embrace, the two of them gasping and panting anew by the time Reed let him up for air.

Reed sat back, and Tucker followed suit. They gazed at each other, taking in the scene, their sticky bodies glistening in the moonlight, sweaty and satisfied and free. When at last their eyes met, their lips parted once more.

This time, not for a kiss.

"Thank you," they said at the same time. Then they grinned in reply and collapsed into a fitful burst of giggles that sounded as relieved, happy, and buoyant as Reed felt.

NINETEEN

Tucker

"I'M TRYING here, geez!"

Tucker gasped, breathless and splashing as he clawed his way, literally kicking if not quite screaming, to the wet tiles at the far end of the pool.

"Almost there," Reed urged him from where he stood, pacing in tight, concerned circles above him on the chlorine-splattered pool deck.

With a trembling hand, wet and pruney from the day's long, eventful practice, Tucker slapped one hand atop the wet tiles at the deep end of the pool and then, moments later, the other. He dangled where he clung and glanced up at Reed where he stood just above.

"Did I do it?" he panted, heart pounding.

Reed's smile was all the answer he needed. He knelt down, shirtless, sweaty, beaming, and grabbed Tucker by both forearms. His grip was strong and reassuring. "Tucker, you did it. All of it. You swam, buddy. You swam all the way here."

Tucker felt all of twelve years old but couldn't deny the sense of childlike pride that filled him to the very core. "You sure? You're not just shitting me to make me feel better?"

Reed's expression changed. "Who hurt you, pal? Why don't you trust me after all this time? I know how important this all is to you. I shit you not, you swam. The entire length. Of this pool." He slapped the wet cement for emphasis. "All by yourself. And it's a big-ass pool. Just look back for yourself and see how far you came."

Tucker sagged with relief, clinging desperately to the deep end but gasping, and with more than just exhaustion. He glanced back at the length of the Olympic-size pool, impressed by all he'd accomplished in such a short time. "I did, didn't I?"

Reed sank down beside him and slipped his feet into the pool up to his shins. "No paddleboard, no training wheels, no me right beside you, holding you in place. That was all you, bro—every kick, every slap, every lap." He slapped his shoulder again. "I'm proud of you, Tuck. Really, sincerely proud."

Tucker blushed and glanced away until he spotted the metal ladder just to his left. He contemplated gripping the pool deck and easing himself over but, suddenly emboldened, pushed off from the wall and paddled, clumsily but steadily, toward its curved, gleaming arms. With pruney fingers he gripped either side of the shiny metal rails and propelled himself up each rubbery step on wobbly legs until he stood, damp and panting, on the warm gray concrete.

Reed remained seated and gave him his serene, smoky gaze as Tucker padded over on wet feet to sit next to him. The pool deck was warm beneath his haunches, sore from the day's long practice. Longer, Tucker realized, than ever before.

"Look at you," Reed teased as he reached over to squeeze Tuck's thigh but then quickly removed his hand. "Struttin' around like you own the damn pool or something."

Tucker blushed anew, enjoying the warmth of the sun on his shoulders and the quiet nudge of Reed's thigh against his own. "Was I strutting?"

Reed chuckled, face nakedly and unabashedly gleeful. "Oh yeah. The only thing missing was some funky soul struttin' music in the background."

"Stop."

"Seriously, Tuck. I am exceedingly proud of you. Like, I've coached a lot of swimmers in my life, but I've never taught anyone *how* to swim before. Like, from scratch. It's exceedingly hard, and these last few days of really focusing and trying your hardest, you've managed to make it look easy."

Tucker squirmed beneath Reed's enthusiastic praise. It wasn't the kind of feedback he was used to, not on the cutthroat and competitive set of *Suburban Dead*, that was for sure. And certainly not back in dog-eat-dog Hollywood. Reed was right to observe he was distrustful of such praise. And naturally, it was just like his nurturing coach to compliment him anyway.

"You're just saying that," Tucker blurted.

"Why, Tuck? Why would I say that if I didn't mean it?"

Tucker leaned closer, until it wasn't just their hips nuzzling but their shoulders as well. "To get me in bed, I suppose."

Reed snorted, shook his head, and leaped to his feet as if he was, well, a swim coach used to doing such acrobatic feats a few dozen times a day. He stood above Tucker and extended a warm, dry hand for Tuck's wet and wrinkled one. "You're the actor here, remember, kid? Not me."

Tucker took his hand and allowed Reed to help him to a standing position. It was, amazingly, the most romantic thing anyone had ever done, male or female, friend or foe, lover or wannabe seductress, in his entire sordid life. He glanced down and smiled. "I don't have to act with you, Reed."

"Now you're making me blush, Tuck."

Tucker rolled his eyes at the cheesiness of the situation, despite enjoying it completely. Reed squeezed his hand and then tugged him along, past the still-churning pool and toward the locker room.

"What about our stuff?" Tucker looked at the date-night deck chairs and cooler, the T-shirts, flip-flops, sunscreen, and other assorted detritus of their daily routine at the camp pool.

"Trust me, Tuck, in a few minutes you'll forget all about that stuff."

"Why?" Tucker asked, though the sudden heat of Reed's grip hinted at the afternoon activities to come.

"You deserve a little reward for today's, uh, *performance*," Reed muttered as he dragged him into the locker room, familiar by now with its tile floors and matching partition wall separating the shower area from the wooden benches lined up just beyond. "And I want to be the one to give it to you."

"Here?"

Reed stood by the opening in the waist-high wall, tugged at the knot in his baggies, and cracked them open, the Velcro sound echoing through the sterile white room with a familiar, erotic scratch.

Reed winked. "What, Tuck? You're standing there telling me that none of your man-on-man fantasies involve a locker room?" He spread his arms wide, baggies still half clinging to his narrow waist. "You know," he teased, really digging into the role of tempter, "steam swirling, water spraying, two guys side by side until one of them can't take it anymore and slowly reaches out to see what the other one feels like. Tastes like...."

Tucker wasn't sure he could blush any deeper, but as usual, Reed had managed to seduce an even richer, hotter flush from his already burning cheeks. "What are you, a mind reader or something?"

Reed had but to wriggle his lean, narrow hips and the baggies slid slickly down his thighs and pooled at his big bare feet. He was, as ever, thick and getting thicker, smooth and pale amidst the sea of tiles that lined the locker room all around them.

Tucker found it curious that, despite how much time they both spent in the sun, Reed always managed to remain pale and smooth, like a statue carved out of the purest marble. All that flesh, serene and supple, was highly erotic. "What, you think you're the only one with a few fantasies up his sleeve, Tuck?"

Tucker struggled with his own swim trunks as he nodded at Reed's smooth, semihard erection. "Obviously not," he muttered as, in turn, his own bathing suit dropped with a wet *thwock* to the tiled floor at his feet.

Reed glanced at Tucker's own thickness, his smile hungry. "Obviously."

He turned then, shapely backside pale and firm and flexing with each short step into the shower area. Tucker followed, belly taut with friction, desire, lust, and above all, the delicious sting of anticipation.

He had no idea what Reed had in mind, but he was literally powerless to prevent whatever happened next or, for that matter, how many times. And suddenly, quite surely, that was exactly what Tucker wanted—to be told, to be led, to be controlled, moved, posed, handled by an expert lover like Reed. Suddenly he wanted it in a way he'd never wanted anything in his life before.

As if sensing Tucker wanted to be led, Reed reached out a nurturing hand and tugged him over the threshold, into the showers, and Reed stood behind Tucker at a single spigot.

"Ready?" Reed whispered in his ear, breath hot and damp on the back of his neck. Their bodies touched, just barely—Reed's chest against Tuck's back, his groin against Tuck's rear, their flesh quivering with anticipation.

Tucker nodded, then croaked around the sudden lump in his throat, "For what?"

Reed's chuckle was coarse and deep as, inching closer, he reached over to turn the dial. Spray enveloped them, lukewarm at first, then hotter, but never quite hot. Tucker gasped all the same, as much from the way Reed clung to his desperate body as from the spray dancing across his head, shoulders, and back.

Reed kissed his neck so tenderly that Tucker's shaft leaped up and down involuntarily, throbbing and aching with the dance of pending release. Inching slightly away, but dragging a patient rasp of wet fingertips along the crest of Tucker's quivering backside, Reed used his free hand to pump several squirts of the neon green body wash from the dispenser on the wall beside the sputtering spigot. Tucker swallowed hard and waited for what might come next.

"Stand still." Reed warmed the gel soap between his palms and nodded as Tucker shifted from foot to foot. "You want every inch to be clean, right?"

They both stepped away from the shower's spray, dripping and desperate and facing each other in the steamy, sultry stall.

Tucker smirked as Reed finally put his hands on his shoulders and smoothed the soap into a rich, frothy, fragrant lather that flared his nostrils and stuttered his heartbeat. "I thought you preferred me dirty, Coach."

Reed snorted, and their eyes met. "I do, movie star, but let's just say I'm not a big fan of the taste of chlorine, okay?"

Tucker froze. Reed used the slight pause as an opportunity to lift Tuck's left arm and lather it from wrist to armpit, then the other.

"Taste?" Tucker croaked.

Reed chuckled. He had moved on to Tucker's belly by then, coating his quivering abdomen with the rich lather, sidestepping his package to softly soap up each hip. Then he crouched and ministered to Tucker's long, pale thighs. He did so slowly, as he had every inch of Tuck's body above his waist. It was an intoxicating sensation, quietly overloading Tuck's circuits until he was powerless to resist.

"Sure," he said nonchalantly, as if it weren't yet another of Tucker's longstanding fantasies quietly coming to life before his very eyes.

Or should he say, between his legs.

Reed winked and gripped a hand on either thigh for support as he crouched before his wet, nubile lover. "This is our second date, right? So mouths only? But definitely, absolutely mouths. Wasn't that the deal we made last night?"

Tucker, suddenly nervous, nodded hesitantly. "Sure, absolutely, I mean, I guess… I just thought we'd have dinner for one of these date nights, right?"

Reed was still crouching, balls so thick and full they nearly danced along the soapy white tiles at his feet. He lathered Tucker's knee as the shower spray beaded off the thin black stubble that coated his head and ran down his chiseled, handsome face.

"Oh, I'll be feasting all right." He leered up at Tucker from where he crouched, thighs wide, cock thick, eyes full of desire, and lips temptingly thick and moist. "On you, Tuck."

Tucker made another audible gulp as Reed made quick work of lathering his legs and slowly working his way back up to his swollen loins.

"That is," Reed murmured, stroking Tucker's cock and balls with richly lathered hands, the feeling as sensual and sloppy as last night's late-night hand job at the edge of his quietly creaking bunk bed, "if you can last that long."

Tucker rolled his eyes, even as they struggled to tumble back into his head like the wheels of a spinning slot machine. In all his fantasizing over the years—his secret yearnings and pent-up desires—he never imagined anything, ever, feeling this insanely good. Reed was right—even after last night's draining, ecstatic mutual masturbation, Tuck struggled to keep from blasting the shower walls with his own splattery goo.

Reed must have sensed it. He tempted Tucker's aching loins with a veritable sponge bath as he eagerly lathered every thickening inch of Tucker, top to bottom, base to tip and back again, to bring him to the very edge of ecstasy and then just as teasingly drift his hands away to glide back up his body until they were standing face-to-face in the shower's glistening spray.

"And even if you don't," Reed added, leaning in to whisper hot nothings in Tuck's ear, "we've got all night together, Tucker. Just you and me and our wet, hungry lips."

TWENTY

Reed

"STAND. STILL. Brat!"

Tucker squirmed, his back against the tile wall beside the still-shuddering shower spigot. His smile was bashful and charming, boyish and playful where his body, glistening and aglow from the recent lathering, was all man.

"It's slippery in here, Reed."

Reed stood to his full height and smothered Tucker's protests with a withering kiss that left his lover with his back against the wall, breathless, panting, and subdued. "It's gonna get a lot more slippery in a minute, Tuck."

Reed enjoyed the blush that suddenly rose to his lover's taut apple cheeks, still damp from the clingy curls atop his head. Reed glanced a kiss off Tucker's cheek and moved closer to his blushing ear to whisper, "And a lot more wet too."

"Stop," Tucker protested by rote, but Reed had no intention of doing any such thing. And clearly, from the thickening curve of Tucker's downturned banana cock, the kid wanted no such thing as well.

Reed kissed him silent once more, releasing him with a gasp. He nuzzled his neck, then his collarbone, then each nipple, wet and taut, with more and more suggestive kisses.

He enjoyed the powerlessness of Tuck's situation—wet and glistening, pinned against the shower wall, dripping and panting and not sure what might happen next. Reed peppered his hard, wet body with kisses, tasting his soapy cleanness and his youthful enthusiasm and enjoying the panting sounds of Tuck's obvious, aching pleasure.

While his lips explored his lover's lean young body, Reed's hands had a mind of their own, caressing either side of Tuck's face and following the hard, taut line of his shoulders, then down his arms, and across the small of his back to the soft, damp, dimpled orbs of his backside. Tucker gasped at the sensation of being caressed and adored, making Reed cling all the tighter as their loins pressed and danced against one another's in the damp, shimmering shower spray.

They danced like that, in and out of the steamy spray, chest to chest, lips to lips, knob to knob, wet and thick and panting and slick with desire, in more ways than one.

The water bounced off their hard, taut bodies until at last Reed released his eager lover and turned the spigot off, and the sudden absence of sound and spray only highlighted their panting, murmuring appreciation for one another. They were both clean and warm from the sun, and the rich, soapy lather drizzled past their bare toes and down the gurgling drain.

At last Reed reached across with both hands to clasp Tucker's, fingers damp and trembling, and drag him gently away from the showers and out toward the waist-high wall where, as ever, two soft white towels waited, folded as if they'd just had maid service.

"You do think of everything," Tucker muttered absently as Reed took one of the towels and began to lovingly and suggestively dry off Tucker's towering form. He was making small talk and nervous squeaky sounds, as if to prolong the inevitable or perhaps to savor it all the more.

Reed knew the feeling all too well, but was powerless to stop the insatiable desire that simmered deep in his hungry belly and translated to the tantalizing sponge bath and more that awaited them in the quiet, deserted locker room.

"Trust me." He dragged Tucker to the nearest wooden bench, yanked him down to a seated position, arranged him at the foot of it as if setting one of the scenes from his popular TV show. "Right now I'm not thinking of anything but what you'll taste like between my lips."

Tucker nodded, and Reed laid out his towel at the very edge of the bench. He sank to his knees atop it, still dripping wet and savoring every moment of it. As he came face-to-face with Tucker's glistening, bushy crotch, he smiled.

Reed dried every inch of his nervous lover—soft fuzzy balls, thin, curved prick, tight, dimpled ass, and taut, quivering belly until he clutched Tucker on either side of his waist, unable to wait a moment longer.

Tucker was still uncertain, hesitant, his manhood curved downward in all its shimmering glory. Gazing at it, Reed watched it quiver and throb with anticipation, much as his own did as it dangled, full and heavy, against the edge of the rough wooden bench. He allowed himself the moment, squeaky clean and almost innocent—two lovers in the glow of foreplay, hearts pounding, breath rasping, bodies tense and expectant in the soft, flattering light of the empty locker room.

The towel long gone, forgotten and curled in a distant corner, Reed ran hungry fingertips along Tuck's clean skin, down the lengths of his thighs and back up again. He palmed those taut cheeks and drew him closer with every squeeze and nuzzle. There was so much to see and explore. It was heady and almost overwhelming, even though Reed had been imagining this very instant since their very first visit to the pool.

Tucker's face was still damp from the tousled brown curls, lips partly opened and full. His hooded eyes, uncertain but also eager, searched Reed's as he glanced up from the bench, literally kneeling at Tuck's feet and moments away from tasting his lover's essence, so rich and pure. He was painfully aware that this would be Tucker's first time being serviced by another man. He didn't take the role lightly but instead intended to give him the experience of a lifetime, for as long as he could.

Starting immediately.

Reed forced himself to ignore the rest of the enticing young body hovering above him and, with eager, hungry lips, lavished soft, feathery kisses all along Tucker's thin, fuzzy happy trail. At last Tucker gasped and flinched at the delight of Reed's lips so close to his shaft.

With an eager hand clasping each of Tucker's ripe young cheeks, he felt them pucker and dimple as well, an involuntary reaction to the sudden rapture on full display. To lure Tuck all the more, Reed kneaded them gently as he continued to bestow tender kisses on his trembling belly, and felt it quiver and buck enticingly beneath his fervent lips.

Reed bent to his work and tugged Tucker slightly forward on the bench for a better perch as, kiss by kiss, savoring its feathery clean goodness, he dampened Tuck's happy trail until it was as glistening and dewy as the tip of his curved, graceful cock.

Tucker made an appreciative, uncontrolled sound as Reed continued to knead and cling to Tuck's backside, which trembled slightly as Reed continued to torment with thick, wet kisses alongside and around Tucker's member. He knew the playful delay would result in all the more appreciation when at last his greedy lips met the manhood still straining to be serviced.

He began at the base with a soft, tentative flicker of his tongue that sent spasms through Tuck's staff. He followed it with a kiss, his hungry lips pressed against damp, warm skin humming with pleasure. From the base he kissed and pecked his way to the tip, straining now, stiff as a board and hard as a rock. It was absolutely begging to be slathered with attention.

He wasted little time. Reed told himself he would stretch it out, tempt and savor and seduce the poor kid into a whimpering, vibrating heap, but at the first swell of his swollen tip, that dazzling sheen of precum dampening the thick head, he gave in to his own personal fantasies and plopped it into his mouth without prelude or announcement.

He felt it throb and pulse with surprise and, emboldened, he savored its clean, meaty taste and drank more in, inch by inch, until his lips clung tightly to the veiny shaft and he dragged back so painfully slowly that they both moaned aloud with sudden, obvious pleasure.

Tuck squirmed, helpless against the involuntary reflexes that forced the gush and gasp from his breath, the throb in his prick, and the clench of his ass as Reed held on for dear life.

While Tucker was a self-confessed "virgin," Reed had had such a long, withering dry spell that the sensation of another man's heft inside his mouth felt almost as new to him. He let his tongue glide across the shaft and explore the slickness of every vein and dimple.

As Tucker twisted and panted with the pent-up desire of a lifetime spent denying himself the pleasure of another man's tongue, Reed savored the meaty top half of his quivering manhood and glided his lips and tongue in concert, up and down and back again. All the while he squeezed Tuck's backside, kneading it one second and squeezing the next.

Reed knew from experience that the combination was intense, and never more so than when it was one's first time feeling the front and back pleasure, the back and forth pull, the drag and the suck and the squeeze and the lick as it intensified, moment by moment, to an almost unsustainable heat.

Reed did so now, sucking harder, licking longer, lips tighter, greedy fingers digging into the soft, pliant skin of Tuck's rear as he began to use it as a guide, dragging him back and forth along the edge of the bench seat, in and out of his full, bruised lips, clinging tightly to his throbbing, leaking staff.

Reed felt the intensity surge, and Tuck's body hummed with anticipation and desire beneath his fingertips as his shaft throbbed with desire and impending release between his lips. In and out, back and forth, Tuck began to gently thrust and grunt until, at last, he growled an almost unintelligible warning and Reed squeezed his ass firmly, yanking his lips from the fat, bulging tip just as a gusher of jizz bolted from inside and blasted Tuck's panting, heaving chest with an almost inhuman coating of fresh, hot spunk.

Reed released his grip on the kid's quivering backside and, with rapt attention, used one hand to softly heft his throbbing balls and with the other, even more gently stroke his pulsing prick.

Tucker shook as his chest heaved, slick and glossy with a coat of fresh icing that dripped down even as his tip continued to sputter and ooze. Reed used the overflow to coat his still-rigid cock.

Tucker glanced down just as Reed looked up, and their eyes met in a flash of intensity he found almost as reassuring as he did flattering. The kid's cheeks were flushed, to say nothing of the swell of his neck and the top of his chest, which burned bright pink above and amidst the glistening gobs of slick cum.

Tucker opened his mouth as if to say something, then seemed to think better of it, but his eyelids fluttered open and shut as a wicked leer rose to his full, slightly parted lips. They broke eye contact as Tucker glanced steadily downward and nodded with approval as his gaze settled on Reed's lap.

He made a soft murmur of approval and then nodded as if to himself. Reed glanced down, amazed to find himself swollen and thick, knob glazed with his own slick coating of precum even as his throbbing prick swelled with his own mounting anticipation.

TWENTY-ONE

Tucker

"YOUR TURN, big guy."

Tucker watched as Reed licked his lips, face flushed, eyes wide, body tensed and cock throbbing hot and hard above his savory package.

He sputtered, shook his head from side to side, and waved his hands in protest. "Listen, Tuck, you don't have to return the favor. I wanted that. I wanted so badly to do that to you, to do that *for* you. I've wanted it since I first saw you get out of the car that first day. That was totally my fantasy. We can wait, if you're not ready."

Reed was babbling, and they both knew it. And lying straight through his teeth. Tucker chuckled knowingly, his voice deep and low as he reached with a trembling hand toward Reed's cheek. He caressed it as if he'd had dozens of male lovers over the years.

"You said I deserved a reward, right?"

Still kneeling on the twisted towel at Tucker's feet, face upturned, skin glossy with a fresh spray of sweat, Reed's eyes widened slightly. "What, you're telling me that wasn't the best BJ of your life?"

"It was, obviously." Tucker glanced down at the clotted jizz still dribbling down his heaving chest and fluttering belly and dotting his happy trail with specks of obvious appreciation. "But... you're my reward, Reed. Don't you know that by now?"

"Stop flattering me, kid," Reed grumbled, but Tucker ignored him. He squirmed atop the locker-room bench as his balls glanced across the warm, weathered wood, still so sensitive he felt every decadent shiver and shrug. "Or my head will get as big as yours."

Tucker made a leering glance down at Reed's staggering hard-on as he continued to kneel at Tuck's feet. He had never coveted anything more in his entire life than he did that throbbing shaft. "One can only hope, big boy. Now shush, you're killing the mood."

For once, Reed did as he was told. He took Tucker's hand as, awkwardly, stumbling, fumbling, they quietly traded places. Once settled, Reed sat stock-still, a hand gripping the bench on either side of his chastely spread thighs, watching as Tucker lowered his tall, gangly body like a spare folding chair on Thanksgiving, and knelt on the damp towel Reed had used for that same purpose only moments earlier.

Reed gasped at the sensation of Tucker's hands atop either thigh as he gradually spread them wider and inched himself closer, running his big damp hands up and down Reed's legs as he leaned in for a kiss. It was tentative at first, but eagerly, insistently, Tucker insinuated his tongue, desperate and hungry for a taste of his own meaty musk on Reed's full, expert lips.

The kiss grew exponentially, and Tucker gripped Reed's thighs for purchase as he tumbled into the embrace, warm and sticky and fragrant as his own spunk dried on his still-panting chest. He could hardly believe this was happening—here, to him, in this place, with this man, so eager and nurturing and drop-dead sexy.

It was a page lifted straight from one of his personal fantasies, sprung to life in a way more pleasurable than he'd ever imagined.

And they were just getting started.

As he dragged his lips reluctantly from Reed's, Tucker glided his hands farther up Reed's smooth taut thighs. Reed began to mutter, his self-assured nature crumbling under Tuck's caress even as he leaned slightly forward for another intoxicating kiss.

Tuck denied him and chuckled playfully as his palms drifted past Reed's crotch, up his fluttering six-pack belly, and against his chest. "Playtime is over, Coach." He pushed back as Reed gasped with the surprise and shock of a startled lover. "Now, lean back and let me have this."

Reed nodded and hesitantly lay back on the long wooden bench, splaying himself out like a feast to be savored, sucked, and stroked. Tucker dragged Reed closer until the angle was just right, thighs spread wide on either side of Tucker, Reed's swollen, dancing testes dangling just off the bench, his ripe, firm rump nestled at the very edge.

Tucker gripped Reed's left thigh, and with his free hand, he slathered Reed's low, smooth balls with delicate attention. He didn't have to see Reed's expression to sense his pleasure, but he heard it in his appreciative gasp, felt it in the surge of the balls in his hand, and saw it in the rise and fall of his eagerly panting chest.

Reed issued a small, careful "Mmmmmm" as Tucker kneaded his package and then inched his hand upward until he gripped the base of his thick shaft. He held it tightly and watched as Reed turned his head from left to right.

Tucker ignored the other sights and sounds of Reed's rapture—the glistening shine of his smooth, pale body, the throbbing heft of his bald package, the fluttering rigidity of his taut, firm belly. Instead he savored Reed's staff and dragged his gentle grip up the veiny shaft, watching the skin loosen and ripple along with his clinging touch. When at last he grasped the tip and eased a glistening drop of precum from the throbbing head, Tucker licked his lips reflexively and, before he could chicken out, bent slightly to kiss it.

Just that. A simple kiss to taste the drop, the clean and vaguely soapy taste of meat and musk. He grunted in appreciation—a feral sound from deep in his coiled gut—and followed the kiss with a caress, lips grasping either side of the tip as it entered his mouth.

It wasn't the only noise to echo in the vast tiled locker room. Reed gasped aloud and shuddered through his entire body as he gripped the side of the bench with white knuckles and spread his thighs wider, arching his feet, toes flat on the tile floor beneath them as if for better purchase as Tucker began to suck and savor the meaty, full tip as if it was the only thing to exist in the entire world.

Tucker ran his tongue around the rigid edge and sucked it dry at the same time. Then he released Reed with another helpless gasp and ran his lips down the veiny staff and back up again, popping the tip back in, then out, repeating the process until he had licked and sucked and savored every inch of his lover's heft to a glistening, slick sheen.

He gripped each of Reed's thighs and felt the tension coiled there like springs. When at last Reed was a quivering, panting tangle, Tucker smirked and, greedy himself, slid his lips atop the glistening orb once more. Suddenly with renewed purpose, Tucker drew more and more of his lover's prick inside his hungry, clinging mouth, then out. He gorged and feasted as he lost himself to the taste, the sensation, the flavor, the heat, the hum of Reed's deep, dripping desire.

Tucker instinctively knew better than to try and fit all of Reed's impressive girth in, at least not on his first try. Instead he braved as much as he could, as often as he could, as slowly as he could, as long as he could, lips clinging to the meatiness as Reed, just as instinctively, began to pump and thrust inside the tasty grip.

Tucker squeezed his thighs for purchase as he kneeled in place, his lover pumping and thrusting, Reed's balls toppling and tumbling against the edge of the long wooden bench, Tuck's lips tighter and wetter around the vaguely thrusting shaft. He felt the surge and the gush moments before it came.

"Tuck!"

Reed's plea was half desperation, half warning, and Tucker tugged his lips from their tight purchase and shifted his attention to the glistening staff as the tip burst forth with an explosion of epic proportion. It rested on Reed's smooth, shaven pelvis, pulsing and throbbing thick white jets all the way to his shivering chin, onto his already glistening chest, then his belly, until it slowed to a crawl and puddled on the slick, pale expanse just beneath his belly button.

Tucker replaced his lips with a soft, tentative grip between his fingertips. He felt the pulse and the jets as they slowed to a sticky, audible drip. And then curiosity got the best of him and he bent once more to lick the last drop of lust from his lover's throbbing tip.

TWENTY-TWO

Reed

"YOU KNOW, Reed, I've been wondering how come *you* have the better room."

Tucker stood indignantly just inside the cabin, hands on either hip like an actual counselor surveying a dozen unmade beds. "Sorry, make that the *much* better room."

Reed was genuinely amused. He reached into the dorm fridge under his desk and grabbed two of the beers he'd stashed on a previous late-night recon mission to the mess hall kitchen and back. "I just assumed yours was the same until last night, dude."

Tucker grew even more indignant and almost—almost—refused the cold bottle of beer Reed offered. "I mean, you've had this setup the whole time, and I'm over there in the cheap seats like some kind of civilian or something!"

Young Tucker twisted off his cap with a spiteful jerk of his wrist as he glanced around accusingly into every corner of Reed's rustic cabin.

"Again, Tuck, I figured they set us both up in the counselors' cabins, you know?"

"They most certainly did not, you frickin' diva." Tucker continued to cast his eyes around the spacious lodge. Reed was just glad Tucker's eyes weren't boring into his or he might discover the real truth—obviously, getting to camp a day earlier than Tuck, Reed had been able to scout out the grounds to his heart's content and had naturally chosen the counselor's cabin for himself.

Never in a million years, of course, did he ever imagine the two would see each other's rooms, let alone in such an intimate context. And now that they had, the lie had gone on too long for Reed to fess up. His only hope was subtle, sexy subterfuge.

Reed sank onto his usual desk chair, and it creaked in all the familiar ways under his relaxed, sated weight. He'd never felt more spent than he had after Tucker's expert draining, spread-eagled and dripping with sweat on the edge of that wooden locker-room bench. Tucker had seemed equally chilled out after their mutual blow jobs, and they both tumbled back to Reed's cabin to turn in early and recharge for another day after a quick snack in the mess hall.

Big mistake. "You're being a tad dramatic, Tuck."

Tucker seemed unapologetic as he waved his hand grandly at the cabin's interior. "Maybe I am, maybe I'm not, but you've had this giant-ass bed without another bed on top of you and then not hitting your head every night when you get up to go and pee in the bathroom three miles away in the dark because you're not used to sleeping in a bunk bed at twenty-three and why would you when you could be sleeping in your penthouse apartment back in LA where there's a bathroom literally five steps from your California king?"

Reed was openly chuckling by now. "Okay, and who's the diva now?"

Tuck sipped his beer, looking flushed and radiant after another successful day in the pool and an even more successful hour or two in the steamy, sticky locker room.

"Look, Reed, I'm due, okay?"

Reed nodded playfully. He liked seeing this side of Tucker—intimate, relaxed, even mischievous. "No doubt, and might I add, if they ever do kick you off your zombie show, from the performance I've just seen, you've got quite a future on the stage. Say in a Shakespearean drama of some sort?"

Tucker finally saw the humor in the situation. He snorted good-naturedly above his beer and gradually unpuffed himself. At least slightly.

There was a beanbag chair in the corner, under a scary-movie poster and one of those stick-to-the-wall basketball hoops. As he slumped down into it, all six foot two of his lean, lanky ass, Tucker Crawford looked about twelve years old. "Fine, I get it. But you could have at least invited me over before now."

Reed gave him a scolding glance. "I believe I tried the other night, remember?"

Tucker nodded, lips full and fat around his beer bottle—not unlike how they'd looked, glistening and plump around Reed's most intimate plaything only minutes earlier. "I guess I just didn't think I was strong enough to resist temptation a few days ago, you know?"

Reed slid deeper into his desk chair, more relaxed than he'd felt in months, maybe even years. It was more than just the release of six gallons of jizz back in the locker room. Tucker, and being with Tucker, simply had that effect on him. "And now?"

Tucker grinned and wriggled deeper into the beanbag until he too looked more relaxed than ever. It was amazing how being in the company of the right person could be such a tonic for the body, mind, and soul. And how long he'd managed to live without it.

"Now I don't have to resist you, Reed."

"The hell you don't." Reed wagged his half-empty beer bottle at his younger companion. "The deal when I agreed to this little sleepover idea of yours was that you'd keep your hands off for the rest of the night, remember? I don't recharge in twelve seconds like you young Hollywood studs."

Tucker leered from across the room. "How do you know if you don't try, pops?"

Reed fixed him with a coach's scowl. "We're not all virgins in this room, kid. And unless you want a swift kick in the ass and a point to the door, I suggest you cool your jets and settle in for a long night of spooning, perhaps romantically, and spooning only."

Tucker surrendered and flashed that big, jovial grin. Reed knew, and Tucker probably did too, that at the first fidget or touch, they'd both probably collapse into a sweaty, sexy, writhing heap of bad intentions and massive, bursting hard-ons. Still, one had to project an air of propriety in these situations, at least until the lights went out and the bodies drifted closer and closer together under a blanket of sweltering Georgia humidity.

"Don't flatter yourself, pops. I just want a good night's sleep after today's, uh, festivities."

"Then we're in agreement, Tuck. So as soon as you finish that beer, we can crawl into bed and rest up for another busy day tomorrow."

Tucker winked and polished off his beer in two quick gulps. Then he set the bottle on the windowsill next to him. Plaid curtains of a hideous green and yellow that probably hadn't been manufactured in years, fluttered on either side of the open window, where the warm, sultry August night crept gently through. Tucker wobbled from side to side in the deep, cozy beanbag, struggling until he nodded at Reed. "A little help?"

Reed shook his head and stood, not quite reluctantly, from his creaky wooden desk chair. Lately, anytime he had the chance to get closer to Tucker, it was well worth the effort. Even if it took his last ounce of energy to shuffle across the room and extend an eager hand.

"I should have warned you, it's kind of hard to get out of."

"Yeah," Tucker grunted as he took the hand and did little to nothing to help Reed pull him out of the bulging black chair. "You should have."

At last Tucker stood, too close by far, body warm and lean in the room's dim light. Flashes of the last two days—sticky and sweet and lurid—fluttered across Reed's memory as he glanced up at his young companion. He went to say "Good night," or "Hurry up," or "Let's change," but the minute he opened his lips to speak, Tucker kissed him passionately, mouth still full of his own savory tang. Reed balked unconvincingly and then fell across Tuck's chest and leaned into the kiss.

"I knew this was a bad idea," Reed grunted breathlessly when he finally managed to push Tuck away and stumble a few steps back toward the bed.

"Just a kiss before bedtime." Tucker promptly tugged off the T-shirt he'd worn to the pool that day and tossed it down into the hole left by his impression in the beanbag chair beside him. "No harm in that, right?"

Reed rolled his eyes as he marveled anew at Tucker's long, tempting body, every detail fresh and new as if he hadn't been savoring it nonstop over the last two sinful days. "I sense harm in every inch of you, Tuck."

Tuck chuckled wryly as he unbuttoned his khaki shorts and slipped them straight off his narrow hips and down to the floor with little more than a shrug and a wriggle. He stepped from them, baggy white boxers clinging to his sinfully smooth cock. "Not tonight, Reed. You plumb tuckered me out back there in that locker room."

Reed wriggled out of his own T-shirt, then his jean shorts, until he had stripped to a pair of soft blue boxer briefs that barely hid his aching, palpable desire. They stood like that, beside the bed but not in it, bare-ass save for their underwear in the pale moonlight.

Tucker swallowed hard, the way he had back in the locker room. "I'm not sure I can keep my hands off you tonight, Reed."

Reed, in turn, drank in all of Tucker—every sinewy inch, soft and hard in equal measure. "You and me both, kid, but let's try, okay? The old man isn't used to this much, uh, action in one day."

Tucker inched closer just the same. He brushed Reed's lips with his own and then sank onto the mattress. Reed joined him, both of them on the edge of the queen-size bed that dominated the counselor's cabin

Reed had nabbed for himself the first day at Camp Run-A-Mok. "Can I tell you something secret?"

Reed chuckled and nudged Tucker's hip with his own. In bed, it felt almost as intimate as anything else they'd done that day. And almost as sexy.

"Isn't everything we're doing here a secret, kid?"

Tucker nodded, but not happily. "I guess so. But this is a different kind of secret."

"Tucker, I said from day one, you can trust me. I'm not going to hurt you, and I'll never share your secrets, okay?" He reached out to squeeze Tuck's leg reassuringly. For once, for now, it didn't lead to any hijinks.

"I believe you, Reed. I just... I don't ever talk like this with anybody else, you know?"

"Me either, kid, trust me."

Tucker nodded, then stayed mum. Finally Reed tried to tug it out of him. "So what were you going to say that was so secret?"

"Just that everything we've been doing—the touching with our mouths, even just kissing you, Reed. It's just that I've never felt that good with a girl."

Reed nodded. He knew the feeling. "No?"

Tucker sighed, slid deeper into bed, and lay on his back. Reed watched him and marveled at this thing of beauty he was about to sleep next to all night. He knew it was, in every way, a very bad idea.

"Nuh-uh," he confessed as Reed finally joined him. He too lay on his back, Tucker warm beside him as they both stared up at a water stain on the ceiling tile directly overhead.

"And you've only ever been with girls?" Reed turned his head slightly to watch for an answer.

"Pretty much, yeah."

Reed chuckled, and the big bed shook gently beneath his stifled guffaw. "Pretty much? What's that supposed to mean?"

Tucker stiffened slightly on the bed beside him. "It means pretty much, is what it means."

Reed smirked. "It's kind of a 'yes' or 'no' answer, pal."

Tucker sighed heavily, and the bed creaked as he shifted his weight to lean up on one elbow. Peering down at Reed's face, he smiled crookedly. "Well, there was this one guy, in high school."

Reed felt warm inside with the looming confession. Not just the fact that Tucker trusted him enough to share it with him, but with the familiarity of the words themselves.

"There's always that one guy in high school," he murmured fondly as he recalled his own first crush and how it made him feel—confused, alone, awkward, nervous, sad, happy, angry, hurt, but mostly horny as hell. Kind of the way he felt around Tucker every minute of every day.

"You too?" Tucker seemed surprised.

Reed let out a world-weary sigh. "Tucker, I've known I was 'different' since eighth grade."

Tucker seemed genuinely surprised—either that or genuinely impressed. "Wow, really? That's when you started fooling around?"

"God no," Reed snorted. "I was a bit of a late bloomer, actually."

Tucker looked suspicious. "How late?"

"Junior year."

"Yeah, really?"

Reed smirked. "No, it was sophomore year, actually. I just didn't want you to think I was some kind of super slut or something."

"Too late, player. So who was it? Your first, I mean."

Reed glanced up at Tucker and offered him a smile he felt all the way to his tugging heartstrings. "If I recall correctly, this started out being your confession, remember?"

Tucker nudged Reed's hip with his knee and sent the bed creaking. "We'll get to mine, but your life is so much more interesting."

"Trust me, it's not."

Tucker sighed impatiently. "Fine, we'll compare confessions in a minute, but for now, about this first of yours?"

"He wasn't my first, actually." Reed glanced back through time to revisit the deserted dugout during Christmas break, no one else around, he and Benjy McPherson meeting in the dead of night, hard as rails and scared as hell of being caught. "But he was my first man crush, if that's what you mean."

"I guess I do, yeah."

"His name was Benjy McPherson," Reed confessed with a bittersweet smile. "He was a junior, a year older than me. We met in summer school, both of us rejects, flunking out but not wanting to repeat another grade. We'd smoke after school behind the minimart halfway between the streets where we lived. Never did anything that summer but stare and flirt and talk and plan, but then school came, and between my swimming and his basketball season, we barely saw each other.

"Then winter break came, and he waited for me on the last day of school. We waited everyone else out—all our friends and girlfriends and teachers and even the janitors. It seemed to take forever for everyone to leave, the two of us lurking behind the big generator in the back, out by the dumpsters.

"When the last car had finally left the school parking lot, we finally unlocked our bikes and stood, waiting for the last car to drift away. When the sound of its engine was long gone, Benjy started walking his ten-speed to the ballfields behind the school. It was like he knew just where he wanted to go and, the minute we were finally alone, headed straight there. He never looked back or said a single word. I just knew that I was supposed to follow. So I followed."

Reed looked up to see if Tucker was still listening. He was staring down at him raptly, as if literally hanging off every word. The air in the cabin was still, humid, fragrant with their soapy sweat, and caressed every so often by the gentle breeze that rustled the curtains on either side of the window above the bed. Tucker said not a word, like Benjy that day so very long ago, but he nudged him with that same knee and nodded expectantly.

Reed's heart was pounding with the memory. He hadn't thought about it in years, but now, speaking it aloud, it felt like he had traveled through time and space and was reliving the moments as much as he was retelling them. As he continued, his voice was low and deep, hardly above a steady hum. "There were three of them. Three dugouts, I mean. It was a big school. We leaned our bikes behind the concession stand, where no one could see them from the road or even the employee parking lot if one of the janitors forgot his keys or something and had to come back. Benjy picked one of the ballfields and opened the gate, then led me to a dugout, empty and long and quiet. It wasn't dark, though. Just quiet. We sat there for a while, just talking, but not much. But I noticed we sat really close all of a sudden, closer than we'd ever sat before. We're talking, like, hip to hip...."

"Kind of like right now?" Tucker was still looking down at him expectantly, as if breathlessly awaiting what he might say next. They had inched closer to each other atop the unmade bed, Tucker's skin warm and smooth alongside his own.

"Just like right now," Reed continued somberly. "It was unnatural for guys to sit that way. Even I knew that. Then again, everything we were doing was out of the norm—hiding out, waiting for the school to let out, being so alone in such a deserted place, hip to hip and skin to skin. But I didn't care. We were alone in that dugout, and this was Benjy McPherson, *the* Benjy McPherson, the man of my dreams. At least at that moment in time. We talked and talked, about what I have no idea. I liked comic books. He liked video games. Probably that kind of stuff. It was late in the afternoon but early in the evening, a kind of in-between time, and I remember that the sun was casting shadows on his face. He had glasses, kind of thick but not nerdy, and curly red hair that I just wanted to touch. To run my fingers through all those curls, just once. The talking stopped after a while. One minute we were yapping about Spider-Man or something and the next, nothing. Just crickets. I didn't care. I was happy just to sit there with him, the only two people left at school, and as far as I was concerned, the only two people still left in the world. He put his hand on my leg at one point. I jumped. We laughed, but I didn't move away. He knew then, why I was there. And I knew why he was there. He leaned in, slow and soft, and kissed me. I kind of knew it was coming. I'd kissed girls before, at dances and stuff, and did the same thing before I kissed them—looked in their eyes, leaned in to make sure it was what they wanted too, you know? It was a little kiss at first, just to test the waters, I guess. But it got hotter and heavier and… and… by the time he let me up for air, I'd cum."

"Say what?" Tucker's voice was just above a ripple in the soft, late-summer breeze. His eyes were wide. "You came? From a kiss?"

Reed blushed as he peered up at his latest lover. "It was so new and so good and so hard and strong, and I wanted it so much and I couldn't help it. I mean, I'd dreamed about that moment for months. Fantasized about it all that last week of school, knowing it would be the last time I'd see him. So, like, all of that was like foreplay, built up in my mind. By the time he finally kissed me, so hard and hot and wet, I was loaded and ready to blast off. I guess I did. I barely knew it was happening until I felt this… goo in my shorts and realized I was hard and pulsing, you know? I looked down, and sure enough, jizz all over the front of my jean shorts. Like, a gallon's worth. So did he, and he laughed. But not for long."

"Why not?"

"Because he'd cum too."

Tucker's chuckle shook the bed in a most pleasant way, and their quiet mumbles and snickers made the mattress vibrate as if they'd put a nickel in the slot in some cheap hotel room. "No shit?"

Reed smiled at the memory. "He was wearing these khaki shorts, and Jesus, he blew a massive load all over the front. I don't know if he was going commando or just came that much that it blasted straight through his tighty-whities, but we laughed about it for almost an hour. Then we had to stay there, sticky and gooey and embarrassed, until it dried and didn't look so bad before we could go home."

Tucker's smile was pure gold. It matched the light in his curious eyes. "Then what happened?"

Reed sighed and shifted to put his hands behind his head and stretch out on his side of the bed, closest to the edge. "Then we'd meet at that dugout every chance we got, all that winter break. It might be at noon on a random Tuesday or midnight on a Thursday. One time we were there at four in the morning, crickets chirping, both of us jumping at every broken branch or croaking frog but literally unable to stay away from each other."

"And?"

"And what? That's not enough?"

"I mean, how far did you go?"

Reed chuckled at the memory. "The same place. We'd sit there, talking and kissing and making each other explode without ever really touching each other."

Tucker gave a surprised little grunt. "Really? Hands-free every time? Not a single stroke or squeeze or nothing?"

"Not a thing. Ever. I think, once we found out we could satisfy each other just with anticipation and desire and kissing, it felt less gay somehow? Does that make sense?"

Tucker nodded. "It shouldn't, really. Two guys kissing is pretty gay. But somehow, I know exactly what you mean."

Reed nodded. "Somehow, Tuck, I thought you might."

Tucker's face was a begrudging mask of respect. "God, that's really sexy, Reed."

"Yeah, I know." His voice had somehow grown deep and husky with the long-buried memory, his belly taut with a fresh wave of renewed desire.

"Like, I could almost cum just from listening to you talk about some guy making you cum. That's so sexy."

"Same, bud, same." He sighed and wriggled deeper into the mattress as he tried to ignore the way Tucker's boxer shorts strained at the story's more intimate details, not quite surprised at the twenty-three-year-old's stamina.

Reed finished his tale, as if to delay the inevitable. "And that's how I knew I was who I was, Tucker. That's how I knew *what* I was. I knew no girl had ever made me that excited just from kissing. Hell, I'd gone all the way with a few girls, and I'd still never felt that good or cum that hard. I'd kind of been lying to myself until that first time Benjy kissed me, and I told myself it was time to stop lying. To myself, anyway. And I've never looked back, kid." Reed looked up at his lover, eyes boring into Tucker's in a way he knew the kid would finally understand. "And neither should you."

TWENTY-THREE

Tucker

"SO THAT'S why you're such a good kisser, huh?"

Reed still lay on his back, tempting and smooth in the moonlight swimming through the open window beside his bed. His lips wore a glossy sheen from talking, his hands behind his head as if he knew just how good that looked as Tucker peered down at him, heart gently pounding from the intimacy of his story and the vivid, lurid details that accompanied it.

Reed looked up at him uncertainly. "Am I?"

Tucker licked his lips in anticipation. "Pretty sure, but let's test my theory, just to be certain." He leaned down almost chastely and pressed their lips together as the emotions and the hormones flowed anew. It was a passionate, swollen kiss, lips plump and aching with desire. When they were both breathless, gasping for air and taut like live wires, Tucker simply leaned back up, peered down at Reed's flushed, handsome face, and smirked triumphantly.

"Yup, pretty darn good."

Reed chuckled, the sound pure and deep in the late-night air of the stuffy cabin. As usual, a thin layer of sweat coated their bodies, as if Mother Nature herself insisted they look irresistible to each other and destined not to make it through a single interaction without giving in and pleasuring each other, one sweaty moment at a time.

Tucker, still propped up on one elbow, gazed alternately at the rustic counselor's cabin and back down at Reed. He sighed heavily and confessed, "I have a Benjy of my own."

Reed somehow managed to look surprised and not surprised at the same time. "Yeah? What was his name?"

Tucker glanced past his lover to a crooked bulletin board on the opposite wall. "Avery Abercrombie."

Reed snorted. The hour was late, their bodies were spent, and nothing was left in the tank. By rights they should have been dead to the world, zonked out in each other's sweaty arms, half-naked and blissed out. Instead they muttered late into the night, hearts still pounding, eyes still wide, confessing in ways Tucker imagined neither of them ever had before.

At least he certainly hadn't. Reed's eyes met his own above a curious, crooked smile. "Sounds like a male model."

"He was anything but," Tucker mused, wearing his own curious smile. "At least, not from a distance. He was geeky and awkward and shy and either stuck out like a sore thumb or melted into the background, unseen."

"But *you* saw him, right?"

Tucker nodded. "Not at first, not out in the hallways or the cafeteria or gym or anything, but he joined drama our senior year. Not first semester, like I did, but second semester, in the spring. He was new, and we'd all formed our little cliques during the first semester, and I felt kind of bad for him. He didn't help himself much, always being clumsy and awkward and goofy, and the more I watched him, adorably sexy."

"Yeah?" Reed looked dubious.

Tucker continued, "Anyway, this one day we were rehearsing for the *Final Follies*. It was this dumb skit the departing seniors put on every year—kind of a big deal, if you cared about that kind of thing."

"And you didn't?"

"Me? I just couldn't wait to get out of school. Start my own life, my real life, somewhere far away. Anyway, the *Follies* were *very* important to the 'Drama Kids,' you know the type. Anyway, at some point while we were rehearsing, he knocked over a potted plant or something, and the teacher snapped at him. He took it to heart, apologized and got back to work, but a few minutes later, I saw him slip out the auditorium's side door and sneak outside. I knew he was probably never coming back, so I followed him. He was leaving really fast. I caught up and stopped him. He was... crying."

Reed looked appropriately sad. "No shit?"

"No shit. Luckily it was after school. No one was around at the time, and plus the back of the auditorium emptied into a parking lot no one used unless it was during a performance. I caught up to him at the loading dock and calmed him down, and we kind of pulled ourselves up and sat there, talking. He knew who I was through reputation, and seemed kind of surprised I'd followed him, let alone commiserated."

Reed nudged him gently. "What reputation was that, stud?"

"Hardly, I just meant… letterman's jacket in track, senior year—the usual high school BS. Anyway, I explained that the drama teacher's bark was worse than his bite, but we both knew I was lying. I don't think he really cared much, and I was just kind of glad to finally speak with him, one on one.

"He said it wasn't the teacher's fault that he was crying. Not really, anyway. When I asked why he was crying then, he blurted out that he'd just broken up with his boyfriend. Then he kind of gasped and realized what he'd just said and who he'd said it to—the straightest boy at Elm Crest High, according to my school rep, anyway—and he made me promise I wouldn't tell anyone. I swore I wouldn't, and I honestly meant every word when I promised, but I knew he wouldn't believe me. He was the first gay guy I ever met."

Reed furrowed his brow above a doubtful frown. "I doubt that very much, Tuck. Just probably the first gay guy who ever admitted it to your face."

"Well, yeah, I know that now, but back then I was a little more innocent."

Reed nudged Tuck's thigh with his own. It was sticky and warm and close. "I bet you were," he mumbled vaguely. Tucker ignored him.

"Anyway, it was mid rehearsal and we were weeks away from the *Follies*, and I knew it was a low-stakes kind of afternoon, so I kind of blew off the rest of the period and asked him out for coffee."

"Right there? On the spot?"

"It wasn't like that. Or at least I told myself it wasn't. I didn't say, 'Hey, you wanna go out on a coffee date with me and peer romantically into each other's eyes for three hours?' I think I said something like, 'Caffeine might help. I know just the spot.' It wasn't a date, not at first. I just really didn't want him to quit, and I thought if I could get him somewhere private, away from our teacher and the other drama kids, he might open up and I'd be able to convince him to stay."

"Why not?" Reed pressed. "I mean, you said you'd never even noticed the guy before. Why did you suddenly care so much whether he quit drama or not?"

Their eyes met in the shimmering dark. Reed was so beautiful, with his chiseled features and that pale, smooth, marble-hard skin aglow in the soft moonlight. Looking at him sometimes made Tucker feel literally breathless. Somehow he swallowed and plunged ahead.

"I had finally noticed him, I guess," Tucker confessed. "And knowing he was into… guys… was new and shocking and yet vaguely comforting. I wanted to know how it all worked for him—having a boyfriend on the down-low, being in a relationship like that. It was so new to me, so foreign, and maybe I was a little jealous? I thought, at some point, maybe if I kept his secret… he'd keep mine?"

"So you knew already? About yourself, I mean?"

Tucker didn't quite nod, but didn't shake his head either. "I suspected. Let's say that. But it was confusing, because girls made me super horny, and I always dated hot ones, easy ones, I guess, who were always up for whatever, whenever, you know. So I definitely knew my way around a woman's body. But there were times in the locker room or at the lake on the weekends or at the gym, where I'd catch snatches of a cute guy's chest or just a flash of bare skin or a sweaty smile, and I'd get just as jazzed, you know?"

Reed glanced past him, up at the ceiling, and nodded quietly without meeting Tuck's eyes. "I certainly do, kid." His tone, world-weary and somber, made it clear he absolutely did. It was, as ever, reassuring.

"So it was all confusing, but it felt really natural that day, when we finally got to the coffee shop, sitting with him all the way in the back, like we had the whole place to ourselves, watching the door to see if someone we knew might walk in. But they never did, and we spent, like, three hours there that day."

Tucker's voice trailed off, raspy in the dead of night. He found himself raking his fingertips lazily, absently, across Reed's bare chest. Neither had noticed, or if he had, Reed hadn't said anything.

"Maybe it was the danger?" Reed offered, making no move to stop him.

"Come again?"

"The danger, Tuck. Of something new, something dicey, something forbidden. Or maybe just the thought of getting caught, getting outed, having to explain yourself, or maybe desperate to explain yourself. You know, maybe that's what excited you so much that first day?"

Tucker chuckled and tweaked one of Reed's nipples playfully. "Are you… trying to talk me out of how I felt about my high school crush?"

"Not at all. I just… maybe?" Tucker could feel Reed's curious chuckle deep in his chest. "I guess?"

"Trust me, I did the same thing all that semester. But once I'd noticed him, once we'd spent that long, endless day together, there was no looking back. Turns out he was in, like, half my classes. And gym class too."

"Uh-oh."

Tucker chuckled, still rasping his fingertips innocently back and forth across Reed's chest. "Oh yeah. Avery really was beautiful, once you saw him up close and personal. Naked and wet and alone, he was a real piece of work, and what's more, he didn't know it. And I wasn't confident enough to tell him yet either. But I started living for sixth period gym every day, I'll tell you that much. He didn't like to shower with the other guys. I mean, I guess for obvious reasons. Duh. I never minded myself. I mean, I had a crew back then, and we were pretty tight in that random, casual way guys are senior year, you know? Beers and bullshit and babes, right?"

Reed nodded silently, still gazing past Tucker at the stain on the ceiling. "Oh, I remember." The strained look on his face made it clear he did, and not necessarily in a good way.

"Right, so they were impatient, and I always had some excuse to drag things out so they'd be long gone by the time I hit the showers. I'd ask the coach stupid questions or find a knot in my sneakers or dig through my locker until finally they just gave up on me and quit waiting around anymore. And that gave me a few precious minutes alone with Avery. He was pale, like he never got out in the sun. And skinny—bony almost—and awkward, but somehow it all worked together and resulted in this peak specimen. The first time we showered together, he kept his back to me the whole time, like he knew what I was really there for. But over time—we're talking weeks, then months—he loosened up."

Tucker peered down at Reed. "He was smooth, like you. Not shaved, just sparse. Short, spiky hair and wispy armpits and the same downstairs, you know? Nothing much to cover up the old joystick. Then again, I only ever saw him naked when he was wet, so maybe it was bushy when he dried off. And he was big. Big in that way super skinny guys always are, you know?"

Reed met his eyes at last and smirked playfully, his sinewy arms still behind his head, armpits smooth and radiant in the moonlight. "Tell me about it," he said with another suggestive hip check. Already thick with the memory, Tucker's manhood shivered at the touch, surprisingly ready for more.

Tuck just rolled his eyes and ignored him. He was too deep in his story to get sidetracked now. "It became like this hidden dance, lurking in the shower stalls, an empty spigot in between us just in case Coach walked in, or anybody else. Just two guys hurrying up before their next class. But if no one did, we'd stand and lather and stare and look away and rinse and stare and then turn the showers off, one after the other, and follow each other out, dripping and naked and wet. Sometimes he'd be in front, sometimes I would be, and we'd grab our towels and dry off in front of each other. It was so hard not to get hard, you know? All that drying and tugging and tapping and stretching and straining alone, inches from each other. And sometimes I couldn't help it. I would. I'd try to hide it, but I could tell by the blush in his pale cheeks that he knew. Other times he'd get hard, toweling himself off by his locker, and try to hide it, but sometimes not so much. Other times not at all. Like he wanted me to see how hard he was. Wanted me to know that I'd made him that hard. In those moments we were more than naked, you know? It was obvious, so obvious. I can't believe nobody caught us, all those times, all those stolen times, naked and dripping and inches, just inches, away from each other."

Tucker's voice trailed off, husky and sentimental. Reed waited patiently for more, but when it didn't come, he nudged Tuck out of his reverie and asked, "Did anything ever happen?"

Tucker glanced down and grinned. "I'm getting there, okay?"

"Sorry, it's just that I'm kind of invested in this narrative now, okay?"

Tucker sighed, fingertips still drifting up and down Reed's six-pack. "Well, it doesn't have a happy ending, if that's what you're wondering."

"Do love stories ever? Especially between two high school guys who can't admit they're in love?"

Tucker glanced slightly away, as if embarrassed to admit it. "I wouldn't call it love, per se."

"No? Sure sounds like love to me."

Tucker shook his head firmly. "More like lust. Because, when he wasn't stroking himself under his towel or waving it in my face, Avery was a bit of a bore, actually. Like, the more I got to know him, the more I realized he only ever talked about video games and anime and other guys he was crushing on in school *besides* me."

Reed's face blanched appropriately. "Rude."

Tucker clucked his tongue approvingly. "Right? It was like, the more he knew I was into him, the more obvious I made it, the more boring and petty and cruel he got. He was almost, like, catty that way. That's kind of why I was glad it ended the way it did."

Reed's eyes widened slightly. "Oh? How's that?"

"More like, where's that?" Tucker was vaguely evasive.

"Okay then, where's that? The locker room? The pool? The dugout?" He gave a chuckle and nudged him once more.

"The lake," Tucker recalled, not very fondly. "Where everything started and ended in those days."

"Oh?"

"Back in the day, I used to smoke, cut classes, wear the punk-band T-shirts, ditch every Friday and start the weekend at the lake with a six-pack and crummy metal music before anybody else even got there."

Reed chuckled merrily, if quietly, in the dark. "Wow, cliché much?"

Tucker blushed and nodded. "I know, I know—the troubled child, the broken home, the acting out—I get it. But it felt real at the time, and maybe the way it all ended was exactly as it should have ended, you know?"

Reed rolled his eyes. "No, I don't know because you keep dancing around the money shot."

Tucker tweaked a nipple playfully, as if using the sexy gesture like a punctuation mark. "It was Senior Skip Day, before all the mad rush of award ceremonies and yearbooks and dances and dinners that last month of the semester. I had already checked out of school by then and was pounding out sets for *Suburban Dead* on location every day, but I sensed this was my last chance with Avery, so I worked a half day, then kind of made some dumb excuse and left the set for the afternoon. By the time I got to the lake, the party was in full swing. They'd been at it since that morning. The kegs were tapped, bottles and cans were everywhere, the whole class was there, getting down and hooking up."

"And Avery?" Reed sounded breathless with anticipation.

Tucker chuckled. "He was there, at the party, off to the side, per usual. It was kind of like he was… waiting for me? Or maybe I'm just flattering myself in hindsight. Either way, he perked up when he saw me. We kind of made small talk, looked around to see if anybody would notice, but when we saw they were all too drunk or horny or hooking up, we kind of grabbed a six-pack and just kind of… drifted away from the crowd. It was the lake where we always partied—lots of woods and nooks and crannies and ways to lose yourself. So we did, and how. Found a little fallen tree to sit on, cracked open a few beers, and listened to see if anyone had followed us.

"They hadn't. We breathed a little easier, or at least… I did. I think we both knew this was it, our last chance. He was going to graduate and work for his father at some office job, I forget what now. I talked a little about the show and what I was doing there, told him I definitely wasn't going to graduate and that I'd already rented a trailer not far from the set with what was left of my savings and my first fat paycheck. Then we just kind of sat there. The time for talking was over. He'd never had much to say anyway, at least nothing very real. We had nothing in common except this *thing* between us. We were sitting close, knee to knee. It was almost summer, hot as hell even in the shade. We drank the beer—not to get drunk, just to quench our thirst. Or maybe to get drunk. Either way, it didn't work. I was still thirsty two beers in and just gave up. I didn't need to get drunk anyway. I was high on him. He knew it. Asked why I'd come to the party if I was already checked out of school and working my first real job. I told him I hadn't come for the party. He winked and asked if I'd come for him. I told him I had, then told him that I would. That I would cum for him, if that's what he wanted."

"Jesus, Tuck."

Tucker marveled at his own teenage bravery. "I know, right?"

"Slut."

"Total slut. Super slutty move. But it was just this once. Just for him. I wanted him so bad. Or maybe it wasn't him. It probably wasn't him, I just wanted *it* so bad. To feel it with a guy, you know? Just to see what it was like, if it'd be better with him than it was with all those girls. If I'd love it, or hate it, or be bored with it, I just needed to know. And I was determined to find out. Right then and there, in those woods, no one around, the world had forgotten all about us, and his pale skinny ass in these stupid plaid shorts and a Hawaiian shirt because he was just that guy, you know?"

"I do," Reed mused, nodding up at him. "So what did he say?"

"He was kind of surprised. I'd never been that forward with him, even though I'd stared at his junk all semester long, gotten hard in front of him, because of him. He asked if I was straight. I said I thought I was, until I met him. He said he had that effect on a lot of guys. I kind of rolled my eyes, but he was serious. I told him I could see why. I wanted to flatter him. I *needed* to flatter him. I guess, in a way, I was kind of using him. I needed this to happen, and I knew he was the only likely candidate for it to happen, so I would have literally told him his shit didn't stink if I thought that would help. Instead I just kept flattering him, really piling it on. I guess it kind of worked. And then we stopped talking, like I'd cracked some code or said the secret, hidden gay password, finally. He shifted a little toward me. He put a hand on each thigh, I guess to steady himself. I flinched and gasped, and when my mouth was still open, he kissed me."

Tucker grew silent, remembering that moment all too well. The taste of another man's lips on his own, a boy's lips really, soft and sweet and as uncertain as his as they fumbled there, in the dark of the forest that towered overhead.

"He tasted like beer." Tucker's voice resumed, to finish the story. "I didn't care. His breath was hot. He took off my shirt. I didn't care. I was hot and sweaty. We both were. I tried to fumble with his stupid Hawaiian shirt buttons, but he batted my hand away. He kissed my throat, my underarms, my chest, fumbled with the button of my shorts. I was so hard and wet, and the button popped off, God knows where, and the zipper stuck about halfway down, but he grabbed me through my tighty-whities. Tugged those down as far as they could go and started rubbing me up and down and… and…."

Reed was glancing up, a knowing smile on his face. "You didn't."

Tucker nodded almost proudly. "I so did. Like a cannon. Everywhere, all over, nonstop, like I'd never come before. Like I was just straight pissing jizz, raining it all over the damn forest, practically. He made this face, this disgusted face, and he stood up and wiped his hands on his stupid Hawaiian shirt. Called me a rookie, an amateur, and then he just stormed off."

"Oh shit."

"No shit, 'oh shit.' I felt so stupid, so useless, like I'd gotten it all wrong. Screwed up my one chance to get everything right. He'd stormed off, all hot and bothered, and I figured he hadn't been very discreet. That maybe that was his revenge, storming out of the forest, clothes half-buttoned and sweaty and sticky so everyone would know what we'd just done. Like he wanted them to know."

"So what did you do?" Reed looked up, an almost childlike curiosity covering that pale, glowing face.

"I waited a while, but I was still sticky and my pants were literally soaked and the freaking zipper wouldn't go back up and the button was gone forever, lost in the woods. So I had to stumble down to the lake and go in, like I'd been swimming, and when I walked out of the woods I had my shirt over my shoulder like I'd just taken a dip, my pants drenched, the rest of the six-pack in hand, and nobody even noticed. It was all for nothing. They were all hammered. It was nearly dusk by now. We'd been in there for hours, I guess. So nobody ever noticed."

"And?"

Tucker glanced down. Their eyes met in the shimmering splinter of moonlight, and he shrugged. "And? And I drove away from the lake and back to my crummy little trailer on location and never saw Avery again."

"Never?"

"Nuh-uh. I already told you, I never graduated, obviously. And that lake party was like my gross, sordid, weird, embarrassing, triumphant mic drop to the last of senior year. I quietly dropped out of school the following week and started working on the show full-time."

Reed nudged his hip insistently, like they were two coeds at a slumber party spilling some major tea and there was still some left in the kettle. "Whatever happened, though?" His voice was impatient, bordering on whiny. "To Avery, I mean."

Tucker smirked, almost embarrassed to tell the tale. "Okay, I might have seen him again, just… not in person."

"Come again?"

"I did, actually," Tucker confessed, still blushing from recalling his brief encounter in the woods. "What I mean is, that day in the woods, he was telling me all sorts of stuff I kind of didn't believe. Like he was going to work for his dad during the week, but on the side he was going to try and find a sugar daddy, and one way to do that was to post videos of himself, uh… you know, online?"

Reed snorted, eyes big and knowing. "Jerkoff vids?"

Tucker nodded. "Like I said, I figured he was kind of bluffing that day, but a few months later I remembered it out of the blue and went looking online. I thought it would be hard to find him after all that time, but he wasn't very discreet. His screen name was AveryAllNight, and wow, he hadn't been kidding."

"You watched them?"

Tucker clucked his tongue and rolled his eyes dramatically. "I mean, duh, that's what I was searching for. I'd never gotten as far as all that with him, though I'd seen him naked enough times, sometimes even hard. Still, this was another level, and I had to admit, he still had it."

"Gross, Tucker. You mean you touched yourself watching him touch himself?"

"What? Like you've never done it?"

"Sure, yeah, but not to someone I know."

"What's the difference?"

"I dunno, nothing, I guess. I just can't picture *you* doing that, Mr. Straightlaced Hollywood TV Star Guy."

"Me either, until I saw one. You should check them out sometime. They're pretty hot."

"They're probably just hot because he was your first guy crush."

"Maybe, sure, but they're also objectively hot."

TWENTY-FOUR

Reed

"MAYBE SO." Reed wriggled in his boxer briefs so Tucker wouldn't see how hard he'd gotten as the poor kid told his bittersweet tale of longing, lust, and ultimately, letting go—a tale that Reed knew all too well. "But nothing will ever be as hot as that story was just now."

Tucker sighed, looking dreamy and pensive in the moonlight. Still propped up on one elbow, face aglow with the ever-present humidity of mid-August in Georgia, his eyes seemed both faraway and dangerously close.

"You're telling me," he purred, still running those soft, purposeful fingertips up and down Reed's torso, even more purposefully now that the tale had been told and all that was left was the fallout, the air in the room heavy with unspoken words and unfulfilled desires. As if peering deep into Reed's mind, Tucker glanced down and smirked. "It almost has me wanting to recreate it, Reed."

Suddenly, perhaps inevitably, Reed wasn't entirely against the idea. "What, your clandestine meeting in the woods with Avery?"

"That and your dugout make-out sessions with Benjy."

Reed's eyelids fluttered open and shut at the thought. He nodded suggestively at the bulge in Tuck's straining boxer shorts. "What, you got a time machine in that pocket of yours? And here I thought you were just glad to see me."

Tucker ignored him. "My memory's as good as any time machine, Reed," Tuck promised, a solitary fingertip circling his left nipple in tighter and tighter circles, as if the kid knew just how sensitive the area was and how the slower Tuck touched him, the harder Reed got. "We've got everything we need to make good on those broken promises, right here, right now."

Reed swallowed, no longer fighting the desire that had been mounting ever since they'd climbed into bed together over an hour earlier. Hell, who was he kidding? Make that ever since Tucker had asked to sleep over that night.

As if Reed might have ever said no.

"So what's stopping you?" His throat was as taut and clenched as his belly under Tucker's feathery, teasing touch.

Tucker's eyes widened above his curious smile. "*You*, dumbass. You're the one stopping me. You told me hands off all night, remember?"

Reed challenged him with a playful eye roll and thick wet lips. "And? Since when have you ever listened to me, kid?"

Tucker licked his lips. "So you mean we should kiss each other to climax?"

Reed blushed suddenly to hear the words spoken aloud. "Something like that, sure."

"No hands?" Tucker squeezed one taut nipple playfully and then removed his fingers altogether.

Reed nodded coyly. "No more hands, Tuck."

Teasingly timid, Tucker licked his lips until they were plump and ripe and glistening wet. "No mouth either?"

"Only mouth to mouth, stud, remember?" Reed was suddenly and quite obviously, given the straining fabric of his sticky boxer briefs, warming to the idea.

Tucker nodded quietly, eyes suddenly distant, as if thinking of something he'd forgotten or perhaps hadn't yet imagined. "I mean," he said quietly, his face drifting closer until he was whispering hot nothings in Reed's ear, making them both squirm as their half-naked bodies tightened the gap and danced alongside one another's in the squeaking bed.

"A little grinding wouldn't hurt, would it?"

Reed had heard enough. Suddenly hungry, the way he'd been all those years ago in that quiet, sultry dugout with Benjy, the way Tucker had been after those quick, steamy showers back in high school with Avery, he dragged his hands from beneath his neck and wrapped them around Tucker's instead.

"Quite the opposite, Tuck. Now quit talking about it and start being about it."

Tucker wasted little time. He lowered himself, gently but eagerly, on top of Reed and ground chest to chest and crotch to crotch, their legs entwined awkwardly even as their lips did as well. His thick, hot kisses rendered Reed breathless and whimpering in record time.

His hands drifted away from Tucker's neck, skimmed to either side of him, and gripped the already twisted sheets as Tucker kissed him into silence. Suddenly inspired, his wiry young lover grabbed him by the wrists and tugged them over Reed's head, never letting him up for air the entire time.

When at last their lips parted, bruised and sticky, Reed didn't quite have the strength to protest. Instead he willingly gave himself over to the sudden rush of fantasy fulfillment, both of them reliving their youths in a way that was far less awkward and far more forgiving with the distance of time.

Tucker straddled him, a hand steadying himself on either side of Reed's chest, palms down on the squeaking mattress. His face contorted in half a dozen emotions as, gently at first, he began to grind his pelvis against Reed's, the sensation staggering in its intensity, even through their underwear.

Reed looked up into Tuck's eyes and watched them flutter and open in concert with his rasping gyrations. Tucker settled into a persistent rhythm, bulge against bulge, the thin fabric between them doing little to stymie the sensation, the moisture, the heat and mounting desire.

"I've never done this before." He paused as their cocks throbbed and swelled against one another.

Reed smirked, already panting from the kissing and the dry humping. For emphasis, he gripped the wrought iron railing that served as a headboard. "You've never done anything before, virgin boy, remember?"

"More than ever before," Tucker insisted. He paused to kiss Reed breathless once again and then removed his tempting lips to murmur sweet nothings in his ear. "And maybe, before this week is over, enough not to be… a virgin anymore?"

His tone was hesitant, his eyes even more so. "Tucker, you're not ready for that yet."

Tuck rolled his eyes and purposefully dragged his long, thin cock against Reed's. Reed shuddered beneath him, desperate for exactly what Tucker was talking about but knowing instinctively it was too much, too soon.

This wasn't some random Grindr hookup or late-night booty call between old lovers. This was fresh and new, unspoiled and unsullied. When and if they ever consummated their… whatever this was… for each other, fully, intimately, deep inside one another, it would have to be mutual, gentle, and a lot further along in their relationship than the first few days.

Reed might have been a slut, but only with equal partners. He wasn't about to take advantage of Tucker's curiosity and inexperience, no matter how eager the kid was to be deflowered right then and there.

"Who says?" Tucker teased, his pelvis drifting up and down until the waistband of Reed's boxer briefs slipped low enough to release the pink, throbbing tip of his leaking hard-on.

Reed gasped, grunted, and thrust gently back. "*I* say, Tuck. Because you're my responsibility now, and I don't want you telling some new lover three years from now about how I ruined your one chance to lose your virginity the right way, the loving way."

Tucker smothered Reed with a reassuring kiss that made it clear he was giving up on the idea. For now, anyway. "Such a prude."

Reed thrust, bucked, and spread his legs wider, slick staff drifting even farther out of his waistband as if it had a mind of its own. "I'll show you a prude, you tramp!"

The two murmured and giggled, the night deep and sultry as it swallowed them whole. Reed was no longer sleepy, his heart pounding as their lips and bodies thrashed atop the twisted sheets and squeaking mattress.

He had no need for more than Tucker's lips against his, his breath hot and sweet in his mouth, his body lean and tender as it danced atop his own. His hands gently drifted from the headboard and went wherever they desired—up and down Tucker's taut, wiry biceps to caress and clench at the base of his lean, narrow back, to squeeze a cheek here or press against a nipple there. They were all hands and legs and chest and waist—a sweaty, sticky, meandering stew that built in intensity with each murmur and writhe and pant and squeak.

In many ways the moment was reminiscent of a flashback sequence—the camp cabin, the squeaky bed, the adolescent insistence on dry humping, the sweaty, smooth innocence of Tuck's face as it alternated between blissful release and fraught desire, the moonlit night and clandestine nature of doing something secret, sexy, and even a little sweet in the middle of the night while the rest of the world slept somewhere far, far away, almost on another planet.

As the night swallowed them, sexy and sweltering and dark and deep, Reed panted and sighed in his young lover's ear and wished they never had to return to real life ever again.

TWENTY-FIVE

Tucker

"NO FAIR, Tucker." Reed smiled as Tucker struggled to drag his lover's boxer briefs down to his knees and then, with another quick tug, off and onto the floor.

"No?" Tucker murmured in Reed's ear, desperate to feel flesh upon flesh as he rubbed his own crotch, still bound by his damp, sticky boxers, against his lover's throbbing bulge. "You want me to put them back on?"

Reed chuckled and shook his head almost frantically, as if Tucker had any intention of doing such a thing. "No, that… that feels too damn good. Jesus!"

Reed wasn't lying. Just feeling the heat and heft of his lover's cock through the thin fabric of his own underwear was tantalizing enough, in ways he'd never imagined. At first he'd thought the idea silly—dry humping at their age—especially after the many ways they'd already pleasured themselves with hands and mouths and everything in between. But now, bodies glistening with sweat, limbs intertwined, he'd never felt so hot and bothered in all his life.

Clearly Reed felt the same. Tucker glanced down and admired the way Reed's staff shimmered in the moonlight, slick with excitement and throbbing with pleasure as Tucker gently clasped his own hard-on, the fabric of his thin cotton boxers dragging across the slick shaft as he stroked with dubious intent.

He wanted to touch it, to stroke its velvet skin and feel the heat and moisture glide across his trembling fingers. He wanted to lean down and enrobe it in his mouth, full lips dragging along every inch and tasting its meaty heft until it exploded in a fiery display all across his trembling belly and glistening chest.

But he was more than willing to play by the rules, especially if it felt this damn good to behave. Then again, it could always feel just a little. Bit. Better.

To that end, Tucker smothered Reed with a sweaty, sticky kiss and held it as long as it took him to quickly tug at his own waistband and, with a slick drag and wriggle, toss his boxers to the floor of the cabin, where they landed with a whisper atop the hardwood planks at the foot of the bed.

Reed murmured, mouth still buried under Tuck's passionate embrace until, gasping, they both turned their heads to an opposite side, sighing as, at last, their swollen members writhed and danced along each other's.

"Jesus," Reed gasped, a hand on either side of Tucker's flexing, bobbing ass as he dug in and used the soft, mounded flesh to guide him up and down his swollen prick.

The friction was powerful—a combination of heat and rhythm that thrilled them both. Tucker's arms strained with tension as he continued to hold himself up, palms flat on either side of Reed's chest, a knee on either side of his right thigh, and grind up and down his lover's knob as Reed squeezed and kneaded his thrusting ass as if guiding him with every drag and pull and squeeze.

Reed twisted himself slightly onto his side and dragged Tucker with him until they lay face-to-face on the bed, clutching each other tightly around the waist as they continued to press and pull their bodies against one another, the friction growing with the new position.

Before Tucker knew it, eyes squeezed shut, lips locked with his lover's, Reed pivoted like a wrestler in the ring, thrusting and twisting in equal measure until Tucker's back was pressed flat against the mattress and Reed knelt above him with a curious smile.

"How... how did you do that?" Tuck gasped as Reed gripped his wrists and tugged his hands above his head. Tucker instinctively gripped the wrought iron headboard and held on tight.

Reed winked and wriggled into position as he hovered just above Tucker's groin. "Practice, kiddo, lots and lots of practice."

Tucker blushed and lay back when he felt the first hint of pressure from Reed's package as, sac against sac, he began to drag and press their balls together in increasing tenderness and frequency, the heft and drag intensifying as Reed lowered himself once more, their pricks shaft to shaft and vein to vein as Reed began to grind in earnest.

It was a soft, silken experience that never quite quickened but instead grew in passion and desire with each erotic glance of manhood on manhood, the rasping intimate as Reed hovered at just the right height and ground at just the right pace.

Reed was an expert lover but not a greedy one. He could have thrust and pumped until he blasted hot jets of lust across Tuck's panting chest and then lay back, sated and snoring. Instead he held himself aloft, not too low, not too high, the pressure of prick on prick just right as, stroke by stroke, Tucker felt his belly tighten, his balls throb, and the breath catch in his throat.

Reed too seemed to sense the approach of a staggering climax. Sweat from his smooth, clean body, damp and aglow in the middle of another hot and sultry night, dripped onto Tucker's as the heat and sensation grew but never quickened or reduced. Methodically, rapturously, their flesh seemed to meld in the late-night heat, sweaty and sticky and throbbing and hot.

Tucker came first, naturally, with a throbbing, clattering explosion so powerful it splashed up the length of his body and splattered his chin. They laughed, surprised at its intensity, its intimacy, eyes meeting in the clear, bright dark.

"Impressive." Reed's voice was husky and silken as he leaned gently down. With an expert tongue, he scooped up a glistening pebble of spunk, and before Tucker could protest, smothered him with an intimate kiss redolent of his own manhood and savory with his own sin.

Afterward, Tucker panting and breathless, sticky and wet, Reed finally deepened his rhythm and lowered himself gently to grind harder and heavier across Tucker's still-throbbing staff until at last he came as well. Quieter, thicker, lower, heavier, the splatters dappled Tucker's belly and joined with his own in a tapestry of icing that flattered them both.

Reed collapsed at last, arms and legs trembling until he sank onto Tucker's torso, their sweat and spunk mixing as they shared one last sweltering kiss, and then, like the Velcro of his swimmer's baggies tearing apart, Reed rolled stickily onto his side and lay panting and sweaty on his back.

He lifted his arms above his head, and Tucker turned, coyly, and lay on his side, arms circling his lover's neck until, like puzzle pieces, they sealed every empty inch between them and drifted, cojoined, into a deep, peaceful sleep, naked in the moonlight and dead to the world around them.

TWENTY-SIX

Reed

"YOU SURE about this, Tucker?"

Reed pedaled the mountain bike slowly, matching Tucker's languid pace as they rode side by side toward the tiny town of Redfern, Georgia.

"Sure," the kid bluffed, sounding all of fifteen. "Why not?"

Despite the withering Georgia heat, Tucker was dressed like an undercover FBI agent, a Camp Run-A-Mok ball cap pulled low over his sweaty curls, an Eastern Georgia State windbreaker he'd found in Reed's closet zipped tightly up to his throat. Below the ridiculous getup, Tuck wore his trademark khaki shorts and topsiders with no socks. Evidently Tucker was confident that the *Suburban Dead* fans in Middle of Nowhere, Georgia, wouldn't recognize his thighs and calves.

Reed was dressed casually for their surprise outing, in a crisp white V-neck T-shirt to beat the sultry midday heat and a pair of madras shorts paired with peach-colored flip-flops. It was as if, for every article of undercover clothing Tucker wore to cover up his true identity, Reed dressed down to look as comfortable as he felt.

It had been another long, eventful day, even after their draining, writhing night—a quick breakfast standing across from each other in the mess hall kitchen, three straight hours of Tucker swimming actual, if floundering, laps in the pool, and sedate, non-jizz-worthy showers in the locker room, and, bored and restless after nearly a week of the same deserted campground, Tucker had announced it was time for them to go on a date.

"A real date," Tucker reminded him now, as the small one-stoplight town closest to the summer camp crept into sight. "Like you promised."

Reed gripped his handlebars nervously. After his recent scandal, Tucker wasn't the only one shying away from the limelight these days. "I'm not sure I ever promised you a real date, lover boy. You just seem to expect it in this sentimental version of romantic love you seem to have."

Tucker rolled his eyes, swerved gently in his direction, and spooked Reed into veering wildly left. Tuck laughed at his dramatics. "Listen, it's a season of firsts for me. You, me, us, all we've shared. I want this. I think we both deserve this, Reed. Don't you?"

Reed had inched back by Tuck's side and nodded profusely as they passed a gas station that looked as out of date and deserted as the empty summer camp behind them. "Of course we do," he teased, not wanting to sound ungrateful. "I'm not sure I can choke down yet another charcuterie board or wedge of pâté after all that rich Hollywood food this week."

"Exactly." Tucker tensed as they passed an elderly couple straightening a Half-Off Sale sign in the window of a hardware store straight off the set of *The Andy Griffith Show*. The couple nodded at them but didn't glance over. Reed took it as a good sign. He knew Tucker was worried about being spotted, especially while dining with another man, but if they were going to venture out together, best to do it in a long-forgotten town like Redfern than in the thriving populace of LA. "Besides, I think I was getting literal cabin fever back there."

Reed smirked and steered gently back toward Tucker to give him a taste of his own medicine. "Well, we have been spending a lot of time in my bed, hot pants."

"Stop." Tucker blushed for more reasons than one.

Reed did as he was told, but only to survey the limited offerings presented by Redfern's Main Street. After riding up one side and down the other, they were left with only five or six decent options at 4:17 p.m. on a mid-August Thursday—Brickhouse Brewery, Corrine's Café, Lonnie's Lunch Counter, Luigi's Pizza Parlor, or Reggie's Down-Home BBQ Shack.

Reed sank back and followed Tucker's lead as he rode past every storefront, sometimes multiple times. He peered inside, sniffed around, nodded, shook his head, and second-guessed himself until at last they drifted up to the rusty bike rack in front of Reggie's BBQ.

Reed frowned as Tucker slid his bike into the rack. "God forbid this town has a sushi bar," he complained.

"Oh, come on." Tucker patted his shoulder playfully. "A nice cold beer, a little corn on the cob, we'll go half-and-half and sample the menu, you know? Make it a big, fat, greasy, sauce-slathered cheat day. Whaddaya say?"

Reed was just glad the kid was venturing out and so happy about it in the bargain. With a wink and a good-natured hip check, he glanced at the empty parking lot and snickered. "You sure this is deserted enough for you?"

Tucker looked bashful all over again, his long, angular body hunched over as if to hide his full height. "I'm just trying to be careful, you know?"

Reed sighed as Tucker cracked open the door and glanced inside. "I know." He pushed Tuck playfully as they both tumbled in, chuckling good-naturedly. "You can't get more careful than a deserted restaurant, kid."

Despite its vaguely drab brick exterior, Reggie's Down-Home BBQ Shack was surprisingly modern on the inside—varnished wood floors beneath their feet, a kind of blues-and-soul soundtrack gurgling from state-of-the-art speakers nestled above their heads, chalkboard-painted walls featuring hand-drawn daily specials, and a smattering of neon signs featuring pigs and various other farm animals. But mostly pigs.

Lots and lots of pigs.

They gave each other wide-eyed, chin-rubbing, WTF glances before a middle-aged black man in a bright yellow ball cap and T-shirt to match emerged from double kitchen doors to greet them.

"Welcome to Reggie's," he drawled in a thickly Southern, authentically grizzled voice. He nodded toward the deserted dining room with an almost self-conscious grin.

"Y'all can seat yourself, obviously," he said with a world-weary chuckle and a halfhearted wave. "I'll go on and bring you something cool to drink. What are you two feeling today?"

Tucker was literally scratching his chin, but Reed had noted a drink special on the nearest chalkboard wall. "How about two of your Loaded Lemonades?"

The older man nodded with a merry wink. "Always my go-to," he murmured as he handed over two wooden clipboards that featured a single page of daily specials on a typewritten menu.

Reed let Tucker lead him to a battered booth in the back—near the window but not in front of it. He vaguely felt like he was accompanying a big-time mobster who didn't want to sit with his back to the door for fear of getting rubbed out by some rival gang.

They sank onto opposite benches, Reed grateful for the comforting heft of solid, thick pleather beneath him. They'd had little sleep since that first tentative kiss, and after the long, languid bike ride in the wilting heat, a cozy booth, a cold adult beverage, and Tucker's sweet eyes were all he wanted at that very moment.

"I think you're safe for now, James Bond," he teased as, reluctantly, Tucker unzipped his windbreaker and folded it carefully on the booth seat beside him. He looked more flushed than ever from the Southern air. Not that Reed was complaining. Tuck never looked better than rumpled, hot, bothered, and dappled with a layer of slick, glossy perspiration.

"Doesn't that feel better?" Reed nudged his toe beneath the table.

Tuck nodded almost bashfully and took off the cap as well. He set it just as carefully down on Reed's borrowed jacket, then tousled out his feathery brown curls as he too seemed to sink back into the booth bench as if it had been made just for them. "Nice, huh?"

Reed took in the funky storefront restaurant and smiled in appreciation. "I've got to give it to you, kid. You do come up with some good ideas."

Tucker smirked playfully, coming into his own now that they were virtually alone in the cozy eatery. "Well, someone has to."

"What's that supposed to mean?"

Tucker glanced toward the hostess stand up front—a wooden counter covered in Georgia license plates from years past. Seeing their gracious host nowhere in sight, he leaned slightly forward and murmured, "Can I ask you something personal?"

Reed snorted ironically. "You've only ever asked me something personal, Tuck."

Tucker ignored his snarky tone. "Would we, I mean, do you think we would have done all that stuff, back there at camp, if I hadn't suggested it first?"

Reed didn't have to think long to answer. "Not at all," he grunted as he tossed an arm over the top of his side of the black booth bench. "I wasn't about to touch you with a ten-foot pole until you made the first move."

Tucker seemed vaguely disappointed. Or impressed. It was hard to tell with him. He was, after all, an actor. They stood their ground in half-serious silence until the old man reappeared, grubby sneakers swishing across the scuffed vinyl floor on his way to the table. He had a pitcher full of lemonade and two short, stubby glasses, all tucked in the middle of a dented round tray. "Y'all looked thirsty, so I took the liberty of making you a pitcher. Hope you don't mind."

"Not gonna complain about that," Reed said, a little too loudly, as if to compensate for the way Tucker seemed to shrink slightly in the stranger's presence. "We appreciate that, sir."

"I'm Reggie," he grunted as he hoisted the heavy glass pitcher onto the table between them. "Owner, chef, and chief bottle washer around these parts. But you don't have to call me sir, for Pete's sake."

"Nice to meet you," Reed murmured, not offering their names. "This place is awesome."

"Never been in before, I take it?" Reggie asked with a vaguely judgmental tone.

Tucker looked helpless on his side of the booth, as if afraid to answer for fear he might say the wrong thing. Reed took the reins of the conversation before it got too awkward. "We're... not from around here."

Reggie winked knowingly. "You don't say."

There was a short round of nervous laughter, and then he straightened up and gave them both a quick but not too probing glance. "Well, anyway, hopefully today's experience will make you regulars."

"You're off to a great start." Reed chuckled as their eyes met above the sweaty pitcher of ice-cold spiked lemonade.

"Y'all hungry yet or want to sit with that awhile?"

Reed was about to answer when Tucker broke in, softer than usual, as if suspecting he'd have to pipe up at some point in the conversation before old Reggie got suspicious. "Do you have anything to nibble on while we sip?" He sounded every bit as if they were supping at some hipster gastropub on Fire Island. "Like an appetizer sampler? Something like that?"

Reggie slid the round tray by his side and wiped thick brown fingers on a black apron that covered his yellow Reggie's Down-Home BBQ Shack T-shirt. "I think I got you covered. Y'all mind if I go on and take the helm for the rest of your meal, dish up some of my finest and see if I can't convince you to come back a time or two while you're in town?"

Tucker perked right up as if he'd suddenly forgotten all about being incognito lest some roving paparazzi on the deserted streets of Redfern, Georgia, spot him supping with his gay lover in the middle of a Thursday afternoon in August. "That. Sounds. Fantastic."

The only thing missing from his overenthusiastic reply, Reed noted, was a fluttering of jazz hands and a tapping of his twinkle toes beneath the table. Reggie chuckled an obvious smoker's rasp and nodded. Then he backed away from the table as if to give them space. "I'll be sure to space things out so you don't get overloaded. You two in a hurry?"

"Far from it." Reed nodded in concert with their jovial host. By the time Reggie turned back toward the kitchen, Tucker had already poured them each a short, squat glass of their adult beverage of choice.

"Cheers." He clinked glasses merrily, as if they were high atop some rooftop bar in Beverly Hills, the toast of the town after some big movie premiere or whatever stars did in Tinseltown.

"What to?" Reed teased, suddenly right at home.

Tucker, as ever, seemed to give it some thought. "To new beginnings." He took a sip, and Reed followed suit, quietly savoring the bittersweet tang of spiked lemonade. It filled the hollows of his cheeks and made him wince with sharp delight. "Oh, that's nice."

"Right?" Tucker asked, like perhaps he'd been the one to order.

"So." Reed flattened the paper place mat beneath his drink. "You're thinking this is all a… beginning?"

Tucker chuckled. "I knew you'd notice that, you predictable old fart."

Reed chuckled back, harder than he'd intended to. "I'm just saying, I don't want to get my hopes up."

As ever, the blush rose easily to Tuck's face. "You'd want that, though? A beginning, with me?"

Reed sipped his drink, if only to give him time to assemble a sane response. Unfortunately nothing about any of this was even close to sanity. "Obviously, Tucker," he croaked, sudden emotion, unexpected and out of nowhere, getting the better of him. "I know I've been a slut in the past, I know it's cost me dearly, I know I'm far more experienced than you, but I believe what's happening here has put us on an even playing field."

Tucker was unwaveringly curious. "How so?"

Reed girded his loins. Nothing with Tucker was ever going to be easy. "Let's just say, the way I feel when I'm with you, and not just during sexy times, but all the time, I've… I've… never felt this way before."

Tucker sipped his drink, lips full and wet on the stubby, thick glass. "Me either."

Reed fiddled with the paper edge of his gently used place mat. Reggie might have been a jovial, helpful host, but his sanitization methods remained questionable. "Not with some girl?" he asked, sounding like he was teasing but definitely not.

Tucker merely shook his head, but Reed pressed. "Not with some other boy? You know, after Avery left you in the woods?"

"Obviously not," Tucker huffed. "What about you?"

Reed didn't answer right away. It would have been untruthful. Instead he racked his memory—recent and far distant—and tried to imagine anyone he'd ever felt remotely this serious, this passionate, this affectionate about. In the end, he came up painfully short.

"Not even close, Tuck," he said, voice still tight with emotion. He noted the poorly hidden scowl of Tuck's expression. "What? What's with the face?"

Tucker gave a wry, humorless chuckle, face bathed in the late afternoon glow from the nearby window. "Nothing. I was just hoping you were madly in love with somebody else."

"What the hell for?"

"Because then there'd be no chance of us working out, you know?"

Reed sighed. Dread—real fear of never seeing Tucker again—filled his chest and tightened it like a vise grip. "I'm trying real hard to see how there's a chance of us either way, Tuck."

The smell of food, fragrant and spicy, announced Reggie's presence before he ambled good-naturedly around the counter, bearing a rustic chef's board heaped with steaming, savory goodies. "Now, don't let all this food scare you, fellas, but I might have gone a smidge overboard whipping up something special for y'all."

"Might have?" Tucker snorted, forgetting himself and leaning forward to inhale the fragrant smells wafting from the thick slab of wood and its various toppings.

Reggie slid the slab across the table and gently pushed the sloshing pitcher to one side as he let it rest, midtable. Thick fingers hovered over each savory morsel as he introduced them, one by one. "Now, I suggest you start off with these honey-and-sage biscuits. My wife Glenda makes them, and man, I'm telling ya. Pure heaven on a plate. Next, I'd move on to these hickory-bacon-wrapped fried green beans. We grow 'em ourselves, and I just picked them this morning from the acreage. Next up is a pile of fried bread-and-butter pickles, paired with an avocado ranch dressing to cool down the spice just a smidge. Past that we have our barbecue shrimp skewers, and to polish it off, a few grilled apple slices drizzled with caramel sauce to cleanse your palate before the main course."

"Main course?" Reed was genuinely flabbergasted. "You mean there's more?" His tone implied they were being punished somehow.

Tucker sat, equally stunned and quite speechless. Reggie wasn't letting him off so easily. "What about you, kiddo. Cat got your tongue?"

Tucker fixed him with a wide-eyed glance. "Listen, no offense, but we walked in out of the blue just expecting some pulled brisket and vinegar slaw on a paper plate, you know? I'd just, maybe do some better branding or signage or something, because this is some serious gourmet cuisine right here, and I'm not quite sure the curb appeal speaks to the exquisite blend of taste and smell that diners might find if they venture inside."

Reggie chuckled and rasped, "Well that's quite a mouthful. Mind if I print that on our next menu run?"

"I'm serious, Reggie, this is…." Tucker gave a little chef's kiss for accent. The older man waved a hand, as if too flattered for his own good, and shuffled off, still chuckling that smoker's rasp. "Y'all enjoy now. That should keep you busy while I whip up the main course."

"Main course my ass," Tucker murmured as he handed Reed one of the multicolored appetizer plates stacked beside the napkin holder atop their table. "I won't be able to fit into my bathing suit for tomorrow's lesson."

Reed was feeling flirty, the smells of home-cooked barbecue, the sounds of rhythm and blues on the speakers overhead, the late afternoon sun streaming in, and Tucker, across the table from him, lean and handsome in his powder blue tank top. "I mean, you promised we'd go skinny-dipping anyway, so…."

Tucker was licking his thumb after having plopped a bacon-wrapped green bean onto his small salmon-colored plate. "Don't threaten me with a good time, pal."

Reed nibbled on a fried bread-and-butter pickle, and the savory dressing did cool the sizzling tang as promised. He washed both down with a slug of spiked lemonade, too sweet and cold and strong for his own good. He fixed his gaze on Tucker across the table and found his eyes, clear and bright, looking back almost expectantly.

"It has been a good time, right, Tuck? I'm not… not imagining all this?" He held out his arms to encompass not just the deserted restaurant or even the small Georgia town outside the nearby window but the whole of their shared experience, every nuzzle and nibble and whisper and murmur and pounding, shuddering heartbeat.

"The best," Tuck enthused. He risked a glance at the empty host stand and then reached his free hand across the table and smothered Reed's with his soft, warm palm, still vaguely greasy from his fried green bean. "I mean that, Reed. No matter what happens next, this...."

Reed slid his hand over on the table until they were palm to palm, holding hands like a real, honest-to-God couple inside the quiet, empty dining room. "I know, Tuck. You don't have to say it. I... feel the same."

Tucker squeezed his hand, and they forgot the savory bounty on the thick wooden platter between them. "You have to, Reed. If you didn't, if you don't feel the same way I do, with the same intensity, my heart couldn't take it."

Reed squeezed his hand as, on instinct, they drifted apart before Reggie could round the corner again and bear witness to their sweet, secret, sacred love.

"Mine either, kid." He'd never meant anything more in his entire life. But never had the stakes been so high before either. Reed and Tucker came from very different worlds and, when their two weeks were over, would go back to them, changed forever but still miles and hours and tax brackets apart. Reed wondered idly, though he dared not share his doubts with young Tucker, whether or not their love for one another, or whatever this was, could withstand the reality of such separate, distant lives.

TWENTY-SEVEN

Tucker

"THIS IS getting to be quite the habit, kid."

Reed lay in Tucker's arms, fragrant body nestled close to his, their skin sweaty and sticky from their latest teasing late-night tryst.

"Yeah." Tucker held him close as their heartbeats quietly returned to normal. "A good one."

Tucker was flat on his back, sheets damp and twisted around one sweaty ankle, the air trickling in through the open window refreshing on his flushed skin. His heart was still racing. Reed's too. Tucker wasn't sure how much of that was from what they'd just done to each other or what it all meant to them. He wasn't sure where one ended anymore and where the other began. Everything they had, everything they did, was mixed up and twisted and glued together—body, mind, soul, and increasingly, heart.

Either way, they didn't need to say more. All of it had been said, one way or the other—over beers or barbecue, by the fire pit, or in the swimming pool, eye to eye or face to face or lips to lips, with whispered urges and murmured hot nothings and panting, gasping, begging grunts, demands, and requests.

They could have lain there all night, not saying another word, listening to each other breathe, skin to skin, comforted by the other's heartbeat, but something about that day, what had happened, how it had happened, demanded discussion.

As usual, Reed weighed in before Tucker's sated mind could recover from the intimate pleasure they'd just shared, naked bodies merged beneath the fluttering curtains above his big counselor's cabin bed. "Thank you, Tucker," he murmured, voice vibrating in Tuck's chest.

Tucker suspected he knew, but asked anyway. Maybe, quite possibly, just stalling for time before reality crept in yet again with another simmering Georgia sunrise in a few short hours. "For what?"

Reed's voice was low and calm when he replied. "For this," he murmured as he wriggled closer, belly flat and sticky against Tuck's hip, smooth legs intertwined with his atop the rumpled bedsheets. For them, for now, the act of lying together with nothing between them save a fresh layer of sex sweat was as natural as bathing together, brushing their teeth together, or even nibbling on a granola bar together across from each other in the mess hall kitchen. "For us, but mostly for today."

"Why today?"

"Because I know that took a lot for you, to risk that. Going out there, out in the world, with me by your side. Sitting at that table, even holding hands for a few minutes, like real lovers."

"We *are* real lovers," Tuck practically scolded as the vehemence, the protectiveness, the defensiveness came over him in a hot flash of emotion.

Reed nodded. "Okay, yes, but you know what I mean. *We* know that, but the rest of the world doesn't. So, you and me, out there in the world, big and proud and together, it was still a risk. We both know that."

"It did feel like a risk at first," Tucker confessed after a few tense heartbeats. "But the more time I spent with you outside of our cozy little bubble, the more I started to see... possibilities."

Reed snorted, breath warm in Tucker's ear as Tuck nuzzled his throat playfully, arms wrapped tightly around his waist as if Tuck might actually float away. "More like impossibilities, you mean." Reed's voice was low and thick against his ear.

"That's what I thought too." Tucker peered at the moonlit ceiling and wondered how long the image of that stupid water stain would stay seared in his memory. "Life outside of this camp, this bed, this embrace, seemed impossible, but today kind of made it real."

Reed was quiet for too long, his body stiffening as Tucker felt him move gently aside, flushed skin peeling stickily away as another long night wore on beneath a blanket of simmering heat and shimmering moonlight.

Tucker turned his head and watched as Reed sat up, his back to the windowsill, smooth skin glossy and slick beneath the ever-present moon, as if he'd drifted beneath the only light in the room. He glanced down at Tucker expectantly, and dutifully, feeling this was a *very big moment*, Tuck gathered what was left of his energy and sat beside him.

They'd brought a bottle of wine to bed with them, pilfered from the generous supply in the mess hall kitchen, and Reed reached for it, took a long sip, and then passed the bottle over to Tucker. In the process they gradually turned to face each other, cross-legged and knee to knee in the middle of the big, creaky old bed.

Reed waited until Tucker had taken a long, thirsty drag off the bottle and handed it back. Then he met his eyes in the sliver of moonlight drifting through the open window. "Define real, Tucker."

Tucker slumped like a kid who'd just been asked to take out the trash. "I can't, Reed. Not in the light of day. I'm just talking late-night, fuzzy ideas of a future, you know?"

"Yeah, I know you are, kid. But I'm too old and too stuck in the real world for that kind of an answer. I liked what we shared today, Tucker. And after too." He ran a careless finger along Tucker's inner thigh, making his whole body shiver and his drained balls leap. "That's no secret. And it's no secret that I'm going to miss you, when this is all over."

Tucker's heart crept steadily into his throat. "But why does it have to end, Reed? Why can't we keep doing this? All of this?" He swept his hand to bring in the room, the chair, the dresser, the open door, the closed screen, the posters on the wall, the big bed, and Reed, aglow and glistening in all his smooth, naked glory, taut and lean in the middle of the night.

Reed's tone was just shy of scolding, a far cry from the sad, almost wounded look in his gentle brown eyes. "I can't keep explaining adult life to you, Tucker. You know that."

Tucker jutted his chin back out in defense and waved the wine bottle at the far wall as if pointing to a vision board of their future together. "I'm not a child, Reed. You can tease and play if it makes things sexier for you, and for me, but you know I'm grown."

Their eyes met in the shimmering dark, and Reed's voice was playfully stern as he growled, "Well if you're grown, then quit saying stupid shit unless you're ready to back it up like a big-ass man." As if to emphasize his point, Reed yanked the bottle away from his grip.

Tucker puffed himself up slightly in the middle of the big, sticky bed. "Who says I'm not?"

"You do." Reed took a dramatic swig and then reluctantly handed the bottle back to Tucker. "With your stupid hat and your windbreaker and flinching every time you thought some poor person on the street was reaching for his camera."

Tucker took a drink and kept the bottle to himself out of spite. And don't think Reed didn't notice either. "I have a lot to lose, Reed. We've talked about this."

"Yeah, about what *you've* got to lose. What about me? I've lost too much already. I can't risk losing more unless...."

Tucker pounced and tapped a firm finger against Reed's even firmer chest. "There it is, Reed."

"There what is?" Reed snatched the wine bottle back while Tucker was busy feeling up his glistening pecs.

"That qualifier. 'But.' 'Maybe.' 'Unless.' Both of us are just dancing around the possibilities."

Reed sighed and glanced out the window. He sagged as if in defeat against the weathered sill as the air seemed to seep from his body like a deflating balloon. "Tucker."

"Reed." Tucker teased him, not content just to nudge his knee but instead wriggling ever closer until their legs interlaced, Tuck's thighs on the bottom, Reed's on the top, their puzzle-piece crotches nestled gently against each other in the deep, dark night.

"Stop, Tuck, really."

"I'm not starting anything, Reed. I just want to be close to you. All the time, until I can't anymore. Can't you see that? Jesus, now who's explaining adult life to whom, you big fat baby?"

"Can't you see?" Reed peered deeply into Tucker's eyes. "The closer we get, the more often we do all this, the harder it's going to be to... to... never see you again."

Tucker rocked back as if he'd just been slapped. "Don't say that, Reed. Don't ever say never. It's 2023, bro, we can do this. It's not the 1950s."

"Yeah, well, you're the one stuck in the closet, Tuck."

"I'm not stuck," Tucker insisted. "This is all new to me. I've never even felt this way about a girl before. How am I supposed to know what to do next when I feel this way about... a boy?"

"I guess ask yourself what you'd do if I were a girl."

Tucker reached up playfully and squeezed Reed's nipples. "Grab your tits, I guess?"

Reed snorted, rolled his eyes, and expertly batted Tuck's hands away as if he were a stunt double on one of the *Karate Kid* movies. "Be serious, kid."

"I am, Reed. You asked. That's what I'd do. Touch you, kiss you, bed you, if you were a girl. Just to keep myself distracted from the fact that I wasn't really in love with you."

"That's sad shit, Tucker."

"You think?"

"Yeah, well, I'm not interested in being sad anymore."

"So what's your answer, genius? You're the older man in this relationship. The hell do you suggest we do, then, huh?" He pushed Reed playfully, the friction in their cojoined laps sticky and sweet as ever.

"I wish I had one, kid. Like I said earlier, we're on common ground in the new-new department, dig?"

"So what are you busting my balls for, then?"

Reed winked, as if he too was tired of talking about the future when so much of it was uncertain and downright scary. His hand slipped down and he playfully cupped Tuck's sac. Then not so playfully. "I guess cause they're so damn pretty, *kid.*"

Tucker squirmed and rocked his body slightly back. His package shifted forward, all the better to fill Reed's outstretched hand. "I thought we were having a very important talk." Then he gasped as Reed tugged instead of caressed, squeezed instead of teased.

"It'd be a lot easier to talk to you, Tucker," Reed murmured, his hand drifting from Tuck's sac to the base of his downturned staff, where he stroked purposefully, "if you weren't always naked all the damn time."

Tucker chuckled, reached out to cup Reed's heft in his own palm, and juggled his balls tenderly as they throbbed inside his eager hand. "Whose fault is that, hot pants?"

Tucker snorted, his heart no longer in words, but only in deeds. Reed seemed to agree as his hands drifted from Tucker's crotch to his calves, of all things. Tucker wondered why until suddenly Reed tugged and dragged him onto his back once more.

Tucker gasped from surprise and desire when Reed twisted and contorted himself so they were at opposite ends of the bed, curled slightly, his face in Tucker's crotch and vice versa. Then Reed smirked and his tongue glided across Tuck's damp, sticky sac, face suddenly between his sweaty thighs.

Tucker felt Reed's breath, hot and staccato, as he giggled playfully around feathery kisses on his throbbing package. In turn, he gazed at Reed's smooth balls and teased them to and fro with the tip of his suddenly eager tongue.

And so another first landed in his face as Tucker eagerly shifted gears from their inevitable parting to the sudden pairing of his lips with Reed's thickening shaft. He bent to the task greedily, as did his wily lover, the sounds of their late-night passion, sticky and sucking and sweet, drowning out the internal monologue that threatened to break Tucker's heart before they even said their absolutely inevitable goodbye.

Until then it was easier just to do what they did best—pleasure each other from every angle, in every spare moment, until there was nothing left to share but their bitter, broken hearts.

TWENTY-EIGHT

Reed

"MORNING, SUNSHINE."

Reed started, a can of iced coffee held to his forehead as he stood, half in, half out of the screen door. Sunlight, bright and bold, filled his eyes but wasn't quite blinding enough to obscure the swarthy, sweaty stranger sitting on his front porch.

Holy shit, Reed thought, blinking his eyes wide with surprise. There was a stranger.

Sitting.

On his front porch!

The older man gave a salty wink, thick lips joyless inside a salt-and-pepper goatee as he added, "Or should I say, afternoon?"

Reed stood stock-still, grateful only for the fact that he'd snatched a pair of random boxer shorts, sticky and damp, from the growing pile on the bedroom floor and tugged them on, wobbly leg by wobbly leg, before he drifted to the front door. He'd been half tempted to free-ball it that morning, and why not? Until that very moment, the camp had been deserted—a private oasis, sweltering and hot, just for Tuck and him. It might as well have been a nudist retreat for all they'd cared over the last few days.

Suddenly this corpulent, sweaty interloper had interloped. "Pardon me?" His voice was as husky and dry as he felt.

"We'll see about that," the man said, his beard as abundant and unruly as his thickly cultured Greek accent. "For now, why don't you and I have a little talk?"

Reed let the screen door swing shut behind him as he scanned the grassy green grounds for his lover, his friend, his companion of the last week. He panicked when he found not a trace of young Tucker.

"About?" Reed stalled for time as he leaned against the porch railing and peered back at the sweaty stranger in his favorite rocking chair.

"About you and my impressionable young TV star," the man said, wriggling a half-empty can of the same brand of iced coffee Reed held to his throbbing forehead. "Hope you don't mind," he said, making it clear the man couldn't have cared less.

Reed ignored the wriggling, sloshing can and nodded knowingly. "Now I recognize the voice. You're the guy who hired me. Costas. Costas Imperial."

The man nodded, and the ancient rocking chair creaked in protest as he shifted his weight to give a little silent golf clap. "Correct, son. So that would make me your boss." He made a slimy little face to go with his slimy little smile.

Reed's heart was pounding to match his throbbing head, but he was too tuckered out by his agile young lover to show it. Instead he gave a gently bluffing smile and said, "I thought Tucker was my boss, *boss*?"

Costas smiled cryptically and said nothing. Instead he crumpled the empty can and dropped it at his feet. It clanked against something, and Reed saw it was another empty. No wonder there was only one left in the little dorm fridge beneath his desk. Reed had just assumed Tucker drank them all.

Where is that little shit, anyway? Reed continued to stall for time as he tried to surmise why some big-time Hollywood producer would sit on his hundred-degree porch in the middle of the day waiting for him to wake up from another hot sesh with his lean, limber TV star.

"How long have you been here, anyway?" Reed's legs were sore from the stretching and bending all night, not to mention half the morning. Despite wanting to mind his "boss," he sank into the matching rocking chair on the other side of Costas.

"Well, I haven't just been out here, kid, if you know what I mean?" The big man grunted and jerked his thumb at the cabin's interior. Reed followed the gesture and peered through the screen door to see the cluttered mess inside as if through a stranger's eyes. Spotting the unmade bed, sheets twisted and damp and Tucker's boxer briefs center stage in the middle of the hardwood floor next to the toppled bottle of wine and the two glasses they'd never quite used.

Glancing back at the producer on his porch, their eyes met in the stilted heat. "You went inside?"

Costas's chuckle was a gravelly, thick sound. "Well, you weren't responding to all the noises I was making out here, so after I saw that

Tucker's cabin was deserted and certainly not slept in last night, if ever, I thought I might find him here. But instead I saw your bare ass pointing my way, not moving, and I thought you might be dead."

"So you helped yourself to a couple cans of iced coffee and, what, waited out here for the coroner's van?" Reed's mind reeled as he did the math and came up short.

He sagged deeper into the rocking chair, no longer needing the rest of his bitter cold coffee brew. He was more than wide-awake. He felt not unlike he had that day in the dean's office, ambushed by half a dozen college officials and watching what little future he had plunge down the drain. How in the hell had he wound up in the same boat again?

"I see your wheels spinning over there, kid, so let me save you some time by getting straight to it—how long have you been sleeping with Tucker?"

Reed stammered and sputtered before he simply sank back in the chair and confirmed the wily producer's suspicions with his defeated body language. "How did you guess?"

Costas brayed out a bark of harsh, triumphant laughter. "Well, I wasn't actually sure until you confessed just now, but I've already seen how Tucker's cabin hasn't been used in a few days and, judging from the assortment of castoff skivvies littering the floor of your cabin like some sexual advent calendar, not to mention your earlier state of buck-ass nakedness, well, let's just say it didn't take Perry Mason to crack this particular case."

Reed simmered in a quiet, smoldering defensive heap of fraught defeat. "So, what now?"

"Now?" The chair beneath the portly producer creaked as he leaned in slightly to make his point readily apparent. "Now you buck up, gird your loins, cut your losses, and make things right, Reed. You make things right for you and for Tucker."

Reed finally rose above the shock and dismay of that morning's rapid-fire avalanche of horribly bad events to glare back at the swarthy intruder. "What if they're already right for me and Tucker, Costas? What if things were absolutely, perfectly right until you came sniffing around this morning?"

"You know what I mean," Costas scoffed. He waved his beefy hand and created another instapuff of musky cologne. "We may film in this godforsaken swamp of a state of yours, but Tucker's home, Tucker's future—and it's a bright one, I might add—is back in LA. You and I both know that."

Reed was still defiant, even if he was clearly jousting at windmills. "If his future's so bright, Costas, why can't he have two homes?"

Costas brayed with laughter, blunt but sincere. "No reason he can't, I suppose, once he's established himself with more than one series. Maybe then he'll have the time to come home to see his former swim coach. The question is, playboy, can you wait a few years for that to happen? Or maybe even a decade or so? Will whatever took place during your supposed professional relationship here at Camp Run-A-Mok last that long?"

Reed wanted to assure the cocky Hollywood schmuck that, absolutely, he'd still have a physical and emotional hard-on for Tucker a few years from that moment, but deep inside he wasn't sure Tuck would still have one for him.

Would he still want tired, old, boring, swim coach Reed now that his libido had been aroused and he had a full buffet of younger, hotter, richer, smarter, cooler, hipper, sexier models out in LA? While their fire burned in the humid Georgia woods, both of them had been uncertain that it might last outside the gates of camp. Now a stranger hammered the point home in a way Reed found hard to deny. His silence spoke volumes to both of them.

"Listen, Reed, believe it or not, I say this as a friend. Or at least as someone who wants the best for you both."

Reed peered back at the portly producer, still leaning slightly over in the chair beside him. "You're right, Costas, I don't believe it."

"Be that as it may, son, you have two options. One, you stick around and defy me and make things ugly and uncomfortable for Tucker. Neither of us want that, right?"

Reed frowned, too stubborn to admit the guy was right. "Depends on the second option, boss."

"The second option, Reed, is that you put on some damn clothes, grab the keys to that shiny new Jeep you have parked by the welcome center, and burn rubber out of here before Tucker gets back from town."

Reed was suddenly confused all over again. "Town?"

Costas waved a beefy, hairy hand. "He and Summer needed to get reacquainted, and I suggested a few quick photos in town. We'll leak them in the weeks leading up to the season five premiere and build interest in showing everyone how well Tucker's doing in the pool these days."

Reed saw his opportunity and leaned forward in his chair. "Wouldn't a third option be to stick around and make sure Tucker finished his lessons? We're supposed to have another week together, right? I'm sure I can get him flying in that pool by then."

Reed's voice trailed off in the wake of the big man's crackling laughter. He grunted as he slid a sleek, metallic cell phone out of his jacket pocket and tapped impatiently on the screen with his big fingers. "Give yourself a little more credit, Reed," he said with the confidence of a poker player holding a winning hand. "He's already swimming like a pro. You're far too modest, don't you think?"

Reed's heart pounded as a video played on the big phone screen— the pool and the swimmer instantly familiar. Clear water rippled as long arms sliced through the water, fingertips arching just as Reed had trained them to do, slicing through the water again and again until he reached the deep end, brown curls damp and pruney fingertips clutching the pool tiles. Then he took a breath and went back for more, lithe body stretched out like taffy.

"Holy shit!"

Reed had seen enough, and like a hot potato, handed it eagerly back. Costas chuckled as he reached for the phone. "Does he always swim in the buff?"

Reed couldn't sell the poor kid out, even if Costas clearly didn't mind. "Well, I mean, we'd do it sometimes back in school, to shave off a few milliseconds and make time?"

"Sure, kid, sure." Costas slipped the phone back in his jacket pocket and awaited Reed's decision.

Reed stood, skin clammy in the midmorning heat and keenly aware he was wearing Tucker's baggy boxers. They barely clung to his hungry waist. Costas moved not a muscle and watched him carefully. "Just one question before I go," Reed murmured, knowing he was beaten and not wasting another minute pretending that he wasn't.

Costas reclined with the self-assurance of a winner in his element, no matter where he sat. Reed had to admit, the guy was good. What's more, if he had Tucker's back, and it sounded like he did, the kid was sure to go far. The last thing Reed wanted was to interfere with Tucker's future, bright as it clearly was.

Costas crossed his bulky arms over his barrel chest and nodded. "Shoot, kid."

Reed nodded at the jacket pocket where the cell phone rested. "Where did you get that, anyway? That video, I mean."

Costas sagged back into his chair, as if relieved. "What, you think I'm the only one sniffing around Camp Run-A-Mok this morning? Summer came with me. Your boy toy must have slipped out before you got up this morning and left his drawers there on the floor."

"Sounds like him," Reed muttered. He reached for the screen door but didn't open it yet, as if waiting for more. Like any good Hollywood mover and shaker, Costas couldn't resist fleshing out the rest of the plot for him.

"Summer must have heard him splashing around while she was out looking for him," he explained. "Knowing her, she whipped out her phone before he even knew she was there, pushed Record as if it was second nature, and captured Tucker's dolphin-like swimming skills for posterity. She sent the video to me, I showed it to you, and if you play nice, the three of us will be the only people to ever see it."

"Promise?" Reed knew his tone was plaintive, wistful, almost begging. Costas sensed it too and didn't answer right away. "Costas, you have to promise you won't show that to anyone else."

Costas gave a curious head shake. "It's not unflattering, you have to admit. He's flying down that pool like a real pro."

"Costas, he's naked. Buck. Ass. Naked. Pale butt, furry junk and all. He's shy about that stuff. He's had enough embarrassment, don't you think?"

Costas blushed slightly, revealing he wasn't actually a cybernetic organism. "From what I could see in that video, kid, Tucker's got absolutely nothing to be embarrassed about, if you get my drift."

"I do, but still. Promise me? No leaking, no paparazzi, no scandal, no rag mags, no viral videos anymore, okay?"

"As long as you promise *me*, Reed, that you'll leave before he gets back from town and finds us here, talking like this. Do that and I'll forget this video ever existed."

Reed nodded somberly. Then he drifted through the creaky screen door to gather up what little things he'd brought and shoved them all back into his single duffel bag. He dressed quickly and didn't bother to make the bed. When he returned to the porch, Costas was standing, wiping his furrowed brow with a satin handkerchief from his suit pocket. "I assume housekeeping will sort out the rest?" Reed slung the duffel bag over his shoulder.

Costas patted him on the back, a hearty clap that nearly sent Reed flying toward Tucker's cabin halfway down the hill in front of his own. "Hell, I'll do it myself if I get my TV star back in one piece and without a male love interest in tow."

Reed ignored the leering joke.

"Tell him goodbye for me?" Reed realized he'd never even bothered to trade cell phone numbers with the kid. He hadn't needed to, given their close proximity over the last few days—that and the fact that they both thought they had all the time in the world before their two weeks were up.

"Hell, I'll go you one better, kid. We're having a big premiere to kick off the first episode later this year. I'll make sure you get an invitation. How about it?"

Reed didn't have to think twice. "I'll take a raincheck, Costas. Clean breaks and all?"

"Wise choice, kid," the producer said with another hearty slap that this time sent Reed down the steps he'd been descending already. "It was just talk anyway."

Reed figured as much. As he approached the mess hall, Costas called out behind him, "And don't even think about following them into town, kid. I've got cameramen all over the place, and if I catch so much as one whiff of your pretty face, let's just say the college will hear about this little misstep of yours, capisce?"

Reed ignored him—and the mess hall, and the pool, and the locker room. He strode purposefully in mismatched socks and crusty boxers under a pair of wrinkled khaki shorts that were probably not even his to the Jeep he'd parked nearly a week earlier and hadn't touched since. Instead he climbed inside, turned over the relatively new engine with a crank and a purr, and without looking back, peeled out of his parking space and beneath the Camp Run-A-Mok sign for the very last time.

TWENTY-NINE

Tucker

"HOLY SHIT, Tuck!"

Tucker froze in place with his hand on the pool tile at the far side of the deep end. His ears were still thundering with blood from that morning's impromptu cardio workout, water splashing and gurgling beside him so that he wasn't quite sure what he'd heard. But he was sure of one thing—it wasn't Reed.

He glanced up to see Summer standing above him, radiant in a slinky black sundress that could have doubled as evening wear. That is, if she were so inclined. Her legs were smooth-shaven and glowing in the late morning sun, her face a mask of youthful triumph as she peered down at him.

"Surprised to see me, Tuck?"

"Summer!"

He wasn't just breathless from the early morning workout, but from her sudden presence and what it might mean, what it would *surely* mean, what it probably already meant, for him and Reed. He struggled to hide the almost violent panic attack that surged just beneath the surface, not just of the water, but of his hopefully placid exterior.

This couldn't be good.

"The hell?" Tucker wiped water from his face and blinked up at Summer for perhaps the hundredth time. He hoped against hope that she was just a mirage, but her sultry gaze and one whiff of her familiar five-star perfume made it clear she was very, very real indeed.

Tucker realized how exposed he was beneath the pool's crystal-clear surface. He scanned the two deck chairs next to the pile stacked against the fence, still face-to-face the way sweet, romantic, sentimental Reed preferred them.

There, damp and dripping, the baggies he'd worn that morning hung half off one side of the nearest chair. He'd tugged them on in good faith, but after a few steady laps, as his muscles warmed up and grew limber and sped up his pace, they started to drag lower and lower with each subsequent lap until he'd simply tugged them off and tossed them aside.

Now he clung to the pool tiles, heart pounding and mind racing at her sudden presence. "What are you doing here, Summer? I thought you were guest hosting that new talk show in Atlanta all week."

She shrugged like it was no big deal that her sudden presence at the otherwise deserted campgrounds had just set off a nuclear chain reaction in Tucker's life. "Meh. I already did my episodes and I'm done, so I flew down here real quick, and now Costas wants us to get a few snaps together before the hiatus is over. So I thought we'd head into town and take a few to keep the charade up before then, huh?"

She waved her cell phone, making Tucker wonder what else she'd been "snapping" while he was crushing his solo swim practice while Reed slept off their late-night suck-and-grind fest. He blushed and rubbed the imagery away with a palmful of water, as if to cool off from the rush of sultry, sweaty images that flooded his brain.

He had left Reed dead to the world that morning, crept from bed to go pee. Then he'd stood in the dewy grass just outside the cabin and known he'd never be able to go back to sleep. Rather than pace around the quiet cabin waiting for Reed to wake up or whiling away the hours on the front porch listening to his spent lover snore the morning away, Tucker had simply dragged on his baggies and trotted off to the pool. He figured he'd brush up on his technique before his coach finally woke up and put him through the paces later that morning… in more ways than one.

Now Tucker wondered what might happen if Reed woke up just then, found him gone and stumbled to the pool, morning wood poking through his favorite brand of clingy blue boxer briefs, only to find Summer standing there with her cell phone handy—secrets, lies, and scandals all exposed at once.

"Summer, I'm bare-ass under here," he confessed, face flushing crimson. Obviously he hadn't expected company, except perhaps for a curious Reed, wondering why he'd never come back from the bathrooms that morning after he stole away from the cozy confines of their shared cabin and warm, cozy bed.

Summer nodded appreciatively, eyes hooded and lips moist as she gazed at his body above and below the still rippling surface of the Olympic-size pool. "I can see that, stud."

He gripped the stairs and paused only a moment in his modesty before deciding to go the full Monty and just rise on up out of the pool, swinging and hanging as if he were alone. Hell, Tucker reasoned, they were supposed to be play dating. She should probably at least see his schlong at some point in their fake relationship. "How long have you been standing there, anyway?"

"Long enough to see you've come a long way, baby." The way she was still eyeing him as he finally stood, dripping onto the pool deck, made it unclear exactly what type of *long* she was talking about. That is, until the next sentence confirmed it.

"You're swimming now, huh? Like, actually swimming." For once, Summer didn't seem to be acting. She sounded sincerely surprised, and if he wasn't mistaken, vaguely... proud?

Tucker hemmed and hawed as he stood there dripping and naked, forgetting that he was standing there dripping and naked. "I mean, I've still got a long way to go, but...." He didn't want her to think he was done with his training yet, even though he didn't know how much more Reed could teach him.

At least, not in the pool.

He finally stopped rambling long enough to spot the towel he'd brought along, clear across the pool by the baggies he'd chucked five laps into his morning workout routine.

Summer watched as he padded across the pool deck, wet feet on warm pool tiles, wondering just where the time had gone. It had still been dark when he'd snuck out of the cabin, and Reed was snoring like a lumberjack as he crept through the screen door like a cat burglar so as not to rouse him. Suddenly, it had to be nearly noon. Maybe he was a better swimmer than he'd let himself believe.

He grabbed his towel and, rather than dry off, unfurled it in front of his lumbering junk. Summer had her cell phone handy and snapped away even as he clung to his package with the dampening towel. "Summer, stop that shit. You and that damn camera of yours!"

Summer squealed with obvious glee, ever the publicity hound. "I can't help it, Tuck. Wait'll the crew gets a load of these."

"Summer, so help me God!" Tucker waved his free hand, and the towel fell slightly below his happy trail as he waved it like an old man telling her to get off his lawn.

Summer finally agreed, but probably only because she'd grown bored of his wet nakedness and was ready to move on to bigger and better things.

"Fine, okay, I'll delete these bad boys. But listen, I may have already sent Costa a clip of your swimming prowess this morning, so…."

The news sent him sinking down to the deck chair as if his legs had just given out, the soggy baggies caressing his right thigh as his heart continued to thump and growl against his pounding chest. "Summer, how could you?"

He didn't blame her for looking confused, even surprised, to say nothing of slightly peeved. How could she know how much that extra week of time with Reed meant to him? How much he was looking forward to savoring every moment with him, and not just in bed?

Summer seemed as genuinely surprised by the power of his reaction as he was. "What, Tucker? I was proud of you, that's all. Plus he wanted to know how you were doing, and when I saw you slicing through that water this morning, man, I just had to start filming."

Tucker could only hope Costa was too busy to watch it for the next day or two at the very least. He'd known it was too good to be true to expect that Scream Studios would let him have the whole two weeks to flounder around in the deep end with Reed, but a few more days would at least give him time to sort out whatever might happen for them in the future.

"Come on, Tuck." Summer had clearly forgotten all about the video, or his schlong, for that matter. She seemed hot and tired, skin aglow from the swelling Georgia sun and ever-present cloying humidity. Reed remembered how hot it had seemed that first day with Reed, out by the pool. How quickly he'd gotten used to it since then. "Let's go into town already, 'kay? I'm totally starving, and we can let the team Costas hired snap a few pics real quick and I can get back to LA by dinnertime, deal?"

"Team?"

"He wants the undercover snaps to be authentic, so he sent me down with a few freelancers from Atlanta to make things seem legit."

Tucker frowned and nodded absently. "To make fake romance photographed by fake photographers legit. Heard."

He had a reason to be grumpy. Going into town with Summer was literally the last thing Tucker wanted to do at that moment, but he knew there was no saying no. He dried himself in earnest and glanced around the pool deck for something to wear into town for their fake photo shoot.

"But… my things?" Tucker thought perhaps he might be able to ditch Summer in the mess hall for a fancy can of iced coffee or craft lemonade, sprint back to the counselor's cabin, and fill Reed in right quick, but his feisty, bossy, hot-and-bothered costar was having none of those shenanigans. And, as always, she'd come more than prepared.

"No need for all that." Summer hefted a denim backpack littered with a colorful array of different-size punk-rock buttons and what looked to be a half-dozen rainbow macramé zipper clips. "I don't want you dressing like some shlub, per usual, so I took the liberty of buying you a few more appropriate things before I left Atlanta. You can change before we split, 'kay?"

Despite the fact that it was all for show, Tucker was vaguely touched. It was the sweetest thing Summer had ever done for him. The sweetest thing any woman had ever done for him.

It was just as well, Tucker realized. He finished drying himself off under Summer's watchful gaze and wondered why she was studying him up and down so intently when, most of the time, she hardly had a spare second to return his morning greeting when he strolled onto the set. The last thing he wanted was Summer following him back to his cabin and noticing the freshly made bed, the tidiness of his space, and putting two and two together that he hadn't slept there for the last few nights.

"Is there underwear in there, by any chance?"

Summer chortled throatily, voice husky like a late-night DJ's. "Sure, but you're obviously more than comfortable without it these days, right, Tuck?"

She leered with an almost playfully overacting wink. He flinched. Had she swung by the cabin that morning after all? Seen Reed and him entwined in each other's sticky embrace, arms and legs and groins and junk entangled in the sultry morning heat?

"The hell's that supposed to mean?"

Summer winked, turned on one heel, and sped away so that he had to follow, the hem of her clingy black sundress spinning like a poodle skirt in the bright Georgia sun. "We'll talk about it over lunch, 'kay, Tuck?"

She traipsed off toward the locker room, looking effortlessly elegant as if she were striding down a red carpet. He followed, world suddenly crumbling at his feet while, just hours earlier, it had been overflowing with possibilities. Now Tucker wondered if all he'd have left of his time with Reed were hot and sweltering memories, ultimately doomed from the start.

THIRTY

Reed

"COME ON, Tucker. Where the hell *are* you?"

Reed steered his Jeep leisurely through town and cruised up and down Main Street on the lookout for Tucker's curly brown locks and broad, sexy shoulders. It was another random weekday in downtown Redfern, Georgia, sweltering and stilted in the early afternoon heat as few pedestrians shambled along the tree-lined sidewalks of a quaint and picturesque Main Street.

He'd thought about skipping the off-limits recon mission altogether, just knowing it would get back to Tucker's producer friend somehow, some way. But the thought of just driving away from Camp Run-A-Mok and never saying another word to Tucker felt like a betrayal of the worst sort.

An even bigger betrayal than never seeing him again. So he did a U-turn on his way to the freeway and, ten minutes later, was idling at an intersection, tempted to get out of his Jeep and continue his mission on foot. But he was certain the minute he did, alarm bells would sound on Costa's alien-spaceship-cell-phone tech and alert him to Reed's presence, and a squadron of Hollywood rent-a-cops would dutifully escort him out of town.

Instead he remained in the Jeep, windows down and radio off for a better view, if that made any sense. His heart pounded and sweat stung his eyes as he idled outside of Reggie's BBQ, where he could see the booths inside were empty, the front entryway as well. Of course it couldn't be that easy. He circled the town square with its carefully manicured lawns, towering green oak trees, and white-painted gazebo amidst a smattering of oddly spaced park benches.

At last he parked, snatched the hat and windbreaker from Tucker's ridiculous getup the day before, and donned it in protest, the big-time Hollywood producer's threats to derail Tucker's career if he so much as thought Reed might follow him into town still stinging his ears. Not used to such covert secret spy missions, Reed tugged the cap down over the black stubble on his head and zipped up the jacket until he looked about as incognito as a pervert in a brown trench coat and nothing else on underneath.

Still he managed to infiltrate the center of town without detection, and closer to the ground now, eyes peeled and ears wide open, Reed passed the half-dozen or so eateries offered by the downtown square. It seemed quainter than it had the day before, if only because Reed sensed it would be the last time he ever saw it.

Around the corner from Reggie's and just down the street from a pizza parlor, Reed heard the tones of canned, folksy, hipster-style music and followed the scratchy fiddles and violins until he stumbled upon the Brickhouse Brewery, a vaguely sprawling affair that looked equal parts abandoned warehouse and outdoor patio.

The music was both vintage and whimsical, just the kind of thing you might hear played over the speakers at a trendy brewery tucked away in small-town Georgia. *Who knew?* Reed crept closer and, frozen in midstep, heard Tucker's familiar lazy chuckle from somewhere very nearby.

It chilled him to the marrow. It was merry and bright where Reed's throat was taut with emotion, bittersweet and harried, so constricted he didn't think he could laugh if someone paid him a million dollars.

He'd know that jolly, mirthful, innocent laugh anywhere. He'd heard it a million times in the last few days alone—self-conscious by the pool, buzzed and hungry in the mess hall kitchen, chuckling and merry around the fire pit, nervous in the glistening shower, and sultry and teasing in bed. The sound, cocky and shy at the same time, had been permanently imprinted on Reed's brain. To hear it now, on the very day their coupling had been torn asunder, so crisp and clear and right around the corner, was as surreal as it was heartbreaking.

He inched forward and forced himself to creep closer to peer around the brick-wall façade of the brewery to the lush and almost hidden patio. Rustic wooden picnic benches were lined up side by side, family style, under a canvas canopy to block the sun and offer shade to the only couple currently seated at a table by themselves.

It was Tucker, looking suave and smooth and sexier than ever in a crisp white linen shirt, the sleeves rolled up to enhance his wispily hairy forearms and smooth late-summer tan. It was unbuttoned just enough to be sexy but not enough to be douchey, and his brown curls were gently tamped down by a weathered salmon-colored ball cap he'd also never seen before. Beneath the table, just visible as he sat cross-legged enjoying a cold glass of something purple and fruity, were madras shorts, orange and brown to offset the casual frat-boy preppy vibes Reed found it hard to resist despite his growing confusion.

The girl across from him was radiant and just as blissed out, looking sultry and elegant in a simple black dress that flattered her gym-worthy physique. She sipped a thick glass of purple fruitiness as well, and both hands cupped the chunky glass as if she was a toddler gripping a sippy cup. She was gorgeous, youthful, smiling, and instantly recognizable— Summer Stevenson, Tucker's A-list costar and his reluctant chauffer the day she dropped him off at Camp Run-A-Mok.

How different things were back then. When he spied Tucker for the first time, lean but anonymous as he unfolded from the passenger seat like an inflatable lawn ornament, Reed had been intrigued but not impressed. Sure, the kid was sexy and hot AF, but Hollywood impressed Reed about as much as a fancy car or expensive bottle of wine.

The kid had been a job, a client—easy on the eyes, pretty to look at, good company—but beyond that? Meh. And then sheer fireworks once Reed got to know him. Funny, quick, witty, sarcastic, lean and sexy, tall and handsome, soft in all the right places and hard when it counted—an able and willing lover, up for any challenge, a quick learner for a virgin, and straight jack rabbit when it came to recharging and keeping the lusty shenanigans up all night and well into the morn.

And now, dressed like a fool, sweaty under his ridiculous windbreaker, lurking around corners and crouching behind bushes like some hapless PI, Reed was obviously, helplessly, ridiculously, and endlessly in love. Not just lust. He knew what that felt like, had lusted over different guys a hundred times in his life. This was something new, something seismic, something unmistakably life-altering. And all the more so, Reed surmised, since it was clearly and irrevocably ending.

He sank against the brick wall, ignoring the simmering heat, the ridiculous getup, the folksy music, and even the occasional passerby as he watched the two costars reunite, clinking thick, crooked glasses and savoring a sampling of savory treats on the roughhewn tabletop between them.

He couldn't hear the words they said, only watch the familiar and friendly way they said them, not at all the way Tucker had described their

relationship in his ear as he pillow-talked him through the night while
their sticky bodies lay entwined beneath the shimmering moonlight.

With every bark of laughter and playful snicker and sip of adult
beverages the two costars shared, Reed felt himself growing farther and
faster from his young lover, who clearly existed in an exclusive world
far and away from his own. He'd had Tuck to himself for the past week,
alone and isolated, tempted and tricked out, half-naked at all hours, bare
the rest, and all to himself.

He'd known Tucker's beauty, his charm, his appeal on an individual
basis, but now, seeing him with Summer, sun-kissed and fitted out as
if they were on the back deck of a shimmering yacht, he wasn't just
outclassed and outgunned by the two Hollywood TV stars, he was on the
outside looking in, in more ways than one.

It really was as if the two were filming a scene, complete with the
picturesque setting—lush greenery in ceramic pots surrounding them and
the filtering shadows from the canvas tarp overhead, Bogie and Bacall
taking a break from shooting a scene in *Casablanca*, the rest of the world
be damned. As if to cement the Hollywood moment, a pudgy dude in a
generic gray hoodie emerged from behind one of the shrubs that half
walled off the patio deck from the sidewalk to snap a picture, then three
more, celluloid frames snapping in quick succession.

Unbothered, the two acted as if they hadn't seen it. And perhaps,
sharing A-list gossip over adult beverages, basking in their rarified glory,
they truly hadn't. Instead they hovered over the picnic table for two,
glasses half-empty, toes nearly touching under the table, canoodling like
long- lost friends.

Make that lovers.

Reed struggled not to be jealous. He knew what he and Tucker
shared had been sincere, authentic, organic, even true. He'd watched
enough episodes of *Suburban Dead* by now to realize that Tuck wasn't a
good enough actor to fake the dozen or more thrilling, gushing climaxes
they'd shared nor the more intimate affections of spooning all night,
dappled and sticky and cooing in each other's arms, confessing their
innermost secrets in voices both true and sincere.

But Tuck wouldn't be the only semistraight dude to take a quick
walk on the wild side, sucking and stroking with wild abandon on the
DL, abandoning his straight sensibilities for a brief and temporary trip to

the wrong side of town, only to go "straight" back to Normal Town once the timer was up and his gay expiration date came due.

But he was the first one Reed had ever cared about—truly, sincerely cared about. He sighed and turned with a rasp of his university windbreaker against the roughhewn brick of the hipster brewery.

He shuffled anonymously through the empty streets and emerged back at the town square with no recollection of getting there. Then he slid into his Jeep, backed out, and headed straight for the freeway and, he supposed, back to life as he knew it before Tucker. Before love had crept into his lonely, solitary life and changed him forever.

THIRTY-ONE

Tucker

"So, HOW long have you been cheating on me, fake boyfriend?"

Tucker chuckled self-consciously, enjoying the midday pitcher of sangria at the breezy outdoor patio Scream Studios had picked out for their impromptu photo shoot. He hadn't eaten since God knew when and he'd had an active night even before his Herculean early morning workout, so the sangria had rushed straight to his belly and then right to his head.

Tucker wore a wary smile. "I'm not copping to anything until I know what *you* know first, Summer."

She sighed and toyed with the stem of one of the cherries from the sangria pitcher between them. It sat, icy and sweaty and chock full of fruity, spiked goodness, like breakfast, lunch, and dinner squeezed into a jar. They drank from glass mason jars, piled high with crushed ice and tart, savory sweetness. "So listen," she said, twisting the stem between two expertly manicured fingers. "I'll be honest. I didn't go straight to the pool this morning, Tuck."

"No shit?" He smirked over his half-empty jar of fruit slushy goodness.

"No, I went to your cabin first, and well, I've seen enough empty bedrooms to know when one hasn't been slept in for a few days."

"I slept there," Tucker murmured noncommittally as he admired the peaceful, verdant setting of the back patio where the hostess had sat them earlier that afternoon. Potted plants shielded them from prying eyes while a canvas awning did the same from the withering sun, and rows of exposed bulbs swayed overhead as they sat alone on the small but intimate brewery patio.

Summer clucked a tongue and rolled her eyes knowingly. "What, your first night?"

Tucker rocked back on his rustic wooden bench, surprised at how quickly he'd absconded from Camp Run-A-Mok and, despite his constant yearning for Reed, how comfortable he felt getting back to work mode with, of all people, Summer Stevenson.

"Why are you asking me all this, anyway? Do I look like I've done anything other than struggle and flop and flounder and slap my way through a pool for the last week?"

Summer gave him a coolly appraising nod. "No, you look great. Spectacular, even. A little sun flatters you, Tuck. I can't wait to see our pictures once the tabloids get hold of them." As if on cue, or perhaps the ragtag team of freelance photogs were actually wearing earphones hooked up to some secret microphone tucked deep inside Summer's collar, a sweaty nondescript man in a sports coat slid from around the corner and snapped a few random pics, shutter frames snapping audibly from his vintage camera.

Tucker ignored the intrusion, even more so than Summer, because he knew it was what Costas wanted. And if Costas got what he wanted, perhaps he'd let Tucker have that one extra week with Reed. When the photographer's flash quit exploding like fireworks in the midnight sky, they both rolled their eyes.

Summer confessed, "Listen, Tuck, I went by Reed's cabin too, okay?"

Tucker sagged and reached instinctively for his sangria to drown out the reality of what she'd just confessed. "Please say you're bluffing, Summer," he moaned, unable to hide the depth of his shock, embarrassment, and disappointment. "Please, please say you're just punking me to try and get me to cop to something."

Summer refilled their squat round jars from the sweaty sangria pitcher, and Tucker watched her carefully. She set the pitcher down and then fixed him with a playful, curious expression. "I wish I was punking you, pal, because it's gonna be hard to scrub the picture of you two sweaty hunks, sheets off, asses and other, uh, junk out for the whole world to see, lean and buff and tan. Come to think of it, it's kind of got me hot and bothered."

Somehow, from the wells of defeat, Tucker summoned a wisecrack. "You did seem a little randy back at the pool, Summer."

Caught by surprise, she snorted, just shy of having a mouthful of sangria to spray in his face. She leaned slightly forward, shadows across her face highlighting her creamy lip gloss.

"I'm not gonna lie, Tucker, you've always seemed a little too vanilla for my taste, but after seeing you guys like that this morning, I'm starting to revise my opinion of you."

He rolled his eyes, but he was feeling the sangria, not to mention the secondhand flattery, deep in his gut. It wasn't just what Summer thought of him, or them, or what she'd seen, but the fact that she wasn't tarring and feathering him and driving him out of town. While Summer squirmed with thoughts both real and imagined about what he and Reed had been up to that week, Tuck thought that maybe other people's opinions of him *weren't* the problem.

Just maybe, Tucker realized, it was what he thought of himself that mattered the most. He never batted one eye while he and Reed were alone, clothed or unclothed, kissing or talking or sucking or laughing or stroking or swimming. The feelings were natural, organic, true, and sincerely welcome. It was only when others appeared—Summer on that pool deck, camera in hand, able to expose their illicit affair with one snap of her camera—that plunged his emotions downward into dread territory.

Yet here she was, bubbly and flirty, admiring him in a whole new light, more accepting than he thought she might be, given her normally frosty demeanor and ironclad Hollywood royalty status. Perhaps she didn't even feel the need to be accepting because love really *was* love.

He glanced up from admiring the contents of his glass to find Summer's face curiously close and leeringly curious. "How come you never told me, Tucker?"

"Told you what?"

She rolled her eyes and wagged her sangria glass toward him. "Told me you batted for the other team, stud?"

Tucker took a long, slow drag off the tangy sweet cocktail and glanced around the patio as if there might be a sound crew lurking just beyond that bush, or perhaps beneath the next picnic table, recording every word for posterity—and killer ratings, no doubt. Finding none, he glanced back and shrugged. "I didn't actually know I did until now. Just now. I mean, I always suspected, kinda, sorta, but Reed was my first, uh, encounter, so to speak."

Summer smacked his hand and leaned forward, then back, and gasped dramatically in her own unique way. "You mean, you're telling me, until this hot, sultry weekend with your sexy swim coach, you've never been with another man?"

She was enjoying herself too much, and Tucker leaned over with what he hoped would be a menacing scowl. "No, Summer. I haven't. So you need to be chill right now."

"I am chill," she gurgled, glancing around secretively as if to prove it. "I just, I mean, so all those girls you flirted with every season, they were… what? Beards?"

"No, Summer, stop. I don't know what they were exactly. I liked them well enough at the time. Even dated a few, when the mood struck me. I'm not immune to, uh, feminine charms."

She rolled her eyes, wriggled delightedly in her seat, gleaming skin aglow in the Georgia humidity. "Well, you've certainly been immune to mine, player. Now at least I know why."

"It's not that, Summer. I like you, I do, and you're obviously chef's-kiss sexy. It's just not *my* type of sexy, I guess?" He made a hands-up human "teethy face," emoji gesture.

She seemed to take the comment in the no-nonsense manner it was intended, and rather than appearing offended, topped off their glasses, making Tucker realize his was empty. Again. He nibbled on one of the breadsticks sticking out of an earthen jar and then washed down its savory, herby goodness with a fresh swig of sangria. While he ate, Summer leaned in conspiratorially, voice as breathy as her eyes were probing. "Tucker, right here, right now, just us, you have to spill. Like, what did you guys do, run into each other's arms the minute I pulled away that first day?"

He chuckled merrily, imagining how aloof, distant, and downright cold Reed had been that first day. Hell, those first few days. It was as if he'd been afraid of even glancing Tucker's way lest he see him as something more than a massive Hollywood paycheck. "Hardly," he guffawed.

She clapped her hands gleefully, all manicured nails and smooth, polished skin as she leaned in for more dirt. Tucker wondered what it was about seeing him with Reed, naked and asleep, bare and sweaty to the world, that had made Summer finally sit up and take notice of him. "So when, then?"

"It just happened." He met her eyes and found her curiosity sincere, not salacious. She clearly wanted more, and in a way, he'd been aching to tell the tale ever since their first swollen kiss that humid night on Reed's front porch.

He continued. "A glance here," he murmured fondly, eyes aglow with the memory. "A chuckle there. A beer or two, a crackling fire, side by side in the swimming pool, lingering a little longer in the showers after practice every day, him checking me out, me checking him out, lingering over goodbye every evening, and then wondering all night what he was doing in that cabin of his, all alone in his boxer shorts."

Summer shivered with delight in the shadows of the canvas awning, face aglow beneath the swaying bulbs as their boozy lunch break stretched on into midafternoon. They paused only slightly as their harried waiter dropped off the small-plate appetizers they'd ordered some time ago—olives and pine nuts, honey drizzled whole-wheat croissants, prosciutto and melon wraps, a bowl of shelled pistachios dusted with Old Bay seasoning.

He drifted away without asking if they wanted anything else, which was probably for the best considering they were both giggling and snorting as it was, only half a pitcher of sangria in.

"And then, finally, you kissed?"

Tucker nodded dreamily, knowing he was blushing and not caring in the least. They sounded like two BFFs, dishing the dirt while doing their nails, hair up in towels at a slumber party. Then again, maybe that was the point. From time to time, between nibbling and sipping and cavorting and laughing, a photographer emerged to snap them in candid fits of unrestrained privacy, a glimpse of big city come to town. They ignored it, mostly because, face-to-face, they were so busy dishing the dirt.

Summer nibbled an olive, fingertips sticky with oil. She licked them salaciously, and he could only hope the photogs got a picture of that little morsel. She swallowed, leaned in, and asked, "Who kissed who first, though?"

Never one for close talking, he sat back. "Me," he said, raising a hand as if to signify he was the "me" they were talking about. She slapped his hand where it rested on the table next to his empty jar.

"No. Way!" When he nodded, she asked, "Why you?"

Tucker recalled the moment—Reed's hesitance, his class, his chaste charm. "He didn't want to lead me on. He's older, so he didn't want to be the one to make the first move, I guess. Plus he's a swim coach, young guys in ball-huggers all day. He's learned the art of restraint, I suppose."

She waved her oily fingers and reached for her empty jar. "Not from what I saw this morning, he hasn't." She put down her glass, grabbed the pitcher, and topped them both off.

Again.

She picked her now full glass back up and leaned in even closer. "And I didn't stare, honest, but were my eyes fooling me this morning or is he shaved all over?"

Tucker had had just enough sangria to snort, snicker, and nod eagerly in reply. "*All* the hell over."

Summer leaned back in again. This time Tucker didn't balk. Somewhere in the distance, cameras snapped and photogs jockeyed for position and some lucky freelancer got their money shot, or as close as he was going to get to it this day. "God, dude, that is so sexy."

"Tell me about it," Tucker mused. "That's never happened to me before."

"Well sure," she huffed. "None of this has, right?"

He shook his head. "Not until now."

"So you were a virgin?"

"I mean, a boy virgin." Her eyes widened before he was quick to add, "I still kind of actually... am." He made another human "teethy face" emoji grin and then covered it up with a sip of sangria.

"So, wait? You haven't done the old boom-boom in the bum-bum yet?"

Tucker nearly snorted out his latest sip but was enjoying it too much to waste a single precious drop. "Not sure what any of that means, but if you're asking if we've gone all the way, no. Not yet."

"What exactly are you waiting for?"

"I don't know." Tucker set his glass down, and despite the savory samplings before them, he wasn't actually hungry. He wasn't sure, after this very surreal night and day, what he actually was anymore. "I guess for it to feel right?"

"Wow, Reed really is a gentleman, huh?"

Tucker was insanely proud as he replied, "He actually is."

"Wow." Summer's voice trailed off, and the moment seemed to fade into a vague realization as she nibbled and sipped and nibbled some more.

She finally nodded, as if digesting the tidbits, the revelations, the unfolding of their just blossoming relationship. She lifted her glass, and the crushed ice made a distinctly refreshing sound against the glass jar as she mused, "But why now, Tuck? Why Reed? I mean, I get it. I saw him in all his sweaty, sticky, naked glory this morning, and sure, he's an absolute, obvious hunk, but Hollywood is full of hunks. Hell, we've worked with half of them on the series and you've never even given one of them a second glance. So what gives?"

"Who says I haven't scoped them out when you weren't looking, Summer? I just wasn't about to air my dirty laundry in the middle of Hollywood, you know?"

She slapped his hand again and frowned her dramatic frown. "You don't really think it's dirty, do you? What you and Reed have been doing?"

He was surprised by the question. "Doesn't everyone?"

This time Summer's gasp made Tucker feel like the judgmental one. "Tucker, no, they don't. My God, what century are you even living in? How are you gonna spend all week in another man's bed and then turn around and feel ashamed of it?"

"I don't feel ashamed," he admitted. "Or maybe I do. The house I grew up in, the town where I lived, who my friends were, none of them would understand what I did with Reed. With another man. But mostly I just feel different now. Like you'll think differently of me, like everyone on the set will, anyone who saw us out together."

Summer set down her glass purposefully, and a little bit of the sangria sloshed over the lip and onto the water-stained table beneath it. Her hand, cool from the jar, covered his tenderly.

"Tucker," she urged as he struggled to make eye contact. "Tucker, look at me."

When he did, shyly, as if embarrassed about what he'd said and even more embarrassed about how he felt, she squeezed the top of his hand for emphasis. "The only way I think differently about you now is that I'm happy for you. Happy that you've found someone you obviously care so much about. Happy that you're happy. Okay?"

Tucker snorted and rolled his eyes even as, out of nowhere, those same eyes welled up with unexpected tears. Summer made a startled "Oh my" grunt and then wiped them dry with a napkin.

"You are happy, right, bud?" she asked, pausing with her tear-damp napkin in midair.

Tucker looked away as a fresh trickle of tears accented his croaking reply. "I've literally never been happier."

They chuckled at the ridiculousness of that moment—the merriment, the discovery, the surprise of it all. She held his hand, not as a fake girlfriend, but as a real friend. Squeezed it, like a sister might. He'd never had one of those before. It felt good. "So what are you going to do about it, Tucker?"

He shook his head as he let the fresh tears air dry. Peering back at Summer, her eyes smoky and sincere under her trendy bangs, he croaked, "I have absolutely no idea, Summer."

She squeezed his hand once more and chuckled with shared emotion. "Well, as someone who's had about a dozen on-set relationships she wasn't supposed to have and made them all work somehow, I have a few ideas of my own. Would you like to hear them?"

Tucker refilled their glasses and settled in, as if they were doing a table read back on set. "Do I have a choice?"

She raised her glass and clinked his in a silent toast. "Not even a little, pal."

"Then why ask?" He was feeling flirty, relieved, and for the first moment since he'd looked up to find her peering down at him in the swimming pool, hopeful.

"I guess I'm just being polite?"

"Since when?" He rolled his eyes and topped off their mostly full glasses, as if he needed something to do with his hands.

"Listen, I can't…." Summer sighed and picked up her glass. Then she put it back down heavily on the fruit-splattered picnic table without ever taking a drink. "I can't help but feel that this is, partly anyway, my fault."

"How so?"

"I didn't shoot that video of you swimming," Summer murmured, narrowly averting her eyes as she used the stem of a cherry to absently dunk it in and out of her sangria glass. "And I sure as hell didn't post it, but when I saw it, I can't say that I was sorry, exactly."

Tucker remembered the first time he'd seen the viral video, how lost he'd felt, how betrayed, how utterly bereft and hopeless. "Why not?" he croaked.

Summer shrugged, bare shoulders in the sun. "Because I knew what it would mean for ratings. And I knew, having survived a few harmless scandals of my own, that you'd come out stronger because of it. Not as a person, but with name recognition, popularity, all that collateral stuff that helped make me who I am today. Part of me, the selfish part maybe, thought you might have wanted that too."

Tucker should have been mad. Had been, really, since the day he'd felt punished by the studio, the network, by Costas, his agent, even the rest of his cast, who mostly stayed silent while his embarrassment played into their motives, one at a time. "That little pep talk might have been easier to hear back on set, Summer. Or even back in LA. I could have used at least one ally from the show, you know?"

Her hand went to cover his, and instinctively, before he could think twice, he dragged his back. She reacted as if stung, tugging her own hand back and rubbing it absently. "I get it. I deserve that, Tucker. We all do. And yes, one of us should have made more of an effort to be a friend to you before you got banished down here." She made a casual gesture, a dismissive hand wave, as if to encompass not just the trendy patio where they sat but the little town where it was located and, by association, the deserted summer camp where Tucker had spent, if he was honest, the best week of his entire life. "But we didn't."

Tucker heard her voice trail off and glanced up to find her wincing after her muted confession. He sighed and crossed his arms defensively over his chest, even though he couldn't blame Summer entirely for his plight. "Do continue, Summer. I believe I heard an apology gaining traction somewhere in there?"

She sighed and nodded. "Of course I'm sorry, Tucker. And I wish I could say I knew that all of this would somehow lead to you finding just the absolutely sexiest swim coach alive and you falling in love with him and almost losing your butt boy V card to him, but I didn't. I'm only glad that something that started without thinking of you very much turned into a happy ending of sorts for you."

"You're lucky it did, Summer. I guess I should thank you, but you just reminded me you're one of the villains in this particular love story."

"Okay, I've earned that. Not entirely, obviously. But like every good villain, I'm ripe for redemption. So if I can secure your happy ending, make things right for you and Reed, make it so you can extend your little sex romp vacation back at camp and, if you're still feeling it afterward, extend that romance out into the real world, could you somehow possibly forgive me?"

Tucker sighed and reached over to smother her hands with his own. She exhaled at the touch, and her shoulders sagged with the visible signs of relief. "Summer, if you could do all that, I'll devote my entire Emmy-winning speech to you, deal?"

She laughed heartily and sipped merrily at her sangria. "Deal. Do I get to approve it first, or is that too much for a villain to ask for?"

Tucker made a gesture with his thumb and forefinger and held it up mere inches from her face. "A smidge. Now, you were saying you had a plan to save my doomed relationship from the trash heap?"

"And then some, pal. Trust me, by the time I'm through with you, you'll be walking the red carpet with your man before you can say, 'And the Emmy goes to....'"

They shared a cheesy, amiable grin. Tucker nodded and then made a boozy gesture by swirling his hand in a rather princely manner.

"Proceed," he said, tracking with the royal theme.

Summer wriggled her butt, put down her glass, pinned him with her cool blue eyes, and took a deep breath, as if preparing to free dive for a rare black pearl. "So, here goes—"

She paused to take a sip when a flash popped a little too close for comfort. An overzealous photog, one who perhaps might not have gotten the memo, stood just behind Summer. He saw her reaction, the wince and the flinch, the half turn that meant she was about to release one of her famous A-lister monologues when Tucker stilled her with a quiet, gentle grip on her hand.

He smiled richly, and not just for the camera—smiled with his whole body, down to his gut and back up again, with his eyes as well. "He's just doing his job, Summer."

"Yeah, well—"

He leaned in gently, knowing she'd take the bait and follow suit, as if sharing a conspiratorial whisper. They did, in a fashion. "We can kiss now, if you want. Give him what he came for. Give Costas what he wants. Get you those social media numbers I know you're craving?"

She seemed to think about it and licked her lips involuntarily as if preparing to do just that. Then she subtly but pointedly leaned slightly back on her picnic-table bench, recoiling as if his breath reeked of more than just sangria and rosemary-dusted breadsticks. "No, Tuck, that wouldn't feel right anymore. Honestly? I think we're done with all that now."

"No shit?"

She sipped her sangria languidly, lips ripe and plump and full. Hell, they looked so appetizing he almost felt like kissing them for real.

Almost, that is. "Shit, Tuck, if I didn't know any better, I'd say you sounded disappointed."

He shrugged. "I kind of am, actually."

"Since when?" She made a face worthy of any horror-movie starlet.

"Don't take this the wrong way, Summer, but I was just starting to like you."

She roared with laughter—a rich, merry, and for once, not put-on sound. She slapped his hand and frowned in reply. "No, how could I ever take that the wrong way, Tuck?"

"I mean, we've never really talked much before, and when we did, it was just about work or your famous parents or how to boost the ratings or making me pose for your fifteenth 'set selfie' of the day, so…."

"I get it, Tuck. But canceling our fake romance is kind of part of my plan for getting you and Reed back together."

"Ah yes, your plan."

"My plan, yes. Reed helped you swim, right? Well, I'm going to help you soar." She smiled and crossed her arms over her pert, unbridled breasts in triumph. She wore the same proud look as when she nailed a really hard monologue in one take back on set.

He rolled his eyes. "Fly where?"

She reached over with both hands on either side of his flushed face, and rather than kiss him, she squeezed his cheeks like an overweight aunt he hadn't seen in six years. "Why, fly right into his arms, that's where."

THIRTY-TWO

Reed

"THIS SUCKS."

Reed cracked a breadstick in half and nibbled it distractedly.

Kira looked genuinely surprised and certifiably sexy in her mustard-yellow sweater and fiery red crinkle skirt. "What? You always loved the breadsticks here."

He waved the jagged edge in his hand playfully at her. "Not these," he growled. The bistro was crowded with young, sexy, happy hipster couples, each of them leaning forward with whispered nothings, meaningful glances, and breathless, eager words to share. "*This.*"

Kira's gaze cast a wide net across the crowded café. With her stylishly shaved head, his boss looked every bit as hip, urban, and uptown as the rest of the couples in the snooty bistro dining room, so he wasn't sure she could relate to his admittedly dramatic complaint. She turned back to him, smirking behind her hip rectangular glass frames. "That's right, Reed. I keep forgetting. You've never been in love before."

He frowned above his snooty craft cocktail, which was far too spicy, flavorful, and small for his current mood. He wanted something stiff, strong, and big to salve his wounds, but the perky waitress in the pink-and-green pigtails had all but bullied him into the nightly special instead. It was already halfway gone, and he'd have been better off drinking water. "Is this love? Is this what it feels like? Because, if so, I'll never fall in love again."

"Famous last words, Romeo."

Reed sighed and nibbled the rest of his breadstick. They sat at a high top near the busy bar—the only seating available to them unless they wanted to wait an hour for a booth in the actual dining room. They should have known better. Gaither, Georgia, was a college town, home to one of the more popular B-tier state universities in the county, and this time of year, it was filled with students new and old as they settled into the fall semester by taking advantage of every minute of their precious weekend.

Still, sitting in a crowded uptown bar with Kira was far superior to pacing the hardwood floors of his lonely loft for the third night in a row. But Reed wouldn't have been happy if they'd had the whole dining room to themselves.

He was miserable. To her credit, Kira had given up a rare Friday night with her family to cheer him up. "God, you're as bad as the girls on the team when some jock they knew was bad news from the start inevitably breaks up with them."

Reed chuckled and shrugged. "I guess I shouldn't have poked fun at them this whole time, then, huh?"

As if on cue, his phone pinged, and when he glanced, a new alert for *Suburban Dead* appeared on his screen. The headline, from yet another popular Hollywood gossip blog, read, "Secret Lovers Break Away from Filming to Canoodle in Local Brewery While Costars Labor Cluelessly Back on Set."

Before he could swipe left and make it disappear like all the others, another picture of Tucker and Summer filled the screen—Tuck in his classy, preppy frat-boy getup and Summer in her breezy sundress as they toasted each other playfully with mason jars half full of fruity sangria and smiles full of sun and sex.

Kira watched it all in slow motion as she sipped her cosmo. She rolled her eyes. "Why are you doing this to yourself, Reed?"

He turned his phone over on his leather place mat, next to the oversized silverware in the fancy black napkin. "I turned on the alerts back when I first got the coaching gig, just to see who I was dealing with, you know? In all the hubbub, I forgot to turn them off, and now bam, with those stupid brewery pictures going viral, it's just nonstop."

"You forgot?" Kira put her drink down, favoring him with an ironic grin. "Or you just can't get yourself to turn off your settings so you can torture yourself every time a new alert pops up?"

She reached for the phone, ebony hand sliding across the table at her typically athletic pace. Reed was no slouch himself and just as quickly slid it out of reach.

"No." He patted the top of her wrist playfully as she eye-scolded him across the cozy candlelit table. "At least this way I get to see him every five stupid minutes."

"God, Reed, you are truly pitiful."

He quietly raised his craft cocktail and gave her a mock toast.

"And clearly enjoying your misery, I see." She took a sip from her oversized martini glass, the one with the blueberry-sugared rim.

"Not enjoying it, per se, but I see now why people write so many sad love songs."

She set down her glass and traded it for a breadstick. "I say this seriously now, but it's like you had a delayed adolescence of sorts. This is stuff teenagers learn by freshman year. You get that, right?"

He nodded. She was right, and he was absolutely acting the fool. "Oh, for sure. I guess I just never let myself fall in love before."

"So what's different this time? It can't just be that he's some big star and you're suddenly a groupie for some show you've barely ever watched."

"Not at all. When we were together, it was like the show never existed. I wouldn't have cared if he was the janitor. I can't really explain it, I guess."

Kira glanced slightly past him at two coeds giggling in a booth across the bar. They sat on the same side—clearly lovers—radiant and youthful and blissfully unaware of the outside world. She glanced back and smirked. "You don't have to, Reed. I kind of have a mini-Tucker waiting on me back home, remember?"

Reed grinned over his cocktail glass. "How could I forget? I think I passed about three billboards and two bus-stop benches with her face on them on the way here."

Kira rolled her eyes and flagged the harried waitress over for another round.

Kira's wife, Saffron Ramone, was a former beauty queen and local Realtor who continued to use her beauty to attract clients by advertising all over town. Her radiant, youthful face, olive complected and surrounded by her trademark Cleopatra bangs, was impossible to miss as one rode through tiny Gaither, where she peered down from billboards and out from bus benches in her equally recognizable three-piece suit, usually in her favorite peacock blue.

The two women met and hit it off at the annual fundraiser for the swim team a few years back. They'd been inseparable ever since, and they'd recently adopted Saffron's niece, Chloe, and become an instant family overnight. Sometimes Reed forgot that, like Tucker, Kira was only twenty-three.

The waitress delivered their drinks with her usual frantic pace and, not wanting to bog her down with longer orders, Kira fired off a few of their favorite appetizers. The poor server smiled gratefully, squeezed her arm, and disappeared to a nearby service station to type them in before another table called her over.

Reed sank deeper into his leather barstool. The fancy cocktail was stronger than he'd realized, and he was glad that the Collegiate Café was a mere two blocks away from his stylish loft apartment downtown.

His phone bleated yet again and skittered sideways on the fancy place mat as he somehow managed to ignore the latest candid photo of Tucker and Summer cavorting under another cheesy headline full of Hollywood puns.

He glanced at it for emphasis. "Yeah, well, at least you don't get alerts about Saffron and her lover every three seconds."

She gave him a mock scowl, perhaps to go with her dime-store therapy. "They're not real lovers, remember, Reed? It's just more Hollywood bullshit. Actual make-believe. You should know that better than anyone after spending a week surrounded by it."

"I know they're not real, but it sure felt real that day I was banished, you know?"

Kira's impatience was growing, not that Reed could blame her. There was nothing worse, he realized, than having to sit and counsel a grown-ass adult about something even a toddler wouldn't do. And yet here he was, being counseled and reveling in his own self-pity.

"You weren't banished either," she huffed. "You're just raw and vulnerable right now. Tucker will come to his senses, and when this viral photo shoot dies down in, like, five minutes, he'll reach out to you somehow and you two can see what life is like outside of your little bubble at Camp Run-A-Mok."

"He doesn't even have my number."

"Oh, for Pete's sake, Reed!" Kira was going to get eye strain from rolling hers so much. "He's got the school's number, right? One day soon, guaranteed, you're going to walk into your office and have a message from him, if not fifteen. And you'll forget all about this fleeting broken heart of yours and concentrate on seeing what love looks like out here in the real world."

Reed glanced at her hopefully and wished he could believe one of the few genuine friends he had at Eastern Georgia State. "I know you're right, at least I hope you are. I just have a hard time believing he's going to suddenly just out himself and start hanging around with me on the regular, you know? I mean, dude wore an actual disguise the first time we left camp to get something to eat together—real cloak-and-dagger stuff. I can't picture him going from that to...." Reed waved his hand at the cluttered table between them, the crowded bistro, and all its many patrons. "To this."

Kira nodded thoughtfully and let the statement simmer as she formed a careful reply. One of the things Reed liked about her, respected most about her, was that she wasn't willing to blow smoke up his ass.

"You know, Reed, people can surprise you. I thought Saffron would be the same way. When we first hooked up, we kept it way, way, I'm talking underground down-low, you hear me? We're not exactly in the most forgiving, liberal, LGBTQ-friendly state in the world, right? We worried—or at least I did—that it might hurt her business if we were seen together on the regular, out and about. But our first Christmas together, she surprised me by sending out one of those photo Christmas cards to all her clients—we're talking hundreds of the town's elite—with the two of us arm in arm and all cozy and cuddling on her front doorstep like it was the most natural thing in the world. And look at us now. No one even bats an eye when we're out in public or at some local event together anymore."

Reed found hope in Kira's story, but wrinkles as well. "But you two knew you were lesbians to start with. Tucker had never been with a man until me."

"So he's a late bloomer. From what I hear, he sure blossomed fast."

Reed blushed at the memory. It was hard to believe it had only been two days since he'd driven back to Gaither and his staid, boring life at the university as if the week with Tucker had never even happened. He held on to their intimacy, their romance, the promises Tucker had made as if they were gospel. But now, as another day passed without contact, he had come to understand it was just another fling.

The sooner he accepted that fact, the sooner he could quit acting like a heartbroken teen and get on with the business of growing the hell up.

Kira slid her warm, familiar hand atop his once again. "Listen, Reed, give it a few more days. They start filming again in a few weeks, right?" When he nodded, she grinned broadly. "So if he hasn't come to his senses by then, maybe you and I do a little set visit and see what's the what?"

"Yeah, right."

"They film in Wilmont, right? That's only an hour or so away from here. We'll jet up there Friday after practice, scope things out, and maybe between filming scenes you can get a word in with your TV-star boy toy, huh?"

"Sure, Kira, right."

She waved her martini glass like a fancy mic drop. "It can happen, Romeo. Say the word and I'm up for a road trip, no problem."

A food runner delivered their appetizers—savory samplings on fancy square and triangle dishes that looked like something out of a *Star Wars* movie. The scents and sights reminded him he hadn't eaten all day, and with Kira's pipe dream fading as quickly as the steam above their fancy plates, he squeezed her hand and reached for his giant silverware.

Her words were as empty as Tucker's.

Reed was alone in all this, alone the way he'd always been. And alone was how he'd solve this, one way or another.

THIRTY-THREE

Tucker

"Tell me what you want, Tucker. I'll see what I can do."

Tucker rolled his eyes and paced the floor of his agent's office in downtown Century City. The building itself was sleek and industrial, the office incredibly stark, clean, and surprisingly small. Then again, Randolph Starkey was merely a junior agent at the firm of TalentCo, the young, upstart agency that had signed Tucker the minute the folks at *Suburban Dead* offered him an actual contract.

Tucker paused with his hand on the back of the chair across from his agent's clear Lucite desk. It was littered with résumés, head shots, and contracts as thick as the phone book. No doubt his own was in that pile somewhere. He was, after all, Randolph Starkey's biggest client.

"I've already told you what I want, Randolph, three times already. I want Reed Chancelor on set with me next week, period."

Randolph rolled his eyes for perhaps the dozenth time since their meeting started ten short minutes earlier. "In what capacity, Tucker? The show has already handed over a sizable check to the guy. They're not going to foot the bill for another week on set, period."

"I was promised two weeks of coaching, Randolph. I only got one. Should I do the math for you, or would you like to take the credit for yourself?"

"It was a verbal agreement, Tucker. I've already told you that. Not quite legal and binding, wouldn't you agree?"

Their eyes met across the confined space. Randolph was in his midthirties, petite but well put together in a fitted navy suit and subdued yellow shirt. His glasses were sleek and thin and rectangular—almost futuristic. His expression was equally robotic. "Where is all this coming from, kid?"

Tucker gripped the back of the chair tighter, to steady himself. "All what?"

Randolph chuckled humorlessly and waved his hand to encompass the office and Tucker standing there, fuming and fit for a fight. "All of this. You demanding a meeting during my lunch hour. Storming in here making demands and expecting me to pull strings when I saved your job in the first place. Need I remind you of the fallout from that little viral video of yours last month?"

Tucker smirked, slid into the chair, and leaned slightly forward. "Randolph, I'm being patient. I'm being kind. I'm also being screwed. You know that, right?"

His agent made a petulant, impatient sound that matched his quick glance at the cell phone resting atop his desk. Probably late for a three-martini lunch with some barely legal starlet he was trying to bed. Suddenly Tucker reveled in making him late. "Being screwed how, exactly? By having one of the biggest salaries on the show? By getting two weeks off every three months of shooting? By being wined and dined by every studio in town so you'll work for them the minute *Suburban Dead* wraps for good? How, exactly, is one of the hottest stars in town getting screwed, pray tell?"

Tucker took a deep breath. He remembered Summer's counsel that sunny day back in Redfern—the empty patio, the sangria in their bellies, and her mouth moving a mile a minute with plans for Tucker's otherwise doomed relationship with Reed. "If I truly am one of the hottest stars in town at the moment, Randolph, then what does that make you, huh?"

Randolph sat slightly back, the cocky grin on his smarmy face fizzling like flat champagne the morning after a catered affair. "I'm not sure I catch your meaning, Tuck."

Tucker glanced at the wall. The paper covering it was a reedy, textured fabric, like gray flannel to match the black bookshelves and floor-to-ceiling window facing downtown LA. The head shots of Randolph's clients lined the wall—a dozen or so sleek black frames, each bearing a glossy black-and-white eight-by-ten photo inside. Tucker's head shot was front and center, top left where the eye went first. Next to his was a young pop star who'd just gone to rehab and whose sophomore album had been delayed for the third time this year. Beside her was a fading action star with a blossoming direct-to-video career in his future. Beneath them was another row of similar sad stories, recognizable faces either on their way up the Hollywood ladder or inching back down, year by disappointing year. Randolph's eyes followed, and he winced as they did.

"I'd say if it wasn't for me, Randolph, you'd still be three floors down and just above the mailroom. That's where all the new agents start, right?"

Randolph waved a hand. His fancy watch glinted in the midday sun. "Tucker, I see where you're going with this, but even before I came to you, I was already scheduled for a promotion."

"Before you? Came to me?" Tucker let out a deep, resonant chuckle as if he was in front of the camera. "Now who's rewriting history, Randolph? As I recall, I had a contract from the folks at *Suburban Dead* in hand when I walked through those fancy doors downstairs almost five years ago, and since nobody had heard of the show yet, let alone little old me, they yanked you out of the bullpen, and you reluctantly took me on as a client as if you were doing me some kind of a favor. That was, until you saw the contract, realized the figures they were talking about, and snatched me up faster than you can say 'bonus check.'"

Randolph had recovered his cool composure. He was an agent, all things considered. Fact was, he was probably a better actor than Tucker. Not that that was saying much. "Low figures, by industry standards, Tucker. If anything, I negotiated a much higher figure the following season."

"Perhaps, but still a far sight less than literally any of my costars. Would we agree on that point?"

Randolph reached for a bottled water on his desk, drank loudly, and slid the cap back on. "So I'm a bad agent, is that what this meeting is about?"

"Not at all," Tucker replied cordially, following Summer's script to the letter. "Just a lazy one."

"Beg pardon?" Randolph's desk chair squeaked as he sat up in protest, palms flat on his desk like a small child sitting at his father's desk on bring-your-kids-to-work day.

"Everything I've gotten, Randolph, I've done myself. I'm the one who has to negotiate with Costas for a raise every year. I'm the one who has to go on social media and keep the fans interested in my character every season. If I've lasted longer than ninety percent of the kids I started working with four seasons ago, it's because I hustle and hump every day I'm on set, and twice as hard during hiatus. In return, I'm asking for the two weeks I was promised with my swim coach. Period. Does that sound unreasonable to you, *Randolph*?"

Randolph sighed and scrubbed his face impatiently. More minutes ticked away until he could rendezvous with his midafternoon delight. "Not unreasonable, Tucker. Just... unlikely."

Tucker's fixed smile dimmed to a small thin-lipped smirk. "Then make it likely, Randolph. Or I can have someone else here at TalentCo negotiate next year's contract, capisce?"

As Randolph sat petulantly across from Tucker, absorbing the news with flared nostrils and a flushed brow, a booming voice interrupted the awkward silence in the stuffy, stilted room.

Right on time. Tucker stifled a relieved smile.

"Is he in there?"

Endorphins flooded his body with a surge of fortified relief. For a moment there, glancing at his phone in the wake of his uncharacteristically diva-like ultimatum, he wasn't sure she'd show. Tucker risked a knowing glance at his agent's face and found it contorted with confusion and a hefty dose of irritation.

"What *now*?" he muttered aloud, desk chair creaking as he turned to face the door as if to hear better.

From the other side of the surprisingly thin door, the assistant's voice sounded young, startled, and obviously starstruck. "Ms. Stevenson, how nice to see you," the intern stammered as Tucker's agent reeled like he'd just been slapped. "Big fan here, by the way. Can't wait for next season. Leaving us on a cliffhanger like that? You all should be ashamed of yourselves, girl. Uh, however, Mr. Starkey is in a meeting with a client at the moment."

Randolph Starkey, all five foot four of him, was standing at his full height when Summer strode into the room, regal and classy in a little black dress and stiletto heels. She whipped off her trademark bug-eye black sunglasses and fixed Tucker's startled agent with a dazzling grin.

"Mr. Starkey, I presume?" Before Tucker's stammering, red-faced agent could respond, she stuck out a hand and pumped Randolph's eagerly. "I'm so glad to finally meet you!"

Tucker grinned behind his hand as Summer really hammed it up.

Tucker sat on the sidelines and watched it all happen as if viewing it from another room entirely. He'd always known Randolph was a climber, but watching him with Summer—flushed and perspiring and stammering and gawking—made it clear where Tucker resided on the pecking order of fame.

"To what do I owe the honor?" Randolph yammered, all but urging Tucker to move over and make way for Summer's grand entrance as she ignored the chair right next to him in favor of standing regally in front of the massive floor-to-ceiling window.

As ever, Tucker thought to himself, *a good actress finds the spotlight!*

Summer rolled her eyes and clutched her delicate pearl necklace as if flattered he might ask. "Oh, well, I was just visiting my own agent, Peyton Principle, on the top floor. You know, in the penthouse suite? Anyway, we always get together over the hiatus each season and talk about our goals for the coming fiscal year—coordinate with the media team, field my offers for downtime, that kind of thing."

Summer reached over and squeezed Tucker's shoulder dramatically. Then she glanced pointedly at Randolph. "I heard Tuck here was gonna be doing the same with you this afternoon, so I thought I'd pop in and see how things are going." She let the implied threat of parental supervision linger awkwardly in the air and at last glanced down at Tucker. "So, bud, how *are* things going?"

As they'd semirehearsed that simmering late summer afternoon on that brewery patio a few days earlier, Tucker ignored Randolph and sighed. Heavily. "Not as good as your summit meeting with one of the agency's managing partners, Summer. I've been here, what... fifteen minutes? Haven't heard of a single offer for the off season."

Summer gradually shifted her position so that her left shoulder was facing his agent, who still stood, mouth agape at the star-studded intrusion.

She took a deep breath and then gushed dramatically, "Wow, that's crazy, Tuck. Just now I signed for an indy romance with the director of *Interview With a Zombie 3* and a small role in next year's installment of *Robot Martian Invasion 7*. You know, if you're interested, I could introduce you to the team upstairs. I mean, it kinda feels like you're ready for the big time by now, huh, Tuck?"

Tucker almost forgot Randolph was there as he and Summer improvised and riffed through the brief exchange. It was just like being on set, only the closest thing to the living dead threatening them at the moment was his mouth-breathing, actual dud of an agent. Tucker made a *way*-over-the-top "Oh, golly, jeepers" face before really laying it on thick. "Gosh, could you? I mean, I just feel like my career has already stalled, and I'm just getting started, you know?"

"Now hold on a minute!" Randolph had eased slightly around the desk to sit on one corner, cool-teacher style, while trying to interject between the two costars.

Summer's face looked vaguely irritated, and Tuck wasn't sure she was acting. He was almost certain the next words out of her mouth would be something along the lines of, "Hush, kid, grown-ups are talking." Instead she merely fixed him with a curt semigrin and said, "We're listening."

"Tucker just got here," Randolph assured her. "He was so busy talking about this silly swimming issue that I haven't gotten to the stack of offers we've got coming up for him."

As if to emphasize, Randolph ran his fingers along a stack of scripts near where he'd slid onto the desk. But Summer had seen her opportunity and pounced. "That reminds me, I assume you've approved an additional week of coaching for Tuck already? Right? I mean, wasn't that why you came here today?" Again she squeezed Tuck's shoulder.

He scowled, not acting either. "Wait'll you get a load of this," he started to say slowly, giving Randolph plenty of time to interrupt.

Predictably Randolph stood back up with aplomb but still managed to only come up to Summer's chin. "As a matter of fact, we were just wrapping that discussion up. Obviously, no one wants a repeat of last month's viral video once filming starts up on season five, so of course we'll get him that swim coach." He reached over and squeezed Tucker's other shoulder reassuringly. "I mean, obviously."

Summer improvised yet again, surprising even Tucker with her brilliance, not to mention her giant brass balls. "And obviously, since Scream Studios has already rented Camp Run-A-Mok out through the end of August, they'll be continuing their lessons there, correct?"

Randolph stammered, face falling slightly as if he'd had other plans for the rest of the month. Or more than likely, none at all. "Well, we haven't hammered out all the details yet but... obviously. Why waste the space, right? I mean, if you guys give me a few minutes while you wait out in the reception area, I'll make a few calls and nail it all down."

Summer tugged Tucker's sleeve and dragged him gently up to a standing position. Together they stood shoulder to shoulder, towering over Randolph as he retreated, yet again, behind his clear, angular, modern desk. "Great idea, and while you're doing that, I think we'll skip the wait and just head on upstairs anyway. I'd like to introduce Tucker to my agents if… you don't mind?"

Randolph's hand was on a landline, frozen and white-knuckled like the expression on his crestfallen face. "I mean, no need for all that, right, Tucker?"

Tucker swallowed. Hard. It wasn't necessarily in his nature to be petty or cruel or even to act while the camera wasn't rolling. But much had changed in the week he'd spent with Reed, and falling in love had also included having more affection for the career he had somehow stumbled upon. "I mean, it wouldn't hurt to just have a conversation with someone else here at the agency, right, Randy? I mean—" He waved a steady hand at his agent's Wall of Fame. "Kind of like you don't only have one client, why shouldn't I explore a few possibilities of my own, right?"

Summer led him to the door and walked slowly to give Randy plenty of time to make a counteroffer. "I'm sure that won't be necessary," he said, all but blocking their progress. "Come to think of it, why don't you two sit back down and I'll return some calls while you're here, okay?"

Summer's hand was on the doorknob, turning it pointedly. She glanced back at Tucker and offered a dramatic eyebrow arch. "I mean, as long as you start with that call to Camp Run-A-Mok and finish with Tuck here's swim coach, I don't see the harm in spending a little more time down here in the trenches with you, right, Tucker?"

Tucker escorted her back to her chair. "I mean, what could it hurt?"

Randolph beamed, fingers flying across the keypad as he prepared to fire off a quick call to the camp where, if all went as planned, he and Reed would be returning by the following afternoon.

While he waited for the call to connect, he gushed, "I've got some great offers for you after this season wraps, Tucker. For instance, there's a superhero flick that just lost its costar to a softball injury, if you can believe that. I think you'd be great for the part, and—yes, Mr. Tatum? Randolph Starkey here, the one who coordinated renting out your camp last month. Yes, well, believe it or not…."

Beside Tuck, Summer sank into her seat with a triumphant, elegant grin. Tucker reminded himself to get her autograph before his time on *Suburban Dead* was finally over, because it was clear that, given today's performance, she was going to be a big star one day.

THIRTY-FOUR

Reed

"CAN I help you?"

Reed sat in his broom closet of an office at a desk cluttered with class schedules, spreadsheets, and charts of last practice's performance evaluations and peered at a frazzled stranger in a familiar brown uniform standing just outside the door.

A delivery man, shy, vaguely chagrined, and definitely out of breath, stood in the hallway, struggling with a package almost his exact size.

His voice was as uncertain as his expression. "Delivery for Reed Chancelor?"

Reed put down the single page of typewritten text, centered just so on a stiff piece of Eastern Georgia State letterhead, glad for a chance to quit rereading it for perhaps the seven millionth time that morning.

He cocked his head and mumbled, "That's me, but I'm certainly not expecting anything from anyone, and certainly not anything so *big*."

The driver squinted some more and read the name on the label. "Reed Chancelor, Swim Coach Extraordinaire, Eastern Georgia State. That's you, that's here, right?"

"Swim Coach Extraordinaire?" Reed murmured to himself, a vaguely suspicious feeling growing in his suddenly tensed gut and merging with a hopefulness he dared not entertain. "The hell?"

Reed stood and took two quick steps past his desk to help the poor delivery guy set the box down. Although it was big and unwieldly, the surprise package wasn't necessarily heavy. His mind raced, alert and exposed and awakened after his days-long stupor.

"Who's it from, anyway?"

The delivery guy squinted at the address on the return label. "Scream Studios." He stammered out an unknown address from Los Angeles. "That's all it says."

Reed let out a silky sigh.

"Something wrong?" The driver saw Reed's face as he stood, literally frozen with arms outstretched and mouth agape. He must have looked just like one of the zombies from Tucker's hit TV series.

The question roused him from his daydream. Reed scrambled for his wallet, found a crumpled five-dollar bill folded in the back—change from a smoothie earlier in the day—and foisted it on the hapless UPS driver before he could think twice. "No, nothing's wrong. Thank you." He spoke too loud, too fast, handed over the crumpled five too eagerly, and all but pushed the deliveryman from the doorway. "Thank you very much."

The driver drifted away down the corridor of the athletic building offices, and Reed tugged at the cardboard box until at last it began to give way. He was vaguely aware of the panting, grunting sounds coming from his own mouth as he struggled with the viselike grip the packing container had on the contents inside until his floor resembled a carpenter's workshop, littered with buzzsaw fragments of cardboard, packing tape, Styrofoam, and shipping plastic.

What remained was a canvas poster, big enough to take up most of his tiny office wall should he ever choose to hang it, or if he ever figured out what it was and why Tucker or someone close to Tucker back at Scream Studios had decided to capture and blow it up, let alone send it to him.

He recognized it immediately, of course. It was a photo of Tucker and Summer cloistered together at one of the rustic picnic tables in the scenic, private courtyard of the Brickhouse Brewery back in Redfern, Georgia.

The sight of Tucker's preppy outfit and glowing, radiant skin immediately set Reed's heart racing as he recalled what they'd done to each other, with each other, for each other only hours before the picture was taken—only hours before the outside world intruded and their doomed romance imploded.

It was clearly one of the photos snapped by the hired team of freelance photographers Summer had dragged down with her from Atlanta to document their fake romance, but the quality was all off. In the pictures that had gone viral in the days following the staged photo shoot, the couple was front and center, and a dozen different versions of them canoodling, conspiring, and preening made the rounds. Reed knew that because his phone still pinged with new social media alerts every few minutes.

The quality, the lighting, the framing, the composition of those other photos was far superior to this one, and not just because it was blown up to almost magnified proportions. Not only were the happy couple out of focus, but they were nearly cropped out of the photo altogether, relegated to a far corner of the frame until something else, even someone else entirely, was the subject of the photo's center focus.

Pulling himself away from the vaguely blurry image of Tucker and Summer in the corner of the frame, Reed's eyes dragged closer to the center, past the potted plants, the swaying bulbs, the patio itself, and to the brick exterior of the brewery and the picture's central focus—Reed himself.

Perhaps the photographer thought Reed was another shutterbug, lurking around the corner and waiting to whip out his Nikon camera and join the fray. Maybe he just wondered who this poorly disguised clown was, watching Tucker and Summer cavort and canoodle from afar. Either way, it was clearly Reed in the picture, looking ridiculous in the blown-up image, ball cap down, jacket zipped up, face a mask of shock.

But clearly, whoever sent the poster to his office realized it was him and apparently found it curious enough to… what, exactly? Reed wasn't quite sure. Blow it up into a canvas print suitable for framing and then ship it to him all the way from LA.

He reached to slide it closer to the wall and out of the way but felt something taped to the back corner. He turned the frame to find a brief note scribbled on Scream Studios stationery. Reed's heart grew a size with each syllable as he read the handwritten note taped there. "So you do love me, after all. Yours forever, Tuck."

As if on cue, a bray of laughter, then surprise, then, amazingly, applause, sounded like a bugle horn from outside his office window and dragged him out of his romantic reverie. Reed wiped stupid, soggy, sappy tears from his eyes and tore himself away from the touchingly romantic, even sentimental, gift to seek out the source of the sudden spectacle downstairs.

Outside his office widow, which was surprisingly big for such a sparse room, Reed heard giggles and squeals as he set the canvas down.

The squealing intensified the closer he got to the window, but not just because of proximity. Below, on the vast deck that surrounded a series of swimming pools, the girls' team had clustered in a vibrating pack and leaped up and down as powder blue T-shirts were tossed at them like beads off a passing Mardi Gras float.

"The hell…" he murmured to himself, alone in his office as one of the swimmers opened up the shirt to reveal the telltale *Suburban Dead* logo. "is going on?"

He hastened past the canvas, feeling flushed and embarrassed but most of all flattered all over again. Down the empty hallway and around the corner, he took the steps two at a time and then pushed through the double doors that led to the pool area. He nearly needed earplugs, the noise was so deafening once he stumbled outside.

In a few moments and even fewer steps, Reed suddenly learned why—Tucker was standing on the bottom step, tossing the last of a stack of T-shirts from an open cardboard box at his feet.

And the girls' swim team was eating.

It.

Up.

"Tucker, what the hell?" Reed's voice somehow managed to be stern and professional despite the fluttering butterflies duking it out with the hearts, rainbows, and daisies that filled his nervous belly.

Tucker held up the index finger of his free hand as he tossed another fluttering, unfolding T-shirt into the crowd, and a dozen or so normally mild-mannered, well-behaved, perfectly respectable perfectionists of their craft suddenly lost their damn minds. Reed felt like he'd just stumbled into the front row of a Backstreet Boys concert in the mid-'90s.

While he was reaching into the box for more and still not answering him, Kira emerged from the crowd, struggling into a crisp new *Suburban Dead* T-shirt of her own and beaming with pride as if she had stumbled onto the red carpet at the Met Gala.

"Sorry, Reed, I should have warned you, but…," she shouted over the din of screaming girls and giggling girls and girls fighting over twelve-dollar TV show T-shirts even as Tucker continued to pelt them with more until they each were wriggling into them, one by one, over their one-piece practice suits. "But Tucker thought he might practice with the girls today, you know? Just for fun."

Reed couldn't ignore the tingle that shuddered through his entire body. "Did he now?"

Tucker threw the last T-shirt to the last swimmer, and cheers erupted through the normally sedate swim team as they turned to each other, unfolding and wriggling and squeezing into their new prizes as Reed anxiously awaited a nod or a glance from his surprise visitor.

And then, the minute Tuck turned, the girls were back at him. "Let's go, Tucker," squealed Madison McClain, their best swimmer in the breaststroke division. "Show us what you've got!"

As if on cue, a dozen wily swimmers tugged cell phones out of thin air and aimed them at the not-so-reluctant TV star. One by one, they peppered him with taunts and come-ons as they basically tugged him toward the pool. And away from Reed.

"Girls!" Reed struggled to control the chaos, but as he tried to follow Tucker down the steps and toward the practice pool, a gentle hand tugged Reed back to where he stood.

"This is what he wanted." Kira nodded as Tucker pretended to blush and squirm, all the while tugging off his own matching *Suburban Dead* T-shirt to reveal his glowing, glistening physique to squeals of amplified delight.

"But why here?" Reed mused as cameras flashed and videos rolled. Tucker posed with the swim team in various stages of undress until at last he stood in front of an empty lane, staggeringly beautiful in the low, sagging baggies he used to favor back at camp.

"Jesus." Kira nudged Reed's hip. "That boy is even prettier in person, and that's saying something."

"Careful," Reed murmured as Tucker made a big show of flexing for the cameras and mugging in general. It was strange, seeing his old friend and young lover interact with actual fans, clearly a natural on-screen and off, making Reed's heart swell with pride. "He's taken."

Kira nodded at the writhing mass of swimmers who surrounded Tucker on the pool ledge. "Sure, if he survives one swim practice with our clearly hormonal girls' team."

As if to escape or, Reed mused, to secure a fresh viral video of himself actually swimming for a change, Tucker made the final leap into the pool. The girls applauded—Kira too, Reed noticed wryly from her side—as water splashed their feet and Tucker, just as he had back at Camp Run-A-Mok, began to kick and pull and tug and slice through the water.

Although he probably couldn't hear them, the girls screamed and applauded, cameras at the ready, some snapping pics, some shooting footage, all fixated on Tucker as he kicked and sliced and reached the other end of the pool in record time.

He emerged dripping and glowing and triumphant, clinging as always to the wet pool tiles with one white-knuckled fist while he triumphantly pumped his free fist in the air. The resulting screams were deafening, and not just from the swim team. The adults were cheering him on as well, and Reed hoped Tucker could see through the maddening crowd and find the smile of pride beaming across his old coach's face.

And of course, the fresh tears of joy.

THIRTY-FIVE

Tucker

"SURPRISED?"

Tucker stood, admiring the canvas print he'd packed up and sent the night before where it still leaned against the wall by the filing cabinet in the small, cluttered office that made his agent's back in LA look like a hotel ballroom by comparison. Reed sank heavily into his desk chair, as if to keep his distance from the TV star who'd followed him all the way home.

"Uh, yeah, you could say that." His voice might have sounded aloof, but Reed's eyes were kind and searching.

Tucker sank into the chair across from his desk. He was still damp from his practice with the girls' team and fidgeting in the Eastern Georgia State tracksuit Kira had gifted him as he finally rose from the pool, triumphant and tired, mission finally accomplished.

Well, the viral-video portion of it, anyway.

The happy ending part remained to be seen.

"Why, though?"

Reed gave him a curious glance over his crowded desktop. In the awkward silence, Tucker tried not to notice how depressing, cramped, sterile, routine, and downright basic the office looked and how poorly it fit the dynamic and clever man he knew Reed to be. As he sat there, still smelling of chlorine and finger combing his hair back into place, Tucker felt better and better about visiting Reed and why he'd come to visit in the first place.

"I told you we weren't through yet, Reed."

"You didn't tell me anything, Tuck."

"I never had a chance to, Reed. And for the record, you never said shit to me either, *Coach*."

Reed rolled his eyes the way he had a million times during their week together back at camp. "Your stupid, big, fat, hairy producer never gave me the chance that morning, Tucker."

They both snorted. "Hey, they tricked me too, Reed. I thought Summer flew down to Georgia on her own. I didn't know they'd come together to roust us out of our happy home away from home."

Reed eased back into his squeaky desk chair. Beside the late morning light filtering in through the big window behind him, Reed was the only flattering thing in the room. "We *were* happy, right? I wasn't just imagining it."

Tucker was in full-on rescue mission mode at the moment and in no mood to suffer any of Reed's insecurities or doubts. "Of course we were. Now stop all that and let me explain—"

"And this is really you, right? Sitting there across from my desk? Swimming down there? Taking pictures with the kids? You're not Tucker's stunt double or some Hollywood special-effects magic, are you?"

"Not sure what kind of budget you think Scream Studios is working with these days, Reed, but no, we don't have the money to clone people just yet. So it's me. All me. I'm just... sorry it took me so long to get down here. I had to do some major shucking and jiving back home, and then coordinate with Kira down here, and of course, the folks back at camp, but—"

"Kira?"

Tucker nodded and leaned slightly forward until he met Reed's eyes, so soft and brown and curious. "That's right, Reed. Kira told me a little more about the struggles you've been having with the folks here at school, so I thought a little VIP visit, some good press, and putting you forward in all the pictures might ease things up a bit for you here. That is, if you want them eased up."

Reed nodding knowingly. "So that's what all that was about?"

Tucker smirked. "Partially. I mean, the studio thought it was as good a time as any to unveil my new skills in the swimming pool, and I thought, why not kill two birds with one stone while I'm in town, right?"

As if on cue, Reed's phone dinged. Tucker glanced over curiously to find him peering at the screen, scrolling through what looked like one or more social media sites, nodding his approval and smiling with every swipe of his finger. "Looks like it's working," he said as he handed over the phone.

Tucker leaned forward to take it and saw the first few Instagram and Facebook posts by the girls on the swim team—still pictures of him smiling and tossing out shirts, posing with the team, and then, splashing and gurgling, the first shaky cam footage of him slicing effortlessly through the

water, turning and raising his fist in triumph from the deep end as, in the
background, the girls' team hooted and hollered their approval. Just beyond
them, on the steps, Reed and Kira jumped, hugged, high-fived, and cheered
him on in unison. It brought a surprised grin to Tucker's beaming face.

He was impressed with the footage, satisfied and at peace that
whatever viral moment he'd had a month earlier would soon be forgotten
just in time for them to start filming season five next month. But he was
even more impressed with Reed.

He handed back the phone with its still-pinging screen. "So you set
up an alert about me, huh, Coach?"

Reed rolled his eyes, avoiding Tucker's cocky, knowing glance in
the process. "I set one for the show, Tucker, when I first got the gig, to
see what I was getting myself into. After we broke up, I just never had
the heart to turn it off."

"Broke up my ass." Tucker forcefully tapped the edge of Reed's
desk like a judge hammering down his gavel in a crowded courtroom.
"This was nothing more than a temporary interruption, that's all."

"For you, maybe." Reed waved his hand across his desk, at his tiny
little tin can of a campus office. "But I'm back to real life, as you can
clearly see."

Tucker sat back in his chair. "Yeah, about that."

"What about it, kid? We had our fun. You start shooting soon, I've
got a swim season coming up, and hey, what's with the face, Tuck?"

"Listen, before you get mad at me, I've squared everything with
Kira and she's squared it with the department, and I might have even
gotten the team to approve between tossing out T-shirts and whatnot, but
we're going back to camp."

Reed sighed heavily and crossed his arms over his chest, making
Tucker feel like he was back in the principal's office all those years ago.
"We're not going back to camp, Tucker."

"Yeah-huh we are." Tucker felt, as he must have surely sounded,
like a five-year-old insisting the moon was made of cheese.

Reed's clattery old desk chair creaked predictably as he leaned slightly
forward and pinned Tuck with those soft brown eyes. "Tucker, listen, I'm
glad you're here. I really am. Seeing you live in person, out of the blue,
getting that poster in the mail today, watching you with the kids, and Kira,
and swimming, my God, it's downright heartwarming, is what it is. I never
thought I'd see you again. But I can't keep doing this with you."

"We're not even doing anything yet."

"Exactly, Tuck, and that's the way we're keeping it."

"You're not the boss of me, Reed."

"Tucker, you just spent an entire hour downstairs telling those college athletes that I'm absolutely the boss of you and that's why you can swim the way you do now, so don't come down here telling me I'm not the boss of you because, hey, what are you doing? Where are you going? Stay the hell away from me, Tuck. I'm actually, absolutely warning you to—"

Tucker stomped over to Reed and shook him by the shoulders until they were both chuckling nervously. As if to prove to Reed he wasn't going to actually try anything in his campus office, God forbid, Tucker reluctantly sank onto the edge of his desktop and kept his hands to himself.

For now, anyway.

"The studio has already rented out the camp for the rest of the month. They paid you, handsomely, I might add, though you wouldn't know it from this shit box of an office, to coach me for two weeks. Doing the quick math, that means you still owe me a week of your, uh, undivided attention, *Coach*."

Reed was still shaking his head, but Tucker could see the diminishing of resolve in each stubborn, weakening protest. When he spoke at last, the aching in Reed's voice made it clear he wasn't just acting but in an honest-to-goodness fight with his heart. "And what happens when the week's over, Tuck?" His voice, barely above a whisper, was mostly a hoarse, pitiful croak. "What then? I have to start all over again, and you get to fly off, back to Hollywood, and I get to take another four straight days of lying in bed trying to get over you, only it's even harder this time because there will be no more camp, no more surprise visits, no more viral videos and—"

"Who says?" Tuck burst out as he slid a foot between Reed's legs, but not to flirt. Instead he kicked gently until the rolling desk chair swiveled and scooted out, back against the window, a surprised Reed along with it.

"Who says there'll be no camp next year? Who says I just don't rent it out every August with my year-end bonus money, huh, Coach? Who says I don't just flat-out buy the damn place and we can move in together when my run on *Suburban Dead* ends? And for that matter, who the hell says I wasn't lying in bed the last four days trying to get over *your* stubborn, sorry ass my own damn self?"

Reed sat, hands clenched on the sides of his desk chair as if Tuck might lash out and send him rolling in a whole other direction. Tucker stood to continue his soliloquy as the papers he'd been sitting on cascaded to the floor.

"Oh, that's right," he huffed as he paced back and forth in front of Reed in his ill-fitting tracksuit, the zipper scratching his bare belly. "I didn't have time to lie around in bed feeling sorry for myself for four whole days because I've spent every waking minute since Summer tricked me into leaving Camp Run-A-Mok with her finagling and calling and plotting and planning to get my ass, and your ass—that means our asses—back there as soon as I possibly could. And this is me getting back here as soon as I possibly could, so if you think for one minute I'm going to let you out of your contractual commitment to me and Scream Studios, you are sadly mistaken, Reed Chancelor."

Tucker found himself standing at his full height, chest puffed out, face red, winded from the effort of trying to convince Reed just how in love they both undeniably were. Reed sat, a bemused expression on his face, and watched as Tucker bent to pick up the fallen papers.

"Are you quite through?" Reed murmured from behind him as Tucker slid the paperwork back onto the desk. One item stood out—a single crisp piece of letterhead that began with the words, "To whom it may concern...."

Nosy as hell, Tucker scanned the page quickly and then turned to wave it in Reed's face accusingly. "The hell is this, Coach?"

Reed looked chagrined but defiant as he reached for the sheet of paper. Tucker, still standing, held it out of reach. "Is this what I think it is?"

"If you think it's a letter of resignation from Eastern Georgia State, then yes, Tucker, it is."

Tucker sank back onto the desk, this time before the wind left his sails completely. "When did you decide this?"

"About an hour before your showboating ass showed up on campus to hand out T-shirts like some rock star, that's when."

"But, I mean, what were you going to do if I didn't show up to rescue your tired old ass?"

Reed turned his chair slightly to one side, then the other, and swiveled gently from side to side as he glanced somewhere just over Tucker's shoulder. "I actually don't know, Tucker. I just know that, ever since I got back here, the thought of another swim season on the sidelines, waiting for the college board to take me off of academic probation, seemed more than a little unpalatable to me."

"But the kids this morning, they love you. Kira, on the phone this weekend as we chatted to set all this up, spoke so highly of you."

Reed smiled for the first time in minutes. "I love them too. I'll miss them—all of them, every last one. But I should have quit when the scandal broke, you know? Kira understands, trust me. I think, in a way, she's relieved."

"Kira knows? She never said a word over the last two days of planning this little field trip down here."

"She's loyal, Tuck. That means a lot to me."

"What? Like I'm not?"

Reed peered up curiously from where he still sat, desk chair in front of the picture window. "I never said that, Tucker, but the fact is, I don't know you that way. Not really."

Tucker didn't miss a beat. "Well, this here's your chance to get to know me, smartass. Inside and out. You know, when you and I get in the car I rented and packed with goodies downstairs and get back to Camp Run-A-Mok, as soon as you drag that sorry ass of yours out of that rickety old desk chair."

Reed started to say something, but Tucker interrupted him. "And don't give me some lame-ass excuse about not wanting to be outed or dodging another scandal or whatever malarkey you've got going on in that thick skull of yours, because, wait—what are you doing?"

Reed stood up and, without another word, kissed him. Soft, gentle, warm and familiar, it was neither the beginning of something more nor the end of something less. It was simply a kiss—a calm, quiet, tender, romantic kiss.

"I *do* have excuses, Tucker, dozens of them. Why I shouldn't go with you, why it's a bad idea, why this will hurt harder than anything else I've ever done in my life when it's over, why you're no good for me, why there's no way any of this will ever work and... and...."

"And?" Tucker watched Reed grab an Eastern Georgia State backpack off a lopsided coat rack in the corner of his office.

"And," he said as he slung it over one shoulder and reached for Tucker's hand, "we can talk all about them on the way back to camp, Tuck."

THIRTY-SIX

Reed

"PRETTY SURE this is how every cheesy '80s horror movie starts, Tucker." Reed glanced around at the deserted camp, the dark trees foreboding as they towered overhead, the rustling leaves a warning, the crackling fire cloaking all sounds of a masked intruder stalking them with a bloody machete.

Wrapped in Reed's arms as the fire pit crackled to one side, Tucker murmured, "Yeah. Big, fat gay ones."

Reed nuzzled Tucker's ear as they lounged by the fire pit on an old flannel blanket they'd found in storage and unfolded for a late-night picnic where, obviously, Tucker was the main course.

"Oh, suddenly you're an expert now?"

Tucker kissed the words out of his mouth, which tasted like the white wine they'd been sipping on ever since they adjourned to the fire pit after a dinner in the mess hall kitchen. It was just like old times, but both of them seemed to realize tonight was the beginning of something altogether new.

When Tucker released him, they peered at each other in the fire's glow. Tucker wore a simple white V-neck T-shirt and a pair of navy blue shorts dotted with little pink flamingos. His hair was getting long—shaggy even—and the feathery brown curls framed his lean, handsome face. He looked like he'd stepped off a sailboat. His lips were full and moist, so kissable Reed almost dragged him in for another soul-crushing embrace.

"Reed, honestly? You make me feel like I know everything about everything and absolutely nothing about anything, you know?"

Reed chuckled. He hardly believed he was back at camp, basking in the fire's romantic glow and the familiar throb in his gut that said something very big, very sexy, very new was about to happen any minute.

"Not even a little, kid." He shivered with delight as Tucker reached out to tug at the top button of his collared short-sleeved shirt and tease it open another inch or two as the thick velvet cloak of humidity inched across his exposed flesh.

They sat, as ever, legs crossed and knees touching, the clear sky blue-black as midnight approached and the dramatic splash of light from the flickering fire accented their faces.

Tucked wanted it this way—insisted upon it, in fact. He had finagled and wriggled and molded Reed into place until they sat, face-to-face and intimately connected, a long simmer to ease them back into the cocoon of intimacy they'd shared before real life interrupted them so unexpectedly.

Tucker took his time unbuttoning Reed's shirt, making sure to drizzle a spare fingertip across his glistening skin every so often, sending shivers through Reed's body as he fumbled with Tuck's shirt. He made quick work of the fancy V-neck and tossed it to one side. Tucker returned the favor. He thumbed loose the last few buttons and tugged Reed's shirt off until they slithered against each other, chests bare and slick with humidity as the last of the day's heat seemed to take revenge for their late arrival back to Camp Run-A-Mok.

They were flirty and familiar in the car, but it had taken a hundred miles or more for the initial awkwardness of reuniting to wear off. By the time they got to the tiny town of Redfern to stock up for the long week ahead, they no longer cared who might see them or even how many. Instead they lingered in the grocery store aisles like an old married couple, fussing over wine bottles, counting calories, and nuzzling hips as they neared the checkout aisle. But along the way, every secret glance and murmured come-on, teasing joke and lingering look had led to this very moment.

Now, hours later, they wasted little time in tugging off the rest of their clothes, casting them aside in growing piles as shoes and shorts and belts and socks flew like toys from a chest as a frustrated toddler searched all the way to the bottom for his favorite teddy bear.

As ever, they sat, thigh covering thigh, groins desperately close, bare chests heaving and aglow with perspiration as they continued to kiss and caress each other into a mounting, murmuring frenzy that had been building ever since they met.

Tucker, in particular, was greedier than Reed remembered—or perhaps just eager to fill this last piece of the puzzle and lose his V card once and for all. He ground his package against Reed's, both of them stiff and sticky as the fire crackled and the heat sweltered between and around them.

Reed was more than happy to take the ride and watch Tuck twist and writhe as he reached out with desperate fingers to tenderly caress and stroke Reed's shaft. The friction was incredible—slick and damp and noisy in the heat of the deep Georgia night.

Reed gave in to the sensation and placed his arms out on either side of him, palms down on the faded blanket for support as he let his eyes close and his head fall back, Reed caressed and stroked him to a proper lather that sounded as good as it felt. The rhythm grew intense but never too much—they both wanted the evening to last as darkness surrounded them.

Tucker eased his grip, weight shifting gradually as he eased slightly back, tugged Reed gently forward, and dragged the poor comforter along with him. Once positioned, Tucker leaned forward to slather Reed's cock with deep, moist kisses that threatened to derail their plans for the evening in record time.

Reed had forgotten how slow and probing Tucker's mouth could be, how eager and affectionate his lips and mouth could be around the swollen tip, the veiny shaft, and the tender, wrinkled flesh where both met. He had almost forgotten the heat and the intoxicating pressure as he reached beneath Reed to squeeze and hold firm to his cheeks, which he used as a guide to slither him in and out of his lips' clingy, warm embrace.

"Tucker," Reed gasped as he nearly came, and Tucker released him from between his glistening lips and winked as he continued to stroke him in reply.

"Sorry." Tucker eased Reed's backside down onto the picnic blanket and writhed his way back up his thighs. "I got a little carried away. I guess I forgot how good you taste."

Reed blushed and then reached out to return the favor. "Your turn," he murmured, but Tucker batted his hand playfully away and wriggled higher onto Reed's lap. "We've got all week for that. Tonight I want you inside of me, once and for all."

Their eyes met in the deepening dark, faces aglow as Reed swallowed hard. "Tucker, be sure."

"Oh my God," Tucker said. "I've had nothing but time to make sure I was sure, and now I'm totally, absolutely, four thousand percent sure, so hurry before you dry up again!"

Reed's erection throbbed. It was literally slathered with Tucker's juices and his own. "So that's why you were extra sloppy just now, huh, kid?"

"Well, I didn't hear you complaining," Tucker grunted as Reed sat up to face him. They kissed, and Tucker's lips were slick and tasted of Reed's own savory musk.

When he let Tucker up, he reached down and cupped the smooth, meaty flesh of each ripe, round buttock. "Tell me if I'm going too fast, okay?" He nuzzled Tuck's ear as he gently moved him into position.

"It's okay." Tuck flicked a tongue in his ear as he confessed, "I picked up a few toys the other day and have been, uh, experimenting a little in your absence."

Reed's chuckle was low and deep, like the groan in Tucker's voice as he pressed the tip of his cock against the tight, puckered star of Tuck's velvet hole. The resulting murmur was deep and resounding as they wriggled and squirmed until, ever so gently, Reed felt and could have sworn he practically heard, the pressure and slight "pop" of insertion.

They froze face-to-face, arms and legs akimbo as time seemed to crawl to a stop.

Reed watched Tucker's face closely, admiring the velvet beauty of his smooth young skin as Tuck's eyelids fluttered open and shut with mounting ecstasy. When their open eyes at last met, illuminated by the flickering fire pit at their side, Tucker smirked and nodded as, with gravity and greed, he sank an inch down the heft of Reed's swollen prick.

"Jesus!"

They both gasped in unison, squirming and writhing as, inch by sweaty inch, moment by careful moment, gasp by greedy gasp, Reed stood his ground and, rather than plunge ahead, continued to use the top half of his member to prime Tucker's young, tender rump. Achingly, almost glacially, he slid back and forth, never entering all the way, always mindful of Tucker's tender, swollen virginity as it clung to his stiff, trembling cock.

While he was more than content to while away the evening, teasing and widening Tuck's tender newness, Tucker once again took the reins and sank another two inches down Reed's shaft.

"Tucker!"

Reed shook his head, marveling at Tucker's wicked smile spreading across his flushed, sweaty face. "Damn, who knew pain could hurt this good."

"It's not supposed to hurt, Tuck."

"Do you see me complaining, big guy?"

"I'm not that big, Tucker, your hole's small!"

Tucker's gritty laughter echoed across the empty campground. "Not as small as it used to be."

Reed grunted, struggling to keep from slithering inside his greedy lover. "I knew this was a bad idea…."

THIRTY-SEVEN

Tucker

"I'M NOT a china doll, Reed."

Reed's face, flushed with sweat, offered a wry, devilish smirk. "Be careful what you wish for, kid."

Tucker smothered him in another meandering kiss, sweaty and sticky and charged with the fervent electricity of desire. "You've already given me everything I've wished for, Reed," he insisted breathlessly, as Reed's stiff cock throbbed and filled him almost entirely. "This is just a cherry on top."

Reed grunted and thrust pointedly as Tucker winced with delight at the bittersweet pressure, their groins growing dangerously close as Tucker squirmed to take more of his lover's girth inside of him. "No pun intended, kid."

They chuckled, but Reed was no saint. He used the moment to thrust gently deeper, and Tucker gasped with the intense pleasure the tight, gasping friction caused so far inside him he thought he might lose his mind. Sweaty and grunting, he ground and squirmed as Reed slithered the rest of his meaty staff inside. As their groins pressed tight against one another, Tucker gasped and bit Reed's lower lip during a shuddering, tender kiss.

They were joined thoroughly—bodies aglow with sweat, faces flushed with desire, lips puffy and bruised from a thousand hungry, yearning kisses. Tuck was convinced they'd never fully part again.

He would have been content to sit there like that all night, Reed wedged deep inside, their hearts pounding, eyes stinging from sweat, clinging desperately to his friend, his lover, his counselor, and, tonight, his teacher.

But Reed had other ideas—all of them better than Tuck could ever imagine. They kissed one last time—breathless, eager, hungry, panting—and then parted and gasped for air. Reed met his gaze. "Lean back," he fairly growled.

"But...."

"Trust me, kid, you won't be sorry."

Tucker eagerly did as he was told, as if secretly enjoying the changing of the guard. He'd been the one to lay out the blanket, light the fire, pour the wine, set the scene, and tug at Reed's shirt until he got the frickin' hint. He'd tugged and sucked and flattered and serviced Reed until there was no choice but to proceed, and now he was more than eager to lean back, palms flat on either side of him as Reed held tight, continuing to fill him to his very core.

And then, as if summoning all of his athletic prowess, Reed somehow rose to his knees, swimmer's body aglow in the flickering flames as he slid a hand onto either side of Tuck's slim waist and, with delicate friction, began to move gently in and out of him.

Tucker gasped at the first drag and thrust, his senses on overdrive, his skin flushed, his voice hoarse from gasping and moaning. His cock throbbed and leaked every time Reed pressed deeper and hit that sweet spot.

He moaned anew, and Reed intensified the rhythm of his velvet gyrations. Gone were the initial hesitance between them and the tight resistance, along with the fragile nature of Tucker's long-simmering virginity. By now the juices flowed, the sweat ran, the friction increased as the berth widened and stretched. Sensing his newfound freedom, Reed responded accordingly.

Taken in every sense of the word, Tucker muttered unintelligibly and gasped with every thrust as he threatened to erupt like a geyser each time Reed plunged deeper, harder, and faster inside.

Reed anticipated the climax and timed it expertly. He reached out and took possession of Tucker's swollen shaft. It took only the slightest grip of his hand, the tender touch of his velvet grip on Tucker's turgid prick, and he blasted out and splattered him all the way to his chin with wet, hot goo.

Tucker thought that was it, that ecstasy was fulfilled, but then Reed thrust one last time, his deepest yet, and hit a bullseye he didn't even realize he possessed, and Tuck splattered his chest and face anew with a fresh round of hot, glistening ecstasy.

Somewhere in the midst of his own climax, Tucker felt the gush and goo of Reed's orgasm and watched it on his face as Reed froze and emptied himself inside Tucker's yielding cavern until at last their simultaneous passion slowed to a trickle and Reed slid from inside and they collapsed into a sticky, gasping, limbs-akimbo, heart-pounding heap of sweat and splatter.

And even minutes afterward, spooning and sticking to each other like glue, they continued to shiver and flinch with the aftershocks of their intense, earnest lovemaking.

Tucker smiled to himself as Reed's chest clung to his sweaty back. They had done it. Made love in every sense of the word. And he knew, even as Reed's breath against the back of his neck grew steadier with the approach of deep, post-fucking sleep, that nothing would ever be the same again.

THIRTY-EIGHT

Reed

"TUCK?"

Flat on his back, Reed blinked himself awake and gazed up at the blanket of stars that filled the deep, dark sky overhead. The fire still crackled, if gentler now, and his skin was alive with heat, sweat, and spunk as he rose to his knees.

The blanket was a mess, clothes scattered hither and yon, half of it in a ball, grass-stained and sticky. Tucker's half was completely empty.

Reed wasn't surprised. From the first time they were intimate, Tuck had been a restless sleeper, and Reed often woke up alone and wondered where his fidgety lover had wandered off to now.

He stood, legs wobbly from release. He was naked and reached for his pair of wrinkled boxers to drag them on over his pink, flushed package. With bare feet and torso to match, he strode off toward the mess hall, hoping he'd find Tuck in the middle of a late-night pig-out, croissants and orange juice and whatever other goodies they'd hauled into the kitchen spread out on the counter like a private buffet for two.

Instead he found only the remnants of such a feast—an empty can on the counter, a pack of store-brand cookies torn open and half-empty beside it. He took one and nibbled at it, half-naked in front of the gleaming fridge as he stared inside. He snatched two cans of their favorite fancy iced coffee and left the kitchen lights on as he swung back out onto the grounds, guided by the sound of splashing water.

With a can of cold iced coffee in each hand, he slid through the gate to the pool. Tucker was doing the breaststroke Reed had taught him, quietly pumping through the water in a pair of gray boxer briefs and nothing else.

Reed thought he might surprise him, but Tucker paused at the deep end to catch his breath, clinging to the wet pool tiles like a safety net. "About time, sleepyhead."

Reed slipped gratefully into the pool, eager for the soft, clear water to cool his flushed, feverish skin and bring his core temperature back down to normal. Then again, good luck cooling off when a hot piece like Tucker was around, glistening and smooth, lean and tempting with every smile and gesture.

He sighed and walked until he was waist deep as Tucker gently drifted toward him until they stood face-to-face. Reed handed him one of the cans, and Tucker oozed with gratitude. "God, I need this."

"You sure will."

Tucker arched one bushy, dripping eyebrow, the open can poised halfway to his lips. "Will?"

Reed drifted to one side of the pool, water rippling around the waistband of his clingy boxers as he rested his back against the deck. "Sure, I mean, you're still technically a virgin, bud."

"What? How? Why?" The realization dawned on his youthful face as he drifted ever closer, every inch of his body taut and tan and dripping wet. Amazingly, Reed felt himself thicken beneath the water's surface, a feat he thought he might never be able to achieve again after literally emptying his sac deep inside of his gracious young lover.

"I mean," Reed explained unnecessarily, "I did you right good and proper. It's only fair you return the favor." Just saying the words gave Reed the shivers—the thought of Tucker wedged deep inside of him, that long, curved cock filling every inch, made him fairly whimper with anticipation.

Tucker was close. "I thought it didn't work that way with couples like *us*."

Reed marveled at Tucker's sweetness and naivete. "What, we're a couple now?"

The old Tucker might have blathered, blustered, taken a step back and questioned the comment. The new Tucker, coming into his own, growled playfully as he drew ever nearer. "And don't ever forget it, Coach."

Reed was about to retort when Tucker kissed him silent. "Besides," Reed murmured dreamily when Tucker at last let him up for air, "couples like us make our own rules. Sometimes I take you, next time you'll take me."

"You want it like that?"

"Tucker, I can honestly say I've never wanted anything more in my entire life."

"Good." Tucker jutted out his chin and puffed out his chest, quietly mocking Reed's alpha status. "Cuz I can't wait to make you my bitch."

Reed nearly spit out his iced coffee and struggled to barely swallow before playfully splashing Tuck. "That'll be the day, kid."

Tucker sagged as if playing a role that didn't quite fit. "Yeah, I don't even know why I said that."

"Probably all those dirty movies you watched to get ready for tonight."

"Probably," Tucker murmured. "I couldn't really watch many. They were all so rough."

Reed was glad they were in agreement on this crucial matter. "Yeah, that's not really my style either."

Tucker inched closer and leaned slightly down to nuzzle Reed's ear. "I like your style better, I think."

"You better, Tuck, because we're just getting warmed up."

"Don't threaten me with a good time."

"Oh, it's no threat."

They went on like that, splashing and teasing, murmuring and dirty talking as they circled each other as the deep, dark night wore on and they let the mood take them wherever it might.

Eventually they went to their separate corners like boxers facing each other from across the shallow end, backs to the warm, wet pavement and admiring one another under the pale moonlight.

Reed shook his head, and Tucker noticed. He always noticed. Jutting out his chin, Tuck asked, "What?"

"Oh nothing, but did you *really* get a bunch of toys while you were back in LA?"

Tucker nodded, no longer the shy, bashful closet case Reed had met only a week earlier. "Yeah, like, a shit-ton of them."

"I mean, what was that like?"

"What? Buying them or using them?"

"Both, I guess. I mean, I literally can't picture either, and yet I know you're telling the truth."

"I just went to this one dirty bookstore I pass on the way to Scream Studios whenever I'm in town. Passed it a million times and never thought twice about going in, and then, once I decided to get you back, I pulled over one day and went inside."

Reed chuckled lazily. "What, no disguise? Just freeballed it right inside, big as you please?"

Tucker nodded, almost proudly. "Basically, yeah."

"Nobody said anything?"

"It was only me and one older dude and the cashier, and neither of them looked like they owned a TV, let alone watched *Suburban Dead*, so yeah, I just wandered to the toy aisle and stocked up my little basket. The dude rang them up and out I walked. He never really even looked up."

"Wow, you've come a long way, baby."

Tucker raised his fancy mocha-colored can and winked at Reed from across the pool. "I couldn't have done it without you, Coach."

Reed considered the comment, longer and harder than he was sure Tucker intended it. "I doubt that, Tuck."

"I don't."

"Even without me, without this, without what happened between us, you can't run from who you are, Tuck. You would have met someone who introduced you to the same pleasures I did, eventually."

"Maybe," Tuck conceded unenthusiastically. "But they wouldn't have been half as pleasurable as they've been with you. Because you're you. You're who I want, Reed. All of you, not just the parts that give me pleasure. You get that, right?"

Reed nodded. "I'm starting to, yeah."

"You really do have a hard time trusting people, don't you?"

Reed balked to be called out so thoroughly. "I warned you."

"And I warned you, I never leave a friend behind."

Reed chuckled at last. "I don't think... you never said that, Tuck."

Tucker blushed. "I know. I just made it up. I was hoping you wouldn't remember if I did or didn't."

"Why, though?"

Tucker shrugged. "It seemed like the right line at the right time."

"I guess you *are* an actor."

"Better get used to it, because after this week, you're going to be surrounded by them on the daily."

Reed met Tucker's eyes and found them suddenly evasive. "What? Why?"

"Did... did I just say that out loud?"

Reed growled playfully. "Yeah, Tuck, you did."

"I just mean, in general, you know. If I can get your ass out to LA, anyway."

"Good luck." Reed felt unmoored and rudderless as the night wore on and they drank one another in across the shimmering pool.

They finished their iced coffees and placed the cans on the deck behind them. Their bodies had cooled down, the sweat and spunk washed away by the calm, clear water as they lounged halfway between the deep end and the shallow.

Reed was watching his fingers make ripples in the water, enjoying the leisurely pace of their mounting sexual tension when Tucker broke the silence at last.

"Speaking of LA," Tucker murmured, clearing his throat cordially, "I kind of have a confession to make."

THIRTY-NINE

Tucker

"ANOTHER ONE?" Reed smirked from across the shallow end.

Tucker chuckled nervously, not sure how Reed might take the news. "Promise you won't be mad?"

Reed gave him a quick eye roll. "Have I been mad yet?"

Tucker had trouble keeping his jaw from hitting the surface of the pool. "Only every moment since we first met. Jesus, was that a real question?"

Reed was far from offended. "Like I said, Tuck, you're not the only actor in this pool, remember?"

Tucker trailed his fingertips through the water and watched the ripples drift across the pool and whisper against Reed's smooth washboard abs.

"What is it this time?" Reed prodded, voice low and sleek to match his mercilessly handsome body.

"Nothing bad." Tucker inched slightly closer as if to distract Reed the way Tuck knew his body usually did.

"How not bad?" Reed murmured, eyes feasting on Tuck's bare, wet skin before they met his curious eyes.

"Not bad at all. I mean, if you don't mind…." He bit his lower lip and winced at the same time. He wasn't sure why, after all they'd been through together, all they'd shared, all they'd said and promised, he was so afraid of losing Reed.

Then one look in his sweet, clear eyes told him exactly why.

Those eyes prodded, to match Reed's curious tone. "If I don't mind… what, exactly?"

"Moving to Hollywood for a while?" Tucker flinched as if the sky might fall upon his pronouncement.

Reed's face neither rose nor fell. He didn't scream or shout, and incredibly, didn't throw a wet, dripping fist square at Tuck's exposed jaw. He merely crossed his smooth, wiry arms over his chest. "Define a while?"

Tucker paused, halfway across the pool, the physical equivalent to a record scratch. "Wait, you're actually considering it?"

Reed's shrug was all the reply Tuck needed. "Do I have a choice?"

"I mean, not if you don't want to be a dick."

Reed seemed to sag down the back of the pool deck, and he peered up at Tucker with a cryptic expression that was harder to read than usual. "I was only ever a dick to keep from breaking each other's hearts, Tucker."

"And now?"

Reed's sigh was as resigned as it was heavy. "Now I just want to be with you. Period. Full stop."

"Really?"

"Here, there, anywhere, really. If you're there, I just kinda want to be around."

Tucker brightened. "Do you mean that?"

"Did I stutter?" Reed's stare was as hard as his taut swimmer's body, smooth and pale under the soft moonlight.

Tucker frowned all over again. "See, now you're kind of being a dick again—"

And then Reed pounced playfully, like a tiger attacking his prey. Water surged and splashed until they embraced and twirled like wrestlers in the water. Reed gushed like a schoolgirl as he pressed Tucker with his back to the pool deck. "Just tell me what it is, Tucker." He growled and no longer sounded girly at all.

Tuck pushed him away, but not too far. He enjoyed Reed at his playful best—moments that were few and far between but getting more and more frequent as they grew closer with each exchange. "So, remember when we were joking about you being my stunt double in the pool?"

Reed's mouth opened with surprise, then sharpened with reproach. "But you don't need that anymore, remember? The video, the new video, the acumen in the pool—shit, you were doing the damn breaststroke just now. I'm not necessarily *necessary* anymore."

Tucker splashed Reed more forcefully than he intended, but Reed definitely deserved it after that woolly untruth. "Okay, that's stupid, so we'll circle around to that in a moment, but... turns out the insurance company won't even let me spend more than five minutes in the water at a time, and that's just not feasible given the length of this scene we're going to be shooting for days at a time, so...."

Reed did the math. "So you *do* need a stunt double, huh?"

"I mean, yeah."

"And you're telling me none of the stunt doubles in Hollywood who looked more like you were willing to do it?"

Tucker was getting pruney, and after the earlier fuck fest and workout afterward, sore as hell. He found himself hoisting his body up onto the deck, sitting on the warm concrete and savoring the sensation beneath his almost bare ass as he swung his feet back and forth in the water below. "We didn't actually ask anyone else," Tucker confessed.

Reed inched closer, face a mask of questions and concern but not, Tuck noticed, rebuttal. He used his powerful arms and broad shoulders to lift his body up and onto the deck to sit side by side and hip to hip beside Tucker. It was almost romantic.

What almost? It *was* downright swoon-worthy.

"Who's *we*?" Reed asked as he swished his bare feet in the clear blue water.

Tucker was surprised by the question. "Costas and me, of course."

"Costas?" Reed's face blanched and wrinkled in disgust at the very name. Tuck stifled a grin; that was most people's reaction and far from unwarranted. "Your producer?"

"Yeah," Tucker confessed with a vague feeling somewhat like pride. "Once the dust settled and Summer helped me set a few things straight back in LA, contractually speaking, I made sure that Costas knew exactly how I felt about the way you two ended it on the porch the other day, banishing you the way he did, and after I made it clear we were a couple, period, end of story, well, he finally saw things my way."

Reed favored him with a curious glance that bordered on suspicion. "*Your* way?"

Tucker nodded. "As in, you were the only person for the job, full stop."

"And he went with that?" Reed sounded as suspicious as he looked. After interacting with Costas personally, Tucker couldn't blame him.

"Sure. But only after a knock-down, drag-out that forced me to use every ounce of acting skill I've acquired over the years."

Reed still seemed disbelieving. "That must have been some acting job, Tuck."

"You're worth it, Reed. To me, you're worth everything. A month ago? I would have never spoken to my boss that way, but since you? Since you, I've discovered what it means to stick up for someone you actually care about. I think, in the process, I've learned to stick up for... myself as well."

Reed nodded thoughtfully, as if still processing it all. "You're not letting our personal relationship cloud your professional judgment, are you? I mean, lots of stuntmen in LA, I would imagine?"

"None that I trust more than you, Reed. And when it comes to safety, trust trumps experience ten to one."

Reed seemed to give it some thought, his hip warm and firm against Tucker's as their bodies dripped next to each other's in the middle of the night. "Why Hollywood?"

Tucker nudged him playfully. "I mean, duh."

Reed nudged him back, not so playfully this time. "No, I'm serious. Don't you guys film here in Georgia? Isn't that why you chose Camp Run-A-Mok in the first place? And a local swim coach?"

"Yeah, but for safety reasons, a scene like this has to be shot in a specially made tank on set, with supervision and witnesses. I guess there are all kinds of protocols involved that we hadn't worked all the way through yet. We hadn't really done a water shoot before, so even Costas was surprised."

Reed grew quiet and pensive again. Then, "When?"

"Next week." Tuck made another "teethy face" emoji grin that Reed couldn't see. He was too busy staring at his feet, pale beneath the water, swirling around in gently lapping circles.

Reed nudged Tucker's hip with his own and sent shivers of delight through his already humming body. The idea of being naked and sticky and sweaty with Reed, slithering deep inside his experienced lover and knocking off the last of his V card credentials, made it clear that the time for talking was reaching its expiration date. "How convenient."

"I mean, they wanted to shoot it this week, but I said hell to the no, right?"

Reed glanced over and nodded. "Look at you, making demands and making moves and popping your cherry, all in the same week."

Tucker slid his arm around Reed's neck and dragged him closer. "I couldn't have done it without my coach, Coach."

"Sure you could, kid." Reed eased his body against Tuck's in that seamless way that fit just right. "You just needed someone to remind you who you were, that's all."

"What about you, Reed? Do you know who you are yet?"

Tucker felt him shrug in reply. They drifted apart, and Reed pulled one leg up from the pool and crossed it against the other as they turned to face each other on the wet pool deck. "I thought I did, Tuck. I thought I was the one teaching you things, but it turns out you were the best coach I ever had."

Tucker grinned bashfully. "I'm already yours, Reed. Wherever, whenever, however you want me. You don't have to butter me up anymore."

"I wish I were, Tuck. I wish I weren't some washed-up, old-ass, thrown-away coach letting some Hollywood peckerwood school me on life, the universe, and everything else, but... here we are, *kid*."

Tucker rolled his eyes. "Now who's the drama queen, huh, drama queen?"

Reed chuckled as if a weight had just been lifted. "Well, if I'm gonna be in Hollywood for the duration, might as well act the part, right?"

"And you're not a coach anymore." Tucker inched closer, as if unable to stay away.

"No shit, kid."

"No, I mean, your new title, per the contract awaiting your signature back in our room—if we ever make it back to our room this week—is officially Swim and Safety Stunt Coordinator, so obviously you'll be on the payroll all season. And after that, well, we'll have to renegotiate your various demands if we make it to season six."

"We?"

Tucker pulled Reed closer. "Sure, pal. You and me? From now on, we're a package deal."

Reed shook his head and then shifted deeper into Tuck's embrace, filling every nook and cranny with his wet, smooth body. Reed's voice was hoarse, his heart pounding, his eyes moist as he croaked, "You can say that again."

Tucker held him slightly at bay, if only to peer back into his suddenly leaking eyes. "I'll say it every day, Reed, until you believe it. This?" He waved his arm at the pool, the camp, the empty grounds, and the still crackling fire just on the other side of the fence. "This is no act.

This is all for you. And for me. I want us together, like this, for as long as you'll have me."

Reed sighed and turned away. He bit his lower lip as if unable to meet Tucker's passionate gaze. "I already told you, kid, be careful what you wish for. You may never get rid of me."

"Then lucky me, you stubborn old fart."

Reed chuckled and collapsed into Tuck's embrace just as his own eyes began to seep with relief. He thought his last confession might be the final straw, but instead, it ended up bringing them closer together.

And now, at last, they could walk free and unencumbered through the world, no longer afraid of opinions or chatter or gossip or, for that matter, each other.

"Thank you, Tucker." Reed pushed him away and hoisted himself to his full height, smooth and pale and already thick against the dangerously loose front panel of his dripping boxer shorts.

"For what?"

"This." Reed waved a hand and then tugged him to his feet. "For a future, for… a future together."

"Don't thank me until we're finished, Reed."

"Finished what?"

Tuck took his hand and dragged him gently toward the showers as their feet made wet prints on the still-warm concrete beneath them. "Finished popping my cherry, of course."

Reed followed eagerly, their hands still clutched tightly together, as if the spell they'd cast might yet be broken. Tucker knew the road ahead might be bumpy, with challenges and confrontations galore. They were heading back to Hollywood in a few days, but he knew that, with Reed by his side, they could face them together, for better or worse. And that was enough of a Hollywood ending for him.

That is, until they got settled in Tinseltown and began writing their own love story, one blissful scene at a time. Starting, Tucker supposed, with this one….

Keep reading for an excerpt from
Winging It
by Ashlyn Kane and James Morgan
Book One of the Hockey Ever After series

WARMUP

A TWO-STORY-TALL image of Gabriel Martin's face stared fiercely down at the man himself as he approached his team's arena.

Gabe wasn't normally that broody-looking off the ice—at least he hoped not. Today, though, he had a feeling it wouldn't matter if he was having the best hair day ever. Not even his signature blond curls could make anyone call him the press-given nickname "Anglo Angel" when he was glowering hard enough to peel paint.

In the locker room, he tried to put the morning behind him and focus on his job... but he could still hear the mental echo of the front door closing.

Unfortunately he could also hear the shrill note of Olie's catcall. "Holy shit. Would you look at the size of that thing!"

Gabe grabbed his trainers from the bench and fussed with the laces. He needed a few seconds to brace himself before he turned around. It had been bad enough to break up with his... whatever Pierre was... the day before training camp started *and* subject himself to a restless night's non-sleep. Now he had to face the ass of one Dante "Baller" Baltierra, a specimen large enough to have its own gravitational pull.

In seven years in the NHL and several more in the closet, Gabe had learned how not to look. But if there was a trick to not noticing, he hadn't discovered it.

There was nothing for it now, though. With all the attention the rest of the locker room was giving Baller—high fives and the occasional wolf whistle—Gabe would be more conspicuous if he *didn't* look.

He raised his head and wished he hadn't. Hockey ass was a documented phenomenon, but no one had it like Baller. Gabe had never seen an ass so perfect. And now it was even bigger and rounder.

"That's no moon—it's a space station!" a defenseman piped up from across the room.

Baller took it all with the grace of someone who'd spent his rookie season getting ragged on for the size of his butt. He bowed, then went in for a hug from Flash, who took advantage of his rights as captain and

Baller's previous landlord and ruffled his black hair as he pulled away. Baller fussed with it as though he could push the longer strands on top back into order. "You're all just jealous because my milkshake brings all the girls to the yard."

"Your milkshake spent a lot of time on internet gossip sites this summer," Gabe added as Baller parked it in the stall next to his.

"Why, Gabriel, have you been keeping tabs?" Baller fluttered his eyelashes and faked a swoon. "Don't worry. There's plenty of Dante Baltierra to go around."

One more reason for him not to come out, as if Gabe needed one—it would make it so much more obnoxious when guys flirted with him in an attempt to chirp. Breaking things off with Pierre when he couldn't accept that Gabe wasn't going to be his boyfriend *or* his sugar daddy had been the right thing to do.

He wasn't the first guy to try it. He probably wouldn't be the last either.

"We know exactly how much of you there is to go around, you nudist." Flash swooped to Gabe's rescue just as he finished tying his shoes. He snapped a towel in Baller's general direction. "Put it away. Coach will make you do extra suicides tomorrow if she finds out you're fucking around in here. Two minute," he said to the rest of the locker room—his accent was always thicker after a long summer without English. Then Flash and Gabe headed to the training area to warm up.

"Think she'll put him on our line?" Gabe asked in French as they climbed on neighboring treadmills.

"If she doesn't, it's a waste of talent." Flash shot him a sideways look, giving Gabe a glimpse of the ragged, almost lightning-bolt-shaped scar at the corner of his eye. "You going to be okay with that?"

Only Flash and Olie knew Gabe was gay. And while Flash was always supportive and pretty good at nipping homophobic trash talk in the bud, Gabe wasn't taking chances with the rest of the guys. His own mother hadn't stuck around once he came out. The truth certainly wouldn't endear him to a professional hockey team. He could think about a rainbow parade once the Stanley Cup had his name on it.

"I never should've told you I thought he was hot." Fortunately Baller was such a caricature of himself that Gabe didn't have to worry about catching feelings. He deflected the conversation back to hockey. "He played well on our line last year."

"Yes, I remember," Flash said dryly. He stopped the treadmill for a minute to adjust the compression bandage around his right knee. "I was there. I also watched the game tape. Then I reviewed the statistics—"

"Oh my God, okay, point made." Gabe laughed and shook his head. "I'll stop back seat captaining." But Flash was still looking at him like he expected more. Like he was still thinking about—ugh. Gabe's stomach squirmed. He hated that look. It made him feel like a bug under a microscope. "Seriously, though. It's fine. Baller's... whatever. It won't affect my play."

"Yeah," Flash said, in English this time as the other players started trickling out of the locker room. "I know."

Famous last words.

"What?" Gabe finally asked when he couldn't take Flash side-eyeing him anymore.

"You could tell them," he said quietly. "They're not going to care. They're good guys and they like you."

Gabe took a deep breath and concentrated on not punching the treadmill. He didn't say what he was thinking: *They don't even know me.* And that was how it had to be. "No." He wasn't ashamed of being gay, but he didn't want to be Gabriel Martin, gay hockey player. He wanted to be Gabriel Martin, star Nordiques forward and Stanley Cup winner.

He couldn't do that if he got traded because suddenly his teammates didn't want to pass to him.

Besides, he practically grew up in locker rooms. He didn't have any illusions about universal acceptance.

Flash sighed. "Have it your way."

That was the idea.

DANTE LOVED media day.

That was probably vain of him, but whatever. Dante refused to pretend he was anything other than his whole self. Sure, there was something ridiculous about standing around in gear and running shoes and making sexy faces at the camera, but Dante was a ridiculous guy. Making the camera crew laugh kept him entertained, and with any luck they'd respond by not using the ugliest shots on the team's social media.

Admittedly, the makeup was not his favorite part. He felt shellacked, which the techs had definitely done to his hair. But the point was to minimize the glare from the lights and not to make his brown skin look whiter, so Dante sucked it up and did his best Mexican American version of Blue Steel until Tricia from PR threatened him with a water bottle.

"You love me!" he shouted over his shoulder as he jogged down the hall toward the locker room.

"You're trying too hard!" she shouted back, but he could hear the laugh in her voice.

Dante grinned. He could already see his face on the Jumbotron screen at Quebec City Amphitheatre, the stats beside his name ticking up with every point he scored.

Last year he'd taken a flukey hit to the head and only played a third of the season. This year he needed to do better. A point per game sounded pretty good. A little lofty maybe, but shoot for the stars and all that.

All he had to do was convince his coach that the open slot on the first line belonged to him.

Good thing Dante thrived under pressure.

He chucked his gear in his stall and ducked into the showers to melt the crap from his face and hair. Then he dried off and slung the towel over his shoulder. Time for phase one of his master plan—ingratiate himself with his teammates.

The locker room was a little over half full when he returned. Most guys were changing into street clothes, and a handful of prospects were talking in the corner, heads bent. Dante couldn't make out the words, but their body language said *I can't believe we're finally here*. Adorable. And relatable.

Olie was smirking to himself as he checked over his goalie gear. The locker-room lights glinting off his shiny brown head gave him a kind of halo, but Dante wasn't fooled. The gear-checking was part of his ritual, but the smirk wasn't. Someone was getting pranked today.

No Flash yet, but the captain always had extra media time. Gabe Martin, his right winger, was here, grimacing at his phone. As Dante watched, he silenced the thing and shoved it farther into the pile of stuff at the back of his stall. Dante knew that expression. That meant girl problems.

And *that* gave Dante a perfect opening.

He chucked his towel in the laundry and clapped once. "Can I have your attention please!" It wasn't a question.

When the volume in the locker room dropped, he realized he was naked. Whoops. Oh well. "I know you jerks missed me over the summer. Dinner and drinks at O'Ryan's?"

The prospies whooped. Olie looked up from his gear, met Dante's eyes, shook his head in fond exasperation, and went back to it, so Dante assumed he was in as well.

Now for his real target. Dante grabbed his underwear from the stall next to Gabe's and shimmied into them. Shit, his ass really had gotten huge. He might need to upgrade his boxers to accommodate. "You're coming, right?"

Gabe came out to the bar after games some nights, but he was always the first to leave, just like he was always the first guy in the dressing room or on the ice for practice. He didn't make small talk, which was annoying, because Dante was dying to pick his brain. Gabe could do things on the ice that made goalies cry for their mothers.

Gabe blinked, almost like he was looking through Dante, then shook himself and met his eyes. "Sorry?"

Woof. Whatever was going on in his head, a night out with the boys would do him good. "To the pub? To drown your sorrows?" Dante suggested. "I saw you looking at your phone. I know that look, man. Forget about her and come have fun."

Finally realization dawned in ice-blue eyes. Gabe's cheeks went slightly pink, which made him look every bit like his stupid media nickname—the Anglo Angel. The blond curls did kind of remind Dante of a fresco he'd seen once. "You've got me pegged, eh?"

Heh. *Pegged.* Dante clapped him on the shoulder and reached for his T-shirt. "Not yet," he said cheerfully. "But I bet we can find you a girl who's into that at O'Ryan's."

When he popped his head through the neck hole of the shirt, Flash was staring at him, judgment written all over his face.

Please. Dante had lived with the man, his wife, and their four kids. If Yvette got half a mind to whip out a strap-on, Flash would be on all fours in no time. But Dante wasn't going to say that out loud. He had *some* sense. Probably better to pretend he hadn't noticed the gimlet eye. "Cap! Tell Gabe he should come to O'Ryan's tonight and turn that frown upside down."

Flash's judgmental stare continued for another few seconds. Then he turned to Gabe. "Ouais," he agreed. "Captain's orders."

Dante fist-pumped. "Victory!" Now he could proceed to phase two—charming Gabe into agreeing Dante should play first line.

He reached for the jeans hanging at the back of his stall, but when he bent over to put them on, there was an ominous tearing sound from his boxers.

Son of a bitch. He paused with one foot in his pants.

Finally the snickers reached his ears and he straightened up and pulled his pants off again. "All right, Olofsson. You got me." Switching his boxers for the same brand in a smaller size. That took planning. Dante threw his jeans at Olie's head. Olie caught them, laughing, and Dante and the rest of the room joined in. "Yeah, yeah, my ass is so big it's normal that my boxers don't fit. You're hilarious. Now where'd you hide my underpants?"

O'RYAN'S PUB served food in hockey-player-sized portions and the owner had been a Dekes fan the first time around, so it was a perennial favorite among Gabe's teammates. Gabe liked it well enough—more social than a restaurant and lower-key than a club.

And the sweet potato fries were excellent.

When Gabe walked in, half the team was already sprawled over a few of the larger tables, laughing over beers. Gabe reminded himself that he belonged here as much as any of them and that any weirdness was in his own head.

"Gabe!" Baller waved him over.

Gabe mentally resigned himself to an exhausting evening. Baller had a personality that matched his ass. He was loud, exuberant, larger-than-life. He'd been the Dekes' first-round draft pick a few years back, but the coaches had deemed him unready for the NHL, so he spent a few seasons in the minors until he got called up two years ago. He played most of that first season up and down the lineup, and then last year, he started with Gabe and Flash... until he took a hit to the head and got sidelined for the second half of the season.

He slid into the seat next to Baller. "Are you corrupting the prospies?" It was the same every year.

Baller grinned his crooked grin. "Who, me? It's not my fault your country's drinking laws are so lax."

Next to him in the booth, Olie nudged his shoulder. "Flash's gonna make you babysit on our first road trip in the US. You know that, right?" Gabe caught his gaze behind Baller's back, and they exchanged smirks.

It wasn't that rookies couldn't get into bars, but making them believe they couldn't was fun.

Baller was twenty-two—plenty old enough to participate in bar shenanigans in any country—but he shrugged and waved it off. "My liver will need a break by then anyway." That was probably true. "But for right now…." Baller lifted a shot glass of yellow liquid in each hand and offered one to Gabe.

He might as well get it over with. He just hoped it wasn't tequila.

Around the table, Flash, Olie, and a handful of prospies, most of whom probably wouldn't make the end of camp, raised shot glasses of their own. Nobody said *to the season*, because that would jinx it. You didn't talk about winning streaks for fear of breaking them, you didn't talk about playoffs in case you didn't make them, and God forbid anyone utter the word *shutout* before the clock ran out.

They touched glasses and swallowed the alcohol.

Fucking tequila. Gabe made a face. "You're the worst."

Baller patted him none too gently on the shoulder. "Admit it—you love me and Jose Cuervo really."

The tables filled up, and the servers took their orders. Gabe worried he and Baller would have nothing to talk about or that Baller would take the lull as an opportunity to offer him more tequila.

Instead Flash sucked him into a breakdown of the merits and weaknesses of power-play and penalty-kill units in last season's Cup final that lasted until their plates were cleared.

Baller looked on in bemusement. "You know, we're gonna have like eight months of nothing but hockey talk."

Flash snorted. "You'll learn. Gabe is very… focused."

He said it like it might be an innuendo. Gabe bristled. "Sorry I like winning."

Baller laughed. "No, no, it's cool. I respect it."

So it was nice. Even if he wasn't going to make hanging out with the guys a habit, Gabe enjoyed himself. At least until his phone buzzed in his pocket.

Gabe should've ignored it, but he pulled it out to check. *Unknown caller.* Yeah, right. He'd had two other "unknown callers" since he blocked Pierre's number.

They had met last season in Ottawa, where Gabe grew up and where he'd spent his summers. Pierre had had no idea who Gabe was. Gabe had been attracted to his lack of interest in hockey, and they spent the first few months of their acquaintance fucking like crazy whenever Gabe was in town.

But the fantastic sex had obviously fried Gabe's brain, because it took him months to realize Pierre wasn't being understanding about being Gabe's secret fling. Instead, he was biding his time, hoping to convince Gabe to be his sugar daddy.

Gabe wished he'd figured that out before he invited Pierre up to Quebec before training camp, but it was better to break things off now than have to handle drama during the season. He put his phone back in his pocket only to find Baller watching him.

"Dude, whoever she is, I guarantee you can do better." Then he gave Gabe a not-so-gentle nudge toward the end of the booth. "You gotta get up, though, 'cause Coach scheduled practice for ass o'clock tomorrow, so I have to pick up early."

Gabe let Baller out. "Gentlemen," Baller said with a jaunty wave. Then he disappeared toward the crowd of bodies around the bar.

"Our little rookie, all grown up." Flash sighed dramatically and leaned his head on Olie's shoulder.

One of this year's crop—Tom something—shook his head and hunched his shoulders. "How does he even pick up girls here? He doesn't speak any French."

Gabe caught himself before he sprayed the kid with a mouthful of beer. Olie took it upon himself to answer instead. "He's a professional hockey player. He makes almost a million dollars a year. And he's cute."

"Dat ass," Flash added gravely.

Gabe rolled his eyes at the memory. "Last year he tortured me by singing 'Lady Marmalade' until I taught him some better French pickup lines." That was one of the few times Gabe had gone out with the team.

Brightening, the prospie beside Maybe-Tom leaned forward, all lanky teenage earnestness. "Can you teach me?"

"You should get a native speaker to teach you." Gabe learned basic French in school, and he'd improved drastically since moving to Quebec, but he wasn't going to fool anyone into thinking it was his mother tongue.

"Why didn't Baller?"

"Baller *did*, but Flash was unhelpful," said Baller himself as he reappeared at the table with a beautiful girl under each arm. Gabe made a note to check his watch next time, because that was *fast*. Baller unwrapped his arm from the girl on his left, who had sharp cheekbones and full lips and was blushing shyly. "This is Fleur"—he gestured to the girl on the right—"and Elise. She wanted to meet you," he added to Gabe in an undertone. Then he winked. "Thought she could cheer you up."

Oh fuck. Gabe should've told Baller he was getting spam calls or something. He'd been stupid to hope Baller would forget about it.

"You have your phone?" he asked Elise in French to cover his discomfort.

Elise nodded and produced an iPhone in a pink case with the Nordiques logo. Gabe stood long enough to put his arm around her shoulders while Baller snapped a photo, then shook her hand. "It was nice to meet you, Elise." Now to steer her back to someone who was actually interested. He tilted his head at Baller. "Be careful with this guy, he's fragile. Still sleeps with his teddy bear. Leaves the hall light on." He winked at Flash and added, "François's wife used to tuck him in at night until he finally got his own place."

"What are you telling her?" Baller squawked as Fleur laughed out loud.

"Nothing that isn't true," Gabe said in English. "Have a good night, kids."

Baller didn't look at all reluctant as the girls dragged him toward the door.

Gabe turned back to the table to find the prospies staring at him. He sighed. "What?"

"You just—" Tom gestured emphatically.

"She was *so hot*," the prospie whose name Gabe had forgotten said mournfully. "Is Baller seriously going to go home with both of them?"

Gabe shrugged. "Probably."

"But *why didn't you…?*"

"Superstitious," Flash said, proving he wasn't Gabe's best friend for nothing. "One time he picks up on the road, pulls a muscle in his back doing too much athletic sex. Missed three games."

It was a true story. It just didn't involve a woman and had nothing to do with why Gabe never picked up when they went out.

"But it's still training camp."

"And a bunch of prospies are gunning for spots on the team—including mine, if I'm not careful," Gabe said. "Though if you keep drinking, I don't know about your chances."

Tom looked at the plethora of empty shot glasses littering the table and turned a little green. Gabe smirked and passed over a couple bills. "I'm out for the night. See you kids bright and early."

In his pocket, his phone buzzed again. Gabe took it out and turned it off as he walked out of the pub. For some reason, he had a powerful urge to spend some time in his garage, swinging a club at his golf simulator. Maybe the satisfying *thwack* of the ball would ease the tension in his shoulders.

ON THE third day of training camp, Dante walked to the rink so deep in consideration of The Plan that he ran into Olie outside the locker room.

"Really, dude?" Olie's tone held a definite note of judgment.

Normally Dante had better spatial awareness. "Shit. Sorry." He paused and shook his head in wonder. "How are you this big even without your pads on?" Like, Dante wasn't the tallest guy on the team, but he was *solid*. Colliding with Olie almost made him fall backward on his ass.

Olie flicked him between the eyes, which was when Dante realized he was still wearing his sunglasses. "How bad did you overdo it last night?"

Dante *tsk*ed. "You know I don't kiss and tell." He enjoyed casual sex with interested women, but he was respectful about it. Besides, he had a Plan to see through; he hadn't stayed out all that late. He took off the sunglasses to prove he wasn't hungover. "I was just thinking."

"Don't hurt yourself!" someone chirped as they passed him in the hallway.

Dante sighed dramatically. "Everyone's a comedian." But he grinned anyway. The scrimmages that would help Coach St. Louis decide who to put on that empty first-line slot would start today.

Time to lace up.

Half the team was already on the ice when Dante finished in the locker room, but the coaches were still talking with each other, not running a formal practice, so he wasn't late. For a minute he let himself soak it in. An adopted Latino kid from a Southern state, he'd made it to the NHL. Two years of grinding it out in the AHL, hoping the big show would call his number, and then a frustrating injury that cut his rookie season short.

Now's my chance.

Coach St. Louis blew the whistle, and Dante hit the ice. He wouldn't let his opportunity slip away this time.

Not if he could help it.

Practice started out promising. St. Louis put him on the red-jersey practice squad with Flash and Gabe.

Dante knew he wouldn't pick up right where he left off—he'd been out for a while with a concussion at the end of last season, so he expected to be a little rusty. Of course, Flash and Gabe had played with each other for years and seemed to read each other's minds with every stride or minute movement of a stick. It was awesome to watch and hair-raising to be a part of.

Which only made it chafe that much more when Dante couldn't match them.

Oh, he kept up fine, speedwise. He didn't have any trouble getting where he thought he should be, and not even hulking defenseman Kitty Kipriyanov could knock him off the puck. He got the puck on Flash's tape often enough.

But Gabe was never where Dante expected him to be, and vice versa. It was like they saw totally different angles of attack. They dropped as many passes as connected.

By the time they broke for lunch, Dante was reevaluating stage two of the Plan. It wouldn't be enough to simply get the coach to put him on first line with Flash and Gabe if they played like this. Their possession numbers would swan dive right into the toilet, and everyone would blame the new guy.

And Dante wasn't entirely sure it *wasn't* his fault. His ego would not allow him to be responsible for that kind of catastrophe. So first, he had to fix… whatever was keeping him from connecting with Gabe on ice.

No pressure or anything. Just the fact that he had zero chemistry with the team's top scorer. Like, that shouldn't even be possible.

Maybe Dante just hadn't given it enough time. But he didn't have much more time to give. There was no guarantee St. Louis would put him on the same practice unit again tomorrow. And sure, maybe he'd get lucky and hit it off with another center… but maybe not.

Lunch was catered, because afterward they had the annual sexual harassment/financial literacy/mental health seminar. Dante snagged the seat next to Gabe and started loading his plate with carbs and protein. "So listen." Was that some kind of white wine sauce on the chicken? It smelled incredible. He added a breast to his plate and then offered the tongs to Gabe, still holding the platter. "I wanted to ask a favor."

Gabe side-eyed him carefully, as though he was expecting Dante to dump the chicken in his lap. Obviously Gabe didn't know him very well yet; Dante would never waste food.

"I'm listening." He took a chicken breast, and Dante passed the platter down.

Fantastic. What was in that bowl of orange stuff? Roasted sweet potatoes? Interesting. He served himself a scoop and then glanced at Gabe again.

Gabe's suspicion had evidently been transferred to a dish of steaming creamed spinach. Yikes. Dante didn't blame him; he was passing on that too.

"We can't read each other on the ice."

Gabe went for the pasta instead, then wordlessly offered it to Dante, who nodded his thanks. "Yeah, I noticed. I was there for practice." When Dante said nothing, Gabe prompted, "So…?"

Finally Dante had to accept that, at the moment, his plate simply could not accommodate anything else. He picked up his knife and fork and sliced off a piece of chicken. "So I think I'm still the best fit for the spot on your line"—he wasn't going to pretend he didn't think he was hot shit; that fake humility BS wasn't for him—"but obviously we have to fix that. So will you stay late with me so we can work on it?"

Gabe blinked. "Who's to say I don't have plans?"

"You and the girl whose calls you've been dodging, you mean?"

"You don't know what you're talking about." He rolled his eyes.

"C'mon," Dante wheedled. "I'll buy you dinner after. Steak, even! And maybe we won't suck this year."

That earned him a flat look. Oops. Maybe that was a little insensitive. Gabe stared at him.

"I'll throw in dessert," he offered, desperate. "Beer. Wine. Look, I will fucking cook you a three-course meal if that's what it takes. Just say yes."

"Okay."

"Seriously. I will break out the risotto and—oh son of a bitch." Baller deflated and his shoulders slumped. "You were going to say yes the whole time, weren't you?"

Gabe glanced at him slyly out of the corners of his eyes. He was smirking.

Mierda.

"I think you're the best skater for the job." He shrugged while Dante fought not to bristle at the faint praise. "And it worked last year. I don't know why it's not working now. So yeah, I'm down for extra practice. But I'll definitely need dinner after… what are we calling this?"

He jerked his head toward the conference room doors, where a large sign reminded them of the afternoon's agenda.

Dante quirked his lips. "Social-responsibility community theater?"

Gabe buried a snort in his dinner roll.

A COUPLE hours later, Gabe regretted his choice. Yes, Baller was fast. Yes, he had a great shot.

He was also vibrating at a frequency that felt like it would knock Gabe's fillings out. Shifting from foot to foot, tapping his stick relentlessly against the boards, squeezing all the air out of his water bottle and then letting it slowly wheeze back in, all while Gabe was tying his skates. "Did you drink an entire case of Rockstar during that meeting? You've got the fucking jitters."

"I had three cups of coffee," Baller admitted sheepishly. "Haven't had any all summer. Maybe not the best idea."

You think? Gabe shoved him toward the ice. "Go work it off. We can't practice like this." Forget getting their passes to connect. They'd be lucky if they accomplished more than learning to hate each other.

While Baller did laps, Gabe stretched out on the ice. It was weird. Hockey gear stank like nothing else in every context except when you were on the ice, and then it was... good. *Right.*

"What is this, yoga hour?" Baller called from the other end of the ice, bouncing a puck in the air as he skated. "Come on, let's go."

One day Baller wouldn't be twenty-one anymore, and then he would understand. "Who begged who for this practice session again?"

Baller sprayed to a stop beside him. The snow he kicked up fell just short of Gabe's face. At first he looked like he might laugh. Then he grimaced, and the mask of cocksure exhibitionist slipped just a little, revealing something real underneath. "Sorry. I guess I'm kind of anxious."

Gabe took a deep breath and let it out as he finished stretching out his hamstrings. His irritation eased as the muscle relaxed. He'd been anxious too when he was new in the league and eager to prove himself. He'd just reacted differently. "I get it." Then he jerked his head toward the bench, where one of the equipment guys had left some stickhandling trainers. Not as good as live opponents, but they could make do for now. "Come on, let's get these set up."

They started out running standard plays from the previous season, using the stickhandling trainers as opponents—set right side up to indicate their foot placement, with the obstacle flat to the ice in an arc around them, showing where their sticks would get in the way.

The set plays at low speed went fine. But when they moved the "players" around and started improvising, it fell apart. Gabe would see a shooting lane open and put the puck there for Baller, only to find Baller had gone somewhere completely different.

"All right, what are we doing wrong?" Baller said finally. "One of us is seeing something the other isn't."

They went over the passes that hadn't connected. "… and you're a left-handed shot," Gabe said. "This guy and this guy"—he gestured to the obstacles and their phantom sticks—"one of each, and they're covering more of the middle between them than you think. But if you skate a little farther—"

"I'll be around the defending lefty with a sharp angle at the net," Baller filled in.

"Or you can backhand pass around him to a cherry-picker in front."

It didn't always work, but they got better. To Gabe's surprise, for every two corrections he made, Baller came up with an equally valid one, pointing out something Gabe had overlooked—that they weren't taking advantage of how fast Baller was, or that he *could* actually deke through a narrow opening without losing the puck.

And his shot wasn't just good. It was *filthy.*

Gabe couldn't wait for the season to start.

They were still having trouble improvising, though. Sometimes things on the ice didn't go according to plan. They would still need to be able to anticipate each other's movements. Having a centerman would probably help, but Gabe wasn't going to ask Flash to stay late at training camp. He barely saw his kids during the season. Besides, Flash wouldn't always be there to bridge the gap.

"Maybe we just need to feel each other out a bit more," Baller suggested. "One-touch? With the trainers set up down the ice?"

It was a pretty simple drill—skating down the ice together and bouncing the puck back and forth. They'd both been doing it since before they were three feet high. But it did require them to work together, since the point was to ping-pong the puck and not keep it.

They skated the length of the rink a few times, slow and then at full speed, and it worked. But as soon as they tried to do it the way they'd need to in a game, without looking….

Baller swore in Spanish, obviously frustrated.

"We keep losing the rhythm," Gabe said unhappily.

Baller froze for a moment before a mischievous smile lit his face. "I've got an idea." He skated over to the bench, and a minute later the tinny sounds of music piped through a portable speaker filtered into the air. He gestured as if to say "ta-da." "If we keep losing our rhythm, then let's make sure it sticks."

At first Gabe didn't recognize the song Baller had picked, but he could appreciate the appropriateness of the first line about shooting for the stars.

Gabe started moving, skating down the ice to the beat, dribbling the puck. When Baller joined him, it was easy enough to pass to him on the downbeat. Even without looking, he knew it was going to connect. Baller caught the puck and passed it back on the next.

At the end of the rink, they curved around and headed back up in the other direction, slipping into one of their plays without discussing it. Gabe still had no idea what they were listening to. After another length, he lifted the puck and fired it into the net. He'd just resolved to ask when the chorus started.

"'Moves Like Jagger'? Really?"

Baller laughed. "What, you didn't recognize my man Adam until now?"

Who? Gabe considered asking but didn't want to look more ridiculous. "'Moves like Jagger' isn't exactly high up on my list of favorite songs," he said dryly.

"Your loss," Baller said as he singled out another puck from the pile. "You go behind the net with it this time and I'll come up the boards."

Eventually the song ended. And then started back up again.

"Really?"

Baller grinned. "It's got a good beat." He wiggled his butt a bit to demonstrate, but he still managed to catch the puck Gabe shot at him. Apparently the rhythm was just what they needed. He toe-dragged to the net and dumped it in.

"So do a lot of other songs. New ones, even." Gabe wasn't sure how old the song was, but he had the vague sense its inescapable airplay had coincided with his rookie years.

"Don't be a hater! I'll have you know this song was totally cool at my first middle school dance." And there was another reminder that Dante was barely more than a babe and Gabe shouldn't want to bang that ass like a screen door in a hurricane.

"Besides, it's good for running! Don't you run?"

"Yeah." Shaking away those thoughts, Gabe picked up another puck as they turned around again and made for the other end of the ice, weaving in and out of the obstacles. Baller caught his pass, no problem.

Okay. So maybe the music thing wasn't a terrible idea. Gabe was even starting to like the damn whistling since he was quickly associating it with the rhythm they were sharing and the satisfying swish of vulcanized rubber hitting the net.

Despite his thawing toward the song itself, Gabe didn't find Baller any less annoying when they packed up and he started singing to fill the void left by his phone—obnoxiously and off-key.

This was definitely a "look at your life, look at your choices" moment. This was *not* cute.

Gabe whacked Baller's still-wiggling butt with his stick. "Put that damn thing away before you hurt something. Or someone."

"Oh, fuck you." Baller smirked. "My ass is magnificent."

Unfortunately Gabe agreed. "You're a magnificent ass, you mean."

"Ouch." He put a hand to his chest as though wounded.

"Hit the showers," Gabe told him with a roll of his eyes. "You stink. And for the love of God, find something else to sing while you're in there."

Of course, that led to a rousing shower-room serenade of "Lady Marmalade," which was particularly entertaining when Baller gave up on the actual lyrics and started making up his own.

When he'd dressed again—Baller was still warbling "he starred in a porno that wasn't fresh enough"—Gabe bit the bullet and checked his phone.

Two missed calls. Four new messages. It could've been worse.

His voicemail inbox was empty. Though his phone indicated they originated from a blocked number, the texts were both obviously from Pierre. Gabe deleted them without reading them and headed home before Baller got out of the shower.

ALEX WINTERS is the pseudonym of a busy restaurant manager whose curious young staff would love nothing more than to follow him around the dining room reading his steamiest, most romantic passages aloud. When not writing romantic holiday stories, he enjoys long walks with his wife, scary movies, and smooth jazz. Visit him at www.awintersromance. com to see what stories he's brewing up next!

Website: www.awintersromance.com

Twitter: https://twitter.com/awintersromance

Facebook: https://www.facebook.com/profile. php?id=100084802422320

Instagram: https://www.instagram.com/a_winters_romance/

Pinterest: https://www.pinterest.com/awintersromance/

Amazon Author Page: https://www.amazon.com/author/ awintersromance

Goodreads: https://www.goodreads.com/author/show/23210941.Alex_ Winters

Spotify: https://open.spotify.com/ user/31c65bunmmjj2msoeelqva5odsjy?si=b622daca78fc4d98&nd=1